CW00349030

DESERVING LARA

The Refuge, Book 5

SUSAN STOKER

This book is a work of fiction. Names, characters, places, and incidents are products of the author's imagination or used fictitiously. Any resemblance to actual events or locales or persons living or dead is entirely coincidental.

Copyright © 2023 by Susan Stoker

No part of this work may be used, stored, reproduced or transmitted without written permission from the publisher except for brief quotations for review purposes as permitted by law.

This book is licensed for your personal enjoyment only. This book may not be re-sold or given away to other people. If you would like to share this book with another person, please purchase an additional copy for each recipient. If you're reading this book and did not purchase it, or it was not purchased for your use only, please purchase your own copy.

Thank you for respecting the hard work of this author.

Edited by Kelli Collins

Cover Design by AURA Design Group

Manufactured in the United States

CHAPTER ONE

Callen "Owl" Kaufman ran a hand through his hair in frustration. It had been over three months since he, Stone, and Pipe had gone to Arizona to check into Cora's missing friend Lara...and found more than they'd bargained for.

Yes, they'd found Lara Osler, but in the process of getting her away from her toxic boyfriend, they'd been drugged, held against their will, almost died at the hands of a serial killer, and had to steal a helicopter to get away from the estate where they'd found the woman.

If he hadn't been so focused on protecting Lara in the chaos, Owl might've found himself sucked down into horrible memories of a time when he'd been held hostage himself, while in the Army. The difference this time was, he hadn't been tortured. Wasn't filmed for the terrorists' sick pleasure. And his teammate Stone, who'd been captured and tortured as well, this time had been the hero of the day. He'd been the one to appropriate a chopper—owned by the rich asshole who'd convinced Lara to come to Arizona—and fly them to safety.

But that safety was an illusion.

He knew it.

His friends knew it.

And unfortunately, Lara Osler knew it as well.

Carter Grant was a serial killer who'd flown under everyone's radar. He'd been working as a bodyguard for Lara's ex, while kidnapping and torturing women right under everyone's noses. He'd shot her boyfriend in the head and slipped away in the chaos of that awful day.

He was still out there.

And he wanted Lara.

Owl's teeth clenched. He wasn't going to touch her again. He'd promised Lara, as well as her best friend, Cora. Just thinking about what Lara had already gone through at the psycho's hands was enough to make Owl's skin crawl.

But he knew better than most that bad shit happened. All it took was one moment of inattention, and Lara could be snatched out from under their noses. She was terrified. And Owl didn't blame her.

Since their escape from Arizona, she'd hunkered down at The Refuge as she tried to heal. Most people would say she wasn't any better than she was all those weeks ago, but they'd be wrong. She'd actually come a long way since her rescue.

But she still had a ways to go. And Owl vowed to be there for her every step.

Cora thought her friend was still a shell of the woman she used to be, but Owl wasn't so sure about that. Yes, outwardly, Lara was still skittish, didn't talk much, and wasn't terribly willing to leave his cabin. But when it was just the two of them, locked in his home, safe and warm, she was starting to open up... revealing a funny, considerate, and incredibly insightful woman.

And Owl was madly in love with her.

Nothing would come of any kind of relationship, and he knew it. Lara saw him as a protector. She'd clung to him since the moment they'd arrived at The Refuge. For weeks, anytime he'd left her line of sight, she'd panicked. Even in that basement in Arizona where they'd found her, despite her drugged haze, she'd latched onto him as her point of safety, and he hadn't done anything to dissuade her of that notion.

She'd gotten better very recently. Much better. He could go up to the lodge and leave her in his cabin with Cora for a couple hours at a time without her having a panic attack. But if he was gone too long, she'd start shaking and her breathing would increase, prompting a call from Cora. Each time, Lara wasn't able to calm down until she saw him again.

It broke Owl's heart because he wanted her to take her confidence back. Her independence. And having her rely on him so completely wasn't a good basis for any kind of romantic relationship.

But he'd do anything for Lara—even suppress his feelings. He'd be her friend. Her rock. Her protector for as long as she needed him. Then he'd let her go. Watch her leave and spread her wings and fly once again.

"Owl?"

Her soft, unsure voice had Owl shaking himself out of his tormented thoughts. He turned to see her standing in the doorway of the guest room. For the first two months, he'd slept in a chair next to her bed because she couldn't bear to be alone.

She'd recently been able to get through the night without waking up screaming, but every now and then, she still woke and needed reassurance that she wasn't back there. Locked in a basement at the mercy of a madman.

"Hey, sweetheart. Bad dream?" he asked, immediately standing and going to her side. It was the middle of the night, and like usual, Owl's insomnia was kicking his ass. He didn't sleep well anymore. Hadn't since he'd been a prisoner of war.

Lara shook her head as he approached. "No. But I woke up and got scared."

"Come on," Owl said, reaching for her hand.

He felt little sparks of electricity when she willingly took hold of his hand, just as he always did when they touched, but he kept his reaction hidden. The last thing she needed was to have to deal with an unwanted advance on top of everything else.

He led her to the couch where he'd been sitting and gently encouraged her to relax. He covered her with a blanket, then said, "Get comfy. I'll be back with some hot chocolate."

Owl could feel Lara's gaze on him as he headed for the small kitchen. He wasn't a gourmet cook, but he'd learned enough over the last few years of being a bachelor at The Refuge not to starve. Yes, he and his fellow co-owners could go up to the main lodge and eat every meal with the guests if they preferred. Robert was the best cook this side of the Mississippi as far as they were concerned, but as an introvert, Owl sometimes just wanted the peace and quiet of his own space.

He pulled down a large mug and hit the button on the electric kettle on his counter to start heating the water. He scooped dark hot chocolate mix into the mug, added a few marshmallows, and braced himself on the counter as he waited for the water to boil.

4

It took every ounce of his control not to go back to the couch and pull Lara into his arms. Every one of his senses was in tune with her. He heard her shift on the couch, the subtle sound of the blanket moving. His fingers tingled with the remembered feel of her skin against his from a moment ago. He swore he could smell the peach lotion she used as well.

Moving his eyes, but not his head, he looked over at her. Her shoulder-length blonde hair was mussed from her pillow. Her dark blue eyes were a little glazed over, as if she was still half-asleep. She wore a pair of black leggings and an oversized shirt that hid the shape of her body, but given all the time he'd spent with her, Owl knew she was still a little too slender, still gaining back some of the weight she'd lost during her ordeal.

Her nose turned up a little at the end and she was prone to blush at the slightest provocation. She was tall for a woman— they were about the same height, around five-ten—but she was two years older than him at thirty-five. She was a bit clumsy and didn't seem to have a pretentious bone in her body...and Owl loved her all the more for it.

Having her in his space was torture, but he would suffer in silence as long as it meant Lara felt safe. No one knew of his feelings for his roommate, and if he had his way, no one ever would. Lara had a life away from here. She was the executive director of a preschool back in Washington, DC. Her kids missed her, all the parents loved her, and her boss had actually told Lara that she'd hold her job for her as long as she needed.

She'd be leaving eventually. Owl knew it. Cora knew it. Hell, everyone knew it. Owl would let her go because he loved her that much. He'd never hold her back. He'd do anything for this woman. Selflessly. Because she was worth it. Because after what she'd been through, she deserved the world. He'd give it to her if he could. But all he could do was ensure she could eventually get back to her life safely. Without looking over her shoulder.

Tex, the computer genius who'd brought him and his friends together years ago to form The Refuge, was trying to track down Carter Grant, the most wanted man in the country right now. The cops couldn't find him. The FBI had lost his trail. But the serial killer couldn't hide from Tex for long.

Owl had dreams of going after Grant once he was found. Of being the one to end the threat to the woman he loved. He'd probably die in the process, as he wasn't like his ex-special forces friends. He had basic hand-to-hand combat skills, but he wasn't as highly trained as a SEAL or Delta Force operative. Though he did have something his friends didn't—motivation. He loved Lara enough to sacrifice himself to make sure she could live a long, happy life, free of Carter Grant's threat hanging over her head.

His friends would rake him over the coals if they knew he'd willingly sacrifice himself to save Lara. But since the chances of Tex *not* telling the others that he'd found the serial killer, and letting Owl go after him alone, were slim to none, his likely demise wouldn't really be an issue. He just knew that, if necessary, Owl would one hundred percent give his life for Lara's.

The sound of the water bubbling in the kettle brought him out of his musings once again. Owl reached for the handle and poured the water into the mug, smiling at the rich scent of chocolate that wafted to his nose. He'd used plenty of extra chocolate, because that was how Lara liked it.

He stirred the drink, then turned and headed back to the couch. Owl could sense her gaze on him, and it made him feel warm inside. He sat next to her and held out the mug. "Careful, it's hot."

"Of course it is, it's hot chocolate," she said softly, with a small smile.

Owl lived for those smiles. They were rare, and he treasured each and every one.

"True. Let me know if it's strong enough for you. If not, I can add more mix."

She blew on the drink, then took a cautious sip. Her blue eyes met his. "It's perfect."

"Good," Owl said, leaning back against the couch.

They sat in silence for a long moment, something else Owl loved about her. She didn't feel the need to chatter unnecessarily. She was as content to sit in silence as he was. She'd told him once it was because of her work. All day she listened to children babble on and on, and while she loved it, she was just as glad to get into her car at the end of the workday and enjoy the sound of silence.

"Couldn't sleep?" she asked.

Owl shrugged. "No."

"You really should take the pills the doctor gave you," she scolded gently.

None of his friends knew the extent of his insomnia. They didn't know that if he managed to sleep for three or four hours a night, he considered himself lucky. His brain wouldn't shut down long enough for him to get a full night's rest. And since Lara had arrived, his worry for her and his need to be there when she woke from nightmares made *sure* he didn't sleep through the night.

"It's fine," he told her.

Lara frowned. "It's not. You don't get enough sleep, Owl."

"I'm used to it."

Her brows furrowed.

Her concern for him felt good. Really good. "Seriously, I'm fine. It's *you* I'm worried about. Why'd you wake up tonight?"

Lara's gaze went back to the mug in her hands as she shrugged.

"Talk to me, Lara."

She sighed. "I just...I'm such a burden."

"What? That's not true," Owl insisted.

She gave him a sad smile. "It is. I can see the worry in Cora's eyes when she visits. Everyone here is on edge, worried Carter will sneak onto the property in the middle of the night and cause havoc. And you..." Her voice trailed off. "I know you didn't expect to have me attached to your hip for this long."

Owl reached for her hand and squeezed it. "As far as I'm concerned, you can stay with me as long as you want."

"You don't mean that," Lara protested.

"The hell I don't. Look, I get it. I've been where you are. When Stone and I were rescued, I was a paranoid son-of-a-bitch. I didn't trust *anyone*. Couldn't even go to the grocery store without having someone with me to watch my back. It hasn't been that long, Lara. Cut yourself some slack."

"I've read what people online are saying," she whispered.

Owl mentally swore. He'd read what assholes on social media were saying as well. When the story came out, some people actually blamed *Lara*. Insisted she must've done something awful to *deserve* what Carter had done. The victim blaming was vicious and horrible to read. And since Carter Grant was actually a very good-looking man—tall and muscular, dirty-blond hair, mid-thirties, hazel eyes—some sick assholes even said they wouldn't have minded being in Lara's place.

They were all fucking idiots. Had no idea what they were talking about. It was easy to sit in their houses, safe and warm, and cast judgement on Lara and every other woman who'd found herself in Carter's clutches.

"Fuck them," Owl spat.

"But they're right. I went to Arizona of my own free will. I wasn't kidnapped."

"Maybe so, but that didn't make it okay for Michaels to lock you in the basement, and it *certainly* didn't give Grant the right to abuse you the way he did. You can't read that shit, Lara. It'll eat you alive, and those people online have no clue what they're talking about. Trust me, when Stone and I got home, people did the same thing. Armchair quarterbacked everything about our situation. They said we were pussies. That we should've fought our way free. That we weren't 'real' soldiers. If I took to heart everything they said, I would've put a bullet in my brain a long time ago."

"Owl," Lara breathed with a look of concern on her face.

"All I'm saying is that you can't read that stuff. I mean it. You won't talk to Henley—who could help you a hell of a lot better than I do—and you barely talk to Cora about what happened. Since I'm the only one you've opened up to, you need to listen to me. Stop. Reading. That. Hateful. Vitriol. Hear me?"

Owl wished like hell Lara would talk to Henley. Their resident psychologist would be able to help her much more than he could. But since she refused to speak about what happened with anyone but him, Henley had given him some tips that would hopefully help. But it was times like this when he felt as if he was completely out of his league. He just prayed he didn't screw Lara up even more.

"I hear you," she said.

"Good. The only people's opinions that matter are yours,

mine, Cora's, and everyone else here at The Refuge. The people who actually know what you went through. Fuck everyone else."

Her lips twitched.

Owl's heart soared. Every time he could make her smile, it felt like a miracle. Especially given the first entire month after she'd arrived at The Refuge, when she was so damn broken.

"Now, you want to stay out here with me or head back to bed?"

"Here," she said without hesitation.

"TV or book?" Owl asked.

"TV."

"You want to continue with that documentary we started yesterday? Or something else?"

"Can we watch *Cinderella*?"

"Of course." Owl picked up the remote and queued the movie. He didn't mind in the least watching the cartoon for the hundredth time. If that was what Lara wanted to watch, that was what they'd watch.

Honestly, he was relieved about her movie choice. He'd heard more than once from Cora that Lara was a romantic. That she believed in soul mates and true love. At least, she had before everything that happened. But the fact that she still enjoyed this movie, that it was a comfort to her, made Owl believe the woman Lara used to be was still in there. She might've been battered and bruised, but she was there.

Lara snuggled into the corner of the couch, her gaze glued to the television. Owl couldn't keep his eyes off her. He wasn't tired in the least, but he was thrilled when, not even fifteen minutes into the movie, Lara nodded off. He was pleased she felt safe enough to let down her guard around him and sleep.

Owl had seen this movie just as many times as Lara had since she'd been here, but he didn't turn it off. He let it play. And prayed that one day, the woman next to him would find her own Prince Charming. A man who would love and cherish her as much as *he* did. He knew it couldn't be him, but he wanted that for her more than he'd ever wanted anything in his life.

CHAPTER TWO

Lara woke up and stayed stock still, trying to get her bearings. She'd learned the hard way that pretending to be asleep could save her some pain...at least for a while.

It didn't take long for her to realize that she wasn't in that basement. Wasn't mostly naked. Wasn't at the mercy of Carter Grant.

She was at The Refuge. In New Mexico. Her best friend had gone above and beyond and refused to believe she wasn't in danger. Cora had persuaded the former military men who lived and worked here to come to Arizona to find her.

Lara opened her eyes and saw Owl asleep in the other corner of the couch. His head was resting back on the cushion and his mouth was partially open as he snored quietly. Lara took the time to study him while he was unaware.

Callen Kaufman, known as Owl to his friends, wasn't like any other man she'd ever met. He kind of looked like Ed Sheeran— had reddish hair, bright green eyes, and a closely cropped beard and mustache. He was younger than her thirty-five by two years and looked kind of preppy. They were the same height, which Lara loved. She didn't have to look up or down to see his eyes. He was fit and strong, but not hugely muscular like the other men who lived and worked at The Refuge. He didn't ooze testosterone. But Lara knew without a doubt that if push came to shove, he'd do whatever it took to protect her from any danger. Had already done just that, in fact.

She didn't have clear memories of her rescue from that house in Arizona, but one thing she *did* remember was staring at Owl's back as he stood between her and Carter Grant like a sentinel. Guarding her. Then she remembered his arms around her, but instead of being alarmed at the touch of another man she didn't know, Lara had just...melted into him.

He was her safe place, had felt it instantly, and she somehow knew that if he left her side, she'd find herself right back in Carter's clutches.

It was unreasonable and irrational, but she couldn't shake the feeling that without this man, she'd be right back in the nightmare she couldn't wake up from.

Over the last couple weeks or so, she'd finally been able to force herself to let Owl out of her sight. She struggled hard to make strides, to convince Owl she was getting better...but the truth was, she was just as messed up in her head now as she'd been in that basement.

Carter Grant was going to get a hold of her again. She had no doubt about that. He'd bragged about the other women he'd captured. The things he'd done to them. Especially loved telling her in detail how he'd killed them...and laughed because he hadn't been caught.

But it was what he'd whispered in her ear one night after he'd finished playing with her that tumbled over and over in her mind.

You're my favorite. I'm not giving you up. Ever. You're mine.

She closed her eyes and took a deep breath.

She wasn't nearly ready yet, but the time was coming when she'd have to leave. The last thing she wanted was to lead Carter to The Refuge. To her best friend. To the men and women who lived here.

Her original plan had been to go to Alaska and hide out in one of those off-the-grid cabins. But she wasn't so sure about that anymore. She didn't know *where* she wanted to go, all she knew was that she didn't want anyone else to be hurt because of her.

Lara opened her eyes and stared at Owl once again. On the surface, the man always looked calm and collected, but he was just as broken inside as she was. And for some reason, that made her lower her shields around him. He'd been through what *she* had. Well, not exactly, but he'd also been held against his will and tortured. He'd opened up and told her a few things that, according to him, he'd never told anyone else.

She was also the only one who knew about his insomnia. Other than his doctor in town, of course. It made her feel special that he'd told her something so private, even if she would have discovered it on her own eventually, given all the time they spent together.

He'd been so patient with her, not caring that he'd basically had to be in her line of sight twenty-four hours a day to ensure she didn't freak out. He didn't make her feel like a burden. Like she was crazy. He was kind and patient and bent over backward to do whatever he could to make sure she felt comfortable and safe.

Of course, she didn't think she'd ever feel truly safe again. But she wasn't going to admit that. Not even to Owl.

If she could ever love a man, it would probably be the one sleeping on the other end of the couch. But her dream of happily ever after had died a horrific death. She wasn't as trusting as she once was. She second-guessed every single thing anyone said or did. She was newly cynical and wary of everyone's motives. Once, she might've been a romantic, but Ridge Michaels, the man she'd thought loved her so much he couldn't bear the thought of moving back to Arizona without her, had destroyed that part of her.

She was *glad* he was dead. Didn't care that his family had been through the wringer after it came out that they'd employed a literal serial killer. That women had been tortured and murdered on their property in Phoenix.

Lara was harder now. Less naïve.

But Owl made her feel a tiny bit like her old self. At least when it was just the two of them in his cabin. She could relax around him because he'd made it abundantly clear he wasn't interested in her romantically. He touched her, but usually just her hand, or at most a brief, platonic hug when she was at her lowest. She never saw anything but concern in his eyes. Nothing that would indicate he was interested in having some sort of relationship. Nothing beyond friendship, which she was grateful for.

But...a part of her, deep down, couldn't help but wonder what it would be like to have Owl as her own. To do what she could to help him sleep at night. To let him take her in his arms and hold her tight when she got scared.

Shaking her head, Lara pressed her lips together and took a deep breath. No. Owl was her friend. She'd been forced on him, and he'd probably be very relieved when she left. She'd tell everyone she was going back to DC, although that was the last place she ever wanted to see again. Instead, she'd go somewhere else. Maybe overseas. She didn't know.

All she knew was that she didn't ever want to feel helpless again. Didn't want Carter Grant to find her and lock her away in some dark, creepy basement so he could live out his sick fantasies with her for the rest of her life.

She needed to work harder to convince everyone she was back to her normal self. Going up to the lodge for meals. Interacting with the others here at The Refuge. Even if that was the last thing she wanted to do. She wanted to stay here. Holed up. Safe with Owl. But no one would believe she was ready to move back to DC and get on with her life if she didn't start acting like it.

So she'd put on a front. Lara had a feeling she could trick the men who lived here easily enough. She didn't know them, and they didn't know her.

But Cora would be much harder to deceive.

Thinking about her best friend made Lara a little teary-eyed. She'd heard from Owl all about what Cora had done for her. The lengths she'd gone to in order to convince someone, anyone, that Lara was in danger. To go to Phoenix and see for herself whether or not Lara was all right.

How she'd researched The Refuge, bid on Pipe at that bachelor auction, stood up to that bitch Eleanor, sold *literally* all her belongings, and put herself in grave danger by coming to Ridge's house.

Lara would never be able to repay her, even though Cora insisted that they were now "even." But befriending Cora back when they were in high school was *nothing* like what Cora had done for her.

What Cora didn't know was, back in high school when they'd met, Lara had needed a friend just as badly as Cora. Her parents weren't abusive, but they simply weren't that interested in their daughter. Other kids thought Lara was stuck-up because of her family's money, and because Lara never initiated any kind of conversations. She was smart, too smart to fit in with most other kids, and she'd had no interest in dating.

Cora was the best thing that had ever happened to Lara. She was outgoing and not afraid to say what she was thinking. She was Lara's opposite, and she adored her.

Years later, when Cora was hours away from being homeless, she'd added Cora to her bank account and made her promise to use her money if she ever found herself in that kind of situation again. Of course, Cora being Cora, she'd refused to touch a dime.

The truth was, Lara needed Cora much more than her friend had ever needed her.

Not a day went by when Lara didn't mentally kick herself for not listening to Cora when she'd tried to tell her Ridge Michaels wasn't genuine. They'd gotten into a big fight over the man, which had led to Lara impulsively agreeing to go to Arizona with her then-boyfriend. If she'd only listened to Cora, she wouldn't have fallen into Carter's clutches.

Thinking about everything the serial killer had done to her made Lara shiver in fear and revulsion.

A moment later, she felt Owl stir, then a second blanket was being draped over her.

"I can turn the heat up if you're cold," he said softly.

Closing her eyes, Lara tried to control her erratic emotions.

Even in his sleep, Owl had felt her shudder...and misinterpreted it. Had anyone ever been so attentive to her before? That answer was easy. No.

"Thanks," she told him.

He stood then, and Lara watched him as he headed for the bathroom just down the hall. She had no idea what time it was, but it was still dark outside. When she'd first arrived, and Owl had discovered she was terrified of the dark, he went into town and bought a dozen nightlights. They were plugged into every available outlet, throwing off enough light to allow her to see, but not so harsh as to prevent her from sleeping.

Those first few days, she'd slept out here on the couch, with Owl at her feet. Then she'd forced herself to go to the guest room, but sleep was elusive. That was when Owl began sleeping in the chair next to the bed. Every time she woke up, her eyes would pop open in terror, only to see her own personal body-guard right there at her side. Most of the time he was awake, quick to reassure her that she was all right. That she was safe in New Mexico.

She often felt guilty that she was so needy. So dependent on Owl. But he never made her feel as if looking after her was a hardship. Never complained that he didn't have a moment to himself because she freaked if he was out of her sight for more than a few minutes.

Cora and Owl had saved her life. And Lara still wasn't sure if she was grateful or pissed at them as a result. Some days, she felt as if everyone—including herself—would be better off if she was gone. She wouldn't be dealing with the debilitating fear and depression that she suffered now if she was dead.

Owl came back into the room carrying another blanket. He'd

obviously made a detour after using the restroom. He settled himself back into the corner of the couch and stared at her.

Lara's muscles tightened at the look on his face. Determination. Stubbornness. She braced for whatever he was going to say.

"You need to talk to Henley."

She was shaking her head before he'd finished his sentence. "I'm doing okay," she insisted. The last thing she wanted was someone getting inside her head. Discovering how messed up she *really* was.

And finding out that she was planning on leaving and disappearing for good.

"You are, but you aren't. Trust me, I know."

"You *don't* know," Lara said, the bitterness leaking through in her tone.

"I do," Owl insisted.

"You know what it's like to crave the drugs you were forced to take because they dull your senses, so you don't have to feel what's being done to you? To be touched against your will? To be told that you'll never get away and you'll be someone's plaything for years to come?"

Where the words were coming from, Lara didn't know, but she couldn't stop.

"Really, Owl? You know what it's like to feel as if every time you step outside, you're going to be snatched up and stuffed into a trunk and stolen away? To be terrified every second of every day, knowing the person who tortured you is still out there? Waiting for the perfect time to grab you again and shove you back into a basement, strip you naked, and jack off to your terror?"

Lara was panting by the time she stopped, every muscle

tense and her head pounding. Her hands shook with adrenaline as memories swam through her brain.

"I know what it's like to be touched against my will. To be beaten to within an inch of my life...for fun. To look up at a red blinking light and realize my humiliation is being filmed to be blasted on the Internet for millions of people to watch. I completely understand the fear of being recaptured and put right back into the same situation I'd just escaped from.

"I also know how it feels for my best friend to be tortured, simply to hurt me even more. To hear his cries of pain and know I can't do a damn thing to help. And yes, my captors are still out there. Some were killed during our rescue, but others weren't. Dozens of men who delighted in every strike, every slash of their knife. I know without a shadow of a doubt if they had a chance to get me back in their clutches, they'd not hesitate to make me their prisoner again."

Owl's gaze was intense, but his tone wasn't accusatory. It was almost...gentle. And Lara couldn't help but feel ashamed by her outburst. But Owl wasn't finished.

"I also know how it feels to be happy one minute, then feel so depressed the next it's all I can do to get out of bed. I hated the pitying looks I got from people who recognized me from those damn videos. I didn't want to see a therapist. I was a man —I could deal with all the shit in my head without help. But after I sat in my kitchen one night with a knife in one hand, and a bottle of painkillers in the other, I realized it was time. I cried like a baby in my first session with my therapist...and damn if that didn't help.

"I'm worried about you, Lara. I can listen, be by your side, reassure you that I'll do everything in my power to make sure you're safe, but I don't have the training Henley does. I swear to you that she's good at her job. And anything you say to her will be held in the strictest confidence. At least try. Please. One session."

Lara closed her eyes. She felt off-kilter...and ashamed. What happened to her was horrible. Terrifying. Life-changing. But she wasn't the only person who'd been through something awful. Owl was proof of that. Hell, all the men who ran The Refuge were. As were all the guests.

She was being selfish. And that made her feel even worse about herself.

"Look at me," Owl ordered.

Reluctantly, Lara lifted her gaze to his.

"I might not have experienced the same things you have, but I know how you're feeling. And I'm in this for the long haul. You can stay here as long as you want. If you need me to handcuff my wrist to yours so you can feel safe, that's what I'll do. He's not going to win, Lara. I promise you that. If it takes me the rest of my life, I'm gonna do whatever's necessary to make sure he can't hurt you again. Got it?"

For the first time since she'd found herself locked in that basement, Lara felt a spark of...hope.

She swallowed hard, then gave Owl a barely there nod.

"Good. Now, do I need to dig out a pair of handcuffs?"

Her lips twitched. "Kinky," she said softly.

A grin formed on Owl's face. "I can think of worse things in life than to be shackled to you, sweetheart."

When he said things like that, some of the old Lara surged to the surface. The woman who would've swooned if a man spoke to her like that in the past. But she wasn't that woman anymore. She was hardened. Cynical. Terrified.

But she found herself relaxing all the same.

Owl looked down at his wrist. "It's five. You want to get up and watch the sunrise at Table Rock with me?"

Lara blinked in surprise. "Table Rock?" she asked. "But that's like...miles away."

He shrugged. "It's an easy hike."

"It's cold outside."

"Not that cold. Spring has finally arrived."

Still, she hesitated. Carter could be lurking in the woods. Waiting to grab her.

"We've got cameras all over the woods. And I'm not supposed to tell you this, but fuck it—there are buried bunkers throughout the forest as well. If something happens, if I feel even a second of concern about someone being out there who shouldn't be, I'll get us to a bunker and we can hide out until the others search the area and make sure we're safe."

Lara blinked at him. "Really? Why?"

"Why do we have bunkers? Because...when we built this place, none of us were in a great space mentally. We needed the reassurance those bunkers gave us. And they've come in handy. Alaska hunkered down in one when the human trafficker came for her, and Jasna was rescued from that asshole who kidnapped her and brought to one to make sure she was safe."

"Oh," Lara said, at a loss for words. She'd heard all about what happened to the other women at The Refuge and was amazed all over again at their resilience.

After a long moment of silence, she took a deep breath and nodded. "Okay."

"Okay?" he asked, one brow rising in surprise.

"Yeah. I'll go to Table Rock with you."

He smiled then. And Lara realized just how much he'd been holding back with her. She'd been with him for months, and she didn't think she'd ever seen such a genuine look of pleasure on his face. He held back because of concern for *her*.

Once again, those tingles in her body returned.

"Great!" he said quickly, obviously afraid she would change her mind. "Go change. Put on some thick socks, those fleece-lined leggings Henley bought for you, a long-sleeve shirt, a sweatshirt, and I'll grab my parka just in case you get cold." He stood and put the blanket he'd just retrieved from his room on the couch, then held out his hand to her.

Without thought, Lara reached for it.

The second his fingers closed around hers, she panicked. Same as always. She didn't like to be touched. Didn't like the feel of someone else's skin on hers. But also like always, the fear faded almost instantly. This was Owl. His hands were warm and calloused and gentle. Not cold and abusive like Carter's.

He let go of her as soon as she was on her feet but stayed near. Lara realized that he did that all the time. Stood by her side just in case she got dizzy, or wobbly, or if she panicked.

This man had definitely become her rock, and she couldn't help but want to please him. To make sure he knew how much she valued his presence...and his advice.

Once he was sure she was steady on her feet, he turned to head toward his bedroom.

Lara's hand shot out and she touched his arm.

Owl froze, only his head turning to look at her. Both of them understanding the importance of this moment.

It was the first time she'd ever initiated any kind of contact with him—with *anyone*—since she'd been rescued.

"I'm sorry about what you went through," she said gently.

Owl's piercing green eyes bore into her own. "Thanks."

"And...I'll talk to Henley."

The relief she saw in his gaze was intense.

"Thank you," he said again.

"Will you..." Her voice trailed off.

"Yes."

Lara felt herself smiling, even though there was nothing funny about this conversation. "You don't even know what I was going to ask."

"Doesn't matter, sweetheart. You want or need something from me, I'll bend over backward to give it to you."

The tingles were back.

"What if I asked you to put on a Bigfoot costume and slink through the woods, making sure to be caught by those cameras you said were out there, just to make everyone else freak out?"

The chuckle that rumbled through Owl made Lara feel as if she'd won the lottery. He was a serious man. He didn't laugh a lot. So being the one who'd elicited that kind of reaction felt oddly amazing. It was the first time in months that she'd felt anything other than fear or worry about her own situation.

"I'm totally doing that now. I can't wait to see Tonka's face when he sees Bigfoot tromping around," Owl told her.

"Well, now that the idea's out there, I'd love to see the Bigfoot thing too. Maybe we could get two costumes and I could tromp around with you."

"Deal," Owl said with a smile.

The moment felt charged. Different. As if they were simply a man and a woman, rather than a broken sexual assault victim and her savior. That thought brought back the question she wanted to ask him.

"I'll talk to Henley...but will you be there with me when I do?" she asked.

The easygoing expression on his face disappeared, replaced by a frown. "I'm not sure that's a good idea."

"I understand if you don't want to hear about everything that happened," she started uncertainly.

Owl shook his head. "It's not that. Don't *ever* think that. I just want you to feel as comfortable as possible opening up to Henley, and it might be awkward if I'm there. You might not want to be as truthful."

"*Without* you there, I probably won't be as willing to tell her anything at all," Lara countered. "I feel safe with you. I don't know Henley. I mean, I'm sure she's wonderful, but telling a stranger everything that happened isn't...it's not...I don't know if I can do that."

"Maybe Cora would be better," Owl hedged.

"No. Absolutely not. She's my best friend. She'd get pissed off and want to go hunt down Carter on her own. She's amazing and wonderful, and I know I'm the luckiest woman in the world to have her, but she's not exactly the most calming presence."

Owl's lips twitched, but he stayed serious as he studied her.

When the silence got awkward, Lara regretted asking him. "Never mind," she mumbled.

"I'll be there," he said quickly.

"Great. Now I've guilted you into agreeing," she said, dropping her gaze.

"Look at me."

It was the second time he'd ordered her to do that in the last hour. But she couldn't ignore the concerned dominance in his tone. She lifted her gaze.

"I'm honored and overwhelmed by your trust in me, sweetheart. I would rather walk across a football field full of glass, in my bare feet, than do anything that might make you uncomfortable. There's also nowhere I want to be than by your side as you start on your healing journey...but if you ever change your mind, don't be afraid to tell me or Henley. I won't be upset. I won't take it personally. If there's something you want to talk about with her that you don't want me to hear, I can go take a walk or something. Okay?"

Lara couldn't think of anything she might want to talk about that she wouldn't want Owl to hear. But a niggling voice in the back of her mind called her a liar.

She couldn't talk about her deepening feelings for this man. Not in front of him.

Nothing could come of them. He was helping her out as a friend to Cora. As a friend to Pipe, since he and her best friend were going to get married one day. Besides, she was just feeling things for the man because he'd rescued her. Kept her safe.

"Okay," she agreed quickly, not wanting him to change his mind.

The tender look in his eyes made her knees weak.

"Go on, get changed. I don't want to miss the sunrise," Owl told her, effectively breaking the intimate bubble that had formed around them.

It wasn't until she was dressed, and she and Owl were outside walking on the trail toward Table Rock, that Lara realized she wasn't scared.

She was outside. In the dark. And she wasn't afraid. It felt like a miracle.

But she wasn't stupid. She knew it was because of the man at her side. Owl had taken hold of her hand as soon as they'd left his cabin and hadn't let go.

After feeling nothing for so long, for the second time this morning, Lara felt hope.

Hope that maybe, just maybe, she'd be able to climb out of the fog of despair she'd been in for months.

And all of a sudden, her plan to leave, to hide out somewhere far from her best friend and The Refuge, didn't seem like such a great idea. She still hated that her presence put everyone in danger, because without a doubt, Carter would hurt anyone who got in the way of what he wanted.

Maybe it was stupid, but Lara could no longer deny that she didn't want to live the rest of her life alone. And she definitely didn't want to live in fear. And if she was living somewhere by herself, she had a feeling that's what would happen.

With Owl's help, and Henley's, and Cora's, Lara wanted to believe that spark of hope meant the possibility of living a normal life again was within reach.

CHAPTER THREE

Owl held onto Lara's gloved hand and stared out at the rising sun. He was exhausted, which was nothing new, but somehow the coming of this new day felt different. More positive. As if the rising sun signified a shift in the status quo.

He was as relieved as he could be that Lara had agreed to talk to Henley, but he wasn't so sure about being with her when she did. For one, he wasn't convinced he wouldn't react the same way she'd claimed Cora might, if he heard every gory detail about what Carter Grant had done. The little he knew already made him want to tear Grant limb from limb. Hearing more about the horrific abuse might push him over the edge. The thought of anyone hurting Lara made his heart ache. He wanted to put her in a protective bubble to make sure nothing and no one ever harmed a hair on her head ever again.

But that wasn't how the world worked. He knew that better than anyone. She'd be much better off learning how to deal with the shit life dealt out. But that didn't mean he still didn't want to keep the worst of that shit from raining down on her.

Lara had made some strides since the day he'd carried her out of that house in Arizona. She still didn't sleep great, had issues being alone, was paranoid of every strange sound, and was a long way toward trusting anyone. But given the improvements he'd seen, he knew she'd get there.

This woman...she was everything he'd ever wanted in his life. Kind, gentle, smart. And much stronger than she thought. It wasn't that he had issues with Cora or the other women his friends had ended up with. Each of them were exactly what the other men needed. But it was Lara who made the anxiety he'd always lived with settle.

What they were doing now was a great example. They'd arrived at Table Rock, and he'd spread out the blanket he'd brought for them to sit on. Neither of them said a word as the sun slowly rose above the horizon. Most women would feel the need to fill the silence with chatter. But not Lara. She sat beside him, her hand in his, and simply absorbed the wonder of the moment.

Maybe it was their shared trauma. They'd each been so close to never seeing this kind of thing ever again. So the fact that they could enjoy it now meant...everything.

When the bright orange and pinks faded from the sky, Owl heard Lara sigh. He turned to look at her.

She had a small smile on her face as she glanced at him. "Beautiful," she said quietly.

"Yes," Owl replied, talking about more than the sunrise. Her straight blonde hair was hanging out the bottom of the stocking cap, splayed around her shoulders, and static electricity was making a few strands stick out a bit. She had on one of his old coats that was at least two sizes too big. Cora had bought her some warm gloves from town, along with a pair of boots.

Her cheeks were pink from the cool morning air and for the first time since they'd arrived back at The Refuge, Owl saw more than misery in her ocean-blue eyes. He couldn't look away.

"What?" she asked a little self-consciously. "Do I have something on my face?" She reached up to wipe at her cheek with the hand that wasn't entwined with his.

"No," Owl told her. "I just...I like seeing you like this."

"Like what?" she asked with a tilt of her head.

"Calm. Relaxed."

Lara turned to look back out over the beautiful scenery, and Owl mentally kicked himself for ruining the mellow mood. Her shoulders were back to being hunched and her muscles were tense again.

"When Stone and I were rescued, I was grateful. Of course I was. But I went through a phase, a long one, where I was resentful as well," Owl said.

At that, Lara's head turned so she could look at him again. He didn't wait for her to comment before continuing.

"A part of me, a huge part, wished that I had died while in captivity. I would've been seen as a hero. Helicopter pilot goes down in enemy territory, gets tortured, and dies serving his country. I probably would've had an interstate named after me or something." He chuckled, but it wasn't a humorous sound. "Instead, I came home broken, bitter, and untrusting. It sucked knowing the entire world saw me when I was at my very lowest. Even today, those damn videos are still out there. Once something's on the Internet, it never completely goes away. There's no telling how many assholes saved those clips and have them on their hard drives.

"Not only that, it felt impossible to get back to the man I used to be. What I didn't realize at the time, and had to learn after lots of therapy, was that I would *never* be the person I was before. That Callen Kaufman was gone. And I had to figure out how to be the new me."

"How did you get over that feeling? The one of wishing you'd died?" Lara asked.

"By doing things like this. Sitting still, appreciating the things around me that made me feel small. I know that sounds strange, but—"

"It doesn't," Lara interrupted. "Sitting here this morning, seeing all this," she gestured to the impressive view in front of them, "makes *me* feel small. Insignificant. Until this morning, all I could think about was that basement and what happened to me there. This sunrise has reminded me that life rolls on. It doesn't care about me...one tiny little person in the scheme of things. You know what I was thinking about when the sun was coming up?"

Owl was so proud of her, he could barely get the words out. "No, what?"

"Destiny Miller."

When she didn't continue, Owl asked, "Who's that?"

"She's one of the kids who attended the preschool I worked at back in DC. She was four when it happened...She was walking down the street with her dad, holding his hand. He was holding her nine-month-old brother in a car seat in his other hand. Apparently, they were going down to the store on the corner to buy some milk, since they'd run out. He'd wanted to give her mom a small break from the kids. She was at home, sleeping in for once. Someone ran up to them...and just shot her dad dead. But you know what?"

"What?" Owl whispered, horrified down to his core by what had happened to that little girl and her family.

"Destiny came to school the next day. She was so devastated, everyone could see that, but she ended up consoling *us*. When she saw me crying for her, she wiped my tears away and told me not to be sad. That her daddy was now her guardian angel, and he'd watch out for her and her brother for the rest of their lives."

Lara turned to stare out in front of her once more. "Bad stuff happens all the time. To people who don't deserve it. Like Destiny and her family. And she's just one of hundreds, thousands...millions of people who have crap happen that isn't fair. Cancer, fatal car accidents, house fires, robbery...the list goes on and on. And *life* goes on. It doesn't stop. The sun still comes up every morning and goes down each night.

"If Destiny could manage to have a positive mindset about what happened, at four years old, then I need to figure out how to do the same."

Owl was speechless. His throat was so tight, he wasn't sure he could speak at that moment. He'd admired this woman before, but now? He realized she was the strongest woman he'd ever met. Yes, he was surrounded by strong women, but in his mind, Lara blew them all away.

"I just..." she went on. "Don't know how. I can't think of a single positive thing about what I went through."

Owl swallowed hard to clear the lump from his throat. "Cora met Pipe. Your best friend proved exactly how important you are to her, and how much she loves you. You're here this morning watching this amazing sunrise. Your situation made the case against Grant stronger and brought renewed interest and desire to catch him once and for all. Brick started self-defense lessons here at The Refuge to help other women."

Lara closed her eyes, and her grip on his hand tightened.

"It's not easy," Owl said. "I wish I could tell you that it is. That one day you'll wake up and just be better. That the negative and destructive thoughts in your head will—*poof!*—be gone. But they won't be. I have days when I still struggle with everything I went through."

"How do you get past it?" Lara asked, her eyes still closed.

"I watch sunrises. I help Tonka shovel cow shit. I talk to Stone. I do crosswords. I sit on my couch in my sweats, don't bother to shower, and eat junk food all day. I allow myself to have a down day. I'm not Superman, no matter how much I might want to be. Give yourself some grace, Lara. No one is expecting you to bounce right back to your old life except you."

She sighed and opened her eyes again. "He's never going to stop," she said in a barely audible tone.

Every muscle in Owl's body tensed, but he forced himself to take a deep breath and not reject her words. "Then we'll just have to make sure when he *does* make his move, we're ready for him."

Lara turned to stare at him with wide eyes. "You aren't denying that he's going to come after me? That I'm not safe here?"

"No," Owl said simply. The thought of Carter Grant coming within ten feet of this woman made him feel homicidal. But Lara needed him to be level-headed and calm right now.

She bit her lip and her brows furrowed before she said, "I think that's the first time anyone's admitted that I'm still in danger."

"Carter Grant is insane," Owl said. "And he's smart. He used to be special forces. He has the skills and the patience to wait out the renewed interest in finding him. Pipe should've killed him when he had the chance, but I understand why he didn't. He was more focused on getting all of us out of that house alive. I can make you a promise, though."

"What?"

"If I come face-to-face with that bastard, *I'm* not going to hesitate to kill him for you."

Lara's lips twitched.

"That's funny?" Owl asked.

"No," she said immediately. "I'm amused by my gut reaction to hearing you say that. Most women would be appalled by knowing a guy wants to kill someone. But it just makes me feel safe. Safer than I've felt in several months. God, I'm so messed up."

"No, you aren't," Owl countered. "You're human. And honestly, I think this is the healthiest you've been since you've gotten here."

"Yeah," Lara agreed. "I feel like I need to thank you for—"

"Nope," he interrupted.

She frowned. "You don't even know what I was going to say."

"Don't care. You don't need to thank me for anything."

"Owl, I've been glued to your side for months. Hell, for a while there, you could barely go pee without me completely losing it."

Owl leaned a tiny bit closer. So many things were on the tip of his tongue that he wanted to tell her. But he settled for, "I haven't done anything I didn't *want* to do."

The air between them was charged, and Owl wanted more than anything to lean forward and put his lips on hers. But that would be wrong on so many levels. She was just beginning to regain some of her confidence. By leaving his cabin, she'd gone from being petrified to the beginning stages of healing. He didn't want to do anything that might undermine that.

Eventually she'd move on. Go back to her life. She'd probably remember her time at The Refuge with mixed feelings. She'd feel grateful for what he'd done for her, and for him and his friends letting her stay in New Mexico, but this place would also bring up bad memories of a time when she felt lost and scared.

Lara licked her lips, and the strength it took for Owl to ease back was almost superhuman. "I heard Robert tell Cora that he was going to make maple pancakes this morning. You feel like heading up to the lodge to try them out?"

Lara blinked as if she'd been in a trance, but he had to be projecting his own feelings onto her. Hoping to see something that simply wasn't there.

"Will you come too?" she asked.

"Of course," Owl said. Hiking out to Table Rock was enough of an accomplishment for one day. He'd never make her go to the lodge alone.

"Can I watch you play your simulation game after?" she asked.

Owl stood...and realized he was grinning. In the space of minutes, things between them felt so much lighter than they had over the last few months. The threat of Grant was still out there. He felt it, and he knew without a doubt that Lara did too. But for this moment, he could pretend all was well.

"Game? I'll have you know, woman, that the flight simulator is no game."

"It looks like a game. You have two joysticks and even pedals, and you put on that headset and you get to mock-fly around the desert, cities, through storms, and other dangerous situations," she said with a wry look.

He and Stone had both purchased flight simulators a few years ago—the same ones that the Army used to help train their Night Stalker pilots and keep them sharp between missions—when they'd decided to keep their flying licenses up-to-date. And now that Brick and the others were seriously considering purchasing a helicopter for The Refuge, it was even more important to keep their skills sharp.

"You wanna play?" Owl asked.

"Me? Oh, I couldn't. I'd crash," Lara said as they started heading back down the trail toward the cabins.

"So? It's not real. It might help take your mind off other things," Owl said with a small shrug.

"True," she mused. She looked over at him as they walked.

Owl loved that they were the same height. He didn't have to look down and she didn't have to crane her neck up when they were talking. He'd also dreamed more than once about how well their bodies would line up in other, more intimate ways.

"All right. You can teach me to become a Nightrider then."

He chuckled. "Night Stalker."

"Whatever," she said with a grin she didn't even try to hide.

Owl liked this side of her. The fact that she was actually teasing him was such a good sign. She wasn't like her friend Cora. Even before she'd been kidnapped, apparently, she'd been the quiet one of the two. More laid-back. So her teasing was a welcome surprise.

"All right, after breakfast, I'll teach you to fly."

"I can't wait."

And it actually sounded like she *was* looking forward to it, not just trying to placate him.

If someone had told Owl even a month ago that this is where they'd be today, he wouldn't have believed them. But he'd underestimated Lara. She was stronger than even *he'd* given her credit for—and he already thought she was damn strong. She'd not only agreed to talk to Henley, but she'd gone on a hike outside the cabin, had opened up to him a little more, had agreed to eat up at the lodge, and had actually smiled more than once.

This was a good day. A *great* day.

And even though her getting better meant their time together would end even sooner than he'd like, Owl would do whatever it took to keep her on the path to regaining her confidence and getting her life back.

CHAPTER FOUR

"Pull up! Bank right! Higher! Oh, shit!"

Lara did her best to follow Owl's directions, but it was no use. The chopper went into a flat spin and she flinched when the screen turned red.

She pushed the goggles up onto her forehead and sat back on the couch, letting the joystick drop to the cushion. "Let's face it. I *suck* at this. I'm not coordinated enough to use the pedals at the same time as the joystick and the other thingy."

Owl chuckled. "It's only been a week. Give yourself some slack."

Seven days had gone by since their first walk out to Table Rock. Since then, a lot had changed in Lara's life.

She was still scared out of her mind that Carter Grant would appear out of nowhere and snatch her away, but she now wanted her life back more than ever. She missed her old self. Not that the old Lara was all that exciting, but at least she wasn't a hermit who refused to go outside.

What gave Carter the right to mess up her life the way he had? Why did he think it was okay to abuse her and scare the crap out of her? It wasn't right and it wasn't fair. And this week, for the first time, she got *mad*. At the situation. At Carter. At how unfair life was.

In addition to that first stirring of anger within her, she'd gone hiking every morning with Owl, eaten at least one meal up at the lodge each day, and had gone over to Pipe and Cora's cabin and sat on their rooftop deck with her best friend—while Pipe and Owl actually visited inside.

She was taking baby-steps to reclaim her life.

She'd even attended a self-defense session that Pipe ran, but that hadn't gone as well. She'd left early, memories coming too close to the surface while she'd listened to Pipe talk about hand-to-hand fighting. She might've been out of her mind with fear and the drugs coursing through her system at the time, but she'd seen the brutal fight between Pipe, Owl, and Carter.

She wanted to try the self-defense lessons again...but not quite yet.

While she'd hoped to wean herself off her dependence on Owl, that was going slowly as well. Just a few days ago, he'd gone down to the barn to help Tonka with the animals, and a strange sound against one of the windows of the cabin had Lara retreating under her bed in the guest room, where she'd had a full-blown panic attack.

Owl had almost lost it when he'd returned and couldn't find her. He was two seconds away from calling all the guys to tell them that she'd disappeared when she'd managed to find the courage to crawl partway out from under the bed and call his name. It turned out to be a stray branch that was hitting the window and making the noise, but it had shown Lara that, despite some milestones this week, she still wasn't very far along in her recovery.

To her relief—and confusion—Owl didn't seem to mind that she was still using him as a crutch. He never made her feel bad for needing him nearby. The more time she spent with him, the more Lara's shields lowered with the man. He was everything she used to want...considerate, patient, attentive, and he definitely spoiled her.

After the panic attack, she'd been forced to admit to herself...she was falling for him. But she knew a deeper relationship was doomed to fail. There was no way he'd want to be with someone so needy. He deserved a woman who could stand by him when life went sideways. Not someone who would climb under a bed and hide because a freaking *branch* was banging against a window. He was an honest-to-God hero, and she was...not.

But while she was here, she selfishly decided to soak up every ounce of friendship and support he was willing to give. Eventually, he'd get sick of being her crutch and she'd have to figure out what to do, but for now, she was going to enjoy the feeling of safety that Owl provided.

Well, as safe as she *could* feel with a serial killer out there, looking for her.

It was literally only a matter of time before he returned, and while Lara didn't ever want to see him again, she had to prepare herself for that eventuality. What other choice did she have? Roll over and give up? She wanted to say that she'd fight, but honestly, she wasn't sure *what* she'd do. She only knew that if it came down to Carter taking *her* or hurting her new friends, she'd choose the former every time.

"You go again," she told Owl, shoving the controllers at him and pushing the pedals toward his feet. "I love watching you fly. You make it look so easy."

"It *is* easy…when you know what you're doing," he said with a small smirk.

Lara rolled her eyes. She'd believed him the first time she'd tried the simulator. But when she'd crashed about two seconds after the chopper got in the air, she realized Owl was simply that good, that he made it seem effortless.

He took the controllers and handed over his tablet. There was an app on it that allowed her to see what he was seeing as he went through the simulations. He put the goggles over his eyes and adjusted the difficulty level from beginner to advanced, then the chopper lifted off the ground.

Lara watched in awe as he maneuvered around mountaintops while being shot at from the ground. He managed to pick up a team of Navy SEALs who were pinned down by enemy fire and then lift off and fly out of the mountain canyon as if he was on a pleasure cruise, rather than a simulated life-or-death flight.

A few nights ago, Stone came over with his own equipment and the two men flew together. It was even more impressive than Owl flying through the simulations on his own. Their respective choppers flew so close to each other, she was sure their rotor blades would hit, but they skillfully flew side-by-side without issue.

They'd talked just a little about their flight from Ridge's house in Arizona. How horrible the conditions were with the wind and sand. How it reminded them of some of their missions in the Middle East…except back then, they didn't have a crappy helicopter to deal with.

It was several minutes into their discussion when Owl turned to her with an anguished look on his face. "I'm sorry. We weren't thinking. We shouldn't be talking about this in front of you."

She'd been able to reassure them both that since she'd been unconscious at that point in her rescue, talking about the flight wasn't bringing back any bad memories.

The truth was, she was fascinated by hearing them talk. Stone and Owl were obviously extremely skilled pilots, and she felt thankful that they'd both been there to get her away from the house. Without them, the outcome would've been a lot different.

Lara watched as Owl's hands easily maneuvered the joysticks. He had long fingers, and she loved how they felt around hers as they took their walks in the morning, even though they were both wearing gloves. Spring in the mountains of New Mexico was turning out to be unusually chilly this year, according to Owl.

"Watch and learn," he joked, jerking Lara out of the daydream she'd fallen into.

She looked down at the tablet and saw Owl was flying his simulated chopper over the ocean. The waves were mean looking, yet Owl was skimming the surface without any issues whatsoever.

"The key is to move with the motion of the waves," he said as he deftly maneuvered the helicopter.

Lara shook her head as, once again, he made operating such a huge machine look like child's play. She smiled as Owl continued to fly the simulator. He was obviously in his element. Intellectually, while she'd already known he had to be a very good helicopter pilot, and had participated in many dangerous missions while in the Army, it didn't hit home *how* good he was until the first time he'd demonstrated the simulator.

True, the simulation wasn't a real chopper, but the ease with which he handled the joysticks and the small smile on his face as he "flew" made Lara understand that this man was born to fly. It clearly made him happy and helped calm him. She had no idea how he'd survived being a POW without being in the air.

She had no stake in what happened at The Refuge, but she was very glad the owners were seriously considering buying a chopper.

"...you think?"

Lara blinked—and realized she'd missed Owl's question.

"I'm sorry, what?"

The helicopter on the tablet suddenly stopped in midair and fell like a stone into the ocean. Looking at Owl, she saw he'd shoved the goggles onto his forehead, and he had an expression of concern on his face. "You okay?" he asked.

"Uh...yeah? Owl, you crashed."

The teasing smile he gave her made tingles shoot down to her toes. "Good thing it's just a simulation, huh?"

Lara shook her head in exasperation.

"You thinking about your session with Henley later today?" Owl asked gently.

Honestly, Lara hadn't thought too much about it at all. But now that Owl had brought it up, she frowned. "I'm not sure talking with her is gonna work."

He was shaking his head before she'd finished speaking. "Your first session went really well."

Lara snorted. Honest-to-God snorted. She ignored the way Owl's lips twitched. "Right," she said sarcastically. "I was a hot mess. Henley did most of the talking."

"The first time I met with a psychologist at the hospital in

Germany, after I was rescued? Before all the crying...I tried to punch him," Owl said lazily.

Lara gasped and her eyes got huge. "You did not!" she said after a moment.

"I did," Owl replied. "I was angry at just about everything and everyone. I didn't appreciate him digging, wanting me to tell him every little thing that happened to me."

"Did you get in trouble?" Lara asked worriedly.

"Nope. I was still weak as shit from my captivity and the guy subdued me in seconds. He actually praised me, said being able to get my emotions out was a good thing, even if it was just physically, and if I wanted to go head-to-head with him, he'd be more than willing to meet me in the gym and let me box it out."

"Wow."

"Yeah. He was amazing. He ended up being the catalyst to my recovery. I only knew him for about two weeks before Stone and I were finally cleared to head back to the States, but I still email him every now and then and let him know how I'm doing. All I'm getting at is that things are usually awkward at first. You need to learn that you can trust Henley, that she's on your side, and that takes time."

Lara pressed her lips together. It wasn't that she thought Henley didn't want to help her; it was more than obvious the other woman was empathetic and probably very good at her job. But just like Owl, the *last* thing Lara wanted to do was rehash what she'd been through. What Carter had done and said to her while she'd been mostly out of it because of the drugs he'd forced her to take.

Just thinking of the drugs made Lara uneasy. She ran her suddenly sweaty palms up and down her thighs.

Owl reached over and took one of her hands in his. It was

one of the very few times he'd touched her without first asking her permission, or letting her choose to take his hand or not. And the feel of his bare fingers in hers felt instantly calming.

"Cut yourself some slack, sweetheart. It hasn't been that long at all. But...if you really don't want to keep your second appointment with Henley, I'm not going to force you. No one will force you to do anything you don't want to."

The fact that he was giving her an out made Lara's spine straighten. She'd never been a quitter in her life, and she really didn't want to start now.

Then she thought of her best friend, and how much Cora had been through in her life...how she kept on chugging along. That was even more incentive to get her to shake her head. "I want to. I...want to get better." That in itself was a revelation for Owl, she knew. Because for a while there, she'd proven herself unwilling to do much of anything. Had been content to hide and not talk to anyone.

But she had to admit, the more she got out and about on The Refuge, the more she *wanted* to. "You'll still come with me, right?" she asked tentatively.

"Of course," Owl said, squeezing her fingers before finally letting go.

Lara felt the loss of his warmth down to her toes, but she forced herself to lean back on the couch as if it didn't impact her.

"You want to try again?" Owl asked, taking off the 3D goggles and holding them out to her.

"I'm not sure I'll ever get the hang of this," she said with a grimace, but she reached for the goggles anyway.

"You will," he said firmly. "It just takes practice."

She watched as he switched the difficulty level back to beginner and took the controllers from him with a sigh.

"All right, slow and steady," Owl said.

Lara thought that could probably be a motto for her entire life. She'd always moved cautiously—except for one time. With Ridge and her move to Arizona. And that certainly hadn't worked out very well.

Forcing her mind away from the colossal bad decision she'd made, Lara concentrated on trying not to crash the simulated helicopter.

* * *

She shouldn't have had so much for lunch.

That was the only thing Lara could think as she sat across from Henley.

After she'd crashed the fake chopper a few more times, Owl had called it quits and they'd headed up to the lodge for lunch. She'd sat at a table with a woman who'd been stalked by a co-worker for months. He'd recently been killed in a confrontation with the police, right outside her front door. The woman admitted that she still wasn't able to go about her normal activities without looking over her shoulder, and every time her doorbell rang, she had flashbacks.

There were also two former military men at the table, and while Lara didn't know their stories—as they didn't volunteer any information about why they were at The Refuge—she could see that they were hyper-aware of everything around them and anyone who walked into the room.

Kind of like Owl and his friends. She hadn't missed the way Owl's head was constantly on a swivel, how he scrutinized each and every person who walked into the lodge. For some reason, that comforted her. She could let down her guard, just a little, while she was with him out in public. That was why she'd latched onto him so desperately when she'd left that house in Arizona. Even while heavily drugged, a part of her knew he'd never let anyone hurt her.

Henley cleared her throat, and Lara realized she'd actually tuned the other woman out. She gave her a sheepish look. "I'm sorry, what?"

Henley gave her a gentle smile. "If you don't want to do this, you don't have to," she said.

"I don't want him to win," Lara blurted. She had no idea where that thought came from, but as soon as the words left her lips, she realized how true they were.

"How would he win?" Henley asked.

"He liked how scared I was," Lara admitted out loud for the first time. "He reveled in it. At first, he liked how hard I fought. He handcuffed my wrists to the bed but left my legs free. I kicked at him whenever he got close. He *loved* that. He'd pull out his dick and jack off to my struggles."

Lara was breathing way too fast, and she could feel her heart pounding in her chest. Just like it had back then.

"Did he talk while he was doing that?" Henley asked in a controlled, calm tone.

"He never *stopped* talking," Lara whispered. "He told me everything he was thinking. How much my fear turned him on. That he adored how red and blotchy my skin got when I was thrashing, how he loved seeing my breasts heave with every panicked breath, and the more my pupils dilated with panic, the more turned on he got."

Lara squeezed her eyes shut but immediately opened them

again when memories threatened to overwhelm her. She turned her head, not sure what she was looking for, but realizing what it was the second her gaze landed on Owl. He was sitting forward in his chair, his gaze pinned on hers...and just like that, she began to calm. She wasn't in that basement. She was safe here. Owl wouldn't let anyone get to her.

"When did he start drugging you?" Henley asked.

Lara inhaled and forced herself to study the other woman. She had one hand on her belly, slowly stroking, as if she didn't even know she was doing it. Though Henley wasn't really showing yet, Lara knew she was pregnant. She'd heard stories about what had happened to her daughter, how she'd been kidnapped by a local teenage ex-patient. That ordeal had to have been extremely distressing, and yet here she was, helping others. Moving on with her life.

Cora had live-streamed the wedding ceremony Henley and her husband, Tonka, had out in the barn just a few weeks ago. At that time, Lara wasn't ready to leave Owl's cabin. She remembered the look on Tonka's face. He'd looked at Henley as if she was the most important person in his life. And when he'd looked at Jasna, his stepdaughter, his look was much the same.

Owl had told her a little about Tonka's situation. What happened to him while he'd been in the Coast Guard. If he and Henley could move on with their lives after the horrible things they'd endured, it gave Lara hope that she could too.

"He didn't like that I started spitting at him," Lara admitted softly. "When I'd talk over him so I didn't have to listen to what he was saying. At first, the drugs made everything worse. I was so lethargic, he could touch me while he..." Lara's voice trailed off, and she used her hand to demonstrate a man jacking off. It was a crude gesture, but it seemed better than saying the words out loud.

"Did he rape you?"

Henley's question was blunt and almost harsh-sounding, but Lara appreciated her candor.

She looked down at her lap. "No."

"And you feel guilty about that."

She looked up in surprise.

Henley gave her a small, tender smile. "Just because he didn't penetrate you doesn't mean you weren't violated. You didn't give him permission to touch you. What he did was perverted and sick. And many times, words can be just as painful as an actual physical touch."

"He liked seeing his release on me. It itched. I can still feel it. It dried on my skin, and I can still smell him on me. It doesn't feel as if I'll ever get clean of it. Of him."

Henley leaned forward then. "You will. I promise you, Lara, you will."

"How?"

"Time. And the love and acceptance of your friends. You think Cora thinks less of you because of what you went through?"

"She doesn't know," Lara insisted.

"You think if she knew, she'd care?" Henley pressed.

Lara bit her lip. If she was honest with herself, yeah, she thought she'd care.

"She won't," Henley said firmly.

"When he came in with the drugs...eventually, I wanted them. I took them gladly. He taunted me with that too. Said I was an addict. Called me pathetic. But I didn't care. If I could've taken double, triple, quadruple the number of pills he offered me, I would've. When he was...you know...I wasn't there. I was somewhere else. Back in DC. On my couch. Watching TV."

"Good for you for having a coping mechanism."

Again, Lara blinked in surprise.

Henley chuckled softly. "You thought I was going to reprimand you for that? No way. That asshole might've thought he was torturing you more by drugging you, by making you compliant, but he was actually doing you a favor."

"But it made it easier for him to touch me," Lara insisted.

"Yes, but it also allowed you to disassociate. If he knew that you weren't listening to him, that you barely knew what was going on, would it have pissed him off?"

Lara nodded without hesitation. "I learned to moan when he squeezed my boobs or pinched me...which he did often, because he liked to see his marks on me. When I didn't react at all, he hurt me worse."

"Exactly," Henley said. "Listen to me, Lara. You might think that you were completely at his mercy, but in reality, you were controlling that situation as much as you could at the time. You figured out what you needed to do in order to stay alive. You *outsmarted* him. I hope this doesn't freak you out...but I read the report you gave to the police. You said that he claimed you were his favorite, right?"

Lara shivered but nodded.

"Then he's an idiot. Because he thought he had you completely under his thumb, but in reality, you were playing a part. I have no doubt whatsoever that if our guys hadn't gotten there, you would've found a way to escape on your own eventually."

Lara shook her head.

"Yes, you would've. You weren't restrained anymore, were you?"

Lara stared at Henley, saying nothing.

"I bet even though you were drugged, you were already thinking about ways to escape. Maybe even about grabbing his dick while he was jacking off and hurting him."

Lara swallowed hard. "He would've hurt me even more if I'd tried anything."

"Probably. But that's why you were waiting. Until his guard was down completely. So you would be sure to get away."

Lara's heart was beating fast again, but not because she was panicking. How did Henley know what she'd been planning? She was mostly out of it from the drugs when she was found. Passed out before they'd gotten to that helicopter. And she hadn't told *anyone* what she'd been thinking, planning. Not the cops, not Owl. Definitely not the woman sitting across from her.

"I see you, Lara Osler. Cora says that you were the nice one in your friendship." Henley smiled again. "That you were polite and quiet. But I see the fire behind your eyes. The determination. Being nice doesn't mean you're not willing to help yourself when the shit hits the fan."

"I woke up one evening," Lara said quietly. "He was late in coming to visit me. I don't know why. But that meant the drugs he'd given me earlier in the day had worn off more than usual. I wasn't tied down, but I'd been there long enough to know I wasn't going to be able to walk out of that basement. The door was locked and the window was too high and small for me to use to escape. But I got out of bed and walked around anyway.

"In the bathroom, under the sink, I found a piece of metal. It was almost a foot long, sharp at one end, and kind of jagged and rough along one side. I don't know what it was for or why it was there...but I took it. Hid it under the mattress. I thought about doing pretty much what you said. Thought maybe when he was masturbating, I'd cut his dick off.

"He never closed the door when he was there. I think he got off on the possibility that a member of the staff might catch him in the act of tormenting me. Or the idea that Ridge could come downstairs at any time and see exactly what he was doing. I mean...Ridge just handed me over to Carter willingly, so I doubt he cared. He was too busy spending my money to worry about what I was going through. Anyway...the door remained open. And I was scared; wasn't sure I'd ever actually use that piece of metal. But I thought about it a lot."

"You aren't helpless, Lara. Not even close. No, you weren't as strong as your captor and he was able to overpower you. But that doesn't mean you were going to be his victim forever. Waiting for the perfect moment to make your move is smart. You didn't ask to be violated. You didn't do anything to deserve to be in that situation. Sometimes life is simply unfair. You can only hope to have the strength to endure, and when the time is right, rise up and overcome the odds."

Lara pressed her lips together. Henley's words echoed in her brain.

You didn't ask to be violated.

You didn't do anything to deserve to be in that situation.

No, she didn't. All she was guilty of was wanting to be loved. Of wanting to please Ridge. That didn't warrant what happened to her.

And...she *hadn't* just lain there on that bed, resigned to her fate. No, she'd been talking herself into cutting off Carter's dick and getting the hell out of there.

"I think on that note, we'll stop for today. This goes without saying, but I'm going to say it anyway...anything we talk about in here, stays in here. And I want to be your friend, Lara, not just your therapist. But if you aren't comfortable with that, it's okay."

Lara hadn't been so sure that talking to a therapist would do a damn thing. She certainly didn't think it would make her feel safer—after all, Carter Grant was still out there and probably making plans to get her—but surprisingly, she did feel *better*.

"I'd like to be your friend too," she told Henley.

The smile on the other woman's face made Lara feel good. Really good.

"Great. How about we go raid Robert's stash of Christmas Tree Cakes?"

Lara frowned. "What?"

"You didn't know? Oh, man, our resident chef is addicted to those things. You know, the super-sugary Little Debbie cakes that are usually only around at Christmastime? Well, Ryan, our newest housekeeper—though, I guess she's not really new anymore, but whatever—has a connection and is able to supply Robert with several boxes a month."

"Are you kidding? I *love* those things!" Lara exclaimed. "Cora gets me a bunch of boxes for Christmas every year, but I can never make them last longer than a few months."

"I knew you'd fit in here. Well, come on, let's go see if we can steal a box. We'll sit in a corner and stuff our faces."

Lara actually giggled. Then asked, "Will he be mad?"

"Robert? Oh, he'll *pretend* he's furious, and he might even withhold some of his chocolate chip cookies...for like a day. He's a big softie. And since it's *you*, he'll totally not be able to stay mad."

"Are you using my situation to keep from getting in trouble?"

"Totally," Henley said with a grin.

"Well…all right then," Lara said with a shrug.

Both women stood and turned toward the door—then Lara froze in her tracks when she saw Owl standing there. Shockingly, she'd honestly forgotten he was there. She wasn't sure whether to feel bad about that or not.

"Can you give us a second?" Owl asked Henley.

"Of course. I'll be outside talking to Alaska," the other woman said. Then she reached out and squeezed Lara's arm. "You're going to be okay, Lara. You're so much stronger than you think. And that's awesome. We need more kick-ass women around here. I want as many as possible to be role models for Jas and this little one." She rubbed her belly with her free hand, then slipped out of the door to the small conference room they'd been using.

She didn't know what Owl wanted to talk about with her, but she opened her mouth to say something—she wasn't sure what—when he beat her to it.

"You good?" he asked.

Instead of immediately answering, Lara thought about it. She felt a little off-kilter from the glut of up-and-down emotions she'd experienced in the last hour. But eventually she decided that, yes, she was good. More than good. "Yeah."

Owl studied her for a long moment. It felt as if he could see inside her, see all the parts she desperately tried to keep from the world.

"Yeah, you're good," he said with a nod. "For the record, I was proud of you before, but now? I'm practically bursting at the seams with admiration."

Lara felt her cheeks warm and knew she was blushing.

Owl didn't give her a chance to respond. "Come on, I'll have your back as you and Henley break into Robert's stash of

Christmas Tree Cakes. But if he catches us, I'm denying knowledge of anything."

"So much for having my back," Lara mumbled, but she smiled when she said it.

"Hey, you have no idea how possessive Robert is about his Christmas Tree Cakes. Trust me, he'll know within hours that some of his precious stash is missing."

"Maybe we shouldn't—"

"Yes, you should," Owl said. "Because I haven't seen a smile that big on your face since you've gotten here. And if Christmas Tree Cakes is what put it there, I'll make sure you have as many as you want for as long as you live. In fact, I might have to talk to Ryan and see if I can get in on her inside source for the things."

He reached for the door, and when Lara walked through, she felt the tips of his fingers on the small of her back. He immediately dropped them, but she could still feel her skin tingling from the small touch.

Owl had always been very considerate about giving her space...and she was surprised to realize how much she *wanted* him to touch her. After everything she'd been through, it was a relief to know she could still tolerate a man's touch.

Actually, *Owl's* touch. It was an important distinction.

It felt as if Lara's world had been turned upside down in the last seven days, and she owed all of that to Owl. She'd fully planned to fake her recovery, so she could convince everyone she was doing better than she was. But she didn't have to fake *any* of the progress she'd made this week.

She felt like a new person...and she liked it. A lot.

She was very aware that everything could change back in a heartbeat. The threat of Carter Grant was looming, even if she tried hard not to acknowledge it. The time would come when he'd make his move, and Lara was no closer to knowing how she'd react.

But she was beginning to think that maybe, just maybe, she wouldn't completely fall apart, as she'd feared. With each day that passed, Lara felt a tiny bit stronger. As Henley had pointed out, she hadn't asked to be abused. Didn't deserve what happened to her. And after those encouraging words...she wanted more. Wanted more friends like Henley and Cora.

Wanted what her best friend had—a partner. Not Prince Charming, but a real-live man who would stand by her, just as she'd do for him.

There was only one man she could actually see in that role... but she wasn't ready for anything like that. And Lara had no idea if he'd ever want a relationship, especially with her. She'd never be like the old Lara, the romantic who always saw the best in people and was a bit naïve, but she realized that if *she* was all right with that...maybe Owl would be too.

Carter Grant winced as his head throbbed—again. Ever since that bitch had gouged his fucking eye out with her thumb, he'd had migraines from hell. He hated the eye patch. It itched, and the phantom pain from the trauma of his eye being injured was no joke.

Nothing was going the way he wanted. He knew for certain now that he couldn't get within twenty miles of The Refuge. He knew all the former special forces owners would remain on high alert. Knew the place had security their guests had no clue about, including cameras everywhere. And with the patch over his eye, he was way too recognizable anyway.

As long as his property—and Lara Osler was definitely *his*—was hiding out there, he couldn't get to her.

So he needed to get her away from The Refuge. But how? That was the question. He still had more research to do. There had to be a way to get his revenge on the assholes who thought they were untouchable, while also getting Lara back in his bed.

She was perfect in every way. He loved seeing his marks on her creamy skin. The thought that the bruises he'd inflicted were probably long gone made his teeth clench in anger.

Getting off wasn't half as enjoyable—or easy—since she'd been stolen right out from under his nose...and he'd tried damn hard to find a substitute. He'd hired a few prostitutes, but they were far too jaded. They were downright bored when he wanted to jack off on them.

Without their fear, he couldn't get hard.

It wasn't until he tied them to his bed, gagged them, and brought out a knife that their terror ramped up anywhere *near* enough for his dick to get with the program. But seeing his jizz on their skin wasn't the same. They weren't Lara. They had scars and bruises from someone else, and their tits and bodies were too well-used. Killing the bitches held no appeal. And the fact that the police had gotten close to finding him in Albuquerque only pissed him off more. It meant he'd had to relocate, farther away from what was *his*.

He needed to come up with a plan. Pronto.

He had plenty of money, thanks to Ridge Michaels. He'd been siphoning cash from him and his rich parents from the day he'd been hired, so funds weren't an issue. It was access, and staying under the FBI's radar.

Somehow, he'd figure out how to get Lara back and take out the assholes from The Refuge in the process. If he could ruin their business, all the better. He'd learned more than a few things while in the military. The government liked to train their elite soldiers in all sorts of subjects.

He wasn't the best hacker in the world, but he knew enough that he could maybe find a string to follow...one that would lead him to his prize.

CHAPTER FIVE

Three days after Lara had last spoken with Henley, the therapist's words still echoed in Owl's head.

You didn't ask to be violated.

You didn't do anything to deserve to be in that situation.

She'd been talking to Lara, but the words had seeped into his consciousness. At no time, in all the years since he'd been a POW, had anyone said those words to him. Not one therapist. They hadn't come out and said it was his fault he'd crashed either, and yet, that's the guilt that had consumed him for years.

Thinking back now, he and Stone had done everything in their power to keep from going down...to no avail. And just because they'd crashed, that didn't give the men who'd dragged them from their helicopter the right to torture them.

As much as the words seemed to lift a weight off *his* shoulders, they'd also done the same for Lara. She'd encouraged him to help Tonka expand the corral this morning...a task that would take hours. In the past...hell, not even two weeks ago, she would've panicked knowing he'd be out of the cabin for so long. But this morning when he'd brought up the project, she'd seemed completely genuine when she told him that she'd be okay while he was gone.

Owl had promised he'd come back to check on her every hour, and she'd insisted that wasn't necessary. That Cora was going to hang out for a while, then they'd go to her cabin and spend time with some of the other women who lived and worked at The Refuge.

He hadn't been sure what to say to that. On one hand, he was more proud than he could express at how well Lara was doing. But another part of him was a little sad that she didn't need him as much anymore. That as she healed, the time when she'd leave crawled ever closer.

It was a horrible thing to think, making him feel like a selfish asshole.

"What are you thinking about so hard over there?" Tonka asked as he stopped to wipe sweat off his brow. Summer was around the corner, but for now they were having a colder-than-average spring, so the weather wasn't as warm as usual, but with them digging postholes and wrestling with the new fencing, it felt almost balmy.

"Lara." Owl didn't bother to lie. This was Tonka. He trusted him with his life. Besides, the man had been through hell. A different kind of hell than he or Stone had experienced, but hell all the same.

"She seems to be doing better."

"Yeah."

"She going back to DC?" Tonka asked.

"I don't know what her plans are," Owl admitted. "But I'd say yeah...eventually."

"Grant's still out there."

Owl pressed his lips together and nodded.

Tonka stared at him for a long moment.

"What?" Owl asked.

"I want to say something, but I'm not sure how you'll take it."

Owl turned to face his friend. Tonka wasn't the kind of man to gossip, or really even talk all that much, period. He'd gotten much better after getting together with Henley, but he still wasn't someone who freely gave out advice. He generally hung back, observed, and offered his opinion only when asked. So whatever he wanted to say, it had to be important.

"Say it," Owl told him.

"Men like Grant...they don't stop. Once they feel as if they were wronged, or something was taken from them...she's not going to be able to stop looking over her shoulder, no matter where she goes. At least not until he's caught, and maybe not even then. The only thing that's going to stop him is death."

Owl's belly churned. Tonka's lips were pulled down in a frown and he sounded as serious as Owl had ever heard him. He wasn't sure mentioning the name of the man who'd killed Tonka's canine partner while he'd been in the Coast Guard was a good idea...but he had a feeling Tonka was talking about *that* man as much as he was Carter Grant. "Pablo Garcia is in jail. He can't hurt you, or those you love, ever again," he said quietly.

Tonka snorted. It was a bitter sound. "You know as well as I do that it's likely he'll get out. He killed two dogs, not people. That doesn't warrant as stiff a penalty."

Owl did know. And it sucked.

"Garcia vowed revenge against Raiden and me. It doesn't matter how many cameras or men I have at my back, or how much time goes by. I know that someday, somehow, he'll be back. Doesn't mean I won't be living my life in the meantime. It simply means he's always there. In my head. Taking up space. I can't, and won't, forget about his threats. But for now? I'm relatively sure I'm safe. That Henley and Jas are safe. As are all of you, my closest friends. That my baby can be born, and he or she will be all right...for now. But the second I get word that he's been let go or escaped, all bets are off."

Owl frowned. He didn't like this for his friend. Not at all.

"Anyway, at least *my* enemy is behind bars. Lara's isn't. He's out there. Watching. Waiting. He'll make his move, I have absolutely no doubt about that...and neither does Lara. Men like Grant and Garcia, their hate is who they are. They're like little kids who had a toy taken away, and so they're pissed off about it. Don't let down your guard. Not for a second. And Owl...if she leaves? She'll do so not because she wants to, or because she thinks she's safe—but because she wants to keep *you* safe. And Cora. And everyone else here. That's how he'll get her."

Owl felt nauseous. Grant coming after Lara would be stupid. But Tonka was right. And yes, Lara knew it. It was part of the reason she'd been so worried about being alone. Her time so far on The Refuge was going a long way toward healing her, as was talking with Henley, but ultimately, the threat was still somewhere about an eight out of ten.

If Grant really wanted to get his hands on Lara again, he'd find a way to do so.

"How do I help her move forward?" Owl asked his friend. "How do I encourage her to get her independence back when we all know Grant is still out there waiting for the right moment to get his hands on her again?"

"The first and most obvious thing you can do is make her

want to stay," Tonka said with no hesitation. "Here. With you. She's not stupid. She knows she's in danger if she leaves. Why do you think she's latched onto you? Find a way for her to make a life here. Give her purpose. She can be independent while living with you, Owl."

He stared at his friend. Was it that obvious how much he loved Lara?

Tonka's lips twitched. As if he could read his mind, he said, "If you think you've hidden how much you care about her, you're wrong."

"Shit," he swore.

Tonka laughed. The man actually *laughed*. Owl was so surprised to hear the sound come out of his stoic friend's mouth that he simply stared.

He clapped Owl on the shoulder, then gave him a friendly shove. "If you think I'm going to give you advice on your love life, you're sadly mistaken. I'm the last guy you should take any kind of relationship advice from."

"Uh, you're the one with a wife and a baby on the way," Owl said dryly. "You think I should ask Brick, who still hasn't actually gotten married to the woman he loves more than life itself? Or Stone, who I think is *allergic* to women? Or maybe Tiny, who walks around here scowling at everyone?"

Tonka chuckled again, and Owl was beginning to worry that hell had frozen over. Tonka laughing twice in less than a minute? The equilibrium of the world was definitely off.

"Right. So maybe I *do* have advice for you."

Owl realized he was almost holding his breath. He could use all the help he could get because it felt as if he'd been drowning for months. He wanted Lara for his own, but he was also well aware she could do so much better.

"Do what you're doing."

Owl blinked. That was it? *That* was Tonka's sage advice? "Not sure that's helpful," he told his friend.

"The difference from when Lara arrived to now...it's miraculous," Tonka said, his tone serious. "She couldn't let you out of her sight. I bet you were barely able to take a piss without her freaking out in the other room," he added, ironically repeating Lara's own words without even realizing. "And now? You're here. Helping me with this damn fence. And she's where? With Cora and some of the other girls? That, my friend, is a miracle. So whatever you're doing...keep doing it. And for the record, she doesn't look at *you* like she does me or the rest of the guys. You're in there. Just be her friend. Support her. Listen to her when she needs to talk. And be exactly who you are. Because, Owl, you're a hell of a good man."

Owl could only continue to stare at his friend in surprise. Through all the years he'd known him, he'd never been this...He didn't even know what the word was. Supportive? Intuitive?

No, that wasn't fair. Tonka was probably always this way, he'd just been dealing with some pretty heavy shit in his head, just like all the others.

"Thanks," he said after a moment.

"You're welcome. Now, this fence isn't going to build itself. And I have it on good authority that women like when their men are all sweaty and testosterone-y."

Owl burst into laughter. "Testosterone-y? That's not a word."

Tonka shrugged. "So? It's true. It's that lumberjack fantasy or something. You go back to your cabin shining with sweat, maybe with your shirt off, and Lara won't be able to resist you."

Owl rolled his eyes. "Oh, yeah, smelling like cow shit,

covered in dirt, and dripping bodily fluids all over the floor...so attractive."

Tonka grinned. "You've got a lot to learn. Come on, help me fit this post and we can get started on the next hole."

As Owl reached for the post, he thought about what his friend had said. All of it. He wasn't sure where he and Lara would end up...but for once, he had a small sliver of hope that maybe he might have a chance with the woman he was madly in love with.

But on the heels of that came the knowledge that Carter Grant was still at large, and as long as he was free, he'd want to get his hands on Lara.

No way in hell was Owl going to allow that to happen. Lara had been through enough; he'd die before he'd allow her to go through that horrible abuse and torture ever again.

Lara smiled at her friend. They'd spent a quiet and relaxing morning at Owl's cabin, chatting about easy topics that kept Lara's mind at ease. Now they were in the cabin Cora shared with Pipe, expecting Alaska, Reese, Ryan, and Luna to arrive in about fifteen minutes. They were going to sit up on the rooftop deck and enjoy the first semi-warm day they'd had in quite a while.

"Pipe and I want to have a simple ceremony here. Upstairs on our deck. Nothing fancy, just us and our officiant."

"That sounds beautiful. You don't want something like Henley and Tonka had?"

"No. I mean, their reception in the barn was awesome, but no, being the center of attention like that gives me hives.

Remember what a basket case I was when I only had to walk across the stage at graduation? I barely made it through *that*."

Cora wasn't wrong. She had such a bad case of stage fright. Even though all she had to do was walk up three stairs, take five steps, shake the principal's hand, and go down some stairs back to her seat, it was a miracle she hadn't tripped and fallen on her face.

"True," Lara said with a wide grin, remembering that day.

"I've missed that," Cora said.

"What?"

"You. Your effortless smile."

Lara pressed her lips together in consternation. "I'm sorry," she blurted.

"For what?" Cora asked.

"For getting mad at you. For yelling. I know you weren't jealous of me, you've never in our entire lives been envious of anything I've had. I was a horrible friend, and I don't deserve you. What you did...selling your stuff, going to that auction, telling off Eleanor Vanlandingham—although I wish I could've seen that part. I can't ever repay you."

Cora walked over to where Lara was standing and immediately pulled her into a hard hug. Cora was five inches shorter than Lara, but she simply yanked her forward, into her arms, and held on fiercely. "You don't need to apologize. Like always, I should've been more tactful. I knew how much you liked Ridge, I just didn't trust him."

"I know. I should've listened to you. And for the record, not that it mattered, I did already have my doubts about our relationship. My rose-colored glasses were fading. I just...I thought that maybe if I went to Arizona with him, if we got away from DC and all the stress I thought he was under, he'd realize how amazing we were together. I never meant to leave for good. It was just supposed to be for a little while."

Cora pulled back and held onto Lara's arms as she stared up at her. "*I'm* sorry."

"What on earth do *you* have to be sorry for?" Lara asked with a frown.

"That it took so long to get to you. I met with the police and your parents, and they didn't believe me. I even spoke with some private detectives, but I obviously don't have the right connections because they all felt like scammers to me. Wanted payment up front...and I'm not gullible enough to fall for that. When I read about the guys from The Refuge, and researched them, I had a feeling they were your best chance. There was always the risk that they wouldn't want to get involved. I mean, it's not like they were hiring themselves out to track down kidnapped girlfriends, but I was desperate."

"You did good," Lara told her best friend. "But I'm still mad at you," she said as sternly as she could.

"What? Why? For what?"

"Your name is on my bank account. Why in the world would you not use my money to hire them? You sold all your stuff, Cora! That was stupid."

Instead of getting upset, Cora simply smiled. "Yeah, but it made it much easier to move in with Pipe. You know, I didn't have all that stuff to move. I think it ended up being, what, like three boxes of stuff that had to be packed up and mailed out here?"

Lara rolled her eyes. "Whatever."

"I'd do anything for you, Lara. I love you so much, you have no idea."

"I love you back," Lara told her, trying not to cry.

"Right, so we have like two seconds before the others get here and I want to ask you something."

"Yes," Lara said.

Cora rolled her eyes. "You don't know what I'm going to ask."

"Doesn't matter. I'll do it."

"So you'll go skydiving with me?"

Lara winced. "Ummmm." They both knew Lara wasn't a fan of heights. And jumping out of a perfectly good airplane? That was a hard no for her.

Luckily, Cora chuckled. "I'm kidding. I'd never ask you to do that. Will you stand up for me and Pipe when we get married?"

Lara blinked in surprise. "I thought you said that you just wanted it to be you and Pipe and whoever was marrying you."

"I did. But you're my family. The only person I had on my side until I met Pipe and moved here. I literally didn't have anyone else. You gave me money, a place to live, and more importantly, you were my friend. You didn't care how standoffish I was when we met, or how many times I quit or lost a job. You just loved me for me. You'll never know how much that meant to be, how much it still means. I can't imagine getting married without you being there."

"But...what does Pipe think about that? I mean, is he going to have any of his friends there?"

"Who do you think suggested I ask you?" Cora replied.

Lara closed her eyes and took a deep breath.

"Please say yes. And Pipe and I talked about it, and if you want Owl there, he'd be more than okay with that too."

Lara's eyes opened. "Your simple ceremony with just the two of you is growing awfully fast. Next thing you know, all the guys, and Alaska, Henley, Reese, and all the other women who work here will be there too, and the ceremony will be in the lodge with Robert making a five-layer wedding cake, and dancing lumberjacks or something."

Cora laughed. "No way. Just the man I love, my best friend, and the guy marrying us."

"I'm confused. I thought you just said you'd be okay with Owl being there too."

"Pipe thought maybe Owl could get ordained. Or approved. Or whatever it's called. That maybe *he* could marry us. He did some research, and in New Mexico, it only costs like fifty bucks and he can do it all online."

"Have you guys asked him?"

"Not yet. I wanted to get your approval first."

"My approval?" Lara exclaimed. "Cora, it's *your* wedding."

"And you're my best friend. And you're the reason I met Pipe in the first place. The reason I'm here. And...I know you're more comfortable with Owl around. Please?"

Lara was overwhelmed. She loved her friend so damn much. She owed her everything. And the thought that she wanted her at her wedding? It meant the world to her. Especially when she'd come so close to losing her. To losing *everything.* "Of course I'll be there. I'd be honored."

"Yay!" Cora said with a huge smile. She leaned in and gave Lara a shorter but no less heartfelt hug, then hurried over to the counter where she'd left her phone earlier.

"I'm sending Pipe a text to let him know it's a go. He'll be thrilled."

Lara couldn't help but feel excitement race through her. It was both a foreign feeling and a huge relief. She'd been riddled with little else but fear and dread for so long, it almost felt as if she was back to the Lara she'd been before. "When are you guys planning this?"

Cora smiled but didn't look up from the phone as her thumbs raced over the screen. "As soon as we can. Owl needs to get the online certificate and we need to apply for our wedding license, but then it's a go."

"Will the other guys be upset? Feel left out? Or the other women?" Lara asked in concern.

"Nope. They already know we're planning something small and intimate. As long as we let Robert make us a special dinner up at the lodge, and they can all be at that, they're fine. I already talked to Alaska about it."

Lara bit her lip. "Are you sure? I mean, I wouldn't want anyone to be offended."

A knock on the door had Lara jerking in surprise and fear, spinning toward the sound.

"It's them. And just to reassure you, we'll ask first," Cora said as she headed for the door. "Pipe said he'll talk to Owl today. I'm thinking it's gonna be within the week."

"So soon?" Lara exclaimed, more to herself than her friend.

Cora paused before she opened the door and looked at Lara. "When you know, you know. Isn't that what you always said? Pipe is the man for me. The only guy I'll ever love. It's as if my entire being came to life when I met him. It's going to be fine. For both of us, Lara. I know it."

Lara contemplated her friend's words as she confirmed who was at the door, then opened it to greet the other women. It was kind of funny. Cora was the jaded one between them. The one who hated watching romantic movies. She always said she was allergic to romance. And here she was, getting married first, something she'd always said she didn't want. And Lara couldn't be happier for her.

And now *she* was the jaded one. The one who may no longer believe in happy-ever-after. Despite the fact she was surrounded by them here at The Refuge. With Brick and Alaska, Henley and Tonka, Reese and Spike. And now Cora and Pipe.

"Lara! It's so good to see you!" Alaska said happily as she walked toward her.

She greeted the others as well, reveling in the honest affection they all expressed when they saw she was there.

Within ten minutes, the six of them were settled on the deck on top of the house. Lara was sitting with Cora on the love seat Pipe had bought so his woman would be more comfortable when they spent time stargazing up there. Reese and Ryan were in lounge chairs, and Reese joked that she was never leaving, it was so comfortable. And Alaska and Luna were sitting on thick blankets placed on the floor, their backs leaning up against the love seat.

It felt intimate, not only because the deck wasn't all that big, but because if Lara reached out, she could touch not only Cora, but Alaska and Luna as well.

"This is an amazing space," Alaska said when their nonstop chatter paused about fifteen minutes later.

"And you can't even see it from the front of the cabin," Reese agreed.

"I'm getting married up here," Cora blurted.

"We know, you told us," Alaska said with a grin.

"Owl is gonna marry us, and Lara's gonna be here. Afterward, we'll go to the lodge and have a huge dinner."

"Sounds awesome."

"Good plan."

"I can't wait to see what my dad will plan for you guys."

"Cool."

Lara looked over at Cora and had to smile when she mouthed *told you*.

"Lara was worried you guys would be upset that I asked her to be there," Cora said.

Lara shot a frown at her best friend, but Cora wasn't looking at her.

"I don't know why. You guys are best friends, have known each other forever," Ryan said. Lara swore she heard a note of wistfulness in the other woman's tone, but Reese spoke before she could think any more about it.

"Owl's gonna marry you?" she asked.

"Hopefully. I mean, Pipe hasn't asked him yet, but he'll do that today," Cora said.

"That's cool," Reese said.

And that was all they had to say about that. No one seemed to have any issue with missing the actual ceremony. And they didn't seem to care that Lara and Owl would get to be there and they wouldn't.

Conversation turned to Jasna's rapidly dwindling school year, some of Ryan's funnier housekeeping stories, and how many months out The Refuge was currently booked.

"When are we expecting the first round of guests with kids, again?" Reese asked.

Lara looked over at Alaska in surprise. She hadn't heard that The Refuge was going to start allowing kids.

"We've got our first trial in just two weeks. And you know what...we filled those spaces in *two days*. Not that it's a surprise in the least; there are plenty of people with kids who could benefit from a place like this. I get why the guys didn't allow children before now, but I'm also excited to see how it goes," Alaska said with a smile.

"Is there anything special planned?"

"Well, not really. We've got the hikes like usual, and we thought we'd do two bonfires that week instead of just one," Alaska said.

Lara felt Cora's eyes on her, and she turned to look at her friend.

"Uh-oh, what's that look for?" Luna asked.

"What look?" Reese asked, glancing at Luna.

"Cora just gave Lara a look like this..." Luna mimicked Cora by opening her eyes wide and wiggling her eyebrows.

Everyone laughed.

"Seriously, what? You don't think that's good?" Alaska asked.

"It's not that..." Cora hedged.

"Spit it out. You're one of us now. If The Refuge crashes and burns, you'll be homeless right along with the rest of us," Reese teased.

"I just...Lara and I have been around tons of kids. Granted, they've all been preschool age, but they're bundles of energy. We have activities planned for practically every minute of the day that they're in school. I think you're going to need more than just hiking and a bonfire to entertain them," Cora said tentatively.

Lara one hundred percent agreed with her. The first day being on The Refuge property would be a novelty, and the kids would probably be fine getting the lay of the land and visiting the animals in the barn. But after that, they'd need to be entertained. Especially if single parents were involved, and Henley was going to be meeting with them in therapy sessions. Someone would have to watch the kids.

"Shoot. I mean, I suppose we could come up with something," Alaska said, looking at Reese with a worried expression on her face.

"Don't look at me," Reese said immediately, holding up her hands. "I mean, my morning sickness has gotten better, but now I'm super tired all the time. It's annoying. I'd hate to fall asleep while entertaining the kids and have them run amok as a result."

"I could ask my dad if maybe we could do a cookie-making and decorating thing," Luna volunteered.

"I'd help, but I think Carly, Jess, and I are going to be extra busy with all the housekeeping stuff that having more people in each cabin will bring. Brick already warned us, and told us we'd be making more per hour as a result, which none of us complained about," Ryan said with a shrug.

"Crap. All right, I'll get with Brick tonight and see what we can come up with," Alaska said, but her brow was furrowed and she looked worried.

"I can help," Cora said. "I mean, before I came here, I worked every day with kids. If you send me the ages of who will be here, I'm sure I can come up with some activities. I'll need a room in the lodge, though. And things could get messy. And depending on the age range, it could get hectic because, you know, I'd want to make things age appropriate. Can't have ten-year-olds making macaroni necklaces and can't have three-year-olds trying to do diamond painting."

"But we could modify the size of the diamonds," Lara blurted. "We could use small beads for the older kids and buttons for the littles. We could even use the same pictures, just modify them so they're age appropriate."

Lara felt all five women's gazes on her, but she kept her eyes glued to Cora's.

"If Robert would help, we could do gingerbread decorating. I mean, not with a holiday theme, but just regular houses," Cora agreed.

"Depending on how many kids there are, maybe we could have a sleepover in the lodge, to give the parents a break. We could make blanket tents and forts," Lara said.

"Movie night, although that might be more difficult if the kids are too far apart in ages," Cora mused.

"We could let them choose what movie they wanted; kids love having a say over what they're doing."

"Scavenger hunt where they have to do things like find a perfect leaf, make a rubbing, pick up a unique rock."

"Sidewalk chalk."

"Put on some sort of play for their parents."

"Make bookmarks."

"Dance party."

"Pool noodle boats."

"Glitter glow-fairy jars."

The two women threw ideas back and forth. All things they'd done before at the preschool in DC.

"Seriously? You guys would be willing to help?" Alaska asked when she could get a word in.

Lara realized that she'd kind of gone into some sort of tunnel vision. So many memories swamped her. She'd loved her job. Loved the children she worked with. It had been so long since she'd even thought about her kids.

"Lara?" Cora asked quietly.

Taking a deep breath, Lara turned to Alaska. "Yeah. I'd be happy to pitch in."

"Thank God!" Reese breathed.

"You too, Cora?" Alaska insisted.

Cora's eyes narrowed. "Why do I have the feeling your mind is going a mile a minute?" she asked suspiciously.

"Because it is?" Alaska said with a smile. "Don't be mad, but living here is like the smallest small town. Pipe said something to Spike, who told Tiny, who told Brick. Word is that you're restless. You aren't sure where you fit in. What you can do here to earn your keep. But the thing is, you don't have to do a damn thing. If you want to sit on your tush every day up here on this amazing deck, you can. No one expects you to work. This place is a well-oiled machine. I lucked out when I got here because the guys had just fired their last incompetent admin assistant. I just happened to do what they needed. And Henley, of course, already worked here."

"I kind of flit around and help out where I can," Reese said. "I'm taking Spanish classes so we can serve a broader community of people. My brother's wife helps with that, she calls me every day and refuses to speak English with me, so I've been picking it up faster than I probably would otherwise."

"And of course, we already have housekeepers, landscapers, an accountant, and Luna helps her dad in the kitchen," Alaska added. "So there's not much else that we need around here that isn't already being done. But if we're seriously considering opening this place for kids for designated weeks, we clearly need help coming up with activities for those kids and implementing them. I hadn't thought about it enough, obviously, so we also need more of an organized plan. So...I was thinking you could try it out this first time. See if you like it. If you don't, that's okay, we can hire someone from town to be our kid coordinator. But if you *do* like it..."

Alaska's voice trailed off hopefully.

"I'm not...I mean, I'm good with kids, but I'm not good at being in charge. I never have been," Cora said. "But Lara..."

Everyone turned to look at her, and Lara stilled. She wasn't sure what to say or do.

"You're freaking her out," Ryan said firmly. "She's helping Cora with this first group, but that's it. No pressure, right, Alaska?"

"Right," Alaska said without hesitation. "And I'm sure Brick and the others will pay both of you. They don't expect anyone to work for free around here."

"*They* all do," Cora said with a small laugh.

"No, they don't," Reese countered. "They have their cabins, and utilities, and food. That's basically their payment. Sure, they work their butts off to make this place a home, not only for the guests who come, but for themselves and their families too."

"You're right," Alaska said with a nod.

"Okay, valid point," Cora conceded.

Lara felt a little overwhelmed. She was both excited and terrified at the same time. She loved The Refuge. It had become her safe place, even if she never thought that she'd stay long-term.

But deep down, she knew that was a lie. With every day that passed, she couldn't imagine leaving. When she'd first arrived, she'd wanted nothing more than to hide out somewhere remote. Now, the thought of being alone, vulnerable, scared the crap out of her. And going back to DC wasn't appealing at all. She loved her job at the preschool, but not enough to go back to the city. While she still didn't want anyone else getting hurt because of her, she couldn't deny that having others around was a comfort.

And not just anyone...Owl and his friends. They'd more than proven that when shit hit the fan, they'd do whatever it took to

77

eliminate the problem. With Alaska and Jasna, when Reese was taken to the border, with Lara's situation in Arizona.

"I'll get with Lara and we'll come up with a plan," Cora told the others. "We'll have a lesson plan of sorts for the week and give it to Brick for approval. That work?"

"Absolutely," Alaska and Reese said together.

"Now, can we talk about what you want for your wedding dinner?" Luna asked. "I know my dad is gonna be in panic mode when he hears, and he'll want to know as soon as possible what to make."

Lara tuned out the others as they talked about different foods. She glanced down at her watch and saw it was almost one o'clock. She hadn't seen Owl in five hours...and suddenly, her skin began to get itchy. She felt restless steal over her.

Looking out over the railing on the deck, trying to reclaim her calm, all she saw was trees. Something moved in the distance, and she stiffened. Was that a shadow? Was it Carter? Was he watching her? Planning?

Anxiety ramped up inside her and in a flash, all she could think about was getting to Owl. He'd keep her safe. Had done so in the past. Had stood between her and the evil that was the man who'd hurt her.

"Lara?"

She heard Cora say her name as if from a distance, but she couldn't seem to focus. Closing her eyes didn't help. The dark made things scarier. She opened her eyes again and frantically looked around the area. Was Carter moving in even now?

She hated this! Knew she was panicking but couldn't seem to control it. She'd thought she was doing so much better. Had felt so confident in being with Cora at her house. But she was falling apart at the seams and didn't know how to stop the downward spiral. One second she was fine, and the next she wasn't.

Cora scooted over and put her hand on Lara's thigh. "You're okay, Lara. I promise. You're safe."

But she wasn't! Lara was sure of that. Carter was out there. Waiting. And he wouldn't hesitate to hurt anyone who stood between him and what he wanted.

"He's coming."

Lara heard Ryan say the words, but she interpreted them far differently than the woman probably meant.

He was coming. Carter *was* coming. And the only person who could protect her was Owl. And he wasn't here! She was alone. *Again.* And it was only a matter of time before Carter was touching her, doing those awful things...

Without thought, Lara jumped up and frantically brushed off the hands that were trying to comfort her, backing into a corner of the deck and crouching, putting her arms over her head. Doing her best to protect herself from what she knew was coming.

But it was no use. She couldn't get away!

"Shit! Ryan, you texted him?"

"He's on his way. He'll be here in two minutes."

"What do we do?"

"Give her some space."

"Should we cover her with a blanket?"

"No, don't touch her."

"I wish Henley was here!"

"Me too."

Lara heard the conversation between the women around her, but it was as if she was at the end of a very long, dark tunnel. She couldn't focus. Couldn't do anything but wait for the inevitable.

A small part of her was ashamed of acting so pitiful. Wanted to get up and fight. But what was the use? Carter was stronger. He'd overpower her like he did before and hurt her in the process. It was better to be submissive. Docile.

A spark of anger lit in her belly. *Why?* Why should she make things easy for him? She should fight! Like Cora had. She'd hurt the man—badly. Had stuck her finger in his eye. Why couldn't she be like her friend?

The thoughts ricocheted around her head, making Lara nauseous. She wanted to move, to do something to help herself, but she was frozen. Frozen in fear. In indecision.

"I'm here."

Two words. But instead of hearing *his* voice...she heard Owl's. Lara would know his voice anywhere. She lifted her head but still couldn't focus. She whimpered in fear.

"I've got you." The same time those words were spoken, Lara felt herself being lifted onto Owl's lap. She snuggled into him as close as she could get—and it wasn't enough. She wanted to lose herself in him. Make herself one with the man. With him there, she was safe. He'd make sure Carter didn't hurt her again.

"We didn't know what to do."

"Is she okay? Should I call Henley?"

"Maybe we should call an ambulance."

"Give us a minute," Owl said calmly, his voice rumbling through Lara. The more he spoke, the more the blackness in her eyes receded. The more she came back to herself and her surroundings.

"We'll go downstairs. But if you need us, yell," Cora said.

"I will. Thank you."

"No, thank *you*," Cora countered. Then said, "Come on, you guys, let's give them some space."

Lara wanted to thank her friend. For understanding. For knowing she didn't want everyone staring at her.

"You're okay," Owl crooned as he rocked back and forth with Lara in his lap. "You're safe. You're here at The Refuge. I've got you."

His words were a balm to her soul. And Lara was both relieved and embarrassed.

"Owl," she whispered.

"That's right. It's me. I'm here. You're good. Take a deep breath. Another. Good."

With every breath, Lara's muscles relaxed. Humiliation replaced the fear in her veins. "Oh, God, I'm sorry. I didn't—"

"Five hours," Owl said, interrupting her.

"What?" she asked in confusion, not lifting her head.

"Five hours. You went *five full hours* without needing to see me. That's amazing, sweetheart."

She snorted. "Five hours. Big deal," she said sarcastically.

"It *is* a big deal," Owl insisted. "It wasn't too long ago when it was about twenty seconds."

"You've got a big boil on your butt and you're happy you can get rid of it for a measly five hours," Lara complained.

Owl chuckled, and she felt his chest move under her. She was sitting across his lap, her legs to the side but her torso turned toward him, her arms curled against his chest and her head buried in his neck. She had the thought that she probably looked ridiculous.

"But it's *my* boil, and I have no problem with it," he retorted.

Taking another deep breath, and soaking in more of Owl's scent, she realized he wasn't exactly shower fresh. It wasn't that she minded his sweaty smell, it was just new. Picking up her head, she looked at him for the first time. His hair was wet around the temples, his cheeks were pink from working in the sun...and if she wasn't mistaken, his shirt was on backward and was damp with sweat.

He lifted a hand and placed it on her cheek, and Lara gave him some of the weight of her head. "You back?" he asked.

"Yeah. I'm sorry."

"Nope. As I said before. Five hours, honey. Henley told you this isn't going to be a fast process. You aren't going to wake up one day and want to move into your own place. And I'm perfectly okay with that. Cut yourself some slack. You want to talk about what happened? What triggered you?"

"Honestly? I don't know. One second I was sitting here, enjoying talking with the others, and the next, I saw shadows in the trees and that was it."

Owl nodded solemnly.

"I didn't mean to take you away from what you were doing."

Owl's lips twitched. "Honestly? I'm glad you did. Digging postholes and putting in a fence isn't exactly my idea of a good time."

Lara appreciated him trying to make her feel better.

"What do you think about Cora and Pipe's wedding ceremony?"

She blinked at him. "You already know about that?"

"Are you kidding? Cora texted Pipe, who came out to the barn and told me—not asked, mind you, but *told* me—that I needed to get my ass in gear and visit the website he was going to email me and get ordained so he could get his ring on Cora's finger sooner rather than later."

It was hard to believe she was smiling so soon after all the horrible things she'd imagined, but if anyone could make her do it, it was this man.

"And you're going to do it?"

"Of course I am." Then he frowned. "What was that thought?"

"You know you sound like Henley, right?"

But Owl's expression didn't loosen. "Don't care. What put that worried look on your face?"

"I just...are you doing it because you think I'm going to have another freak-out if you aren't here? Ruin their ceremony?"

If anything, Owl looked even fiercer after her question. "You aren't going to ruin anything. And I'm going to marry one of my best friends because I've never been more honored to do anything in my life. I've always felt a little like an outcast here. Stone has too. We're all close, but helicopter pilots are a different breed than SEALs and Deltas. We're like the nerdy little brothers. To know Pipe respects me enough to want me to participate in his wedding? It's an honor. And having you there is icing on the cake. For me *and* Cora."

"I don't know what to wear." It was the first safe thing Lara could think to say, especially when her feelings for this man suddenly seemed confusing and jumbled.

Owl smiled. Then a chuckle left his lips. "I'm sure we'll figure it out."

"Owl?"

"Yeah, sweetheart?"

"When I thought he was coming...I was so scared. I gave up. But then a part of me got mad as hell."

"That's good."

Lara stared into his eyes. She wanted to believe him. So badly. But she felt so messed up in her head. She wasn't sure *what* to believe anymore. What to think.

"And Henley will tell you the same thing when you talk to her tomorrow."

Lara had forgotten that she'd arranged for another session with the therapist the next day.

"And you know what else?"

"What?" Lara whispered.

"I think it's time you participated in those self-defense lessons again. But maybe just with The Refuge staff first. You'll feel more comfortable with people you know around you."

Lara closed her eyes. She didn't deserve this man. She'd made stupid decisions and somehow they'd led to this moment. It didn't make sense, and a part of her felt guilty. But another part didn't care. She would enjoy being here for as long as it lasted.

"Okay."

"Okay," he confirmed with a nod. Then he did something that changed Lara's world forever.

He leaned forward and kissed her forehead.

His warm lips lingered, as if he was memorizing the moment as desperately as Lara.

It struck her then—she'd thought about this moment for so long. About being in Owl's arms. He'd touched her plenty in the last few months, but she'd longed to feel...more. To have his arms around her not in a quick, platonic hug, but in an intimate embrace. Even though this wasn't exactly how she'd imagined it happening, it felt amazing. So right.

And his lips on her skin? Heaven.

Being with him like this, surrounded by his scent, feeling the warmth of his body against her own...she'd never felt safer.

Lara peeked up at him shyly, and saw a look of satisfaction on Owl's face. It seemed that he was just as happy to have her in his lap as she was to be there.

He pulled back and smiled at her.

"Let's get you downstairs. You can reassure everyone that you're okay. Then we'll go home and I'll take a shower and we'll find something to watch on TV. That sound okay?"

"Do you think we can get some lunch somewhere along the way? I'm hungry."

It was such a mundane thing to say, but for some reason it felt momentous. Probably because for the last couple of months, she'd never admitted when she was hungry. She'd eaten, but only when Owl or someone else suggested it was time.

"Yeah, I think we can do that. You want me to ask Robert for something, or have me make grilled cheese sandwiches?"

"With tomatoes and pickles?" she asked with a small smile. Deep down, the blackness and ugliness that was Carter Grant lingered, but she was determined to push that, *him*, to the recesses of her mind. She'd have to deal with him one day...but that day wasn't today.

Owl wrinkled his nose. "If you want."

Lara smiled. He hated pickles, and putting them on a sandwich was completely gross in his opinion. But he'd do it for her.

"I want," she told him.

"Right, then that's what you'll get. Can you stand?"

"Of course." But when she got to her feet, Lara found she was a little wobbly. Owl's arm went around her waist a second later, supporting her. He led her to the stairs and insisted on going down first—and backward, holding onto her the entire way.

Lara was a little embarrassed when she first went into Cora's cabin to say goodbye, but her friends quickly made her feel more at ease.

It wasn't until later that night, when it was dark outside and she was sitting on the couch under a fluffy blanket, her feet in Owl's lap, and they were binge-watching a show about the British royal family, that Lara thought more about what had happened that day.

Her best friend was getting married, wanted Lara there, she'd gone five hours without the need to have Owl within sight, she'd agreed to help Cora entertain the kids coming to stay at The Refuge in a couple of weeks, and she felt as if she was getting closer and closer to the other women who lived and worked on the property. And not superficial friendships either. The concern on their faces after Owl had brought her down from the deck had been real.

And it felt good. Really good.

Yes, she'd had a flashback, and it was a bad one. But she couldn't shake that feeling of anger that had welled up deep down. Even if she'd planned to give up, to let Carter do whatever he was going to do, that small spark of fury gave her hope. It was the same feeling she'd had after finding that piece of metal she'd hidden under the mattress.

She wasn't there yet, but maybe in the future she'd be able to do more than just freeze when Carter finally made his move. She might not win, might not be able to get away from him or prevent him from hurting her, but just knowing that her psyche might be ready to fight for what she was building here at The Refuge, made her feel like a different person than the Lara Osler who'd naively flown to Arizona with a man she hadn't even loved.

CHAPTER SIX

"Jab! Jab! Jab! That's right. Harder. Stop trying to protect him. Hit him like you mean it!" Pipe ordered.

Owl kept his gaze locked on Lara as she punched the pads he wore on his hands.

This was the second self-defense lesson she had attended, and all the women were really into it. He thought they might not take it too seriously, but he'd been wrong. Every single one of them had somber expressions on their faces as they followed Pipe's directions on how to hit and punch. They didn't joke around. Didn't make light of what they were doing. Which made sense considering everything that had happened to some of them.

Lara wasn't super coordinated, but every time she made contact with one of the pads, he felt it down to his toes.

Minutes later, Pipe was still verbally encouraging the group when, all of a sudden, Lara dropped her arms and stared off into space for a moment.

Then she spun and headed for the door.

Owl didn't hesitate to follow. He tossed off the pads and reached her just as she was pulling the door open.

"Lara?"

She looked up at him—and her eyes were full of tears.

Immediately concerned, Owl wrapped an arm around her and pulled her close. She landed against him with a soft *oof*...but she didn't freeze up. She did the opposite, in fact. She wrapped her arms around him and lowered her head to bury her face in his shoulder.

"Lara? You okay?" Cora asked. She and Pipe had obviously seen Lara's almost-exit and had come to see what was wrong.

"I've got her," Owl said.

"But what's wrong?" Cora asked.

Thankfully, Pipe put his arm around her waist and kept her from coming any closer. "Owl's got her," he murmured.

"But—"

"Owl's got her," Pipe repeated a little more firmly.

"Fine. Lara? If you need anything, just let me know later, okay?"

The woman in his arms didn't respond verbally, just nodded against him. Owl gave Pipe a chin lift. Gratitude rose within him for his friend. He was relieved Pipe had faith enough in him to get to the bottom of what was bothering Lara.

He steered them both out of the room and heard Pipe raise his voice to the others to keep going, to keep punching the shit out of their attackers. He would've smiled in any other situation, but he needed to find out what had upset Lara.

He could've brought her to one of the empty conference rooms in the lodge, but he wanted her to feel safe. And the safest place he could think of was his cabin. They'd both spent a lot of time there over the last few months, and thanks to her presence, it truly felt like a home.

Thankfully, they didn't run into any guests on their way out of the lodge or as they headed toward his cabin. Owl had them both inside within minutes and locked the door behind them. He steered Lara to the couch and sat down next to her. She immediately folded her legs and curled into him.

Owl shifted so he was resting against the cushions, Lara held tightly against him. He didn't bother asking what was wrong; she'd talk when she had composed herself. He'd learned that about her. That when she had a nightmare or a panic attack, it didn't help to bug her to talk about what was wrong. Giving her space to work through things in her head first was what she needed.

So Owl did what little he could. Held her tightly and made sure she knew she was safe.

"You're good, sweetheart. Take deep breaths. That's it. I've got you. You're safe here, the doors and windows are locked, no one's getting in. And if they do, you know I'll stand between you and them, just like I did before." He kept up the reassuring words, not really knowing what he was saying.

Owl rested his cheek against her hair as he gently stroked up and down her arm. He had no idea how much time had passed when she sighed against him. Her warm breath wafted over his chest, and it took every ounce of control Owl had to keep his dick from hardening. Dealing with his arousal was the very last thing this woman should have to endure right now. Although it was getting more and more difficult to keep her from seeing how much she affected him. The longer he was around her, the more he wanted her.

But that's not what she needed from him. She needed to feel safe. Needed his friendship. Without strings.

Lara lifted her head and bravely met his gaze. His hand came up and smoothed the hair back from her face. "Better?" he asked.

She nodded.

"Want to talk about what happened?" Henley had encouraged him to try to get her to talk when she had an anxiety attack, after she'd calmed down. Had told him that sometimes talking through whatever it was that triggered her would make it seem less scary.

"Sometimes it all feels so useless," Lara said softly.

"What does?"

"The self-defense. The security. Looking over my shoulder."

"It's not," Owl said with a shake of his head. At her skeptical look, he continued. "You never know what's going to come in handy at some point in your life. How the smallest thing could make a difference. Could make *all* the difference."

He could tell she didn't believe him. Thought he was simply trying to make her feel better. And while he *was* attempting to do that, he also wanted to get through to her.

He decided to tell her something he'd never told another soul. Not any of his therapists, not Stone, none of his friends here at The Refuge.

"When I was being tortured...one time, my captors got bored with their usual daily routine...you know, beating the crap out of me, seeing who could knock out more of my teeth. They decided to break the bones in my hands.

"You've seen me with the flight sim, you know how important my hands are for flying. The thought of them taking that away from me was unthinkable. If they managed to disfigure my hands, with the conditions we were being kept in, I had no doubt they'd get infected and the likelihood of any doctor being able to put them back the way they were was slim to none.

"The one thing they wanted during *every* torture session was for me to beg. I refused. I didn't want to give them the satisfaction. But that day, in order to keep them from breaking the bones in my hands, I begged. I got down on my damn knees and begged them for my life. For Stone's. To let us go. To stop hurting us.

"They loved it. I think that was the video clip that actually went viral. Me on my knees, crying, trying to divert their attention from the idea of breaking the bones in my hands."

"Owl..." Lara murmured.

"I'm not telling you this for your sympathy," he said after taking a deep breath. "I do have a point. Anyway, it worked. They were in such a hurry to upload the damn video that they threw me back in my cell and left me, and my intact fingers, alone. The next day, we were rescued. But in the process, one of the Delta Force Operatives was shot. He dropped to the dirt right after the team blew my cell door open. There was a firefight, and his teammates couldn't stop to give him medical attention. So while they engaged with the captors, I rendered first aid to the man who'd been willing to give his life for mine.

"His heart had stopped. I don't know if it was shock, loss of blood, or what. But in the middle of that firefight, I started CPR. Conditions weren't ideal." Owl snorted at the understatement. "But I was that man's best hope at the time. We were both extremely lucky. After only a minute or so of compressions, his heartbeat returned. He wasn't out of danger, but at least his heart was pumping again.

"My point is this: If my hands were broken, if my captors had

done what they'd planned, there's no way I could've adminis-
tered CPR. The pain would've been too unbearable to do
compressions the way I needed to. That man would've died right
in front of me. So...my decision to beg, this small but shameful
thing, had huge ramifications."

Lara's gaze was glued to his.

"Learning how to punch might not mean that you can knock
someone out with one right hook—but it could surprise
someone enough for you to run. So I'll say it again. Our smallest
decisions can have far-reaching consequences."

He could tell she was mulling over his words carefully, which
made him fall for her all the more. She could've dismissed him.
Come up with alternatives to the situation she'd just heard.
Maybe one of the soldier's teammates would've been able to do
CPR. Maybe Owl would've been able to do the compressions
even with all his fingers broken. But instead, she listened with all
her heart and soul.

"I'm sorry that happened to you," she finally said.

Owl nodded. "Just as I'm sorry about what happened to you."

"I want to be brave. I want to stand up to him. Some days I
think I'm ready. That I'm so mad about what he did, I have no
doubt when I see him again I'll be able to beat him. But other
days, I'm so terrified. I know that I'll be that same scared
woman who gladly swallowed those pills, if only to dull the pain
and humiliation he was inflicting on me."

Owl wanted to correct her. She'd said *when* she saw him
again, instead of *if*. But he wasn't stupid enough to think that
Grant wouldn't do everything he could to get his hands on Lara
again.

"All you can do is prepare. I wish I could sit here and tell you
exactly what to do in any future situation you might find yourself

in. Unfortunately, I can't. But I *can* tell you this—you are not the same woman you were a few months ago. I know down to my bones that whatever happens will not be a repeat of before. And if I was a betting man, I'd put all my money on you."

Lara's eyes filled with tears, but Owl refused to break eye contact.

"And I'd go even further and say that God forbid I was ever a POW again, I'd want you by my side. Because I have no doubt whatsoever that you'd surprise the hell out of our captors. You'd find a way to outsmart them, simply because of who you've become."

"Owl, I...you...Crap."

He smiled, then got serious again. "Your instincts are spot on, sweetheart. Hitting my hands with gloves would be nothing like a real life-or-death situation. Whoever you're trying to hit won't stand still. They won't have padding on their hands or face. Punching them would hurt. A lot. It would take more than one little smack to make them let you go. And they'd probably be hitting back. It's kind of like my flight sim. It seems real to you because you've never flown an actual chopper. But it's not. The smell is different. The feeling of the instruments is different. Choppers are loud, even with the headsets on. There's usually chatter in your ear from your copilot and others on the ground as you fly. But that doesn't mean the simulator doesn't have value. It's just different."

"You're telling me the self-defense classes aren't useless."

"That's what I'm telling you. And I'm definitely not an expert on hand-to-hand fighting, but Pipe is. He's got great advice. Stuff that you can store away, up here." Owl tapped her temple gently.

"Like going for the soft-tissue spots," Lara said dryly.

"Exactly."

"Cora was amazing," she whispered. "I was mostly out of it, but I saw her jump on Carter's back. She really hurt him."

"She did," Owl agreed. "And you know what? He let go of Pipe."

"And hurt *her* by throwing her across the room," Lara said dryly.

"True. But her actions gave Pipe the opening he needed to disable him enough so we could get the hell out of there."

"If I have the chance, I'm killing him," Lara said fiercely, staring at Owl boldly as if waiting for him to be shocked, to talk her out of it.

"Okay," he said.

"Okay?" she questioned, obviously surprised by his reaction.

"Yup. And I am too."

"Oh."

"You want to go back up to the lodge and the lessons?" he asked, knowing deep down that's what she needed. He would prefer to sit here on his couch with her snuggled into his side, but he wanted her to get back on her feet even more. To soak in every bit of advice Pipe could give her. Because an uneasy feeling in his gut told him she'd need it.

"I think so. Owl?"

"Yeah?"

"Thanks." She picked up one of his hands and brought it to her mouth, where she kissed his knuckles. "I'm glad your hands are okay."

A jolt of arousal shot through Owl once more. Seeing her lips on his skin made him think of her lips somewhere else. It was inappropriate as hell, and he kind of hated himself for thinking such carnal things, but he couldn't help it.

"Me too," he said unsteadily.

When she lifted her gaze to his this time, Owl could've sworn he saw the same arousal he was feeling reflected in her eyes. But it was probably wishful thinking.

"Come on, lazy bones. If we hurry, we can probably catch the tail end of Pipe's training."

Owl stood, taking Lara with him. He should've dropped his hand from around her waist, but he couldn't bring himself to do it. All too soon, she'd be strong enough not to need him...and he was dreading that day more and more.

* * *

Lara was only a little embarrassed when everyone turned to glance at them when they re-entered the conference room Pipe was using for the self-defense lessons. But thankfully, no one made her feel weird about leaving halfway through. Then again, she didn't really expect them to. The women she'd gotten to know at The Refuge were good down to their cores.

This time, when she was practicing kicks on a very patient and trusting Owl, instead of thinking about how useless this would be against Carter, who was bigger and stronger than she'd ever be, she imagined kicking his knee out from under him. Pipe said over and over how the goal wasn't to completely overpower an attacker, it was simply to incapacitate him long enough to get away.

During a break from practice, while Cora was demonstrating on Pipe the different places to hurt someone, and how to use other parts of your body than just hands and feet—using elbows, knees, and even your head as a last resort—Lara became hyper aware of Owl standing next to her.

They were so close, his arm was brushing against hers. She could smell the soap he'd used in the shower that morning. She was keenly aware that if she moved even a little, she'd be pressed up against his side. And she had no doubt that if she did that, he'd lift his arm and put it around her waist so she'd fit against him even better.

Blinking in surprise at the sudden jolt of arousal that shot through her, Lara held her breath. She'd thought that after... Well, *after*...she'd never feel arousal for a man again. That Carter had ruined any kind of desire to be intimate.

But she was definitely feeling desire at the moment.

She thought back over the last few months. Owl had been nothing but careful with her. Giving her the space she needed. Only touching her now and then. But with every day that passed, and she felt less scared and needy, Lara wanted the man even closer. And not just because she needed him to feel safe. He did that for her, of course, but more than that, she *liked* him.

As a person. As a friend.

As a man.

Glancing at him, she saw he was paying close attention to what Pipe was saying. She recalled him mentioning once that he wished he'd gotten a lot more hand-to-hand training. Now, it was obvious he respected his friend and was getting as much out of the lesson as the women.

He must have felt her staring, because he turned his head and caught her eye.

"You good?" he asked as his brows furrowed in concern.

Lara gave him a small smile and nodded.

He reached around her and squeezed her upper arm briefly, before turning his attention back to Pipe.

That simple touch sent sparks down her arm, straight to between her legs.

Damn! If that simple embrace made her feel so tingly, what would their entire bodies touching skin-to-skin feel like?

Lara blinked, shocked at the idea. Did she really think she could be intimate with Owl? After what she'd been through?

Yeah. She thought she could.

Owl wasn't Carter. Wasn't anything like *he* was. Owl would rather die than hurt her in any way.

And just that suddenly...Lara wanted him.

The question was, did he want her the same way? Maybe he was simply being the kind man he always was. Maybe he thought of her like a sister. He might be horrified to learn that she thought of him in a sexual way.

"Lara? Are you sure you're okay?" he asked.

She jerked. Shoot, he'd turned to look at her again, and she'd missed it because she was thinking about what it would be like to be naked in bed with the man. *That* thought made her lick her lips in anticipation. He'd kissed her a couple times, tender kisses to her temple or forehead, and suddenly she wanted to know what his lips might feel like against hers.

He'd be firm but gentle at the same time. He wouldn't force her. He'd go at her speed.

"Lara?" he asked again.

She felt her cheeks heat and desperately tried to hide her arousal. "I'm okay."

"I think we're almost done. You want to bug out early?"

Lara shook her head. She desperately wanted to talk to Cora. She needed her best friend's perspective.

"Okay, but if you need some space, just let me know and we'll go."

She didn't know what she'd done to deserve this man at her side, but suddenly she wanted to do whatever she could to keep him there. "Thanks."

Owl was right, Pipe was winding down.

"Remember that just because you're women, that doesn't mean you're helpless or incapable. You're just as capable as anyone who might be trying to hurt you or the people you love, and probably twice as smart. If someone is bigger or stronger than you, that doesn't mean they're automatically going to win. I think my Cora proved that point nicely. The key is not to panic. Use what you have at your disposal, and never, ever give up. Understand?"

Looking around, Lara saw Alaska, Henley, and Reese nodding their agreement. Henley had her hand on her belly and Tonka stood behind her, his hands on her hips. Alaska was next to Brick, his arm around her waist, and Reese gazed up at Spike with an adoring look on her face, which her husband returned tenfold.

Just being in a room with these women—women who'd been through hell, but managed to come out the other side bent, not broken—was an inspiration to Lara. Simply being around them made her feel stronger. She wished she'd managed to venture out of Owl's cabin weeks ago, but she refused to feel bad about that. She'd needed the time. The space to feel safe.

Lara felt like a caterpillar who'd just emerged from its cocoon. Life was much different as a butterfly than a caterpillar, but no less dangerous. She just had to learn how to navigate this new world she'd found herself in.

"Wasn't that great?" Cora asked as she approached Lara.

"It was. Sorry I left for a while."

"No worries. You okay?"

"Yeah, I think I am," Lara said with more confidence than she'd felt in a long time. She wasn't sure if it was the story Owl had shared with her or what. But she had the insane thought that she actually *wanted* Carter Grant to find her. To get their showdown done and over with, so she could get on with her life once and for all.

"Are you guys hungry? I'm starving!" Henley exclaimed as she approached them with a huge smile.

"Yes! Let's go see what Robert's making for lunch. Maybe we can convince him to let us eat early," Alaska said as she joined them.

"As if you have to convince him to let you do anything," Brick said with an eye roll. "You all have him wrapped around your little fingers."

"Don't be jealous, honey," Alaska told him with a small smile, patting his chest.

"Jealous? Who's the one who made you moan with—"

Alaska reached up and slapped a hand over his mouth as she blushed bright red. "Yeah, yeah, yeah," she told him.

Brick grabbed her hand and tugged it down, kissing her palm. "Take your time. I'll go relieve Tiny from the reception desk until you're done eating."

"Thanks."

"Of course," Brick said. Then he leaned down and kissed her lips before heading for the door. Tonka and Spike had already left, so it was just the girls, Owl, and Pipe left.

"You want to go with them?" Owl asked Lara. "Or we can go see Robert and bring lunch back to the cabin if you want."

"I think I'd like to eat with the girls today."

The pride she saw in his eyes made Lara feel good.

"Okay. Sounds like a plan."

"There's a group who signed up to hike out to Table Rock before lunch today, you want to join me in taking them?" Pipe asked Owl.

In response, he looked at Lara.

She loved how attentive he was to her. But she also felt guilty. Because she hadn't been able to let Owl out of her sight, *he* hadn't been able to do a lot of the stuff around The Refuge that he usually did. She didn't like that she'd been the reason the others had to take up the slack.

"It's fine. I want to finalize some of our plans for the kids with Cora after lunch. We can stay here in one of the conference rooms and talk after we eat...if that's all right," Lara said, looking at Cora.

"It's perfect, actually. I had some questions about how much time some of the activities might take, so we can work on the timeline for each day and figure out who will work with which age groups, and how we want to break up the activities," Cora replied.

That decided, Pipe hugged Cora, and Owl shifted Lara a little farther away.

"You sure you're good with this? I can stay around the lodge if you need me to."

"I know, and I appreciate it more than I can say. What you said earlier...you know..." She glanced down at his hands. "It helped. A lot."

"Good. Both Pipe and I will have our phones with us if you need anything. Don't hesitate to reach out."

"I won't."

They stared at each other for an awkward second or two before Owl smiled. He reached for her hand and squeezed it, then headed for the door with Pipe.

For a moment, Lara thought he was going to kiss her. She even leaned forward a little in anticipation.

She definitely needed to talk to Cora, and maybe the others too. The conversation might be embarrassing, but she needed advice. Man advice.

CHAPTER SEVEN

Fifteen minutes later, Alaska, Henley, Reese, Cora, and Lara were sitting around a table in the kitchen, stuffing their faces with the sandwiches, sliced veggies, and cookies that Robert was preparing for The Refuge guests. He'd grumbled about them barging into his kitchen and demanding food before it was ready to be served, even while quickly accommodating them.

"You look...good," Alaska told Lara a little hesitantly once they were all seated.

"I actually feel good today," Lara said. "And I feel like I need to apologize to you guys. I—"

"No," Reese and Henley said at the same time.

Henley reached out and put her hand on Lara's arm for a moment before sitting back. "You really don't. First, because we all get it. Seriously, we do. And second, because you've done only what you've needed to heal. And no one here is ever going to accept an apology for you doing what you need to do. We understand."

Alaska leaned forward and pinned Lara with her gaze. "Small spaces," she said quietly. "I never used to mind them, but there are days when I break out in a sweat simply thinking about opening a closet. A freaking *closet*! It's stupid. It's ridiculous. And yet, sometimes my brain goes back...there. And it's just too much. But you know what? I've learned when I have those bad days to cut myself some slack. I went through hell and was lucky to come out on the other side. I know it, Drake knows it, and everyone here knows it. There's no judging here, Lara. None."

"I have some mornings when I don't feel as if I can let Jasna get out of my car when I drop her off at school," Henley added. "Like, I literally want to grab hold of her arm, jerk her back into the seat, and drive away like a bat out of hell. Her being taken was so hard because I had zero control. And it *sucked*. But then I look at her beautiful smile and realize how amazing and happy and whole she is. She isn't afraid of the world, even after being kidnapped, and I'm so very thankful for that."

"And it pisses me off," Reese said with an adorable wrinkle of her nose, "but I have no desire to ever travel again. I went down to South America by myself and didn't think twice about it. But now? Nope. I'm officially a homebody."

Cora shrugged when the others looked at her. "I was scared," she admitted. "But I was held against my will for like, an hour or whatever. Most of my fear comes from thinking of the people I loved getting hurt. That means you, Lara. And Pipe. And all of you guys. I'm still waiting for the moment when you all come to your senses and wonder what the hell you were thinking, being my friend, but in the meantime I'm going to enjoy the hell out of finally being a part of the popular crowd."

"First of all, we are anything *but* the popular crowd," Alaska said with a small snort. "But none of us care. And secondly..."

you're stuck with us, Cora. There's nothing wrong with you. Nothing at all."

Everyone murmured their agreement.

Henley turned back to Lara. "So, you see? We all have fears and things we struggle to overcome. And that's just *us*. I won't even get into our men. Or every single guest who comes to The Refuge. And if you're thinking for one second that any of us will hold your actions against you, you need to learn to stop. In fact, I'll go so far as to say I think you're doing an amazing job. It wasn't too long ago when this," she gestured around the table, "would have been impossible for you. So celebrate the small wins, Lara. Will there be setbacks? Of course. But that's a part of healing."

"I'm proud of you," Cora said, emotion making her words gruff.

"Me too," Reese echoed.

"Me three," Alaska said with a smile.

"Me four," Henley agreed.

"Right," Lara said, struggling for a moment to contain her emotions. "So...I have a question, but I'm not sure how to ask," she blurted.

"You can ask us anything," Alaska said, sincerity lacing her words.

"I don't think I can trust my instincts when it comes to people anymore. I never would've thought Ridge could do what he did to me...you know, leaving me to Carter's mercy. But he did. And at one point, I thought he was someone I could spend the rest of my life with. So now, I...I'm worried that what I'm feeling is...because of gratitude. Or that I'm stupid and crazy for feeling the way I do. I don't know." Lara was aware she was rambling. That she wasn't making any sense. Suddenly, talking to all these women at once didn't seem like the best idea. She should've just sat down with Cora.

Alaska's eyes seemed to dance. "Please tell me you're saying what I think you're saying. Are you talking about Owl?"

Lara's cheeks heated. She shrugged. "He's been...amazing. He hasn't complained once about me needing him within sight for months. He's never made me feel like a burden, even though I know I am. And lately, I...he...Has he had many girlfriends?"

Reese and Cora were grinning like fools, and Alaska looked like the cat who'd gotten the cream. But it was Henley who spoke. "Owl? No way. Ever since I've known him, he hasn't seemed interested in any women. Not at all."

"Oh," Lara said, a thought occurring for the first time. "Does he *like* women?"

Everyone laughed.

"He likes one woman in particular," Cora told her friend.

Lara blinked in surprise...and tried to tamp down the disappointment and pain that followed those words.

"*You*, silly! He likes *you*!" Alaska exclaimed.

Relief swept through Lara. "I'm not so sure," she said. "I think he's just being nice."

"He is," Henley said. Then she elaborated. "But no man, and I mean *no man*, would do what he's done if he wasn't emotionally involved. He can't take his gaze off you when we're talking in our sessions. I'm talking laser-focused on you, Lara. If you gave the slightest indication that you didn't want to be there, he'd act. I have no doubt."

"He's always got his eyes on her," Alaska agreed.

"Because he's waiting for me to...freak out," Lara suggested.

"Nope. Not even close," Reese said with a shake of her head.

"Like Pipe looks at me," Cora explained gently.

Lara closed her eyes as hope rose within her. She'd seen for herself how Pipe looked at her best friend. As if the sun rose and set with her.

She felt someone touch her, and she opened her eyes. Cora had taken her hand.

"I can understand why you'd be reluctant to trust yourself. But Owl is not Ridge. The men here...they're different. They would never lead a woman on. They'd never make her think there's something deeper than there is if no feelings exist. From what I've seen, and from what I've heard from Pipe, Owl is a good man. Do you like him?"

Lara licked her lips and nodded.

"Have you told him?"

"No. I don't want...what if he really doesn't feel that way? What if it makes things weird?"

"What if it doesn't?" Cora countered.

"Carter's still out there," Lara reminded her friend. "What if he hurts Owl, or you, to get to me?"

"If he does, that's not on you. You deserve this, Lara. You deserve *him*," Cora said.

"He doesn't deserve me though. A paranoid, scared-of-the-dark victim who's being hunted by a serial killer," Lara said a little bitterly.

"Anyone who earns your love would be *lucky* to have you," Alaska said fervently. "We've seen your friendship with Cora. How you'd do anything for her, and we all know the depths she'd go to for you. If you think that kind of relationship is normal, or common, you're dreaming. Anyone who's the recipient of that kind of loyalty and love would do whatever it took to keep it. To earn it for himself."

Lara looked at her new friend.

"Give him a chance," Alaska urged. "He's not going to let you down."

"It's him," Cora said, making Lara's focus shift back to her. "The one. The man you've been looking for all your life."

Lara swallowed hard. She wanted to believe that. But she was scared. *Terrified.*

"Trust him," Reese encouraged.

"I want to, but I don't know how to let him know I'm interested," Lara admitted, getting to the real reason she wanted to talk to the women in the first place.

"Kiss him," Cora said firmly.

"I agree. I don't think you need a lot of words. All it's going to take is the slightest indication that you're interested in him the same way he's interested in you, and he'll take things from there," Alaska said.

"How do you feel about intimacy?" Henley asked gently. "You know, after everything that's happened recently."

Lara thought about that for a moment before saying, "If it was anyone but Owl, I'd say that was a hard no. But...Owl won't hurt me. He'll go easy."

Henley nodded approvingly. "He will. But if anything makes you uncomfortable, you need to speak up. If he actually hurt you, even inadvertently, it would destroy him. After what he's been through, the last thing he'd ever want to do is make you feel uncomfortable."

Lara nodded.

"With that said...I agree with Cora. Kiss him. I think if you tried to *tell* him how you feel, that you're interested, it's likely that he'd try to talk you out of it because he'd think it was for your own good. That maybe you're just interested because he helped save you. But if you *show* him your feelings..."

A shiver went through Lara. She could almost feel Owl's lips on her own. She wasn't completely convinced she could make such a bold move like her friends were suggesting, but at least if he wasn't interested, she'd know immediately.

"Hey! We're having a party and I wasn't invited?" Jess asked as she entered the kitchen.

Lara smiled. She liked the other woman. She was one of the three housekeepers employed at The Refuge.

"What're we talking about?" Jess asked.

"Lara was worried she's been too weird for us, we convinced her otherwise, and she likes Owl and was asking advice on how to let him know," Cora summed up.

"Cora!" Lara protested.

"What? Just catchin' her up," she said innocently.

Most of the time, Lara loved her friend's blunt personality. But at the moment, she had to admit she was feeling a little embarrassed.

"What'd you tell her to do?" Jess asked, grabbing an apple off the counter and taking a bite.

"Kiss him. I would've suggested going into his room at night and crawling into bed...naked, but I figured that was a bit much," Cora said with a giggle.

"I knew Eric was the man for me the first moment I met him. But he was shy. *Really* shy. I realized things were going to take forever if I didn't make the first move, because he wasn't catching on to the little things I said or did to try to encourage him. We'd met to go on a hike just outside of town, and there was a little girl who'd fallen on the trail and skinned her knee. He was so good with her, my ovaries just about exploded.

"After he'd put a Band-Aid on her knee and made her smile, the girl and her mom left. I just couldn't control myself any longer. I pulled him off the trail, backed him against a tree, took his hand and shoved it under my shirt over my boob and kissed the crap out of him."

Lara stared at the woman with big eyes.

"Wow! What happened?" Reese asked.

Jess grinned. "He fucked me against that tree, then I spent the night at his house and never left. I'm telling you, the shy ones are *monsters* in bed."

As the other women catcalled and laughed, Lara felt those tingles between her legs once more as she thought about what kind of lover Owl might be. The fact that she wasn't freaking out over the idea of sex made her feel as if she might actually be healing from her ordeal, more than any other strides she'd made.

Alaska fanned herself with her napkin. "Whew! Is it hot in here?"

"Scorching. I think I need to go find my man," Henley said.

Everyone laughed again.

"Lara?" Jess said.

"Yeah?"

"Kiss him. Owl is head over heels for you. I've never seen anyone so protective of someone else before. And before you say that being protective isn't an indication that he likes you as more than a friend—you're wrong. It's the *best* indicator. Eric doesn't have a temper, but all it takes is for someone to say one derogatory word about me or my job to get him riled up on my behalf. You won't find a better man for you than Owl."

Lara was very glad she'd decided to eat lunch with these women today. "I will," she blurted.

"When?" Cora demanded.

"I don't know. When the time seems right."

"The time will never seem right," Jess argued. "I mean, in the middle of the woods against a tree probably wasn't the best timing, but it worked out."

"So, what, you think I should just walk into the lodge and plant one on him?" Lara asked sarcastically.

"Yes!"

"I'd pay to see that!"

"Absolutely!"

Lara laughed at her friends. "Whatever."

Cora squeezed Lara's hand that she was still holding. "I'm so happy for you."

"Don't be happy yet. He might not want to change things up between us," Lara said.

"He does. He will," Cora said confidently.

"On that note, I need to go out front and relieve Brick from the desk. He doesn't love being there," Alaska said.

"And you do," Henley said with a smile.

"I do," she agreed. "I know, I'm weird."

"We all are," Reese said with a shrug.

As if Alaska's leaving was a signal, the others all got up to put their dishes away and head out themselves, until it was just Cora and Lara left in the kitchen.

"Do you really think he likes me...that way?" Lara couldn't help but ask.

Cora grabbed her hand again. "Do you really think I'd be encouraging you to open yourself up to Owl if I didn't think down to my toes that he would be receptive?"

"Well, no."

"Then there you go. I've watched *Cinderella* with you how many times? A hundred? A thousand?"

"It hasn't been that many times," Lara protested, even

though she knew it was probably somewhere between those two numbers.

"He's your Prince Charming. Not rich, but you don't need money. Not from a royal background, but I have a feeling that would be a pain in the ass. He's struggled and suffered...so he knows what you've experienced."

Lara blinked in surprise. Cora didn't know what Owl had told her, but she was so on the money with that comment, it was almost scary.

"He's your match, Lara. You've been looking for him your whole life. You've had some bumps in the road along the way, but you did it. You found him. Now you just have to find the courage to reach for what you want. And...I think I need to say it. *Hold on.* For all you're worth. Don't let go, no matter what."

"What if he wants me to?" Lara couldn't help but ask.

"He won't."

"How can you be so sure?"

"Because he needs you."

"I think it's the other way around," Lara said dryly.

"Nope. If you think men don't need their women, you're wrong. You need each *other*. Owl is perfect for you, just as you're perfect for him."

"I hope so. I think it would break me for real if he rejects me."

"He won't," Cora said firmly.

Lara smiled. "How did we get here? With you being the one who's all boy-positive and me being reluctant?"

"Fate," Cora said with a small smile. Then she hooked her arm in Lara's. "Come on, let's go figure out our schedule with the kids who'll be descending on The Refuge."

Feeling excitement well up inside her, Lara nodded. She was

happy to be helping out, to be doing what she loved. With every day that passed, she felt more like her old self...albeit with a little more caution thrown in.

She couldn't forget that Carter Grant was out there somewhere, but her determination to live her life was slowly returning. Lara couldn't control the future; all she could do was live in the moment. And that's what she was going to try to do.

CHAPTER EIGHT

After Owl and Pipe returned from the hike with the guests out to Table Rock, they headed to the lodge. Brick had requested an owners' meeting and no one hesitated to agree.

When he entered, Owl wasn't sure what the huge grin Alaska shot his way was about, but he immediately asked where Lara was. After sticking his head into the small room where Alaska said he could find her with Cora, and seeing for himself that Lara was all right, he made his way to the larger conference room where his friends were convening.

Tonka was the last one to join them, and as soon as he was seated, Brick spoke.

"We talked about the possibility of getting a chopper for The Refuge after Stone and Owl borrowed that helicopter to head down to the border to rescue Reese. And after what happened in Arizona, I think it was made even more clear that having a chopper at our disposal would be a good addition. We could help with searches for missing hikers, and maybe even transport fire-fighters in the case of wildfires.

"I've talked it over with Stone, and we agree that the best place for a hangar and helicopter pad is near his cabin, where we'd been planning on building a few more cabins. But this isn't a cheap proposition. We'd have to forego the extra cabins for now, and more staff to help with the housekeeping and admin. But more importantly," Brick looked at Stone and Owl, "you two would bear the brunt of buying and maintaining the chopper. You guys are the pilots, and you know about upkeep and safety and pretty much everything that has to do with owning a heli-copter. What do you two think?"

Excitement rose within Owl. After he and Stone had crashed and been tortured, for years he wasn't sure he'd ever wanted to fly again. But he'd kept up his training and licensure because he hadn't been able to let it go. And flying down to find Reese with Stone had felt so right. Climbing into the pilot's seat was like coming home.

And while the circumstances in Arizona hadn't been ideal, and he really didn't like flying the R66 chopper, the adrenaline rush he'd gotten from the rescue was eye-opening.

The one thing he knew without a doubt he could do better than just about anyone on earth, was flying. In the sky, he didn't feel as if he was lacking. It didn't matter how well he could shoot, or how good he was at hand-to-hand combat. Up there, he was the best of the best. And he loved it. Being an Army Night Stalker pilot was one of the things he was most proud of in his life. And the thought of being able to continue to fly and help others with his skills—and not have to worry about being shot down by terrorists—sounded like a dream come true.

But Brick was right. There was a lot involved with owning a

helicopter. Safety being the top of the list. They'd need to find mechanics who could help troubleshoot and fix issues they couldn't, they'd need to figure out how to get fuel, and while The Refuge was profitable, they weren't a charity, so they'd need to decide when and how much to charge people for their services.

Maybe they could even offer rides to their guests, so they could see the beautiful landscape of Northern New Mexico...for an additional price, of course.

Even though building a hangar and a landing pad would be a pain in the ass, Owl couldn't help feeling thrilled by the prospect.

He looked over at Stone, trying to determine what he was thinking about all of this. When their gazes met, Owl knew his friend and fellow pilot was on the same page.

"Yes," Stone said firmly as he turned back to Brick.

"Hell yes," Owl agreed.

Their friends all grinned.

"Are we really buying a fucking helicopter?" Tiny asked with a huge smile on his face.

"I think we are," Brick agreed. "Although, now we have to find one. I've talked to Tex, and he's connecting me to some contacts who can help find what we're looking for."

"A Bell," Stone said. "Maybe a 505. They're reliable, a lot of law enforcement departments use them. The avionics system is top notch and easy to read, and it has a good-size cabin. It's not the largest bird on the market, but for what we need, I think it'll be a good fit."

"Agreed," Owl said. "And it only needs one pilot, which comes in handy."

Stone grinned at his friend. "What? You don't want to fly with me anymore?"

"Shut up. You know there isn't anyone I'd rather have in a copilot seat than you."

"You mean pilot seat. *You* can be the copilot."

Owl grinned at the banter. The truth was, they were both perfectly capable of being pilot or copilot, but it was fun to argue about it.

"Okay, that's settled then. I'll call a contractor in town and start discussions on clearing some land and getting the plans drawn up for the hangar and pad. If we get a bite on a good deal before it's done, we can probably rent a space at the regional airport in Los Alamos."

"Wow, you aren't wasting any time, are you?" Spike asked.

"Since when do we waste time on anything once we've made up our minds?" Brick asked.

"True. Look at us. Married, kids on the way, we don't fuck around," Tonka quipped.

When their laughter died down, Brick turned to Owl. "I'm gonna need you guys to take the lead on this. Which means traveling to check out any potential choppers. Take them on test flights, things like that. We could arrange to get it transported back here to The Refuge, but I'm thinking maybe the two of you wouldn't mind flying her back here from wherever we buy one. But that means..." His voice trailed off.

"Lara," Owl said, knowing what his friend was getting at.

"Exactly."

Owl's first thought was that there was no way he could do it. He couldn't leave Lara, not when she was still so vulnerable.

"I can do it," Stone volunteered without hesitation. "Owl can stay here."

But the thing was, Owl didn't *want* to stay here. He wanted to run his hands over the bird. Do a proper inspection. Feel her rumble under him. Buying a helicopter wasn't exactly like buying a car, but close in many ways. He needed to see how she handled. And every pilot was different; things he discovered in test flights wouldn't be the same things Stone noticed. It would be smart if they both made the decision on such an important purchase.

"Lara is doing much better. We're not talking about leaving tomorrow to go check out a possible helicopter, are we?"

"No," Brick said. "I mean, Tex is on the hunt for us, so I'm guessing it won't take too long, but we need to talk to Savannah as well, make sure our numbers are good so we can do this. I don't foresee a purchase happening immediately."

"Let me talk to Lara," Owl said. "I'm thinking she might be all right in a couple of weeks, enough that I can go with Stone."

The expression on Stone's face told Owl that his friend wasn't so sure.

"I have faith in Lara. I think she'll be okay," Owl told his friends.

"What if she goes with you?" Tiny suggested.

"That's a great idea," Stone said immediately.

"She's been here since we found her. It might do her good to get away. See some new scenery," Spike agreed.

"What about Grant?" Pipe asked quietly. "We all know that threat hasn't been neutralized."

Owl frowned. He knew his friend was still blaming himself for not killing the man when he had the chance—and he hated that. Taking a life was something none of them had ever done lightly. But the man was a literal serial killer, and Pipe regretted leaving him alive. There was a better-than-average chance the man had already killed again since they'd rescued Lara. They all worried about that very thing.

"There's no way he'd know where she was," Tiny said. "I

mean, he probably knows she's *here*, but it's unlikely he'd know where Stone and Owl might go to pick up a chopper. Hell, by the time he realized Lara wasn't at The Refuge anymore—if he somehow even learned *that* much—she'd be back."

Owl liked the option of taking her. He wasn't thrilled at the thought of leaving Lara, but having her come? Being able to share what he loved with her? Yeah, he was definitely on board with that.

He refused to think about the possibility of her not liking to fly. She'd been unconscious when they'd left the house in Arizona and had no recollection of that flight, which was probably a good thing. And flying for pleasure was way different than being in the middle of a life-or-death situation.

"I think that'll work. She can give you her opinion from a layman's perspective," Spike agreed. "You know, if the seats are comfortable, how loud it is, if she can understand what you're saying in the headsets. That might seem silly, but if we're going to be giving tours and people are going to pay big bucks for them, we don't want bad reviews because the seats suck or they couldn't hear a damn thing."

"That's a good point," Brick agreed. "So...Owl and Stone, you're okay with this? You want any of us to come with you?"

Owl thought about the offer for two seconds before shaking his head. He saw Stone doing the same. He wasn't going to ask Tonka or Spike to accompany them, because their wives were pregnant. Brick was the heart and soul of The Refuge, and no one wanted to take him away if they could help it. Pipe and Cora were just starting their lives together, and Tiny hated flying.

A small part of Owl was scared shitless about being off The Refuge property and completely responsible for Lara's safety, but if something *did* happen, he had no doubt he'd do whatever it took to make sure she was protected.

Even if it meant sacrificing himself.

That thought should've been startling. That he was willing to give his life for hers. But given how he felt about her, it wasn't. Just weeks ago, he'd made a vow to himself that if it came down to her life or his, he'd gladly give up his own. And he felt even more strongly about that decision now.

As he thought about it, his fear waned and excitement over the prospect of getting Lara away from here grew. Showing her that she could reintegrate into the world outside of the safe bubble The Refuge offered. Not that he wanted her to leave, but he also didn't want her to stay simply because she felt she had no choice.

"I'm okay with it if Owl is," Stone said.

"And I'm okay with it if Stone is," he countered, the two men smiling at each other.

After another twenty minutes of talk about financing, and setting a tentative time for Owl and Stone to meet with the contractor later that week to walk the grounds and decide exactly where the new hangar should be and what it should contain, the meeting broke up.

Owl hung back to talk to Stone.

"You sure you're good with this? It'll mean we'll be way busier," Owl said.

"Hell yes. I love this place, and I love helping with the hikes and landscaping, and clearing the trails, but working with birds again? I'm definitely all right with being busier. What about you?"

"I'm in," Owl said with a grin. Then he sobered. "And you really don't mind if Lara comes with us?"

"Not at all. She's…"

"She's what?" Owl asked, concerned about what his friend might say.

"Good for you. You seem more settled lately."

"Yeah," he agreed. "She understands me in a way not many people can."

Stone nodded. "Happy for you."

Owl snorted. "There's nothing between us, Stone."

"Yet."

He grinned slightly. "Yet," he agreed.

"What are you waiting for?" Stone asked.

He gave his friend an incredulous look. "He tied her to a bed. Drugged her. *Jacked off* on her. She's still working through that shit in her head. I'm thinking getting into a romantic relationship this soon probably isn't the best idea."

"What does Henley say?"

Owl shrugged. "I don't know. I haven't talked to her about it."

"You should."

"I'm not so sure about that. I'm thinking Lara just needs more time."

"Life can change on a dime," Stone said with a small frown. "We know that better than most. One moment you're living the dream, and the next you're being beaten to within an inch of your life and you don't know if you'll live to see the next day."

"I understand that. You *know* I do. But the last thing I'd ever want to do is hurt her, Stone."

"So, you're moving slow then," his friend said.

"Yeah. And maybe going with us to check out whatever chopper Tex finds will be the catalyst to her seeing me as more than a crutch."

"If I can do anything to help with that, just let me know. I mean, having a third wheel around probably isn't the best thing for romancing your girl."

Owl didn't crack a smile. "You aren't now, nor will you *ever* be, a third wheel. I haven't said it before, but...you know that I wouldn't have survived that hell without you, right?"

"Yeah. I feel the same way."

A few seconds went by before Stone broke the emotional moment. "Holy shit, we're getting our own chopper," he said with a grin.

"I feel like it's Christmas and my birthday all over again," Owl admitted.

"Same," Stone agreed before clapping Owl on the shoulder and turning for the door.

Owl smiled and followed his friend. He needed to talk to Lara, maybe ease into the conversation about the possibility of leaving The Refuge. He wanted to be careful, avoid freaking her out, but he hoped and prayed that she might be excited about the opportunity to not only spend time with him outside of New Mexico, but the chance to take a little more control of her life back.

CHAPTER NINE

Lara had chickened out over a dozen times since she'd gotten the advice to simply kiss Owl as a way to let him know how she felt.

He'd been so excited a week ago, when he'd escorted her back to his cabin and told her all about the possibility of The Refuge getting a helicopter. She was excited for him, and she belatedly thought it could have been the perfect time to kiss him, to share in his joy. But she hadn't.

Since then, they'd both been busy, Lara spending more time with Cora, finalizing the plans for the families who would arrive in a week. And Owl with Stone, researching everything chopper-related in case the purchase went through. They'd met with a contractor, and she'd watched from a short distance as they described exactly where the hangar would go and what it would look like and how many trees needed to come down in order to make the landing pad safe. To Lara, it didn't seem as if they were asking for *enough* trees to be taken down, but she trusted the men to know what they were doing.

But deep down, anxiety was building within her. If The Refuge got a helicopter, it was likely Owl and Stone would be the ones who would go inspect and possibly buy it. Which meant he'd be leaving The Refuge.

The thought of him not being around made her uneasy. Carter was still out there. If Owl left, would that be the break Carter needed to come after her? And beyond that, Lara wasn't sure she'd be able to go a week or more without Owl at her side.

The more she thought about it, however, the more she accepted the *real* reason she didn't want Owl to go...and it had nothing to do with potential panic attacks.

It was because she'd miss him desperately.

She'd spent almost every minute of every day in his presence for months. She'd talked to him, laughed with him, and felt safe enough to let down her guard to sleep because she knew he was nearby.

The fact of the matter was, she enjoyed being with Owl. And she'd never felt so comfortable with another man. Ever.

She'd thought she'd been in love in the past, and she'd definitely felt a kind of short-term infatuation for guys. But what she felt for Owl was completely different. He settled her. Made her feel strong. As if she could handle whatever else life felt the need to throw at her. No one else ever made her feel that way.

Which made it even more frustrating that she hadn't been able to drum up the courage to kiss him. The few times she'd considered it, something happened to make her back off. Someone walked into the room. She sneezed and the moment was gone. She simply lost her nerve.

Despite that, with every day that passed, Lara fell for him even more.

Now, this evening, Cora and Pipe were getting married. After the ceremony, they'd head to the lodge for the dinner Robert had painstakingly planned. And the mood around The Refuge was celebratory and romantic.

No one seemed put out that they wouldn't be there to see the actual ceremony. That was one of the best things about The Refuge and the people who lived and worked there. The friendships formed here were real. Deep and true. Not based on what anyone could do for anyone else. If Cora and Pipe wanted a private and intimate ceremony, that's what they would get, and no one felt left out or annoyed by their decision. They were all simply happy their friends were together.

Earlier in the week, Alaska had grilled Lara on her size and favorite color, then surprised her by coming to Owl's cabin with three outfits for her to choose from to wear to Cora's ceremony. It was one of the most thoughtful things anyone had ever done for her, and Lara was almost overcome with gratitude.

While the two dresses Alaska had brought for her to try on were beautiful, Lara felt the most comfortable in the third outfit. It was a simple pair of gray slacks, coupled with a gorgeous soft-pink blouse that had long sleeves and felt like silk. The bottom layer of the shirt was form-fitting, while the outer layer was flowy and swished and flowed like the sand on a windy beach when she moved. Lara had fallen in love with it as soon as she'd seen it in the box.

And the best part wasn't even how comfortable it felt on... but the look on Owl's face when he saw her.

He looked utterly stunned.

On one hand, Lara felt a little embarrassed that he was so

blown away by how she looked, because that probably meant he'd gotten very used to the oversized shirts and sweats she'd worn since she'd known him. On the other hand, she couldn't deny that she loved the look of awe on his face when she'd walked into the room to model the outfit for him and Alaska.

She felt just as awed when he strolled out of his room, ready to walk her over to Pipe's cabin. He'd changed into a pair of black slacks and a white long-sleeve button-up shirt...

With a pink tie that perfectly matched her shirt.

It should've been a little cheesy. But instead, his choice to match her outfit made Lara feel giddy. How many times had she seen couples dressed alike and smiled at how cute they looked? Others might make fun of those people, might roll their eyes and think it was ridiculous, but not Lara.

"You look nice," she told him, internally wincing at her less-than-effusive word choice.

"And you look absolutely beautiful," Owl told her.

"You don't think I should've chosen one of the dresses?" she asked nervously, running a hand down one of her thighs.

"No. This is perfect. *You're* perfect."

For a moment, the air between them seemed charged. He'd stopped close enough to her that all it would take was one step forward and she'd be in his arms. She wanted to kiss him. Desperately. Wanted to do what she'd been dreaming about for a week now.

At that moment, his phone dinged with a text.

A few seconds went by and Owl didn't move. He didn't reach for his pocket to see who was messaging him. He simply stared into her eyes. Lara licked her lips, wondering if he was going to make the first move to act on the obvious attraction they were feeling.

When his phone dinged again, he sighed and reached for his pocket.

He read the text, then lifted his gaze to hers once again. "That's Cora. She wants to know where the hell we are because she's ready to marry Pipe already."

Lara chuckled. "She's never been super patient."

The smile on Owl's face was easygoing and relaxed, and Lara did her best to memorize it. "Then we'd better go before she marches over here to get us."

And another opportunity to let this man know that she wanted to be more than friends was lost.

Owl went to the closet and grabbed her jacket and helped her into it, his fingertips brushing against her shoulders. Lara shivered as he shrugged on his own coat. Spring was still cooler than normal for the area. Early mornings and nights were chilly, but at least not cold enough to need gloves anymore.

Especially not when Owl immediately reached for her hand after he'd locked the door to the cabin. They stepped off his porch, and Lara realized she was content. Her life wasn't perfect. She still had panic attacks and, more importantly, Carter Grant still hadn't been apprehended.

But Lara was...surprisingly all right. A couple of months ago, she never would've thought she'd be where she was today, emotionally. She'd been so broken. Had thought she'd never be able to be happy ever again. But the people here at The Refuge, most especially Owl, had helped her see that while bad things had happened, she could rise above those things and come out stronger on the other side.

Her talks with Henley helped a lot. But it was thinking about Owl and Stone, and what they'd been through, and seeing them doing so well today, that helped the most. They didn't deserve what happened to them. And she hadn't made a wise decision by going to Arizona, but that didn't mean *she* deserved what happened to her either.

The fault was Carter's. No one else's. He was an evil man who did evil things. And while Lara was still scared shitless of the fact he was on the loose and probably planning horrible things when it came to her, with every day that passed, she felt less scared. More capable.

"If you get overwhelmed at any point tonight, just let me know and we'll go," Owl said as they walked toward Pipe's cabin.

Lara squeezed his hand. "I will. Thanks." She felt his gaze on her and turned her head to look at him. "What?"

"It's just...in the last couple weeks, you've made incredible progress. I'm so proud of you."

She smiled. "Thanks. Talking with Henley has helped; I can never thank you enough for encouraging me to try therapy. Hearing *your* story helped even more. And...I don't know...being here, with you, seeing how happy Cora is, watching the other women interact with their guys, observing some of the guests and how hard they're working to overcome their demons...it's all been very eye-opening and has helped put what happened to me in perspective."

"I'm glad. But I think you're not giving yourself enough credit. You're incredibly strong, Lara. You would've gotten where you are today without being here at The Refuge. I have no doubt."

He was wrong, but it felt good that he thought so. That he thought she was strong. There were definitely days when she felt anything but, and he'd put up with a lot from her. Her clinginess, her panic attacks, her inability to do much more than huddle on his couch for weeks on end.

All her life, Lara had wanted a partner who would give as much as he took. Who would take care of her as much as she took care of him. And she thought she'd found that in Ridge Michaels. Who knew it would take him completely screwing her over to find what she'd *really* been looking for all along?

They reached Pipe and Cora's cabin, and the door opened as they approached.

Lara gasped when she saw her friend standing there, impatiently gesturing for them to hurry up and get inside.

Cora was wearing a black knee-length dress. It showed off her curves and looked absolutely amazing on her. It had been a very long time since Lara had seen her so dressed up.

"What took you guys so long?" Cora demanded. "We've been waiting forever!"

"It's only two minutes past when they said they'd be here," Pipe said, coming up behind Cora and wrapping his arm around her waist. He wore a pair of jeans and a black short-sleeve polo shirt that showed off the tattoos on both arms. He looked handsome, and the way he stared at his wife-to-be made Lara's heart melt.

"Yeah, yeah, yeah," Cora said as she backed up to let Lara and Owl inside. "I just need to grab my shoes and we can go up to the deck."

"You need any help?" Lara asked.

"Yes!" Cora exclaimed. Then, after a long pause, she grinned at Owl. "You're gonna have to let go of her."

Lara felt Owl squeeze her fingers before doing just that. Almost immediately, she missed the feel of his hand in hers. But she dutifully followed Cora to the bedroom.

Cora shut the door and turned to Lara. "Have you kissed him yet?"

Lara's lips twitched, and she shook her head at her friend. "No."

"Why not?" Cora demanded.

"Because every time I think about doing it, the timing is off. Like today...when I thought maybe he might kiss me, you texted and broke the moment," she said wryly.

"Shoot!" Cora said, her brows pinched together.

Lara couldn't help but laugh. "It's fine. If we were any later, you would've lost your mind. Anyway, if I'd kissed him already, you'd definitely know by now. And I'm hoping that once we *start* kissing, maybe it won't end there."

Cora's head tilted as she studied Lara. "You're different," she said after a moment.

"What do you mean?"

"Well, when we first got here, I wasn't actually sure you'd be able to get past what happened. And I don't mean that in a bad way; I wouldn't have blamed you. I was *hoping* you'd be able to find the person you used to be, find your way back to her. But now...I don't think that's going to happen."

Lara frowned.

"You were quiet. Shy. You were content to fade into the background. And other than at work, you didn't like to make decisions. You just went with the flow."

Lara thought back to the person she was in DC and knew her friend had her pegged exactly right. She'd never liked being the center of attention. She much preferred to hang back, to let life swirl around her. But after the things she'd been through, the thought of standing against some metaphorical wall and letting others decide her fate held no appeal. The lack of control she'd had while in that basement in Arizona had fundamentally changed her. Now she wanted more control of her life.

"You're right," Lara said.

"I know," Cora said without a hint of conceit. "I'm so proud of you, Lara. I was so worried about you. I wanted to do more, but I didn't know how to help. And another woman, someone who didn't love you as much as I do, might have become jealous or pissed that you turned to Owl instead, but not me. I wouldn't care if you never talked to me again if it meant you were going to be all right."

Lara's eyes filled with tears. Some people had lots of friends. Dozens of people they called their best friends. But all Lara needed was one. One person who had her back, no matter what. And Cora was that in spades.

"I love you," Lara blurted.

"I love you too, but if you make me cry on my wedding day, I'm gonna be pissed," Cora said, blinking quickly to try to prevent the tears in her eyes from falling.

That was another change. Cora had never been a crier. But obviously the events of a few months ago had affected her too.

Without thought, Lara stepped forward and yanked Cora toward her. Since she was tiny, it wasn't too difficult. She hugged her best friend hard.

Cora returned the embrace just as fiercely. Then she took a deep breath and stepped back. "Right, mushy time is over. How do I look?"

"Amazing. Beautiful. Like a princess," Lara said without hesitation.

Cora rolled her eyes. "Whatever. I told Pipe I wasn't going to wear a white dress, and honestly, I don't think he cared *what* I wore for our wedding. But after I tried on a hundred different outfits and still couldn't find one I was happy with, he suggested this dress." She ran a hand self-consciously down her thigh as she shifted uneasily in front of Lara. "It's the dress I wore to the auction. I wasn't so sure...I mean, it's not as if this dress cost that much, but I dug through the few boxes of crap I still owned that Pipe arranged to be packed and shipped here from DC and found it. When I put it on, you know what?"

"What?" Lara asked, loving this story.

"It felt right. I mean, it's black, so it's not typical for a wedding, but I actually feel pretty in it."

"As you should, because you are!" Lara told her. "What shoes are you wearing?"

Cora smiled and walked over to the closet and pulled out a pair of two-inch black heels. "They're from Payless. And yes, I was wearing these that day too."

Personally, Lara thought her friend's outfit was perfect. And even better since Pipe had suggested it.

"Well, put them on so we can do this," Lara said with a smile.

Cora put the shoes on the floor and slipped them onto her feet. She straightened and smiled at her friend. "I can't believe this is happening," she whispered.

Lara's smile grew. "I can. It's about time someone realized what I've known for years and years. That you're an amazing woman and you'd make someone an equally amazing partner."

"Thanks," Cora whispered.

"Come on. Let's go. I'm sure Pipe is anxious to get his ring on your finger."

"Lara?" Cora said, not moving.

"Yeah?"

"I would've waited as long as it took for you to be able to stand up with me."

It was Lara's turn to get teary-eyed.

"You'll always be my best friend. Just because I'm getting

married doesn't mean that our relationship will change. At least I hope it won't. And even if you go back to DC and I'm here… don't think you're gonna get rid of me that easily."

Lara chuckled through her tears. But the immediate visceral reaction she had even *thinking* about leaving The Refuge was almost scary. She hadn't thought about going back to the East Coast. Not once. In one of the few phone calls she'd had with her parents, they'd mentioned it, but Lara had never entertained the idea. She couldn't imagine going back there. And not only because this was where Owl lived. DC held too many bad memories. And if she saw Eleanor Vanlandingham, after hearing how she'd treated Cora at the auction…she wasn't sure what she'd do to the woman.

Taking a deep breath, she decided to lighten the mood. Cora would hate it if she actually cried right now. Because then she'd go out into the other room, Pipe would ask what had happened and if she was all right, and it would delay their ceremony. So she said, "If you tried to blow me off, you wouldn't like what happened."

To her relief, Cora chuckled. "Right. I'm shaking in my boots," she said, then walked toward the door, snagging Lara's arm as she passed. "Come on. I want to marry my man, go eat some grub, then come back here and have my wicked way with him all night."

"Like that's any different from any other night?" Lara teased.

Cora stopped in her tracks and stared at Lara for a moment before grinning and shaking her head. "I think I like this new Lara. Teasing me about sex? I can't *wait* until you and Owl get it on and we can talk sexual positions and how good our men are in the sack."

Lara didn't comment, just went along docilely as Cora headed for the door once more.

The pang of longing deep down almost hurt. She wanted exactly what her friend described. More than she could put into words. Wanted to be able to sit down and talk sex and relationships with her best friend. But honestly, she wasn't sure what would happen in the future. Owl might see her as nothing more than the broken woman who was the best friend to one of *his* friends' wives. She didn't *think* that was the case, but she'd been completely wrong when it came to her love life before.

Luckily, she didn't have too much time to think about that because as soon as they entered the main room, Pipe walked over and pulled Cora in his arms. He kissed her long and hard, then headed for the front door without a word.

"Guess it's time," Lara joked, feeling a little like a third wheel.

"You think they'd even notice if we didn't join them on the rooftop deck at all?" Owl said with a chuckle.

Lara should've been surprised that Owl was on the same wavelength when it came to being a third wheel around their friends, but she wasn't. Not after how much time they'd spent together.

Owl reached for her hand once more and led her out of the house behind their friends. Before she knew it, they were on the deck. Looking around, Lara was impressed. It was just what Cora said she wanted, an intimate ceremony at sunset. Pipe had switched out his colorful fairy lights for white ones, adding more strings along the deck railings, and the sun was low enough in the sky to give the lights an ethereal glow. Cora was beautiful, and Pipe looked so strong and imposing. His gaze never strayed from the woman in front of him.

Owl stood next to his friends and pulled out a piece of paper from his pocket, clearing his throat before speaking.

Unfortunately, Lara didn't hear a word. She couldn't stop staring at Cora and Pipe. Their emotional connection was easy to see. All her life, Cora had been the one who was skeptical of love. She'd made fun of Lara for her romantic side, suffered through countless viewings of *Cinderella*, and couldn't stand Hallmark movies around the holidays. She thought they were cheesy and unrealistic.

And yet, here she was. Her hands in Pipe's, looking up at him just as those heroines in those Hallmark movies looked at their heroes.

Lara closed her eyes. If she hadn't made that stupid decision to go to Arizona with Ridge, if she hadn't been the object of a serial killer's obsession, if Cora hadn't decided to go to that auction to try to bid on Pipe...her best friend wouldn't be where she was right this moment.

She wouldn't have found the one person in the world meant to be hers. She wouldn't be marrying the love of her life.

Contentment spread through Lara. She'd been through hell. Had thought she was going to die. Had endured things no one should have to experience. And yet...suddenly, she knew she wouldn't change a moment. One of the things she'd wanted for years had happened...because of *her*. Her best friend was happy. Truly and deeply happy.

It made everything worth it.

"Cora...you may say your vows."

Lara turned her attention back to what was happening in front of her. Cora and Pipe had decided to write their own vows, and she didn't want to miss them.

"All my life, I've been an outcast. Looking through windows, wanting what I saw happening inside. But the harder I tried, the more elusive those dreams got. As time passed, I realized that I was different. Something was wrong with me. There had to be, because no one ever seemed to want me. My love was rejected time and time again. Until Lara."

Cora turned her head and smiled at her friend.

Lara swallowed hard, trying not to burst into tears.

"She accepted me as I was. Brash, outspoken, and bitter. So very bitter. And then she disappeared. And I panicked. If the one person who actually liked me could leave, what did that mean? And then, there you were, Pipe. On that stage. I couldn't take my eyes off you. You were different. Like me. I saw how people looked at you. How their gazes went from your tattoos, to your long hair and beard...and they judged you. Oh, how they judged. I think I fell in love with you at that moment, but I didn't want to admit it. Because admitting it meant opening myself up to rejection, just like when I was a kid.

"But you burst through all my walls. You made me understand what love truly meant—accepting the other person exactly as they are. I love you, Pipe. More than you'll ever know. But one thing you *should* know, is that you'll never be as loved as loyally as I will love you. You'll never have to wonder if your wife is faithful. You'll never have to question if I've got your best interests at heart. All those rejections I went through as a kid just made my love all the deeper now. I'll support you in whatever you want to do, and I'll beat the crap out of anyone who dares to give you the side-eye because of how you look. You're perfect for me, and I'll always be in awe at how life managed to put you in my path just when I needed you most."

It was hopeless to try to keep the tears from falling. Lara

wiped her cheeks with her hand and gave Owl a small smile when he lifted a brow at her, obviously asking if she was all right.

"My turn?" Pipe asked, prompting Owl.

He chuckled and turned his attention back to the couple. "Sorry, yes. Pipe, your vows?"

"I love you, Cora. And those arseholes who rejected you when you were little were the ones who missed out. Not you. I will always honor and cherish you. *Always*. You're my everything, and I don't give a shit about people side-eyeing me, but if they dare say one word about you, all bets are off. When we have kids, they'll never go one day without knowing down to their bones that they're loved and wanted. And that goes for the ones we adopt as well as the ones we have ourselves."

"Pipe," Cora whispered, clearly overwhelmed.

Pipe dropped her hands and pulled her into his embrace. Her hands landed on his chest while one of his arms was locked around her waist, the other hand on her cheek.

"You're mine, Cora. From the moment I saw you from that stage, I was intrigued. But it was when I was standing in your empty flat, and realized the lengths you'd gone to in order to help your best friend, that I fell in love. Irrevocably, instantly in love. I wanted that loyalty for myself. Needed it. I'm an intense bloke, and you'll probably get irritated with that, but I don't care. You're mine, just as much as I'm yours. Forever."

After exchanging rings, Cora and Pipe grinned at each other, and Owl finished the ceremony.

"With the power vested in me by the state of New Mexico, I now pronounce you man and wife," he said with a huge smile.

Pipe turned his head and glared at his friend. "And?" he demanded.

"And what?" Owl said.

"You're forgetting the best part," Pipe growled. Honest-to-God growled.

Cora giggled as her arms snaked upward and went around her new husband's neck.

Owl grinned. "Oh, you mean the kissing part?"

"Yeah, asshole. The kissing part," Pipe complained.

"Didn't think you needed permission to kiss your woman."

"This is our wedding. You're supposed to say it. So say it already, damn it!"

It was funny to see the friends griping at each other, and Lara thought it was kind of adorable that Pipe wanted the traditional words.

"Right. Fine. Pipe, you may now kiss your bride."

"It's about damn time," he muttered before lowering his head.

The kiss her best friend and new husband shared was deep, long, and so full of love, Lara had a hard time looking away. The way Pipe held Cora. The way his hand spanned the small of her back. The way she went up on her toes to get closer. It was all so damn beautiful, Lara couldn't help but sigh in satisfaction and joy.

"You good?"

Lara jerked in surprise as she felt Owl's hand on her back and he leaned toward her. She hadn't seen him approach; she'd been too busy enjoying her best friend's happiness.

"I'm great," she told him with a huge smile.

Time felt suspended as they stared at each other.

Then, so caught up in the beauty of the moment and joy for her friend, Lara moved without thought.

She leaned in and kissed Owl.

It was a brief kiss, no more than two pairs of lips meeting.

And as soon as it was over, Lara second-guessed herself. She pulled back and looked into his eyes, not sure what she'd see.

Emotion swirled in Owl's gaze, and the hand at the small of her back pressed against her for a moment. What was he thinking? She had no idea. But she took comfort in the fact that he didn't look appalled. Or disgusted. In fact, he looked...awed. Which in turn made Lara relax.

She hadn't messed up by kissing him. Thank goodness.

"I'm so happy!" Cora exclaimed from next to them.

Lara turned her attention away from Owl and turned toward her best friend. Owl stepped back, and then Cora was throwing herself at Lara.

Laughing, Lara caught her, and they swayed back and forth as they hugged.

"Look!" Cora ordered as she held her hand in front of her best friend's face.

Lara chuckled again, catching hold of Cora's hand and holding it still. Pipe had wanted to surprise her with the ring and hadn't let her know anything about it until he'd put it on her finger.

It was classy and beautiful, and so totally perfect for Cora, Lara felt all melty inside again. The band was platinum with an inset emerald-cut diamond, with two princess-cut diamonds flanking it.

"I love it so much!" Cora exclaimed happily.

"It's perfect," Lara agreed.

Cora hugged her friend again, before turning back to her new husband.

Lara felt Owl's hand return to her back. "We'll go on and head to the lodge," he told the couple.

"Cool. We'll be up in a bit," Pipe said, not looking away from Cora.

Lara smiled. She had a feeling it would be more than "a bit," and as soon as she and Owl left, Cora would be gettin' some from her new husband.

She was so happy for Cora, she could hardly contain herself.

"Wait! Before we go, we need a picture!" Lara exclaimed, pulling her phone out of her pocket. She'd had to buy a new one when she'd gotten to The Refuge, because she had no idea where hers had gone.

She couldn't help but smile as she clicked a picture of Cora and Pipe. They looked perfect together, and their happiness couldn't be contained.

Then Pipe insisted on taking a picture of her and Cora. Then Cora wanted one of Lara and Owl. Then they had to do a selfie of the four of them...

By the time Lara and Owl headed down the stairs from the deck, it was fully dark.

"Don't make me send Jasna to come find you two," Owl called out after he'd gone inside and grabbed their coats, meeting her at the foot of the deck stairs.

"Don't you dare!" Pipe yelled from above. "Wouldn't want to scar her for life."

Everyone laughed. Lara had a feeling her best friend would forget about everyone else in a heartbeat. And she couldn't blame her. If she'd just gotten married to the man of her dreams, and was alone on a romantic deck with fairy lights and the stars blooming overhead, she wouldn't be thinking about anything other than getting him naked.

Her gaze swung to Owl without thought. He looked so handsome, and the happiness that oozed from him after being part of their friends' ceremony was clear to see.

For once, Lara wasn't hyper-aware of her surroundings. She wasn't afraid of the darkness lurking beyond the trees. Wasn't thinking about anyone out there hunting her. All she could think about was the brief feel of Owl's lips against hers, and what, if anything, it meant for the two of them.

Halfway to the lodge, Owl tugged on her hand, stopping Lara in her tracks. It was almost too dark to see now, but she felt safe with this man at her side.

"What's wrong?" she asked with a small frown.

But Owl didn't answer. He tugged on her hand once more, harder, and Lara fell against him with a small *oof*. Since they were the same height, she didn't have to crane her neck to look at him.

"Owl?" she said.

"You kissed me," he said in a low, rumbly tone.

Lara licked her lips nervously. "Yeah," she agreed.

His gaze almost burned as he looked into her eyes. "Was that an I'm-caught-up-in-the-moment-and-grateful-for-all-you've-done-to-help-me kiss? Or was it something more?"

Lara's heart beat like a drum in her chest. She couldn't read him. Did he want it to be the former or the latter? The shy woman she used to be struggled to take control. To tell him she'd gotten carried away. To not take the risk of being rejected.

But the new woman, the one who'd survived the awful things that had happened to her and yearned to be loved the way her best friend was, rebelled.

"More," she whispered.

"Be sure," Owl warned. "Because if you're simply trying to

outrun some demons, or excise them, I'm not the man you want to do that with."

"I'm sure," she told him, feeling more and more confidence well up inside. Owl wouldn't be warning her away if he simply wanted to get off. Besides, that wasn't the kind of man he was. She should know, she'd spent more time with him than any other man she'd gotten involved with in her life. And she wanted *this* man more than all of them combined.

It was Owl's turn to lick his lips. He wrapped an iron arm around her waist, and then they were touching from hips to chest. She could feel the warm puffs of his breath against her lips. Every nerve ending tingled. And yet, still he hesitated. As if he didn't want to hurt her. As if he wasn't sure she really wanted him.

That was unacceptable.

Lara snaked her hands upward and cupped his face. Then she kissed him again. This time, pressing her lips against his in desperation. She needed him to know that she had no second thoughts. That she wanted this more than she could say with words.

For a few seconds, Owl didn't move. He stood stock still as Lara kissed him.

Just when disappointment began to creep through her, Owl made a noise deep in his throat and his lips parted. His tongue came out and pushed into her mouth. Lara moaned as his taste bloomed on her taste buds. He'd obviously popped a mint into his mouth at some point before starting his officiant duties, because she could taste it.

His arm tightened as he backed her up, until she was leaning against a tree. Then his hands brushed hers off his face and he gripped the back of her head, moved it where he wanted. His other hand slipped under her blouse and rested on the bare skin of her back. His fingers were chilly but felt amazing against her almost overheated skin.

She gripped his shirt at his waist and held on for dear life as he kissed the living daylights out of her.

When he finally pulled back, they were both breathing hard.

"This changes things," he said firmly.

Lara could only nod.

He leaned in and kissed her forehead. Then her temple. His hand was still tangled in her hair, and he had her completely pinned against the tree. But Lara didn't feel trapped. If she made the slightest move to escape, he'd let her go. She had no doubt of that.

She didn't want him to let go. She loved being in his arms. She felt safe there. Protected.

His gaze searched hers, and Lara did her best to exude confidence and sexiness. She wanted this man to want her as much as she wanted him.

Owl shook his head. "Bravest woman I know."

"If I didn't make the first move, I'm not sure you would've," she admitted softly.

"You're right. There's no way I'd do anything that would remind you of...him."

"You don't," Lara said with a small shake of her head. "Not even close. You won't hurt me. Being with you is nothing like what he did. When you touch me, I crave more. When you look at me, all I see is concern, not perverted lust. I...I met with Henley the other day."

"You did?" Owl asked.

Lara nodded. It was the first time she'd wanted to meet with the therapist without Owl by her side. Mainly because she wanted to talk about sex. She'd been the recipient of Carter's warped idea of intimacy. It was one-sided, and he had no concern whatsoever for what she was thinking or feeling. In fact, he got off on treating her like an object. A thing. A vessel for him to release on.

Henley helped her see once and for all that what had been done to her wasn't about sex at all. It was about control. Carter needed to do what he'd done to feel powerful. It was warped and depraved.

She'd left the session feeling stronger than she'd felt in months. More determined to show Owl that she wanted to be intimate with him.

"What Carter did...It wasn't about attraction or need. Or even lust. I'm not afraid of being with you, Owl. I want that. I want *you*. And I don't want to be just a dependent woman you're trying to help anymore. I want to be me. Lara."

"You haven't been that woman since I tucked you into my guest room that first night," Owl said.

Amazingly, Lara believed him. She might not have seen it then, but in the last month, she'd been more than aware that he treated her with kid gloves less and less. Aware of how he'd touch her in small, intimate ways. How he'd bend over backward to give her anything she might desire. And her friends were right —his gaze followed her everywhere, and not just because he was waiting for her to freak out.

It was all of that and more that had given her the courage to kiss him. If she'd thought for one second that he considered her an annoying houseguest, someone he couldn't wait to get her head out of her butt and move back to Washington, DC, she wouldn't have been so bold.

They stared at each other, caught in the magic of the moment.

Then a breeze came through, and Lara shivered.

"Come on, I need to get you out of the cold," Owl said firmly. His hand slid out of her hair, slowly, as though he really didn't want to move but was forcing himself simply because she was chilly.

This time as they headed toward the lodge, he wasn't holding her hand. He wrapped his arm around her waist and had her plastered against his side as they walked together.

Lara smiled as she leaned into him. She wished they didn't have to go to the lodge. She wanted to go straight back to their cabin and explore what they'd started there in the woods. But the anticipation felt exciting. Besides, she truly did want to celebrate Cora's wedding. Her friend deserved a huge party, and there was no way Lara would miss it.

Carter Grant smiled as he sat back in his chair.

He'd done it. It had taken way too long to get the information he needed, but money talked. And he'd hooked up with a man he'd met a few years ago. Someone who was just as deviant as he was...in a different way. His acquaintance wasn't into hurting and using women, like Carter. His vice was money. He could never get enough. He'd sell his own mother if it meant adding to his bank account.

And since Carter had what the man wanted—cold, hard cash—the guy had no problem agreeing to work with him.

So after months of hard work, racking his brain as he

attempted to figure out a way to get Lara Osler back into his bed, under his control, he'd finally found a way.

The assholes who owned The Refuge, the very men who'd been harboring her in their secure compound, would be her downfall.

They wanted a helicopter, and Carter's new acquaintance happened to have decent hacking skills—and a pilot's license. He also knew where to find the exact chopper The Refuge assholes wanted.

The emails sent back and forth about the helicopter hinted that Carter would soon have his property back. *His* Lara might accompany the two former Night Stalkers to check out the chopper they hoped to buy. The one his accomplice had found just for this situation.

Lara stepping foot away from New Mexico was the break he needed. It was his chance. His chance to get her back where she belonged, under him, at his mercy. He couldn't wait.

With the assistance of his acquaintance, and a shitload of cash—which would totally be worth it—Lara Osler would be his once more, and two of the assholes who'd dared keep her from him would be taken care of. Win-win for everyone.

Well...maybe except for Lara.

She'd find out what happened to those who defied him. If she thought what he'd done before was bad, she'd soon realize she was dead wrong. He'd gone easy on her. But no more.

Carter's smile grew, and he reached down to unbutton his pants as his erection surged. Now that he had a plan, knew that she was going to be his again, he was desperate to orgasm. No bound and gagged prostitute needed. He was so hard it hurt.

It took less than a minute for Carter to relieve himself, and he closed his eyes as he imagined his come decorating his property once more.

He zipped his pants, not bothering to clean the mess he'd left on the floor of his motel room. He had more plans to make. And a secure location to obtain—one where Lara would never be able to escape.

Nothing would keep him from the woman who got away. Nothing and no one.

CHAPTER TEN

Owl shifted restlessly in his seat as he watched Lara dance with Cora. After dinner, the chairs in the dining area of the lodge had been pushed back and someone had brought out a portable speaker and started some music. It wasn't very loud, and there weren't any flashing lights, no special dance floor, but that didn't seem to matter to anyone.

The guests who'd joined them for dinner had gone back to their cabins by this point, and it was simply the men and women who lived and worked at The Refuge, celebrating the joy of two more of their group being joined together in marriage.

Owl would've joined the revelry on the dance floor, but one, he couldn't dance. And two, his dick was so hard, he didn't want to announce to the world that he could barely control himself.

It was still almost unbelievable that Lara had kissed him. When she'd pressed her lips to his up on that deck, he'd been so startled, he couldn't do or say anything. A part of him had thought it was a dream.

As he'd been standing there, marrying his friends, he'd looked over at Lara at one point and immediately fallen into a daydream where it was *his* wedding. His and Lara's.

And then she'd kissed him. It was so close to what he'd been thinking that it was difficult to distinguish reality from fantasy in that moment. He'd lost the chance to do or say anything before they were interrupted.

But that brief kiss had all his hopes and dreams surging to the forefront. He never in a million years would've risked doing what Lara had done. She'd been through hell at the hands of another man, and he couldn't forget all the times she'd panicked at the smallest stray sound, or the thought of being left alone and vulnerable.

The Lara who'd stood on that deck with him and their friends tonight wasn't that same scared woman. She'd made giant strides with her mental health in such a short time.

Owl was under no illusion that she was completely healed. Just as he wasn't. There would be triggers that would send her right back to that basement in Arizona. But she'd get through them, he had no doubt of that.

For her to let him know that she wanted more than friend-ship—in the only way he would've truly believed her—was more than he ever could've hoped for. And Owl had no doubt that her interest was genuine. He could see the way her heart beat hard in her neck. Felt the way she'd held on to him. Could practically taste the desire on her tongue.

She looked at him the way he'd always dreamed. And he wanted her. More than was comfortable.

Of course, Lara had no idea that he loved her already...but that could wait. The last thing Owl wanted to do was scare her away. A part of him still feared she was using him as a stepping stone to getting her life back. That she wanted a sexual relationship just to prove that she *could* have one after the shit Grant had done to her, and then she'd realize she could do better.

But after that kiss in the forest, the one that curled his toes and had him harder than a fucking rock, Owl held out hope that she was as into him as he was her.

He wasn't a manwhore, but he'd been with his fair share of women. And there was something about that kiss tonight that was different than any other kiss he'd experienced. It was more intense, and not just about lust. He and Lara had a connection that went deeper than merely scratching a sexual itch. He'd felt it in that kiss...and now he couldn't wait to get her alone.

Owl hoped one day he could convince Lara that no one could ever love her as much as he would. That no one would make her feel as cherished and safe. He'd do whatever it took, whatever she needed to make the decision to stay with him. Now and forever.

He wanted what Pipe had. What all his friends had. And that was Lara as his wife, her belly round with their child. Laughing and smiling up at him from their couch as he stood over her.

"They look happy," Tiny said as he pulled out a chair next to Owl.

Forcing his thoughts away from the woman he wanted in his bed more than he wanted to breathe, Owl turned to his friend. "Yeah."

"I'm probably overstepping, but fuck it. I'm doing it because I give a shit. You sure starting a thing with Lara is a good idea?"

Owl looked at his friend and considered playing dumb, but discarded that idea in about two seconds. *Tiny* wasn't dumb, far from it. People might take one look and instantly label him as some muscle-bound moron, or even assume he was too pretty to be a critical thinker, but they'd be wrong. Tiny *was* handsome... but he'd been a Navy SEAL, one of the best of the best.

Unfortunately, out of all the guys who ran The Refuge, he was also the most suspicious and cynical. The one most likely to think the worst in any given situation. Owl suspected it had something to do with his past, and he couldn't fault him if that was the case. They all had their baggage to deal with.

"Yes," Owl said simply.

Tiny lifted a brow in response.

"For some reason, she seems to want me. *Me.* The guy who everyone looks at and sees a version of a popular musician. Or the man whose face was plastered all over the Internet, begging and crying while being tortured. They see me as soft or weak. But when Lara looks at me, she sees someone completely different. A man who can protect her. A man who's capable of dealing with the trauma she went through, because he went through something similar. We have more in common than not."

"I'm not sure that's the best reason to get into a relationship with someone," Tiny said quietly.

"Maybe. Maybe not. But I love her, Tiny." Owl said the words almost defiantly. He was ready for his friend to tell him it was too soon. That he only felt protective toward her because of everything that had happened. And those weren't things he hadn't already thought about, but Owl didn't give a shit. He knew how he felt, and that what he felt for Lara was so different than anything he'd experienced with other women, it wasn't even in the same ballpark.

Tiny shocked the shit out of him by merely saying, "All right then."

"All right?" Owl echoed.

"Yup. You're a grown-ass man. If you say you love her, you

love her. And I'll tell you this, she won't find a better man than you."

Owl swallowed hard. Getting approval from the taciturn and somewhat stern Tiny felt good. "What about you?"

"What about me, *what*?" Tiny asked.

"Anyone you're interested in?"

His friend snorted. "No."

Owl tilted his head and studied the man next to him. It seemed to him that Tiny had protested a little too quickly. "Luna's single."

"Are you joking? She's a *kid*. Besides, Robert would cut my balls off if I even looked twice at his daughter."

Tiny wasn't wrong. "What about Savannah? She's not around much, since she can do the books remotely, but she's pretty."

"How about you stop trying to set me up?" Tiny drawled. "Just because everyone around here is getting married and having babies, doesn't mean we *all* have to."

"You don't want that?" Owl asked. "And I'm not judging. I mean, it's fine if you don't."

It took Tiny almost a full minute to answer. Just when Owl thought he wasn't going to respond at all, he spoke.

"I want it. I look at Brick and the others and see how happy they are, and it makes me want it *more*. But..." His voice trailed off as he stared at the dance floor without seeing it.

"But?" Owl prompted.

Tiny shrugged. "I have trust issues," he finally said.

"Don't we all," Owl commiserated.

Tiny's gaze pinned him intensely. "You ever woken up to the woman you thought you'd marry plunging a knife into your chest?"

Owl's eyes flew wide. "Um...*no*."

"Yeah. Don't recommend it. The thought of falling asleep next to another woman is enough to make me never sleep again. Hell, I'm not sure there's a woman alive who could put up with my paranoia and trust issues."

"You'd be surprised," Owl told him.

"I don't like surprises," Tiny grumbled.

He couldn't help but chuckle.

"Shut up," Tiny said, bumping Owl's shoulder with his own.

Owl was still smiling as a new song began playing. His grin grew as he watched the women of The Refuge converge on the pseudo dance floor. They were all there. Jess, Carly, Ryan, Luna, even Savannah. And of course, Alaska, Henley, Reese, Cora, Lara, and little Jasna.

"Y-M-C-A!" they all yelled, using their arms to make the corresponding letters as they sang.

The room was filled with happiness and joy, and if anyone had asked Owl if he knew this was where they'd all be a year ago, he would've laughed his ass off. He and his fellow Refuge owners weren't ogres, but they also weren't exactly what people would call joyful.

At one point, with ear-to-ear smiles on their faces, Cora wrapped her arm around Lara's waist and together, with one arm each, they made the movements to form each letter together.

Owl's throat got tight as a ball of emotion formed. The friendship between the two women was unbreakable, and so damn strong it was beautiful. Thinking about everything Cora had done to make sure Lara was all right was something he'd rarely ever seen.

The song ended, and Cora turned to Lara and hugged her tightly. They shared a few words on the dance floor before Cora smiled up at her, then walked toward her new husband.

Another song started, and when Owl saw Lara look around self-consciously, he was on the move. It was unacceptable that she would feel even one moment of doubt, of worry. Not after the pure joy he'd just witnessed.

He was at her side in an instant. "You thirsty?" he asked, knowing it was merely an excuse to make sure she was good.

"A little," she said, smiling up at him.

Owl steered her away from the others still dancing, over to a table where Robert had set up a drink station. There were soft drinks in a bucket of ice, various juices, bottles of water, and even some punch that he'd hilariously labeled "Baby-Making Punch." It was simply fruit punch and sprite, but everyone had gotten a kick out of it.

Lara reached for a water and held it out to him.

"I'm good," he said with a shrug.

She grinned. "Will you open it for me?"

"Oh! Yeah, of course," Owl said. He twisted the top off and handed the bottle back.

"I mean, I could've opened it myself, but my hands are a little sweaty," she explained.

"You looked like you were having fun," Owl told her, taking her elbow and moving her a little away from the table so others could get to it.

"Yeah," she said a little wistfully. "It's been a while."

Owl couldn't stop himself from leaning in and kissing her temple.

"What was that for?" she asked with a small smile.

"To tell you how pretty you look tonight. How I love seeing you relax with your friends. To let you know how precious I think your friendship is with Cora. She relies on you a lot, and having you here tonight, for one of the happiest moments of her life, meant more to her than you probably know. And...because I wanted to."

Pink blossomed on Lara's cheeks, and Owl couldn't take his eyes off her.

She licked her lips, then looked around. Cora and Pipe were on the dance floor now, swaying back and forth more than actually dancing. Tonka had Jasna by the hands and was twirling her around in circles, while Spike sat at a table with Reese, his hand on her belly as he spoke in her ear. Alaska and Brick were standing off to the side, talking with Ryan and Jess. Stone had left not too long ago, and Tiny was chatting with Robert.

"You look tired," Lara finally said as she turned back to Owl. "I know you're still not sleeping through the night."

Owl shrugged. "I'm used to it, sweetheart. I wake up in the middle of the night and no matter what I do, I can't go back to sleep. It's nothing new."

"Hmmmm, well, maybe you just need someone to tuck you in."

And just like that, the arousal Owl had been feeling all night came roaring back with a vengeance.

His lips twitched. "You want to tuck me in, Lara?"

The pink in her cheeks deepened as she lifted her chin and said, "Yes."

Owl was in awe of this woman. She was obviously feeling out of her league, being so forward, and yet she was doing it anyway. She'd somehow managed to find herself again. And while he was certain he would've liked the old Lara...the one Cora had described to him and Pipe months ago, while trying to convince them to help find her...this new Lara was utterly irresistible. "You want to say bye to Cora?"

"I'll see her tomorrow, I'm sure," Lara said with a small shake of her head.

Owl forced himself to break eye-contact with Lara and looked over at Tiny. Catching his eye, he gave him a small chin lift, then motioned toward the door with his head.

Tiny smiled and nodded.

That taken care of, Owl didn't hesitate to wrap his arm around Lara and pull her against his side, turning her toward the front door of the lodge. He thought he heard her giggle next to him, but was too focused on getting them back to his cabin.

"Are we going to get our coats?" Lara asked, just as he reached for the door.

Swearing under his breath, Owl turned them to head toward the smallest conference room, where everyone had left their jackets before dinner.

He quickly found theirs in the pile and helped Lara shrug into hers. He threw his coat on, then grabbed Lara's hand and practically pulled her toward the door once more.

But they were stopped by Alaska, who wanted to say good night. Then Jasna ran over and wanted a hug. The next thing Owl knew, he was standing back while everyone came over to say their goodbyes to Lara.

He didn't miss that they weren't fawning over *him*; instead, everyone wanted to make sure *Lara* knew how glad they were that she'd come. Now that she was getting back to herself, the woman was a magnet. She seemed to draw people to her because of her kindness, making everyone she came into contact with feel as if they were the most important person in the world.

Owl had a feeling this was why she was so loved at her job back in DC. Why kids flocked to her. They had an innate sense that she liked them exactly how they were. They didn't have to pretend to be something they weren't in order to feel as if they were important and worthwhile.

Ten minutes had passed by the time everyone had told her how much fun they'd had with her tonight...and Henley was quietly assured she wasn't leaving because of a panic attack.

"Sorry," Lara said a little sheepishly when she finally turned to him once more.

"About what?"

"We were leaving," she said with a small shrug.

"If you think I was going to deny your friends a chance to say their goodbyes—and make sure you're all right—you don't know me as well as you think you do."

"I know you," she said quietly. "Your eyes were on me all night. I could feel them. You were making sure I was okay. I knew without a doubt if I had any bad moments, you'd be there, which made me feel as if I could let go...just a little. Not worry about who might be watching or lurking in the shadows."

"Damn straight," Owl murmured.

"Thank you," Lara said, her words heavy with emotion. "You make me feel like the woman I've always wanted to be. Pretty, carefree, popular."

"You're all those things and more, sweetheart," Owl said.

"I'm not, but you make me feel that way."

If it was the last thing Owl did in his life, he'd make this woman see her worth.

"Take me home?" she asked.

Home. Hell yeah. He loved that she felt that way about their cabin. Without a word, he reached for her hand and they walked toward the door. This time no one stopped them and Owl held the door open.

The night was quiet now, and very dark. But he could make his way to his cabin blindfolded and confidently led her down the path. With any other woman, he might take the opportunity to make out in the darkness. To maybe ramp up the anticipation of what might happen when they arrived back at the cabin. But this was Lara. And even though Owl was ninety-five percent sure they were alone, he wasn't going to risk that five percent chance that they weren't. His Lara wasn't fond of the dark, and he couldn't really blame her. He preferred to see his surroundings himself.

He led them to his cabin and quickly unlocked the door and got them inside. He took Lara's coat and hung it next to his own in the front closet. Then he turned to her. "You want something to drink?"

"No. I want *you*."

Owl blinked. He was still getting used to her taking the lead when it came to intimacy. "You've got me," he replied without hesitation.

She gave him a small smile as they stood in the front foyer and stared at each other for a long moment. Then Owl took her hand in his once more and quietly headed for his bedroom.

He led her to the side of his bed, dropped her hand, and took a step back, putting a bit of space between them. "If we're going to do this, you're in charge," he said.

Lara blinked.

"I would rather boil myself alive than hurt you. And while I'm as proud of you as I can be regarding your mental progress, I will *not* be the reason you have a relapse. If at any time you want to stop, we'll stop. Whatever happens between us will be because we both want it, not because you're trying to prove something to yourself. Okay?"

Owl saw her shoulders relax a fraction and was relieved that he'd said the right thing.

"Okay," she said with a nod. "I'd like to go get changed."

He nodded. His dick felt as if it would have permanent marks from where it was pressed against his zipper, but he'd give her all the time in the world if that's what she needed. "I'll meet you back here. Or do you want me to come to your room?"

"Here," she said without hesitation.

Owl stepped toward her once again and pulled her close. He hugged her hard, enjoying the feel of her against him.

She hugged him just as fiercely, her hands pressing against his back as they embraced.

Then she pulled away and he immediately let her go. "I'll be back. Don't fall asleep on me," she warned.

Owl snort-laughed. "Not a chance."

She backed away, not taking her eyes from him as she went. At the last moment, she turned and disappeared through the door, and only then did Owl let out the breath he'd been holding.

He was nervous as hell about this. He worried that it was too soon. That no matter what she said, Lara was trying to prove to herself that Grant hadn't fucked her up for sex for life. He wanted to be the man to show her that she was still utterly desirable. But he also wanted to protect her from herself...and him, if necessary.

Owl headed for his bathroom to brush his teeth. He wanted to be in bed when she returned, if for no other reason than to look as nonthreatening as possible. He hadn't lied. She would be in charge of every single thing they may or may not do tonight.

It was a weird feeling to be both aroused beyond what he thought possible and scared shitless.

CHAPTER ELEVEN

Lara swallowed hard. She wanted this. Wanted Owl. But she had to admit that she was nervous. She wasn't really trying to prove anything to anyone, but now that he'd brought it up, she wondered if that was at least a little part of this.

The thought of being naked in front of Owl made her belly clench in distress. She couldn't help but remember Carter's leering gaze as he touched her, as he bruised her bare flesh.

Closing her eyes, Lara forced herself to take a deep breath. Owl wasn't Carter. And she could do this. *Wanted* to do this.

She changed into the oversized T-shirt she'd been wearing to bed and left her underwear on. This was what she'd worn to bed every night since she'd arrived here at the cabin, minus the leggings she usually had on. It felt weird to be walking around with her legs bare, but she refused to show up to Owl's bed with almost every inch of her body covered.

She stopped in the doorway of Owl's room and stared.

The light from his bathroom was on, as was a lamp next to

the bed. Owl was lying on the mattress, surprisingly wearing almost the same thing she was. A T-shirt and a pair of boxers. The light in the room wasn't extremely bright, but it wasn't dim either. It was actually perfect.

He'd liked all the lights on, so he could see the bruises he left on her skin. But he also liked to leave her in the dark when he was done, and sometimes he'd sneak into her room and scare her even more when he appeared out of nowhere.

Owl seemed to instinctively know exactly what she needed.

Taking a deep breath, Lara started for the bed.

She reached the side and without thought, immediately lay down next to Owl. She snuggled into his chest as he shifted to put his arm around her back, holding her against him.

Neither spoke for a long moment. Then Lara said, "You didn't have to keep your shirt on for me."

"I didn't," Owl said.

That made Lara lift her head. There was an odd note to his voice that she didn't understand.

"I usually sleep in my shirt and sweatpants," he said with a shrug. "Being nude...it reminds me of...The first thing our captors did was strip us. They wanted to humiliate us. Our cells were cold, really damn cold, and being naked, it was...it sucked."

It was almost scary how alike their experiences were. "He took my clothes too," Lara said quietly. "And while he didn't leave me naked, he put me in this scratchy nightie thing. He'd push it all the way up when he was there, and even though it was loose, I felt like it was strangling me. Sometimes he'd pull it over my face. Then, before he left, he'd tug it down over his release. So it was always damp. Uncomfortable. I *hated* that damn thing."

She came up on an elbow and looked down at Owl. "So...we leave our shirts on then?"

He smiled at her and nodded. "That sounds perfect."

Lara relaxed. She should've known Owl would make this easy. "What now?" she whispered.

"Now you do whatever you want."

Lara frowned. "But I want you to enjoy this too."

Owl chuckled. "Sweetheart, there's nothing I can think of that I'll enjoy more than having you in my arms. It doesn't matter if we do nothing more than this. Promise."

"But do you *want* more?" she couldn't stop herself from asking.

"I want it all," Owl admitted. His gaze bored into hers. The sincerity in his words burrowing down to her heart. "I want your mouth. Your body. Your heart. Your soul. I want to fall asleep with you in my arms, and wake up the same way. I want you to be happy, safe, and to live your life exactly how you want. There's so much more I want, but if I told you right now, you'd probably leap out of this bed and run screaming from this house."

She doubted that. Anything this man wanted, she'd do whatever she had to do in order to make it happen. "Right now, I want a kiss," she whispered.

"Then take what you want," he ordered.

Leaning down slowly, Lara did just that. She brushed her lips over his and lifted her head when he didn't move.

"Owl?"

"Yeah, sweetheart?"

"I want you to kiss me back."

He grinned. "Then come back down here and give me those lips again and I will."

So she did. And this time, Owl didn't hesitate to take what she was offering. The hand that had rested on her back moved up and once more shoved into her hair, holding her head where he wanted it. His head tilted and he took her long, hard, and deep. Her lips felt bruised and swollen when she pulled back to catch her breath and stare at him.

Suddenly, it wasn't enough.

She felt ravenous. And she'd *never* felt this way. Like if she didn't get more of this man, she'd break into a million pieces. She'd had sex before, but it had never felt...desperate. Necessary.

Moving decisively, Lara straddled Owl. His hands moved to her hips and held her steady as she fought to catch her breath. Slowly, she shifted so her hands went under his shirt and touched his bare stomach. He was warm, and she felt his muscles contract as she caressed him.

Smiling, loving the power she felt from being on top, Lara eased her hands higher. She couldn't see what she was touching, but she felt his chest hair tickling her palms and when she reached his nipples, her grin widened as he arched into her touch. She played with the sensitive buds for a moment.

"You like that?" she asked.

"Yeah," Owl told her. His eyes were slits now, as if it was difficult to keep them open. She could feel his cock under her but wasn't alarmed by it. This was Owl. Every molecule in her body knew where she was and who she was with. She was safe. Owl would protect her.

An image popped into her brain while she caressed his chest...of him standing next to the bed in that damn basement in Arizona.

He'd been fierce in his determination to make sure no one touched her. Every muscle in his body taut, his hands in fists as he'd stood between her and Carter. His willingness to protect her, a stranger, had seeped into her consciousness even then.

And throughout the time she'd been with him, she'd seen that courage and unselfishness time and time again.

And she was seeing it again now. He lay under her, every muscle tight, aroused, and yet he was giving her the reins. Letting her set the pace. It meant the world to her. It meant everything.

Leaning down, Lara kissed him again. Aggressively. And he let her take what she needed. But the thing was, she wanted everything. She wanted to consume Owl. Take what he'd offered time and time again. His strength. His confidence. It was selfish, but at the moment, Lara didn't care.

She ripped her mouth from his and took a moment to relish the way his eyes were unfocused and how hard he was breathing. She slowly moved down his body, digging her nails into his chest a little as she went. His legs widened, giving her room. Lara pushed his shirt up, just a little, so she could get to the waistband of his boxers.

Looking up his body, she watched as Owl grabbed the pillows and scrunched them, raising his head a bit so he had a clearer view of what she was doing.

Grinning, Lara slowly drew his boxers down over his cock. She didn't take them all the way off, but he lifted his ass, giving her room to pull the material as far as his thighs. She couldn't wait to touch him long enough to move them any farther.

Taking his hard cock in her hand, she heard Owl hiss as she squeezed him. He wasn't overly long, but he was thicker than anyone she'd been with. The purple head of his cock flexed as she gripped him.

"Holy shit, sweetheart. Please."

"Please what?" she asked with a small smirk.

"Anything. Anything you want," he replied.

This power was heady. Her choice had been stripped from her in the harshest way possible. She hadn't been able to say yes or no. All she'd been able to do was endure a psychopath's sick whims. Owl was giving back her power, and she'd never loved anyone more as a result.

Tightening her grip, Lara moved her hand up, then back down his shaft.

"Yes..." Owl hissed.

Looking at his face, you wouldn't think he enjoyed what she was doing, but when a bead of precome formed at the head of his cock, it was obvious. His hands were in fists at his sides as he lay under her, completely at her mercy.

She only faltered for a moment as the scent of his desire hit her. The musky smell reminded her of being back in that basement, but she took a deep breath and concentrated on the here and now.

Looking down, she watched as she stroked him. How the soft skin of his cock moved with her hand. How his balls seemed to draw up as she stroked. Lara pushed her other hand under his shirt once more and tweaked his nipple even as she gripped his cock harder.

His hips rose at that, but he seemed to remember where he was and who he was with and lowered them back to the mattress. "I'm close to coming," he warned her. "And I'm not sure if you want that or not."

Even now, in the middle of his own pleasure, he was protecting her. Her love for him grew even bigger. Did she want him to come? Yes. Definitely. But like this? Probably not. She could almost hear Henley in her head, warning her to take baby steps rather than jump feet first into the deep end.

"I do," she reassured him. "But...I don't want it on me."

Because she had her hand around his dick, she felt him deflate a little at her words, and she hated that.

"Come here," Owl ordered, not letting her dwell on her demons.

Letting go of him reluctantly, Lara moved upward.

"More," Owl said, gently putting his hands on her hips.

She moved up another inch.

He grinned. "More," he said a little firmer, using his strength to pull her all the way up so she was sitting astride his chest. Her pussy was a few inches from his face now, and Lara felt herself getting wet thinking about having his mouth on her. That definitely wasn't something that had happened while she was a captive. Anything that gave her pleasure was off the table. It was all about *him*.

She jerked in surprise when Owl's hands slipped under her shirt.

"This okay?"

She nodded quickly.

His gaze was locked on her face as his hands moved upward. They gently cradled her breasts and his thumbs tweaked her nipples.

Yet again, she was thrust back into the basement, but as she gazed down into Owl's face, those memories faded. This was nothing like then. Owl's hands were gentle and felt good on her skin.

"You're perfect," he mumbled. "You fit my hands like you were made for me."

He gently squeezed her, and it didn't hurt. Not in the least. Lara instinctively arched into his touch.

"That's it. Let me make you feel good. Because that's how

you make *me* feel. You have no idea how much of a turn-on you are right now. You're strong, and capable, and in charge."

Every word out of his mouth was meant to give her control, and amazingly, the longer Owl touched her, the more she wanted him to continue.

Lifting her hands, she placed them over his, through the shirt. She encouraged him to squeeze her harder.

"Easy, sweetheart. We'll get there. Just let me love you gently."

Panting, Lara dropped her hands and braced herself on his shoulders. How long he caressed her, she had no idea. But suddenly it wasn't enough. She was soaked. Her nipples were rock hard and she needed more. She needed to come.

Moving quickly, and dislodging his hands in the process, she shifted to the side and yanked off her panties before lifting a leg back across his chest.

"Make me come," she demanded as she stared down at him almost defiantly.

"With pleasure. Closer, Lara. Put your pussy on my mouth."

His words made desire shoot through her body. She'd never been a fan of dirty talk, but with this man? She loved it.

Scooting forward, she watched as Owl licked his lips in anticipation. She was practically dripping now. He brought one hand up and scrunched the pillow under his head again, lifting himself a little higher, and then he used his other hand to palm one of her ass cheeks.

Lara yelped as he dove forward, burying his head between her legs.

The first lick of his tongue through her slit felt amazing, but it was when he latched onto her clit and began sucking as if his life depended on it that her heart felt as if it stopped beating.

"Owl," she murmured, trying to pull herself away from his intense lovemaking.

But he tightened his hold on her ass and held her against him as he licked and slurped up every ounce of pleasure that dripped from her body.

"So beautiful," he murmured before licking her once more.

Looking down, Lara could hardly believe this was happening. The lovemaking she'd experienced in the past had been very vanilla. She'd lain on her back while her boyfriends entered her. It felt good, but it had never been this...intense.

Her hips began moving without any input from her brain. She humped Owl's face, trying to get as much stimulation on her clit as she could.

"That's it. Fuck my face," he encouraged.

In any other situation, Lara would probably be mortified. But she was so close to a monster orgasm, she couldn't muster the energy to think about anything other than getting off.

She moved a hand between her legs to finish herself off, but Owl wasn't having that. He pushed her fingers away. "That's my job," he said fiercely, before lifting his head and latching his lips onto her clit.

Lara froze for a moment—before suddenly flying into a million pieces. The orgasm was so powerful, it almost hurt. In a good way. It had been so long since she'd felt anything like it, but at the same time, *this* feeling was completely new.

Owl had turned her inside out, and as she shook and trembled, she felt safer than she ever had in her life.

Even as aftershocks continued to jolt through her body, Owl pulled back and stared up at her. "Please...fuck me, Lara. I need you. So damn bad."

She moved. The only thought in her head to ease the longing

she could hear in his voice. She shifted down his body until she was hovering over his cock. It was hard as a rock. The head was weeping with precome, and Owl's teeth were clenched as she reached for him.

He inhaled sharply as she gripped his cock and aimed it between her legs.

She hesitated then, drawing out the moment. Lara wasn't sure why. She felt good, *really* good, and it was obvious Owl was hurting.

"It's okay," he said, his voice shaking. "You did so good, sweetheart. I'll be tasting you on my tongue for the rest of my life. We can stop. It's all right."

Lara suddenly realized what she was doing.

She was testing him. Wanting to see if he'd really stop as he promised.

And that sucked. Because she trusted Owl. More than she'd ever trusted anyone. And here she was, torturing him. He was two seconds away from coming and she was hesitating. Making him think she wasn't sure about him. About *them*.

Without another thought, she lowered herself and took him to the hilt.

They both gasped.

It hurt a little, but Lara barely felt the pain. All she felt was complete. She was full, so damn full, and for the first time ever, she felt as if she'd become one with a man.

Owl's hands had moved again, gripping her hips in a firm but gentle touch. He stared at where they were joined with an expression of awe.

Lara would never forget this moment. Ever. For the rest of her life, she'd replay it over and over again. How Owl had given her control over their lovemaking. Had let her do what felt right.

Giving only what she felt she could give. And right now, she wanted to give him everything.

He was hers. She wasn't giving him up. The protectiveness and possessiveness she felt toward him was new. She'd never felt that way about anything before. But this man? She'd fight to the death for him.

She tried to rock her hips, but Owl's hands held her still.

"Owl," she whined. "I want to move."

"I can't protect you," he said in a tortured tone.

Lara froze.

Owl had never felt anything as amazing as Lara's pussy gripping his cock. He was born to be inside her. She was soaking wet, her juices dripping down his shaft to his balls. He'd eaten her out as if his life depended on it, and he figured that maybe it did.

And he'd almost burst with pride when she'd taken him. But as he stared down at where his cock was buried deep within her body, he panicked.

He wasn't wearing a condom.

"I can't protect you," he blurted.

"What?" she asked, sounding hurt.

"Condom. I'm not wearing one," he said between gritted teeth. He felt every movement she made. Her inner muscles were strangling his dick as if they never wanted to let him go. Not that he wanted to go anywhere. He could live right here, just like this, for the rest of his days. But he refused to do anything that might hurt her. Might make her regret being with him.

Her brow furrowed as she stared at him.

"The last thing I want is anything we do to give you a flashback. And sex can be messy, sweetheart. Especially without a condom. I know what he did to you, and I want to protect you from seeing my come."

Lara sat up straighter, the small movement making him groan. "Wait, let me see if I understand you. You're not worried about protecting me from getting pregnant. You aren't worried about what diseases I might have caught from a freaking serial killer. You're thinking that the sight of your *sperm*, the result of you experiencing pleasure from being inside me, might make me have a panic attack?"

She sounded confused. Owl hurried to explain further. "Yes. For the record, I *want* to knock you up. I can't think of anything sexier than knowing my son or daughter is growing in your belly. And no, I'm not worried about diseases because I was there when the doctor gave you the results of the tests he ran in the hospital in Arizona, remember? So yeah, if the sight of my come leaking from between your legs has even a one percent chance of fucking things up between us, then I don't want to risk it. Rise up for a minute and I'll grab a condom from the drawer. They might be older than is wise to use, but it's better than nothing."

This conversation was anything but sexy, but Owl's cock hadn't lost its hardness. How could it when he was buried in the hottest, wettest pussy he'd ever had the pleasure and privilege to be in?

"You...Owl...You can't."

"I can't what? Get the condom? Of course, I can. I just need you to lift up so I can reach the drawer."

In response, Lara leaned down, resting on his chest. It made his cock twitch inside her, and he felt a small burst of precome release from the tip. Gritting his teeth, praying he wouldn't prematurely go off inside her, Owl wrapped his arms around her.

"No...you can't *want* to get me pregnant," she insisted, staring into his eyes.

"Why not?"

"Because! That's crazy. Guys don't like to be trapped."

"*I* do. Trap me, Lara. Please."

"You're weird."

"Yeah. I am," Owl said without an ounce of concern. "Look, I've learned the hard way how precious life is. How short it can be. I don't know why or how I survived what I did, but I'll be damned if I let the best thing that's ever happened to me slide through my fingers.

"I love you, Lara Osler. You're *it* for me. I want to marry you, have children with you, and live happily ever after either here at The Refuge with our friends or, if you prefer, back in DC, so you can get your job back and kick ass with those kids. I don't care which. As long as you're with me, I'll be happy. And if you don't want any of that, you should climb off my cock and go back to your room. We can figure out something else for your living arrangements. Maybe you can stay with Cora and Pipe. Whatever makes you comfortable. But I can't keep my mouth shut anymore."

Owl was practically panting by the time he finished—and as soon as the words were out, he regretted them. Not only because he knew how much pressure it would put on the woman in his arms, but because he didn't want her to leave, to stay with her friend. He wanted her right where she was. In his bed, his cabin, where he could continue to make sure she healed from the shit life had thrown at her.

In response, Lara slowly sat up once more, and Owl frantically began trying to rebuild the shields around his heart that he'd dropped for this woman. It would kill him, but he'd let her go and not make it awkward for her.

Internally, he snorted. Not awkward...right. He'd just told her that he wanted to knock her up. How could that not be awkward?

Just when he was bracing himself to feel the chill of the air on his cock as she pulled away, she surprised the fuck out of him by reaching for the hem of her shirt.

She whipped it over her head, sitting astride him completely naked.

And. She. Was. Fucking. Perfect.

Her tits shivered with every breath she took. Her nipples were long and hard, begging for his mouth. She had a small pooch of a belly, and seeing her hips spread apart as she straddled him was the most erotic thing he'd ever witnessed.

And then she moved. Not off him, as he'd expected, but up and down on his dick.

"I love you too," she said as she locked her gaze with his. Her fingernails dug into his chest, and he could feel them even through the shirt he still wore. "I went to see Henley alone because I wanted to talk about *you*. I admitted that I loved you, and I told her that I was worried it was some sort of knee-jerk reaction to everything that happened. We talked about it for a long time...and I realized that my love for you isn't because I need to be rescued or protected. It's because of the man you are. I've looked for you my entire life, Owl...just ask Cora. She'll tell you. And it's almost unbelievable that I found you at the exact moment I'd given up."

Owl could barely focus on what she was saying. The feel of her pussy gripping his cock as she raised and lowered herself over him was distracting as hell. He reached for her and grabbed her waist. Stopping her movement.

"You love me?" he asked, wanting to hear the important bit again.

"Yes."

"Say it," he ordered.

She grinned. "I love you."

Owl closed his eyes and let the words sink into his soul.

"Your turn," she prodded.

His eyes opened and he stared up at her. "I love you. So much it's almost scary."

She nodded as if she understood that perfectly. "You really want a child?"

"With you? Yes," Owl told her.

"Then let go of me so I can move, and we can see about making that happen."

"You want kids?"

"With you?" she echoed his words. "Oh, yeah."

That was all it took for Owl to come.

He hadn't planned on it. Had wanted to make sure his woman was satisfied again. But hearing her say she wanted him to give her a baby was more than he could control. Grunting, Owl felt his dick twitch inside her as he emptied himself.

"Shit," he complained when he could talk again.

Lara grinned down at him.

Without pulling out—because honestly, Owl loved being inside her—he reached for her clit. He held her on top of him with one hand and manipulated her very sensitive bundle of nerves with the other.

"I...thought...I was...in charge," Lara panted as she writhed over him.

"You are," Owl reassured her even as he pushed her closer and closer to the edge.

"Doesn't feel like it," she told him with a small smile.

"Anything you want, you get," Owl said.

"I want you," she said.

"Then you've got me. I'm yours. Now, come for me. Let me feel you come on my cock."

Before he'd finished speaking, she was coming again. She clamped down on his dick, and he'd never felt anything as erotic as what he experienced at that moment.

Amazingly, or maybe not so amazingly, Owl felt himself harden inside her.

He wanted to flip her over and fuck her hard and fast, but as he'd said, she was in charge. And he didn't want to do anything that would bring her out of the pleasure haze she was currently in. He rocked his hips, thrusting into her body.

They both moaned.

"More," she pleaded.

He'd never make this woman beg for anything. He lifted her slightly, so he had some room to work, then he thrust into her again, over and over. After a while, his stomach muscles began to tire, but he didn't stop. The sight of their combined juices on his dick when he pulled out only made him harder. They were making a mess of the sheets, but again, Owl didn't give a shit. He'd gladly sleep in the wet spot every night for the rest of their lives.

"I'm gonna come inside you again," he warned. "Gonna shoot my sperm so far inside you that there's no way my guys can't get to your eggs."

"Shut up, Owl. That's not sexy," she complained.

She was wrong. It was absolutely sexy as hell thinking about getting her pregnant.

He was on the verge of coming when Lara took control and sat down on him—hard. Then she squeezed her inner muscles as tightly as she could, fucking him internally.

Owl felt the room dim as he exploded.

When he came back to himself, Lara was lying on his chest once more. His dick was still inside her, but he knew it was only a matter of time before he slipped out. He sat up as best he could, reaching for the blanket and pulling it up and over the both of them.

Then he did something he couldn't have imagined doing their first time together...if ever. He shifted and wiggled until he'd removed his shirt. His boxers were still around his thighs, but he didn't care. The feel of being skin-to-skin with Lara was heaven.

She must have thought so too, because she sighed heavily and snuggled closer.

They were quiet for a moment before she asked, "You think you can sleep now?"

Owl chuckled. "Yeah, sweetheart. I can sleep."

"Good."

He didn't mention that falling asleep wasn't his problem. It was waking in the middle of the night and not being able to go *back* to sleep. But with a naked Lara in his arms, staying awake the rest of the night wouldn't exactly be a hardship.

"Is this weird?" she whispered after a moment.

"No," Owl said without a shred of doubt.

"I don't think so either. But some people will."

"Fuck 'em."

She chuckled against his chest. "No thank you."

Owl huffed out a breath and felt himself slip from inside her body.

"Oh...that felt weird!" Lara exclaimed.

Actually, it felt horrible. But Owl simply shifted Lara in his arms so she was mostly lying on the mattress, which had to be more comfortable than lying on him, and took the opportunity to remove his boxers. He kicked them off, not caring that they'd be lost under the covers. He'd sort out the bed tomorrow.

They lay there for a minute or two, before Lara lifted her head. "Would you be offended if I put my shirt back on?" she asked.

Owl let out a relieved breath. "No. I was about to ask you the same thing."

They shared a smile as they reached for their T-shirts. Then they settled right back into the position they'd been in before. Even though Owl had loved the feel of her against him, he couldn't deny he was much more comfortable wearing the shirt.

"I love you," Lara whispered after a while.

"I love you too," Owl replied, experiencing that overpowering feeling in his chest once more. "Go to sleep. The new guests with the kids will be here before you know it, and I know you and Cora have more stuff you want to plan."

"Yeah."

Owl thought she was going to say something else, but the next thing he heard was her deep breaths as her body relaxed completely against his own.

The responsibility he felt toward this woman was almost overwhelming. But it also felt as if it was meant to be. Life with her would be more complicated than living on his own, but he'd been doing it for the last few months, and found he was looking forward to his future. And that was new, as he'd merely been going through the motions of life since he'd been rescued.

Owl kissed Lara's forehead and smiled when she murmured something in her sleep and snuggled closer. Closing his eyes, Owl couldn't help thinking that life was finally looking up for him. He had a woman he loved and who loved him back, The Refuge was thriving, his friends were happy, they were getting a chopper and he'd be able to fly once again, and the possibility of children was on the horizon.

Life was good, and he'd do whatever it took to keep it that way.

* * *

Three hours later, Owl woke. He was momentarily confused about where he was and who he was with, then it all came back. Lara slept peacefully in front of him. They'd shifted in their sleep to their sides, and he was now curled around her back, holding her against his chest.

He sighed, turning to look at the clock. Insomnia sucked. He'd suffered from it ever since he'd been a POW. Everyone said it would fade, that as he healed physically and mentally, he'd be able to sleep through the night, but here it was, years later, and he still woke up after only a few hours' sleep. No matter what he did, what remedies he tried, once he woke, that was it. He was up.

As he'd thought earlier, at least this time he could lay in his bed with Lara. That made his insomnia bearable. It felt like a dream that he was finally holding the woman he'd wanted for months. He respected her, admired her, worried about her, and yes, loved the hell out of her. And she loved him back.

Then, a surprising thing happened. As he lay there with Lara in his arms, reliving the most amazing sex he'd ever had and thinking about baby names, wondering what kind of pregnant woman Lara would be...he felt himself get drowsy.

Owl didn't have any expectations. This had happened on rare occasions in the past. He'd feel as if he was going to drift back to sleep, but then he'd continue to lay there for hours, depressed when it didn't happen.

The next thing he knew, Lara was pushing him onto his back, grinning down at him.

"Good morning," she said.

"Morning," Owl mumbled—then froze.

In tune as ever with him, Lara frowned. "What? What's wrong?"

"I slept," he said, utterly gobsmacked.

"What?"

"I woke up in the middle of the night, as I always do...but then...I fell back to sleep."

"I'm glad," she said, relaxing against him.

"No, you don't understand. Every single night for more than five years, I've woken up and not been able to go back to sleep. I've had insomnia ever since I was rescued. But last night...I woke up, then fell asleep again."

Lara lost some of the sleepiness in her eyes. "That's great."

"It's you," Owl said reverently.

"I think it's probably the two orgasms you had," she said with a small smile.

"No, it's you," he insisted. "Having you in my arms, knowing you were safe, my brain finally stopped spinning."

She stared at him with an odd look in her eyes.

"What?" It was Owl's turn to ask.

"It's just, for so long, I've desperately needed you by my side, and now…" Her voice trailed off.

"The table's turned. I need you to sleep," Owl said without hesitation.

"You need me," Lara whispered.

"One hundred percent."

"I…is it wrong that I like that?"

Owl shook his head. "Nope. But you do know what this means, right?"

"What?"

"That we can't sleep apart. Ever." He was only half kidding.

"Works for me," she said quickly. Then got serious. "For so long, I thought I was broken. I hated how I couldn't let you out of my sight. It made me feel weak. And now, knowing that I can give you something in return…it makes us feel a little more even."

"It's not a contest," Owl told her.

"I know. And I'm probably not explaining myself very well. But knowing that I can help you, even if it's in this small way, and even if I don't think it's really *me* that helped you sleep last night, it still feels good."

It was her. Owl had no doubt. He'd given up on ever sleeping through the night again, and the first night he'd held Lara in his arms, he'd slept like a freaking baby. It was her all right. She was what he'd been looking for all along. Having her close let his brain shut down, stop reliving all the bad things that had happened to him. And…he had to admit, the orgasms probably hadn't hurt either.

"You hungry?" he asked, suddenly eager to get up and start the day. He felt amazing after the extra sleep.

"I could eat."

"You want me to make that hash brown, ham, egg casserole you like?" he asked.

"I'd love that," she said with a small smile.

"Are you sore?"

She blushed. "A little."

"Why don't you take a long bath this morning then. By the time you're out and dressed, the casserole will be done."

"Okay. Owl?"

"Yeah, sweetheart?"

"I love you."

God, this woman. "I love you too." Then he kissed her quickly on the lips and swung his legs off the side of the bed. He headed toward the bathroom to do his business and glanced back once. Lara was on her back in the middle of the mattress, her arms over her head, stretching, a huge smile on her face.

Yeah, Owl could get used to this...her. In fact, he was already.

CHAPTER TWELVE

Lara wiped her brow as she sank into a chair in the lobby of the lodge and turned to grin at Cora. Her friend was collapsed into the chair next to hers and looked just as exhausted. They'd just said goodbye to the last family that had been there for the four-day trial run, and from her perspective, inviting families to stay at The Refuge had been a resounding success.

She hadn't realized how much she'd missed teaching or being around kids. They had a way of making you forget about your own issues and enjoy the moment. And there had been a lot of enjoyable moments in the last week. Of course, Lara also felt as if she'd been running a marathon. She'd forgotten how much energy children had.

"That was fun," Cora said.

"Yeah," Lara agreed with a nod.

For now, the two friends were alone, and Lara took a moment to appreciate the quiet.

"I'm proud of you," Cora added.

Lara looked over at her.

"I mean it. You've come a long way in such a short time. You're so strong, and resilient, and even after everything that happened, you're still the Lara I know and love, and I don't know how you're doing it."

She was talking fast, like she was hurrying to get her thoughts out, but they made a warmth swell in Lara's belly. "You want to know how?" she asked.

Cora's gaze was glued on Lara's. "Yeah," she said.

"Because of you. When I was in that basement and scared out of my mind and hurting, I knew you wouldn't stop looking for me. When Ridge came in and made me do that video phone call with you, I wanted so badly to blurt out that I wasn't all right, that I was being held prisoner. But Carter was there, I knew he had a knife, and if I said anything, he'd hurt me even more than he already had. So I lied my ass off...but I gave you our signal. Do you remember?"

"Of course I do!" Cora exclaimed. "That stupid ear tug."

"Yeah. Later that night, when Carter had finally left me alone, I closed my eyes and imagined what you were doing. What cages you were rattling to get to me."

"I'm sorry it took so long," Cora said softly.

But Lara shook her head. "No, don't do that. You came. When no one else cared that I'd suddenly disappeared, you knew something wasn't right. *That's* how I survived it. Because I knew my best friend was out there likely raising hell and gathering the cavalry to come and get me. And I was right."

"I love you so much, Lara. If I'd lost you..." Cora's voice trailed off.

"I feel the same, and no one is losing anyone," Lara said firmly. "And the other reasons why I'm not still hiding under my bed, quaking in my boots, is because of Owl. And Henley. And Brick, Tonka, Spike, Pipe, Stone, and Tiny. And Melba. Chuck too. Bubba the horse, Scarlet Pimpernickel. Everyone who works here. The guests, who are an inspiration. It's this *place*. There's something about The Refuge that makes it seem easier to climb out of my head and join in what's going on around me. I *want* to participate. I *want* to see the beautiful panoramic vistas. And I *want* to see my best friend living her best life."

Cora sniffed. "You're making me cry, and that is *not* okay," she complained.

"Cora Rooney is crying?" Lara teased. "Is hell freezing over?"

"It's Cora Clark, thank you very much, and yeah, when people don't give a rat's ass if you cry or not, it makes it much less of a big deal," Cora said.

"You know what, I'm *glad* Ridge was a douche. And that I was stuck in that house."

"What?" Cora asked with a frown.

"I mean, becoming a serial killer's newest obsession sucks, but me being there led you *here*. To Pipe. Look at you, Cora. You're *married*. And you've relaxed enough to freaking cry. I can count on one hand the number of times I've seen tears in your eyes before now. I'm so damn happy for you."

Cora stood and plopped her butt down on the chair Lara was currently sitting in. They were smushed together so close, Lara had to put her arm around her friend so they could both fit.

"I'm *not* glad," Cora said fiercely. "If you think I'm happy that you were kidnapped and tortured, you're insane. And I don't care if I'm happier than I've ever been in my life. If I have an amazing sex life and if I'm married to the man of my dreams... not that I'd ever had dreams about finding a man. And I don't care that I've found the family I never had growing up. I would give it all back if it meant you didn't have to go through what you did."

Lara shook her head. "No."

"Yes," Cora insisted. She grabbed Lara's hand. "The worst weeks of my life were when we got you here to The Refuge. Seeing you so...broken. I hated it. I would do *anything* to ensure you didn't have to experience that kind of fear. But now you're..."

"I'm good," Lara said softly.

"Yeah, you are," Cora agreed. Then she smiled. "And don't think I haven't noticed the way you and Owl have been eye-fucking each other the last several days."

Lara tried to keep a straight face, but she couldn't stop the small smile that formed.

"I knew it!" Cora exclaimed. "You and Owl are gettin' it on! Please, please, *please* tell me that man is good in bed!"

"Shhhh," Lara scolded, looking around.

"No one's around. They're all outside saying goodbye. Spill, Lara. Seriously."

"Owl is...he's amazing."

The smile on Cora's face was so big, she looked like a complete goof. Her voice gentled. "And it's...okay? I mean, emotionally? After what happened?"

"Amazingly, yeah. Being with Owl is nothing like being in that basement. He's very careful to not do anything that he thinks will bring back even the slightest bad memory. He lets me be in charge."

"Ooooh, that's not something I would've guessed," Cora said with a smirk. "I love when Pipe takes control in bed. I'd deny it if anyone other than you were sitting here, but there's something so freeing about letting him order me around."

Lara grinned at her friend. "I'm happy you have that."

"No, we aren't making this conversation about me. I want to know more about you and Owl."

"There's not much more to tell. I've been really busy with the kids the last few days so by the time I get back to the cabin, I'm exhausted. But..."

"But what?" Cora asked when Lara's voice trailed off.

"I'm happy I took everyone's advice and made the first move. But now..." She paused again, not sure how to explain her feelings while not sounding completely crazy.

"You wish he would initiate things," Cora finished for her.

"Yeah. He's been so careful with me. And I love being on top and being in charge of our lovemaking. But I think I want him to be a little more...in control."

"You aren't worried that you won't be able to handle that emotionally?" Cora asked, serious now.

"A little," Lara said honestly. "But I know Owl, and if I do start to slide into my memories, he'll bring me back."

Cora's eyes filled with tears again.

"Lord, what are you crying about *now?*" Lara teased, glad to lighten the conversation a little.

"I'm just so happy you have a man like you've always wanted."

"This might not last," Lara warned. "What is it Sandra Bullock said in the movie *Speed?* Relationships formed under intense situations never last? My situation is probably as intense as they can get."

"Whatever," Cora said, waving a hand in the air dismissively. "I know how much you love that movie, you've made me watch it a million times, and it's not because you love action flicks. It's a heroine-in-peril movie."

Lara grinned at that. She'd had a long conversation with Cora at one point about how she didn't like the term "damsel in distress," because it had negative connotations and inferred that the woman was sitting around, waiting for a man to "save" her. Heroine in peril didn't seem quite as bad.

"I do love that movie," Lara admitted.

"And Owl is your Jack," Cora said with a sigh.

"I think he is," Lara whispered.

"Right, so you need to tell him that you want him to take control," Cora said firmly. "From what I know of the man, and what I've seen in the months we've been here, if he thinks taking control in the bedroom will give you flashbacks or emotionally damage you, he's not going to risk it. So you're going to have to tell him that you honestly, truly want him to take charge. To initiate sexy times between the two of you."

"You're right."

"Of course I am." Cora sat up a little and looked toward the window, then she turned back to Lara. "And they're waving good-bye, so we only have a little bit of time left before everyone comes back and Owl claims you again. Are you excited about going to check out the helicopter with Owl and Stone? Are you nervous about leaving The Refuge?"

Lara frowned. "What?"

"What do you mean, what?" Cora asked, sounding confused.

"I have no idea what you're talking about," she said. "Owl and Stone are *leaving*? And they're getting a helicopter?"

Cora stared at her a moment, then abruptly tried to get out of the chair. "Um...maybe? I need to go check on...Henley. I mean, she's pregnant and all, and—"

She didn't get to finish her sentence because Lara grabbed the material of her shirt and yanked.

Cora fell back onto the chair. Well...onto Lara's lap.

Lara wrestled with her friend as she tried to get away, and it felt amazing. Like old times. Cora might be her best friend, but she drove Lara crazy fairly often, and mock wrestling with her felt like coming home.

She wrestled Cora to the floor and sat on her back, pinning her in place.

"Cora Clark—wow, I love how that sounds—tell me right now what you meant. Owl and Stone are leaving to go look at a helicopter? I knew the guys were talking about getting one, but I didn't know they'd actually *found* one. Are they leaving soon? And what's this about me going with them?"

"It's not fair that you're bigger than me! Sitting on me is a dick move, Lara," Cora complained through giggles. But no matter how much she struggled, she couldn't dislodge her.

"Talk, woman."

"Fine, geez! I thought you knew. Yes, they found a helicopter they want to buy, but Owl and Stone have to go check it out. Test-fly it. For obvious reasons, they need to be the ones to do so. The chopper is up in Seattle, apparently. They're supposed to leave next week, but Owl was leery to leave you, so I think it was Brick who suggested that you go with them."

Lara was stunned. Owl hadn't said a word about any of that. She wasn't sure whether to be excited for them that they'd actually found the chopper they wanted, happy for Owl and Stone that they'd get to do something they loved on a more regular basis—fly—or upset that Owl hadn't said anything about the upcoming trip.

"I'm sure he didn't want to worry you," Cora said from under Lara, quieter now.

Lara had been proud of the progress she'd made. Had reveled in Owl's affection. They'd said they loved each other, for goodness sake. And yet he'd kept this from her. What was he going to do, carry out a packed suitcase the day he was leaving and inform her that she was coming with him?

Or...maybe he'd decided against asking her to go because he didn't think she could handle it.

Could she handle it? Lara wanted to think she could, but the thought of leaving the safe haven of The Refuge sent an instant bolt of terror down her spine. Carter Grant was still out there. They all knew it. It was just a matter of when he made a move to claim what he thought was his.

"Lara?" Cora asked in concern.

Taking a deep breath, Lara did her best to control her suddenly all-over-the-place emotions.

"What the hell is going on here?" a deep voice asked with amusement.

Looking up, Lara saw Tiny, Owl, Pipe, and Brick standing in the doorway of the lodge, staring at them. She was still sitting on Cora.

"We're having a girl heart-to-heart conversation," Cora said with a small chuckle.

Lara was embarrassed that she'd been caught sitting on her best friend and immediately tried to get up. Before she could move too far, Owl was there, holding a hand down to her.

Childishly, she didn't want to take it. Wanted to smack it away. She was hurting because she had to learn about the trip from Cora...and selfishly, she wanted him to hurt too. But because she was an adult, and wanted to avoid the conversation she needed to have with him in front of the others, Lara took his hand.

And the second her skin touched his, it tingled. Sparks shot down to her toes. It was thrilling, and slightly annoying because she was irritated with him.

They hadn't had sex since the families had arrived because she'd been exhausted at the end of every day. And energetic kids aside, just engaging with so many people, for the first time in months, was mentally taxing. But they *had* been intimate. Owl had gathered her in his arms in their bed, and they'd fallen asleep wrapped around each other. And he'd slept. Every night. That was a heady feeling for Lara. He helped her feel safe and she helped him sleep through the night. The fact that he needed her as much as she needed him felt as if the scales were a little more balanced between them.

Now, she felt off-kilter. Why hadn't he told her that they'd found a helicopter they wanted to buy? It was a big deal for him. Having a real-live chopper he could fly anytime he wanted instead of having to make do with the simulation program? That was huge!

And the fact that he and the others had discussed her going with him and Stone to Seattle when they'd go to check it out, but he hadn't brought it up with her? It stung.

"You guys were amazing," Brick said with a grin.

"Oh my God!" Alaska exclaimed as she entered the lobby from the small office in the back. "I've already gotten two emails from the families who left earlier and they were overflowing with praise for The Refuge and, more importantly, you guys! They said their kids cried when they left because they'd had such a great time. I could never have done what you did!"

Brick held out his arm, and Alaska snuggled into him. Everyone was smiling at her and Cora, and it was overwhelming for Lara. Her emotions were already all over the place and this wasn't helping. She needed space. Needed to think.

"Thanks," she said. "I'm gonna go back to the cabin," she informed the group, then headed for the door without looking back.

"Was it something I said?" Lara heard Alaska ask. But she didn't stop. She was being rude, but at the moment, her only thought was to get to the cabin and away from everyone.

CHAPTER THIRTEEN

"What the hell?" Owl muttered as he stared at Lara's back. He took a step to go after her when he felt a tug on his shirt. Turning, he saw Cora standing next to him, looking concerned.

"I messed up," she admitted. "I didn't know you hadn't talked to her. I spilled the beans about the chopper, and I asked how she felt about leaving The Refuge. I didn't realize you hadn't told her about the trip or asked her to go with you yet."

Owl's stomach churned.

"You haven't told her about the trip?" Tiny asked.

"We found the chopper the day all the families arrived. She's been busy and tired. Every night, she came home and collapsed. I didn't want to burden her with that on top of everything she's been doing for The Refuge," Owl said a little defensively.

"I get that," Pipe said, putting an arm around his wife. "Cora's been like a zombie every night. Mumbling about crayons and crafts before falling asleep two-point-one seconds after she sits down to watch TV."

"It's been a while since we've done the kid thing," Cora said. "And back in DC, we were only there during the day. We didn't have to entertain them through dinner or do any of the fun stuff we did here in the evenings."

"I need to talk to her," Owl said, pressing his lips together.

"Give her a moment to think," Cora told him.

But Owl shook his head. "No, she'll *overthink* things."

"Maybe it's not a good idea after all," Brick suggested. "She can stay here with us. We'll watch over her. Make sure she's good."

Owl had no doubt that his friends would take good care of his woman. But something deep down rebelled at the thought of leaving her. She might have been the one who was scared to let him out of her sight, but now he was the one who didn't want to leave *her*. He'd gotten very used to having her with him nearly all the time. Loved the talks they'd had. Enjoyed looking over and seeing her sitting on his couch.

He was completely addicted to Lara Osler, and the thought of spending a week away from her made his skin crawl.

"I appreciate that," he told his friends, "But she needs this. Needs to get out. See that the world isn't out to get her."

"What if something happens?" Tiny asked.

"Then we'll deal with it," Owl said firmly. In the back of his mind, he was as worried as he assumed Lara was about her past coming back to haunt her. But another part of him kind of wished Carter Grant would make a move. He'd rather die than do anything that would hurt Lara, but this not knowing sucked. The knowledge that the serial killer was out there somewhere... it would eventually tear Lara down. So if the asshole was going to try anything, Owl wanted him to do it sooner rather than later. He'd make a mistake, the FBI would catch him, and they could move on with their lives once and for all.

Lara was doing amazing. She still had her setbacks, and with Grant out there, she could never fully relax...and everyone knew it. This trip to Seattle would be the first step in her taking back her independence. Proving that while she might have been through a horrible experience, she wasn't a victim.

Owl just had to convince her that he wasn't an insensitive jerk for not telling her about the possible trip before now. For obviously discussing Lara behind her back with his friends, however innocent, and for not giving her more than a week to think about the possibility of venturing off the property.

"Let us know if you need anything," Brick said.

"Owl?" Cora said before he could leave.

Trying not to be annoyed and just wanting to get to Lara, Owl turned to her.

"Don't let her push you away. You're her Jack."

He had no idea what the hell that meant, but he simply nodded and said, "I won't." Then he turned before anyone else decided they wanted to have a chat and strode toward the door. He needed to make this right and wasn't sure how. He hated the hurt and confusion he'd seen on Lara's face before she'd left. He'd fucked up, and somehow, someway, he needed to fix things.

Lara took a deep breath once the door to the cabin shut behind her. The walk through the wooded path seemed longer and scarier for some reason. It wasn't quite dark out yet, but it was overcast, and that made everything a little more eerie.

She went into the guest room, needing a neutral room to process everything she was feeling.

What hurt the most about what she'd learned from Cora was that it was *Owl* who'd kept things from her. Lara's head pounded with a headache...and her chest hurt from heartache. Maybe he had a good explanation, but she couldn't think of what that might be. He'd had plenty of time to tell her they'd found a chopper, and more importantly, about the possibility of her going with him and Stone to check it out.

She curled into a fetal position on the bed and stared blankly out into the dim room. Did he not *want* her to go? Was that why he hadn't brought it up? That hurt, but honestly, she wouldn't blame him. What did she know about helicopters? Nothing. And if she had a panic attack, he'd have to deal with that rather than the chopper. The last thing she wanted was to be a burden on anyone.

And she'd been more than a burden on Owl for quite a while. Hell, for months he wasn't able to do any-damn-thing without her freaking out if she lost sight of him. She'd come a long way from the woman she'd been right after she'd been rescued, but neither of them knew how she'd react out in the real world. Here on The Refuge, she felt safe. But the second she stepped foot off the property, she was fair game. And she had a feeling everyone knew it too.

The sound of the front door opening and closing had Lara tensing. But Owl's deep voice immediately made her relax.

"It's me!" he called out as he always did when he came home.

Home.

This cabin was home for Lara now. It was her safe place. Her own personal refuge. And the last week and a half had been heaven. Yes, she'd been tired from working with the kids all day, but coming home to Owl was a dream come true. And now she questioned everything about that. She'd been duped before, and while she didn't think Owl was anywhere in the same league as Ridge, she couldn't help but wonder if, once again, she'd let her overly romantic hopes and dreams overpower her common sense.

She wasn't really surprised when Owl appeared in the bedroom doorway a moment later. He didn't walk over to where she lay on the bed, which she appreciated.

He leaned against the doorjamb and crossed his arms.

"I'm sorry."

Lara blinked in surprise. She wasn't sure what she'd expected, but from past experience, she kind of thought he'd lead off with some sort of defensive explanation for not telling her about the helicopter or the trip. She wasn't surprised that Cora had told him she'd spilled the beans.

She didn't respond to his apology.

"When you first got here, you slept like that," he said quietly.

Confused, Lara didn't lift her head, but she couldn't deny that he had her attention.

"Curled in a little ball. Protecting yourself from the world. And the fact that you're doing that again...it kills me. Because *I* did that. I made you feel as if you had to protect yourself from me." The agony in his voice almost made Lara sit up and open her arms to him. But she stayed where she was. Watching. Waiting.

Owl shifted just inside the room with his back to the wall, then he slowly slid down so he was sitting. He lifted his knees and rested his arms on them as he continued to stare at her.

"All those months ago, when you first got here, people were surprised at how unfazed I was when you refused to let me out of your sight. My friends offered to relieve me all the time. Cora begged me to take a break and let her stay with you. But I refused. You want to know why?"

Lara tried to tamp down her curiosity. But she couldn't. She gave him a small nod.

"Because I needed you as much as you needed me. You ever watched any of those military shows on TV?"

She frowned. It seemed like an abrupt change in topic, but she gave him another small nod.

"Yeah, the Navy SEALs shows are awesome. They're alpha, protective, brave, and as badass as it gets. Every woman's ideal when it comes to what they want in a partner. The firefighter shows? They're the same. Those men run into burning buildings when everyone else is running out. In real life, they're heroes. The ones who get the news stories, the movie deals, the books written about them.

"Then there's me. How many times have you even looked twice at the person *driving* in those shows? The guy flying the helicopter that dodges RPGs, mountains, machine gun fire, and every bad guy within a ten-mile radius trying to take him down? Or the guy driving the firetruck? The person who's flying those planes over wildfires, through the smoke and flames, to either drop retardant or the hot shot firefighters?

"Never," he said, answering his own question.

Lara frowned, understanding where he was going...and not liking it at all.

"Stone and I weren't SEALs. We weren't Delta Force Operatives. We're pilots. Damn good ones. But only pilots. We weren't sure the Army would send anyone after us when we crashed. At least, not in as timely a manner as we needed them to. Because there are always more pilots. Eventually, yes, they did send help, but we're pretty sure it's because of the videos that were blasted all over the Internet. Having us in the terrorists' clutches was bad PR for the military. So they sent in one of those badass teams to bring us home.

"Even then, we weren't treated as heroes. We weren't on the news or interviewed for *People Magazine*. Our rescuers were in high demand for interviews. For their perspective on what happened. Because of those damn videos, people were *embarrassed* for Stone and me. Our skinny, pale, naked asses weren't the kind of muscular physiques that made for good entertainment. We faded into the background. We were merely a footnote in the War on Terror. Invisible, which in some ways was what we needed...but it stung too.

"But you, Lara, you *saw* me. To you, I wasn't merely the pilot. I was important. Needed. And it felt *good*. So damn good. I didn't mind that you needed me near. It was wrong of me, I know that, but for so long, I craved being important to someone. So much that I didn't fight your dependence on me.

"And when you started to recover? When you didn't need me around all the time...I was proud. So impressed that you could find your way out of your panic and fear. And I have to admit that I liked how our relationship was changing. You no longer needed a crutch, but you still seemed to enjoy being with me. Talking. Cooking. Doing normal things.

"I didn't tell you about the trip to buy the helicopter, *not* because I wanted to keep it from you, but simply because flying is no longer the most important thing in my life, Lara. *You* are.

"I think I loved you from the moment we left that hospital in Arizona. You were so scared, so traumatized, and yet you still did your best to reassure your parents that you were okay...when you were anything but. You reassured Cora, tried to make her feel better about you being kidnapped. From that moment, I fell hard and fast. Anyone who could be as kind as you, to think about others even while trying to deal with such a horrific ordeal, was someone I wanted to be around. Someone I wanted to have in my life forever.

"I'm excited about having a chopper here at The Refuge, but that excitement is eclipsed by *you*, Lara. I wasn't thinking about horsepower or fuel capacity when you walked into this cabin every night; all I wanted to know was how your day went. Hearing the stories about the kids you and Cora entertained, how much you were enjoying contributing. That was my focus. Then we'd wake up in the morning, and I'd be so overwhelmed and grateful that I'd slept through the night again...the helicopter was the last thing I thought about."

Lara's head was spinning. She wasn't sure she'd ever heard Owl say so much at one time before. She was transfixed by everything he was sharing. He didn't talk a lot about his time as a POW, or what he endured after he was home...but hearing his thoughts now, about what others did or didn't think of his profession, was heartbreaking. And worse—he wasn't wrong.

Those movies he talked about? They didn't focus on the daring pilots of those choppers at all. They showed the helicopters flying in and out of mountain ranges, picking up the special forces soldiers, dropping them off amongst heavy gunfire, but not once could Lara remember any focus being on the pilots.

"And in the last few days, you've also been exhausted. And happy. I got a glimpse of the person your kids out in DC got to see every day. Your inner light shone so bright, it almost blinded me. I didn't want to dim that for even a second by making you stress about a potential trip off The Refuge.

"I'm sorry, sweetheart. I should've found a way to tell you about the helicopter. Tex found a Bell 505. It's almost new and the price is unbeatable. Brick's been emailing back and forth with the seller and our accountant to make a potential deal. Now, he's made an appointment next week for Stone and me to check it out before any purchase. A couple weeks ago, when The Refuge owning a helicopter was more a discussion than a done deal, Brick suggested that maybe you could come with us to take a look at it. It was before you were doing as well as you are now. But even then, I wanted you to come with me, simply because I didn't like the thought of not being around you for any length of time.

"I've gotten used to you, sweetheart. The way you hum under your breath when you're cooking. The mess you can't seem to help leaving in the bathroom when you're getting ready for the day. The way you feel in my arms at night. The sounds you make when I'm deep inside you. I love you, Lara. And I hate myself for the hurt and uncertainty you're feeling. That you're in a fetal position because I made you doubt my love for you."

The silence in the room when he stopped speaking was heavy.

But surprisingly, Lara felt...light.

"I'm not really hurt because you didn't tell me about the helicopter itself. I'm upset because I thought maybe you decided you didn't want me to go, or didn't think I could handle it...and that's why you didn't bring it up. And also because it's something I know you were probably thrilled about, and you didn't let me share in that excitement.

"I want to share in the things *you* love too, Owl. Too much has been about me so far, and I'm tired of it. I want to share my joy over Henley and Reese's pregnancies. I want to celebrate birthdays. I'm sick of everyone tiptoeing around me. I'm not great, but I'm getting much better. Henley has helped me see that life is about how you react to experiences. And I don't want to be Carter Grant's victim. I want to laugh. Make love. Tease my friends and be involved in their lives. And I can't be involved if everyone is second-guessing what they say in front of me because they're scared I'm going to have a panic attack."

Owl nodded. "You're right. I promise not to keep anything from you from this moment on. If I'm happy, I'll share with you. If I'm angry, I'll let you commiserate and talk me off the ledge. If I'm scared, I'll let you comfort me. I fucked up, Lara. I know it, and I'm sorry. Please don't let this break us up."

Just the thought of leaving this man made Lara's chest hurt. She slowly sat up. "Come here?" she asked tentatively.

Owl shot to his feet and was at the side of the bed in a heartbeat. She scooted over, giving him room, and he lowered himself to the bed beside her. They were face-to-face, and he smoothed a hand over her hair and stared into her eyes.

"Forgive me?"

"I think I'd forgive you anything," Lara told him as she wrapped an arm around his waist. The other lay flat against his chest between them.

"Thank God," he breathed as he shut his eyes.

It was clear to Lara that Owl had been just as stressed out as she'd been. He hadn't been in a fetal position, but he'd been just as upset about the tension between them.

"For the record, I *do* see you, Callen Kaufman. And I see an amazing man. Unselfish, giving, and willing to do whatever it takes to make others happy. I also see a sexy, gorgeous man who makes me feel things I've never felt in my life."

"Safe?" he asked.

"That too," she reassured him. "But I'm not in love with you because you make me feel safe. Because you protect me."

He lifted an eyebrow, and Lara couldn't help but think he was kind of cute when he needed reassurance like this.

"I fell in love with you because you never saw me as broken, even when I was."

"You were never broken, sweetheart. Dented, maybe. But not broken."

Yeah, she definitely loved this man. "And the answer is yes, by the way."

He frowned in confusion.

"I'll go with you and Stone to Seattle."

His eyes lit up with excitement. "Yeah?"

"Uh-huh. How can I pass up the chance to see you behind the wheel...wait...it's not a wheel, is it? The controls?"

Owl chuckled. "Yeah."

"Pass up the chance to see you behind the controls of a real live helicopter? I mean, the simulator is great, but I'm thinking it's much different in the real thing."

"It is and it's not. Stone and I bought the best simulator out there. The foot pedals feel a little different in the real thing, and you can't feel the wind buffeting the chopper in the sim, but the controls are pretty accurate."

Lara smiled at him.

He grimaced. "Sorry. I'm a little excited. And I've already talked to Brick about security for you during the trip. We're staying in a place Tex recommended, and we're not going to dally. We're going to go up there, check this chopper out, and come home. And we won't file our flight plan until the last possible minute so if anyone is out there watching, they won't be able to track us. I'm not going to let anything happen to you. No way in hell."

"Okay."

"Okay?"

Lara nodded.

"You hungry?" he asked.

At the mention of food, Lara's belly growled. Loudly.

Owl laughed. He leaned in and kissed her, letting his lips rest on hers for a long moment. Then he pulled back. "I have one more question. Who the hell is Jack?"

Lara giggled.

"Seriously, Cora told me I was your Jack, but I don't know what that means."

"It means you're mine," she said with a small smile.

"Damn straight," he said before swinging his legs off the mattress and holding out a hand to her.

Lara took it, and she felt a tingle inside when he didn't drop it as he started for the door.

She was happy...but in the back of her mind, she couldn't help but think about what Sandra Bullock had said in the movie. The line about relationships starting under extreme circumstances not working out.

She hoped she was wrong. Because if she lost Owl, she'd never recover. She instinctively knew he was her one and only chance at a deep, true, forever kind of love, and she was going to do everything in her power to hold onto it, *him*, for all she was worth.

* * *

Carter Grant couldn't stop grinning.

It was nearly time!

Everything was in place.

In less than a week, he'd have his property back where she belonged. And this time, he'd make sure she couldn't escape.

He'd planned as many of the details as possible. He didn't know exactly when she and the assholes from The Refuge would arrive in Seattle, or on which flight, but it didn't matter. He'd briefed his accomplice thoroughly, and the man would deliver Lara to his new lair. It was remote, and even if she did manage to escape the room he'd prepared...she wouldn't be able to get off the island.

It was going to take almost all the money he'd saved up— okay, stolen from the Michaels family—to secure the house and pay off his accomplice, but it would be worth it. He'd gotten a new identity and changed his appearance. Despite the eye patch he wore, no one would immediately suspect he was a notorious serial killer being hunted by the FBI. His blond buzz cut had grown out in the last few months and was now dyed almost black. A colored contact hid his hazel eye.

He was also smarter than all his enemies. He'd live out the rest of his life on the island he'd bought, with his special toy.

Thinking about Lara being at his mercy once more made his cock harden. He ignored it. He had more important things to do, and he wanted to save himself for what was to come.

Chuckling at the play on words, Carter relaxed into his chair as he ran over the plans for the next week in his head once more. Lara and the two assholes would arrive in Seattle and spend the night. Then they were scheduled to meet with his accomplice, who was posing as the helicopter's owner. He'd allow the trio to take the chopper up for a test flight, they'd complete the financial details...

And after getting his money, the accomplice would kill the two assholes and fly Lara straight to the island.

Then the fun would start.

Carter could hardly wait.

CHAPTER FOURTEEN

Tomorrow was the day they were leaving to head up to Seattle, and Owl had to admit he was nervous for Lara's sake. Yes, she'd been doing so well, hadn't had a panic attack in weeks now, but leaving The Refuge was going to be stressful for her.

Tonight, the two of them were spending a quiet evening in their cabin. They'd played on the flight simulator for a few hours, and Owl was impressed with how good Lara had become for never having been in a helicopter before. Well...while conscious. She wasn't quite ready to join the Army and sign up to train as a Night Stalker, but he loved seeing the joy on her face when she made it through an entire flight sim—on the beginner level—without crashing. She wasn't the greatest at takeoffs or landings, but Owl had no doubt that she'd master those soon enough.

"What are you thinking?" she asked as they cuddled together on the couch. He was pretending to read, and he'd thought she was engrossed in the sitcom on the television. Owl shouldn't have been surprised that she knew he was thinking rather than relaxing. He'd been going over and over their travel plans, trying to come up with scenarios for how to react if the worst happened.

"Not much," he lied. No way in hell was he going to pile more worry on Lara's head.

"Are you excited?"

"Yeah," Owl said with a small smile. And he was. He'd never dreamed that one day he could be part owner of his very own helicopter. And it made it even better that Stone would be at his side. Flying for pleasure would be a welcome change from the countless stressful missions they'd been on in the Army.

The last few days had been filled with details for their trip, emails to the seller, and generally trying to get everything together for him, Stone, and Lara to fly up to Seattle. He'd spent time with Brick, Pipe, and the others, taking their advice for keeping her safe, suggestions he welcomed. The last thing he wanted was something happening to Lara on his watch. He'd never forgive himself.

"Are you sure you still want to go?" Owl asked.

"Yes." Her answer was immediate and heartfelt. Owl felt pride well up inside him once more. His Lara was tough.

She turned to him. "Do you still *want* me to go?"

"Of course I do," Owl said, his brow furrowing. "Why would you think I wouldn't?"

"Because of *him*. Having me around makes everything more stressful."

Owl turned to the woman he loved and palmed her face. "No, it doesn't. I'd be stressed out if you were there or not. And you know what else? I wouldn't sleep. And that would make the trip more dangerous. Because who wants a pilot who hasn't gotten enough sleep?"

Lara rolled her eyes. "Whatever."

"I'm serious," Owl said with no hint of humor in his voice. "For a man who hasn't slept through a night in over five years, you're a miracle."

"So you're with me because I help you sleep," she said, her voice teasing.

"No, I'm with you because you make me happy. You make me feel as if I can be the man I've always wanted to be. You make me yearn for what I thought I'd never find...a family. I'm with you because you're *you*, Lara. I love you."

"I love you too."

Owl kissed her. He wanted so badly to push her backward and take her right then and there. Hard and fast. Show her without words how vital she was to him. But he forced himself to keep the kiss light and easy. He'd rather stick his dick in a light socket than do anything that would bring back any of the trauma she'd experienced.

Lara gripped his shirt tightly and pressed herself harder against him. He loved when she took control. Not only because it meant she wanted him as much as he wanted her, but also because it let him off the hook when it came to worrying about how much was too much when it came to intimacy.

But all too soon, she stopped, pulled back and stared at him. Owl couldn't read her expression. He frowned, worried now. "What? What's wrong?"

"Nothing," she said quickly, biting her bottom lip.

"Talk to me, Lara. Do I need to call Henley?"

"No! I mean, I'm fine. I just...do you like it when I take control of our lovemaking?"

Owl arched a brow. "Do you mean to tell me you don't know if my orgasms are real or not?" he joked.

She smiled at that. "No, I definitely know you aren't faking those. Your come dripping out of me in the morning tells me that."

Owl couldn't stop his satisfied smile. He loved filling her up. Loved seeing his release drip out of her when she got up in the morning. It was a purely masculine reaction, and he probably should be ashamed of himself, but it was so damn erotic, he couldn't dredge up the energy to feel bad. He'd kind of freaked out the first morning, worrying about how she would react, but she'd simply given him a sheepish smile before heading to the bathroom.

He belatedly remembered her question. "I love when you're in charge," he told her honestly.

"Me too, but..." Her voice trailed off.

Owl's blood ran cold. She wasn't happy with their sex life? Had he fucked up somehow? "But what?" he asked, a little harsher than he meant to.

Lara looked up at him. "I'm always on top," she said.

Owl frowned. He freaking loved watching her bob on his dick. Seeing his cock disappear into her body as she sank down on him. The way her tits bounced as she took him. There wasn't one thing about her sitting astride him as they made love that he *didn't* like.

"And?" he prompted.

"I just...I wouldn't mind if you were on top sometimes."

Owl stilled. The image that popped into his brain was so carnal, it was taking everything in him to remember to breathe. "I don't want to bring back bad memories," he whispered.

"He didn't...I mean, he liked to straddle me and get off, but you aren't *him*, Owl. When I'm with you, I don't think about him. I trust you, and I know there are times you hold back with me. I want you to enjoy what we do together as much as I do. And when it's obvious you're doing everything in your power to be gentle with me, it makes me think that you aren't getting as much pleasure out of sex as I am."

Owl was torn between being extremely turned on, and pissed off at himself. He definitely loved everything he and Lara had done together, but he hated that she'd picked up on the fact that he'd been controlling his reactions.

He stood, taking hold of her hand as he did. He pulled her to her feet, then towed her toward the bedroom.

"Owl? Are you upset?"

In response, he gently urged her to sit on the mattress and scoot into the middle. She did so, not taking her gaze from his. When she was lying down, he crawled in and hovered over her.

"I'm not upset," he told her as he caged her in with his body. "I love that you were strong enough, and brave enough, to make the first move as far as we're concerned. Everything about you turns me on. Your brain, your kind heart, and especially your body. I've never been as satisfied as I've been with you in my bed. Watching you take back the control that asshole stole from you has been some of the best experiences in my life." He hesitated.

"But?" she prompted.

Owl's lips twitched upward. His Lara was so damn perceptive. "But," he continued, "if you want to give me some of that control, I'll gladly take it. On one condition."

"What?"

"The second you feel any twinge of unease, you tell me. I'm

serious, sweetheart. It would kill me if I did anything to make you uncomfortable."

"Deal."

Owl's arm shook as he held himself over the love of his life. His brain was screaming, *Do it! Take her!* But his heart was urging him to have caution. To go slow.

Lara smiled up at him, and he could see the muscles in her body relax. He was pissed that he hadn't noticed earlier that she wanted to give up some of the control he'd willingly given. But he'd make it up to her.

Straightening to his knees, Owl ripped his T-shirt over his head. The smile she gave him was enough to make his cock throb. Mentally telling himself to calm the hell down, he lowered himself once more and inched down her body, until he lay between her spread legs. He pulled on her leggings and was relieved when she raised her butt to help him.

As he dealt with her leggings and underwear, she wiggled until she'd taken her shirt off as well. She lay under him completely nude, and Owl once more wondered how he'd gotten so lucky. How this classy, beautiful, passionate woman was all his.

Lowering his head, Owl pushed her legs farther apart, and feasted.

* * *

Lara moaned as she gripped Owl's head. This wasn't the first time he'd gone down on her, but he seemed different tonight. Of course he was. She'd given him free rein to take control. And he didn't hesitate. He ate her out like he was a starving man and she was a four-course meal. He didn't let up when she squirmed under him. He used his lips, tongue, and even his fingers to bring her to the edge time and time again, but he stopped short of letting her orgasm.

"Owl," she whined when he lifted his mouth from her clit for what felt like the hundredth time.

"You want something?" he teased.

"Yes! You!" she exclaimed.

Owl practically leapt off the bed, but he was back before Lara could blink. He'd removed his sweatpants and was hovering over her, one hand on his cock, stroking himself, the other pressing against her belly.

For a split second, Lara was back there. In that basement. Watching as her captor masturbated over her. But then she blinked and all she saw was Owl.

But of course, he saw her reaction. He froze, sitting back on his heels.

"No!" Lara exclaimed, reaching for him. "Please, Owl, I need you!"

"Are you sure?"

"Yes! I love you. I'm here with you, and you would never hurt me."

"Damn straight," he said, then his jaw clenched with determination and he scooted forward, forcing her thighs to spread apart to make room for him.

"You are so beautiful. Dripping for me," he said in a hoarse tone.

"Yes," she encouraged. Hearing his voice went a long way toward keeping her in the here and now.

"Touch me," Owl ordered. "Put your hands on my chest. Feel my heart beating just for you."

She gladly did as he asked, and he wasn't wrong, his heart was thumping hard in his chest. She could feel one of his many scars under her palm, and it further grounded her. Owl had his own demons, and she wanted to be there for him just as he had for her.

She felt the tip of his cock brush against her sensitive folds, and gasped.

Then he was inside. He didn't hesitate, which she appreciated. He buried himself as deep in her sheath as he could go, and nothing had ever felt so right in her life. And it felt different with him on top. Amazing.

"Is this okay?" he asked, holding himself still above her.

"It's perfect," Lara breathed. "Move."

He did. Slowly at first, but with each thrust, his assurance grew that he wasn't hurting her, that she was enjoying what he was doing, and he sped up.

Soon, he was pounding into her, claiming her. Ruining her for any other man—not that he hadn't already done that.

"Yours," he chanted every time he bottomed out inside her.

Lara couldn't help but smile at that. He didn't claim her; he was still giving her the power by claiming she owned *him*. It was semantics, because she did feel as if she was his right back, but she loved how sensitive he was to all that she'd been through.

Owl reached down, grabbing hold of her knee and pulling it up. Then he did the same with the other one. He hooked her legs over his arms and braced himself on the mattress as he hovered over her.

He thrust, and she squeaked because he was so deep inside her now. Much deeper than when she'd been on top.

"Yours," he said again, as he pushed inside her.

"Mine," she agreed.

He stared into her eyes as he took her. She was helpless under him, but instead of feeling afraid and small, she felt powerful. When she ran her hands up his chest, he shuddered as she caressed his nipples. When she put one hand on the back of his neck, she felt the goose bumps rise on his skin. He might be in the dominant position at the moment, but she had just as much power over their lovemaking. It was a heady feeling.

"You like this," she panted.

"Fuck yeah, I do," he told her.

"You're so deep."

"Gonna fill you to the brim," he choked out. "Gonna give you my baby. If you don't want that, now's the time to speak up."

Lara smiled. She wasn't sure why tonight was different than any of the other times he'd come inside her, but she didn't argue. She wanted this man's baby. Craved it with every fiber of her being.

"Do it," she demanded.

Determination lit Owl's eyes, and he stopped holding back. He pounded into her, grunting each time he bottomed out. Pleasure swam throughout Lara's body. Everything tingled. She moved a hand down between her legs.

"Oh, fuck, that's so damn sexy," he said, his gaze now focused on where they were joined.

She stroked her clit as he continued to fuck her. The pleasure rose hard and fast, and Lara was lost in the exquisite sensations.

"Do it," Owl begged. "Come, Lara. I can't hold off. You feel too good. You're too tight and hot."

Her fingers moved faster, and she used her pinky to stroke Owl's dick every time he pulled out of her. She tried to thrust her hips upward but had no leverage. She was completely at Owl's mercy—and that realization was all it took for her to fly over the edge.

A long groan left her lips as she convulsed in Owl's embrace.

Even before she stopped shaking, he pushed all the way inside her and let out the sexiest groan. He moved a hand, allowing her to lower her leg, and grabbed one of her butt cheeks, pulling her closer and shoving himself even deeper inside her body.

Her hand was trapped between them, she was sweaty, and she felt as if she'd been turned inside out, but Lara had never been more sated in her life.

Owl slowly moved so she could put her other leg down, but he kept his hand on her ass as he shifted above her. He pressed his hips closer and lay his body on top of hers. Their flesh slid together sensually as he used his free hand to smooth her hair. Then he palmed the back of her head and held her still as he rested his forehead against hers.

They were both panting, and she could feel his heartbeat against her chest. She should've felt smothered. But having Owl draped over her felt amazingly...right.

"In nine months, we'll get to meet our baby," he whispered.

Lara chuckled. "That sure you knocked me up?" she joked.

Owl lifted his head, and she saw absolutely no humor in his expression as he said, "Yes. There's no way I didn't get you pregnant after how hard I just came."

Lara had the thought she should be feeling uneasy right about now. This wasn't normal. Guys weren't this obsessed with getting their girlfriends pregnant. Hell, she hadn't even really figured out what she was doing with her life. Her parents expected her to go back to DC eventually, and her job was still being held for her there.

But instead, all she felt was...relief. All she'd ever wanted was to be married to a man who loved her above all else, and to have a family with him. Owl *was* that man, she had no doubt about that. And if she was lucky enough to be able to have children with him, she'd never ask for anything ever again.

Many people wouldn't understand, but Lara didn't care. She shifted until her feet were flat on the mattress, and she squeezed her thighs together, holding Owl in a full-body embrace. "I can't wait to meet him or her," she said solemnly.

He stared down at her for a beat, before slowly smiling.

"And for the record...I'm officially handing the reins of our sex life over to you. You can be in charge."

She felt his cock twitch inside her at that.

"Yeah?" he asked.

"Yeah."

The hand in her hair tightened, and the small tug on her scalp sent goose bumps racing down her arms. "I didn't hurt you?"

"No. Not even close."

His dick twitched again.

Then he moved, sliding up to his knees, forcing Lara to lower her legs to give him room. He sat back on his heels and pulled her ass onto his lap. The position felt a little awkward for Lara, but when he put his hands on her chest and pinched her nipples, she didn't even care.

"Just to be sure I knocked you up, I'm gonna come inside you again. And again. As many times as I can manage," he vowed.

This dominant side of her man was a little surprising, but then again, it probably shouldn't have been. He might not be a Navy SEAL or a Delta, but he was used to being in complete control when he was piloting a multimillion-dollar chopper. And the way he flew in the simulator, at once focused and a little reckless, should've been a clue to Lara that her man might not act dominant in public, but behind closed doors, he was one hundred percent alpha.

"Your pussy's gonna be dripping for days. Want you to feel me there throughout the next week while we're gone."

"Owl," she moaned.

"You first though," he said with a small smile, then moved a hand to her clit.

It was going to be a long night, but Lara wasn't complaining. Not in the least.

CHAPTER FIFTEEN

Everyone came to the lodge to say goodbye the next morning. Lara felt like a zombie; she hadn't gotten nearly enough sleep, as Owl had been insatiable. He'd done just what he'd promised, filled her up three times, making her orgasm at least double that amount. She felt like a rubber noodle, and while it might not have been his intent, she was too tired, too sated, to feel any apprehension about leaving The Refuge that morning.

Owl had kept a hand on her almost at all times. As if he couldn't bear to not touch her. At the small of her back, his arm brushing against hers, holding her hand. She'd dreamed of a man like this, but honestly had lost all hope of ever finding him. And now here she was. Lara had to pinch herself to make sure she wasn't dreaming.

When everyone had said their goodbyes, and as Brick was giving Owl and Stone a last list of instructions and information about the chopper and the transaction, Cora pulled Lara to the side.

"You look tired, are you all right?"

The concern her best friend had for her made Lara feel good. "I'm fine. I just didn't get much sleep last night."

"Were you up worrying?" Cora asked with a frown.

Lara gave her a shy smile. "Hardly."

Comprehension dawned on her. "Oh!" she said with a grin.

"Yeah, *oh*."

"I take it giving Owl control worked out for you?"

"Definitely," Lara agreed.

Cora grinned stupidly. Then she sobered. "I'm in awe of you. Out of the two of us, you've always been the smart one, the pretty one, the elegant one. And now you're the Wonder Woman of us too. You can literally do anything you put your mind to. I should be jealous as hell, but instead I'm just so damn proud."

"Cora," she protested, feeling overwhelmed.

"Nope. No crying. I forbid it," Cora said, even as her eyes filled with tears.

So Lara did the only thing she could right then, she pulled Cora into a hug and held her tight.

"Love you," Cora mumbled against Lara's shoulder.

"Love you too," she returned.

They stood like that for a moment before movement caught Lara's eyes. She looked up to see Owl, Pipe, Stone, and Brick staring at them.

She lowered her arms and Cora turned.

"What?" she asked. "Can't two best friends share a hug?"

Pipe chuckled. "No one said anything," he reassured his wife.

"Whatever," she mumbled.

Pipe pulled her into his arms. Cora leaned back against him

and covered his clasped hands with her own where they rested on her belly.

"If you have any questions about anything, don't hesitate to call," Brick told Owl and Stone. "I've looked over all the paperwork, so it's just a matter of you guys signing on the dotted line if you give the chopper your approval after test-flying. As soon as I get word from you that all's well, I'll have Savannah get the ball rolling on the money transfer."

Owl and Stone nodded.

"You've got your licenses, right?"

"Yes, Mom," Stone joked.

Brick winced. "Sorry. Just had to make sure."

Owl had approached Lara while Brick was still talking, standing next to her with his fingertips resting lightly on the small of her back. That touch reminded her of the night before, when she was on her knees and he was behind her, caressing that spot right where his fingers were now as he took her hard and deep.

She shivered.

"If you feel as if something's off, speak up," Brick ordered Lara in a firm tone.

She nodded.

"And, you two, if you get that oh-shit feeling, don't hesitate. Get the hell gone. A chopper's not worth anyone's life," Brick said.

"You hear anything from Tex?" Stone asked with a frown.

"No. Grant's still in the wind. I'm just being cautious."

"Nothing's gonna happen to Lara. I give you my word," Owl vowed.

"Good. But she's not the only one I'm worried about," Brick said.

"We've got this," Stone said.

"I *dare* Carter to show his face," Lara blurted. "Not that he can know where I am or what our plans are, but if he does, he'll be caught in a heartbeat. He can't go anywhere without being recognized...thanks to Cora." Lara smiled over at her best friend. "He sticks out like a sore thumb. We'll be fine."

"Right. Then let's get going. You guys have a flight to catch," Brick said firmly.

Lara hugged Cora once more then headed out to Brick's Rubicon with the others. Stone sat in the front with Brick, and Owl held the back door open for Lara. He climbed in after her, and once she'd fastened her seat belt, Owl immediately reached for her hand.

She shot him a shy smile as she squeezed his fingers. He smiled back and ran his thumb over the back of her hand. That brought another reminder of the night before, of the moments after the last time they'd made love. The sheets were a mess, she felt sweaty, but she'd never been more content. They'd lain next to each other, holding hands, attempting to catch their breaths, and Owl had run his thumb over her hand just as he was now. No words were needed; that small touch said it all.

Then they'd taken turns in the bathroom, put their shirts and underwear back on, and had almost immediately fallen asleep in each other's arms.

Owl was her perfect match. In every way. He made her feel stronger. Invincible. Like she could do anything. They hadn't talked about marriage, but Lara had no doubt that was coming. She wasn't so old-fashioned that she felt as if she had to be married to have a child, but her parents would be disappointed if she wasn't. Not that she lived to please her mom and dad, but since she was sure it was what she and Owl wanted, it wouldn't be a hardship to take that step.

As they drove toward the airport, as if he could read her mind, Owl lifted her hand and kissed her ring finger. It was almost scary how calm Lara felt. She should be freaking out. Leaving The Refuge was a big deal, but with Owl at her side, she could face anything.

Determined to not be a liability, as purchasing this helicopter was important to Owl and his friends, Lara took a deep breath. She could do this. They'd go up north, test-fly the chopper, then start the multiday trip home, stopping at small towns along the way. Easy-peasy.

That night, after arriving in Seattle and very nearly having a panic attack at the airport, Lara's optimism about the trip was waning. It was easy to be brave when she was at The Refuge. But out here, with so many people around, with so many places a man could hide, and so many ways he could manipulate others to get to her, Lara was regretting her decision to come with Owl and Stone.

Recognizing her increasing panic, Owl had been glued to her side, his head on a constant swivel. He'd told her that she was safe probably a hundred times.

Lara wanted to scream that she *wasn't* safe. That she *wouldn't* be safe until Carter Grant was behind bars. But she kept her mouth shut. She was afraid that if she said anything, she wouldn't be able to stop. The last thing she wanted was to mess up this trip. For Owl and Stone, and all the others at The Refuge who were looking forward to having a helicopter at their disposal.

They had just arrived at the hotel, and Stone was checking them in while Owl sat with Lara on one of the couches in the large lobby. She was practically on his lap, squished up against the arm of the sofa with Owl's body plastered against her side, but it made her feel more secure.

Stone walked over to where they were sitting and crouched in front of them, handing Owl a small paper envelope with what Lara assumed were the keys inside.

"You're in room 412. If you want to go on up, I'll make contact with Ricky and let you know what time he'll be ready for us tomorrow," Stone said.

"What room are you in?" Owl asked.

He shrugged. "There was a mix-up and the room was double booked. But it's not a big deal. I can stay out in the rental."

Lara frowned as it dawned on her what he was saying. "No," she said with a shake of her head. "Absolutely not."

Stone's face gentled. "It's okay."

"It's *not* okay," Lara said, panic rising within her once again. "You can't sleep in the *car*. It's not safe. And that's crazy! Why don't you want to stay in the room with us? Is it me? I know I've been a little unsettled, but I promise I'll be better. I won't bother you."

"It's not you," Stone said without hesitation, trying to soothe her.

But Lara wouldn't be soothed. "No! If you're sleeping in the car, we're *all* sleeping in the car. I won't be able to get a wink of rest if I know you're out there alone and I'm in a comfortable bed. If you're uneasy about being a third wheel, don't. And I can sleep on the couch so you're rested for tomorrow. I'm assuming our room has one, but if not, I can sleep on the floor."

"We have a room with two queen beds, Lara. And even if we didn't, you're not sleeping on the damn floor," Owl said with a scowl.

"I am if it keeps Stone out of the car!" Lara almost screeched. Her voice was too loud, but with her panic steadily rising since they'd left the airport, she was on the verge of having a breakdown.

"All right. I'll stay in the room," Stone told her quietly.

"Seriously! I don't understand why you'd do that. I shouldn't have come. You wouldn't have even *thought* about sleeping in the car if I wasn't here!" Lara had worked herself into a state and couldn't seem to snap out of it. "You guys are best friends! You've been to hell and back and now you don't even want to sleep in the same room as us? I don't want to come between your friendship!"

Stone leaned in and gently cupped Lara's face in his hands— and she abruptly stopped spiraling. "I was trying to be polite," he said, softly yet firmly.

"Well...stop it," Lara grumbled.

His lips twitched. "Okay."

"Okay," she agreed.

"You good?"

"I don't know. Are you really going to sleep in the room with us?"

"Yes."

"Then I'm good," Lara decided.

Stone held her for a moment longer, then pulled her forward and kissed her forehead before letting go and turning to Owl. "She's kind of a firecracker. I wouldn't have guessed."

Owl's hand went to the back of her neck and squeezed gently. "For the record, if she didn't set you straight, I would've. What the hell were you thinking, Stone?"

"I was thinking that you guys needed your rest. And you know how bad my nightmares can get. Don't want to wake you up in the middle of the night because I know it's impossible for you to get back to sleep once you're up."

"Not anymore," Owl informed his friend.

"What? Seriously?"

"Seriously. Apparently, holding Lara is the cure for my insomnia."

"Wow. That's awesome."

"It is. And fuck you for thinking I'd give a shit about you waking me up. And for not telling me you're still having those damn nightmares."

Stone shrugged and stood. "They aren't anything new. They come and go. I just didn't want to bother you guys if they happened while we were traveling."

Owl stood, and Lara did the same, wrapping her arm around him, wanting to stay close to his side but feeling bad for Stone at the same time.

"Well, if they do, it's fine," Owl said firmly.

"Don't let her get near me if I have one," Stone warned.

"I won't," Owl told his friend.

"Wait a minute," Lara complained. "If you think I'm gonna sit and watch when he's suffering from a nightmare, you're wrong."

"Trust me, sweetheart. I've got this. I know how to deal with them. And Stone's right. You can't get near him if he's having a nightmare."

"I get...violent," Stone explained as he pushed the button for the elevator. "I'd hate myself if I hurt you."

Lara's heart ached for him. "I understand. I'll let Owl help you then. But...after you're awake, don't be surprised if I mother you."

Stone rolled his eyes. "Whatever. As long as you don't *smother* me for waking you up."

"She needs practice with that mothering thing," Owl said nonchalantly when they were inside the elevator.

"Wait—*what*? Are you pregnant?" Stone asked incredulously.

"No."

"Yes."

She and Owl answered at the same time.

Stone raised a brow in confusion.

"He thinks he has super-sperm and that he *knows* he knocked me up last night," Lara said with a roll of *her* eyes this time. She felt her cheeks warm and knew she was blushing, but pressed on. "So he's assuming I'm one day pregnant, but until I see the line on the test or get the thumbs up from a doctor after he examines my pee, I'm saying no."

"Ah...right. Congrats then. Since I'm the first to know, do I get the honor of having a kid named after me?" Stone asked.

"Did you hear what I just said? I don't even know if I'm pregnant," Lara asked.

The door opened, and the three filed out onto the fourth floor.

"I heard you, but I also know my friend. If Owl says he knocked you up, he knocked you up," Stone said. "He's nothing if not stubborn like that."

"You guys are insane," Lara said. But deep down, she realized

SUSAN STOKER

that bantering with Stone and Owl, observing how close the two men were, made it easier not to dwell on her own situation.

"And no, we aren't naming our daughter Jack," Owl told him.

"Jacketta has a nice ring to it. Besides, you could have boys."

"Of course we will," Owl said. "Our first will be a son. Then we'll have three girls, then another boy," Owl said.

Lara turned to him in astonishment. "We aren't having five children!" she exclaimed.

"Why not? You want a big family. You told me so yourself."

She had. But five? Then something occurred to her. "Are we seriously talking about having five children when we haven't even had one yet?"

"Yup," Owl said with a small smile.

"Whatever."

"Stoney is a gender-neutral name," Stone joked as he opened their hotel room door.

Laughing, Lara relaxed when the door shut behind them. Finally behind a closed, locked door with both Stone and Owl, she felt ten times safer.

"What are we doing for dinner?" Stone asked. "I'm starved."

"Take-out," Owl and Lara said at the same time.

She shot him a smile.

"Take-out it is," Stone agreed as he flopped onto his back on the bed closest to the door. "Let me know when it arrives."

Owl shook his head at his friend. "Guess we can get that pizza with pineapple you love so much, Lara. Or maybe that broccoli pasta dish you like. We can get a family-style dish big enough for us all."

Lara was confused. She didn't like pineapple on pizza, and couldn't remember talking to Owl about it in any case.

But when Stone sat up and grumbled, "Fine, *I'll* take care of

226

ordering dinner," she realized that Owl had been needling his friend once more.

She'd spent some time with Stone, and with all the men at The Refuge, but this was the first time she was seeing the dynamics between the two best friends so up close and personal. They were a lot like she and Cora when they were together, and Lara loved it.

She went over to the bed where Stone was now sitting, scrolling through his phone. She sat next to him and peered over his shoulder. "I could go for a big juicy hamburger, but delivery takes so long the fries are usually soggy by the time it arrives."

"We could do Italian? We've got a microwave in here, and we could zap the noodles if they're not hot."

Lara wrinkled her nose. "Steak?" she asked.

Stone smiled at her with a nod. "Hell yeah."

After they'd sorted that out, and Stone had put in all their orders, he told them he'd go down to the lobby to wait for the delivery person.

"That's fine, as long as you don't sneak out to the car," Lara said a little snarkily.

In response, Stone put Lara in a gentle headlock and gave her a noogie. She screeched and laughed as she tried to get away from him. Stone laughed, kissed the top of her head, and walked toward the door.

Throughout it all, Owl sat in the lone chair in the room, watching them with a sparkle in his eye.

"Be back in a bit. Don't do anything I wouldn't do," he warned. Then right before he shut the door, he stuck his head back into the room and added, "And since she's already pregnant, there's no need for a quickie...if this room smells like sex when I get back, I really *am* sleeping in the car." He shut the door before Lara or Owl could reply.

"Come here," Owl ordered as soon as Stone was gone.

Lara walked toward him and gave a little grunt of surprise when he grabbed her hand and yanked her onto his lap. When he got her settled, he asked, "How are you doing?"

"I'm all right," she told him.

"Seriously, are you good? Because you were spiraling, and it sucked because I couldn't do anything to stop it."

Lara put her hand on his cheek to try to soothe him. He'd been joking with Stone minutes ago, but she could see now that he was pretty wound up. "I won't lie, the trip's been harder than I thought. But I'm better now. Being here...inside...it's better."

"I'm sorry," Owl started, but Lara shook her head.

"Don't be. I'm as safe as I'd ever be with you and Stone. And I couldn't stay hidden away forever. This is fine. It's good. We'll get that helicopter and be on our way home before we know it."

"Home," Owl agreed. He kissed her softly. Then grinned as he pulled back. "We've got at least twenty minutes or so...we *could* have that quickie."

Lara could tell he was kidding. "You and quickie are oxymorons. There's no way you could do quick if your life depended on it."

"I don't know, sweetheart. The second I get inside you, I seem to lose all control."

Thinking of him being deep inside her made Lara squirm a bit. "Right, but you get distracted before you get in there. Do you really think you can see me naked and not make it your quest in life to give me two orgasms before you even enter me?"

Owl wrinkled his nose. "You have a valid point."

Lara giggled.

"I love that."

"What?" Lara asked.

"Your laugh. You haven't done enough of it since I've known you. I'm going to make it my goal in life to hear it more often."

"Being around you and Stone is a good start," Lara said. "You guys are really close."

"Crashing, being hunted down and tortured together...it's a good way to make close bonds really fast," Owl said dryly.

Lara hated that for him, but at the same time, she was suddenly very glad he hadn't been alone during that ordeal. "Are his nightmares really that bad?"

"Worse," Owl confirmed. "They're night terrors. He doesn't talk about them with me, doesn't tell me what they're about, but I can guess. I thought he was doing better, but obviously he's still suffering from them. He was serious earlier, if he *does* happen to have one while we're on this trip, let me deal with it. Don't touch him. He's thrown me across the room more than once, and the thought of him hurting you...neither of us would be able to deal with that."

"I won't go near him. I promise."

"Thank you."

"Is there anything we can do to help him?" Lara asked.

"Don't treat him any differently."

Lara understood that. She hated when people looked at her with pity, although it had been a long time since anyone had done that, and she wanted it to stay that way.

"Now, what can I do to help *you* when you start feeling uneasy?" Owl asked.

"Exactly what you did today. Stay near me. Touch me. Both help a lot."

"Not a hardship. And for the record, you did much better

than you think today, sweetheart. And I'm not just saying that. The rest of this trip will be a breeze. Tomorrow we'll head to the much smaller regional airport, where we're meeting this Ricky Norman guy. We'll take the chopper up first and put her through her paces. Then we'll come back to the hotel, finish up the business side of things, and go back to the airport the day after to start the trip home."

"It'll take like five days to get home, right?" Lara asked.

"Four or five. Depending on how we feel."

"So we'll be home in a week or so," Lara said with a deep breath. "I can do that."

"Of course you can. You can do anything."

"I'm not sure about that. I can't fly a helicopter," she joked.

"Sure you can. I've seen you on the sim, you're a natural."

Lara rolled her eyes. "You said so yourself, the simulator isn't like flying a real helicopter."

"True, but I'm sure if you had to, you could do it."

"Let's hope I don't need to find out," Lara said with a shiver.

"Enough about that. Since a quickie is out...are you opposed to some making out?" Owl asked.

"With you?" Lara teased.

Owl growled and dug his fingers into her sides, tickling her.

Lara shrieked and tried to pull away from him, but Owl's hold was too tight. Thankfully, he stopped tickling her and wrapped his arms around her instead.

They were still kissing when Stone returned, and he sighed dramatically when he entered and saw them wrapped around each other in the chair.

"You want me to leave and come back later?" he joked.

"No! I'm starving," Lara told him.

"Me too," Owl said under his breath, shifting her off his rock-hard cock as he helped her to stand.

Lara giggled and realized how much calmer she felt already, grateful her panic attack didn't last for hours. This trip was going to work out, after all. She just knew it.

* * *

His plan was going to work out. Carter Grant was feeling more and more confident of that as each day passed.

In two more days, he would finally have Lara back. And he'd make sure she never left...until he was done with her. And it would be a long time before that happened.

He'd gotten word from his accomplice that the test flight was happening tomorrow as planned. He wished he could be there. Wished he could see her face when she realized what was happening.

But he couldn't leave the island. He'd decided he was still too recognizable, even with the small changes to his appearance. He was probably the most wanted man in the country right now, and with his goal so close, he needed to lie low. Carter didn't like relying on someone else to carry out the plans he'd so painstakingly crafted, but he had to hope the money he was paying his accomplice was enough to make sure he didn't deviate from his instructions in any way.

"Soon," Carter murmured as he looked over the room where his Lara would be living. It was perfect. The chains on the bed, the lingerie picked out, and the door she wouldn't have a hope in hell of getting through. This time, there wasn't anyone else in the house he had to hide her presence from. She'd be completely isolated and at his mercy. No matter how loud she screamed, no one would hear.

He just had to make it through two more days. Then his property would be returned. Anticipation made Carter almost giddy. He didn't feel the throbbing of his missing eye. Didn't feel an ounce of remorse for what he was about to do. The two assholes with her deserved to die for keeping his property away from him. And Lara?

She'd get what she deserved. And he couldn't wait.

CHAPTER SIXTEEN

Lara gripped the edge of the seat, both in trepidation and excitement. The time was finally here. After meeting with the seller, Ricky Norman, at the regional airport that morning they'd all been escorted to the waiting chopper. Owl and Stone had gone over every last inch of the Bell 505 helicopter sitting on the tarmac. But throughout their examination, Owl had kept his eye on her. She was standing in the morning sun, watching.

Instead of feeling nervous about being out in the open, Lara was calm. No one could sneak up on them, not as exposed as they were out on the tarmac, and long before anyone could get to her, Owl would be there.

The evening before had been full of anticipation. Owl and Stone were like two little kids the night before their birthday. They'd all slept like rocks—thankfully, Stone hadn't had any nightmares—and had woken up before their alarm went off, ready to get to the airport and set eyes on their potential new helicopter.

And the first sight of it hadn't disappointed. She was sleek and shiny, and Owl and Stone practically drooled.

Stone had graciously let Owl take the controls first. Both the pilot and copilot had the ability to fly the chopper. Owl and Stone had a discussion the night before about whether they wanted to remove the controls from the copilot's seat and decided for the moment, at least, they wanted them to stay. The two were used to flying together, and honestly, it gave Lara a sense of comfort to know if something happened to whomever was flying, the other person could take over. The guys might change their minds in the future if they had more interest in tours and needed that front seat to hold paying customers, but for now they were content to leave the chopper the way it was.

All three of them had a headset on since it was so loud in the cab, allowing them to talk to each other and to the small control tower. They were given the go-ahead to take off, and Lara held her breath as the machine slowly lifted off the ground.

This was happening, and she could feel the excitement in the air.

At first, she couldn't take her eyes from Owl. It was obvious very quickly that he was in his element. He had a small smile on his face as he operated the controls. Lara had been in awe of him before, but seeing him flying a real chopper made her even more impressed.

The helicopter moved smoothly through the air as he used the stick to move them forward and the lever on the side of his seat to control the altitude. She knew the basics of the lever and stick, but the pedals were still difficult for her to master with the simulator. Owl didn't have any of those issues. He and Stone kept up a constant stream of chatter about mechanics and wind speed and other technical issues she had no interest in.

Stone had his own set of controls on his side of the chopper, but he kept his hands in his lap as his friend flew them over the gorgeous towns and forests. Every now and then, he'd pass along what one of the screens in front of them was reporting.

Turning her attention to the small window next to her, Lara gazed out at the passing scenery. The Seattle area was beautiful, and they'd been blessed with a beautiful day for the test flight. The sun glinted on the water and Lara was amazed all over again at how many small islands there were off the coast.

As beautiful as this area was, Lara realized that she actually liked New Mexico better. She hadn't seen it from above, obviously, but she loved the forest around The Refuge and was even partial to the dry air, compared to the humidity here in Washington.

"What do you think, sweetheart?"

The sound of Owl's voice rumbling in her ears through the headset made Lara tingle. She turned to look at him. His head was turned and he was staring at her.

"Shouldn't your attention be on the road...er...sky? Whatever?" she reprimanded.

Both Owl and Stone chuckled. The laughter sounded as if it was in stereo in her ears.

"It's not like a car," Stone explained. "As long as he keeps his hands steady on the controls, we'll keep going in one direction at the same altitude forever."

"And if he doesn't? Keep the controls steady?" Lara asked.

Stone shrugged. "Then we'll crash," he said simply.

"Shut it, Stone. I'm fine. We aren't going to crash," Owl soothed. "What do you think?" he asked again.

"Um...it's fine?" Lara wasn't sure what he wanted to know.

"How's the seat back there? Is it comfortable? Can you see

out the window okay? Does the seat belt fit, does it pinch anywhere? You aren't feeling nauseous or anything?"

"Oh, the seats are fine. I mean, it's not like your couch or anything, but it's not uncomfortable. And yes, the windows are amazing. The belt is fine, and you didn't ask, but the headset is so cool! I can hear you guys as if we were standing next to each other back in the lodge. And I'm not airsick in the least. Probably because you're such a good driver."

"We'll see how you feel when it's Stone's turn to fly," Owl joked.

Stone punched him in the shoulder. "Whatever. We both know I can outfly you any day of the week."

The two men were in great moods, which made Lara relax even more. Up here, they were at their happiest. And up here, no one could hurt her. No one could make her do anything she didn't want to do or sneak up on her. She was free. Free from worries, free from fear.

Owl flew them for a bit longer, warning her every time he was going to test one thing or another, so instead of being terrified when the chopper fell abruptly, or when he banked left or right, she was exhilarated. She trusted Owl completely. Experiencing his skill as a pilot firsthand was much more impressive than watching him practice on the simulator back at The Refuge...and that was already pretty darn remarkable.

When he was satisfied with how the craft handled, Owl gave the controls over to Stone. Surprisingly, Lara could discern subtle differences between the two pilots' skills. While Owl's handling of the aircraft was smooth and she could barely tell when they changed altitude, Stone was a touch more heavy-handed, but not so much that it made her sick to her stomach. He was more prone to using the foot pedals to rotate the cabin back and forth, letting him see more of the area he was flying over simply by manipulating the tail rotor.

Lara didn't prefer one technique over the other. With Stone at the controls, she didn't have to alternate looking from the front of the chopper to the side window. Because of the way he continually turned the aircraft, she could simply look out the side.

Once again, Owl and Stone were talking shop, and Lara soaked in the moment. She had a feeling by the time they made it back to New Mexico, she would be more than ready to be done with flying for a while, but for now, it was a new and novel experience.

When they finally touched down again, Lara couldn't help but share Owl and Stone's excitement. They were more than pleased with how the helicopter handled and convinced everything seemed perfect.

They walked toward the main building at the airport and met back up with Ricky Norman.

"So?" the man asked. "Is she everything I told you she was?"

"She's perfect," Stone told him.

"Yup," Ricky said with a smile. "Then we have a deal?"

"We have a deal," Owl told him and reached out a hand.

The two men shook, and Ricky turned to Stone, who also shook his hand. "So, I'll see you three in the morning then? You have all the info you need for the payment transfer?"

"We'll get with our accountant and start the ball rolling as soon as we leave here," Stone told him.

"Good, good. I'll be here bright and early tomorrow morning to meet you and we can sign the paperwork," Ricky said. "Then you three can get started back south."

"Tomorrow," Owl said with a nod, reaching for Lara's hand.

If she hadn't been looking at Ricky, she would've missed the way his gaze dropped to their hands and his lip curled.

She couldn't imagine what offended him so much. Surely two people holding hands wasn't a shock?

But before she could think too much about his odd reaction, Owl was turning and taking her with him as they headed for the doors. Stone was already on the phone with Brick, telling him all about the chopper and how perfect it was. From earlier conversations, Lara knew Brick would then get in touch with Savannah to start the wire transfer.

It was hard to believe it was really happening. The Refuge was going to own a chopper. She looked up at Owl as she squeezed his hand. "This is exciting."

He grinned at her. "It is. Us having a helicopter will save so much time if we need to look for missing hikers or help with rescues. And I have a feeling we'll start making money sooner rather than later with sightseeing tours."

Lara nodded. "Stone was your copilot when you were in the Army, right?"

"Occasionally another Night Stalker, but mostly him. Why?"

She shrugged. "I just wondered how that worked. Did Stone operate the tail rotor while you did the other stuff?"

Owl chuckled. "No. The copilot assists the pilot when we're in the air with things like radio communications and checklists."

"Oh, so you both had controls at the seats, like with this helicopter?"

"Yup."

"That's cool."

"Yeah. Stone and I...I loved working with him. He was always the calm one in situations. We had some close calls together, and you never would've known it by looking or listening to him. He has the ability to keep cool and go with the flow. When we crashed? He was damn near stoic. As we were falling from the sky, he calmly talked me through doing what I could to keep us from crashing uncontrollably."

Lara was fascinated. Owl had told her some things about that awful time in his life, but the memories always made him tense. In contrast, he sounded relaxed right now. "Is there such a thing as a controlled crash?" she asked skeptically.

Owl chuckled. "Actually, yeah. Any crash where you don't die is a controlled one."

"Right."

"Anyway, he was also the one who stayed calm when we were discovered, stripped, and thrown into those cells. It drove me crazy at first. I mean, I couldn't understand why he wasn't more...emotional. But his stoicism was what helped us both stay in control. I owe him everything."

Lara squeezed his hand.

"I think that's why he has night terrors," Owl said softly. Stone was still on the phone and wasn't paying any attention, but it was obvious Owl didn't want him to accidentally overhear them talking about him. "Because he shoves shit so far down, it unconsciously comes up when his guard is down...when he's asleep."

"Probably," Lara agreed.

"Thank you for coming with us," he said, changing the subject. "I know this isn't easy for you, but having you here...it's nice. For both me and Stone."

"It's nice for me too. I feel as if I'm really taking control of my life back. Carter is still out there, I know that, but me being here kind of feels like I'm spitting in his face. Like I'm actually living, even though he doesn't want me to."

"You are. And every day, I learn something new about you."

Lara smiled up at him. "What'd you learn about me today?"

"That you love flying. The expression on your face as we flew was the same thing I feel deep down, when I'm in the air."

She loved that. "Being in a helicopter is so different from a plane."

"Yup."

"We're all set!" Stone said, breaking the intimate moment.

Lara didn't mind. She was looking forward to a lifetime of those kinds of moments with the man at her side.

"Brick was happy to hear everything checked out. He's gonna start the ball rolling with the money transfer. Tomorrow at this time, we'll be in the air headed south."

"We're all good for the first fuel stop and our overnight?" Owl asked.

"Yup."

"Awesome."

"So...what are we gonna do for the rest of the day?" Stone asked.

Lara felt Owl shrug, and she looked up at him.

"Sweetheart?" he asked.

A part of her wanted to go back to the hotel. Wanted to hide out, away from people. Away from anyone who might hurt her. But hadn't she just said that she enjoyed taking control of her life back? How enjoying her life was like spitting in Carter's face? She wanted to hold on to that feeling. Besides, it wasn't as if Owl, or Stone for that matter, was going to abandon her somewhere on her own.

The thing that made up her mind was the deep-seated belief that Owl would do whatever she needed him to do. If she said she wanted to go back to the hotel, he'd take her back there without a second thought and without feeling salty or bitter about it. He'd sit with her in that small room and find a way to entertain them. Stone probably would too. But the morning had been so fun. Exciting. And she didn't want to ruin the good mood they were all in.

"I've heard the view from the Space Needle is awesome. I mean, I'm sure it can't compare to seeing the world from the window of a helicopter, but..."

Owl and Stone's smiles were so big, they looked almost goofy.

"And there's Pike Place Market. Oh! Seattle is the place where they have that gum wall, right? I think it's close to the market too."

"A gum wall?" Stone asked, looking confused.

"Yeah! It's a wall covered in chewed gum!" Lara said enthusiastically.

"Gross," Owl muttered.

"And this is on the top of your must-see list?" Stone asked, the skepticism easy to hear in his voice.

"I just hope they haven't cleaned the wall recently," Lara mused.

"Right, so Pike Place Market, the Space Needle, and disgusting gum wall...anything else?" Owl asked.

"Ivar's?" Lara asked, pushing her luck.

"Who's that?" Stone asked.

"Not who, what. It's a restaurant. They have amazing oysters...so I've heard," Lara said.

"Didn't peg you for an oyster girl, but if that's what you want, that's what we'll have," Owl told her.

"Hopefully they'll have hamburgers," Stone muttered.

Lara couldn't stop smiling. They hadn't even done anything

yet, and she felt amazing. Like her old self. Owl led her to their rental car and lobbed the keys at Stone. "You're driving," he ordered as he settled himself in the back seat with Lara.

"Great, now I'm a chauffeur too," Stone mock-grumbled.

Once she was buckled in, Lara leaned her head against Owl's shoulder. He put his hand on her thigh, and she sighed in contentment. The worry was still there, but she'd managed to push it down far enough inside her where she could pretend she was a normal woman. On a normal business trip with her normal boyfriend.

She wasn't normal, she still had a serial killer who'd vowed that she was his, but for now, just for today, she was going to try to ignore the bubble of anxiety that lived inside her. Carter Grant couldn't get to her. Not with Owl and Stone by her side. She was going to enjoy the day, seeing sights she'd only read about, and then tomorrow, she'd get to do something very few people had a chance to do...travel the country by helicopter.

* * *

"It's a go," Ricky Norman said as soon as Carter picked up the phone.

Carter smiled. Huge. "Any problems?"

"None. They took the helicopter up as planned."

"Was she there?"

"The chick? Yeah."

"How'd she look? Was she scared? Nervous?" Carter asked impatiently.

"Not really. Actually, she seemed pretty relaxed. Especially around that man of hers."

"*What*? What man?"

"The preppy one. The one without glasses. They were holding hands when they left and looking pretty chummy. I thought you said she was your girlfriend?" Ricky asked.

Fury swamped Carter, making it hard to think. Speak. Finally, he growled, "She's *mine*."

"Right. Whatever you say. The money for the bird is supposed to be wired later today, but you still haven't paid me."

"You'll get your money when you deliver the goods," Carter told him between clenched teeth.

"I'm thinking that's not fair," Ricky said. "I'm taking all the risks. Disabling cameras at the airport, getting rid of two people, kidnapping a third. It's likely I'll be a wanted man after this. I'm thinking I need at least half up front."

"No," Carter spat.

"Right. Then the deal's off."

A film of red fell over Carter's gaze. He was so pissed right now, if Ricky was in front of him, he'd kill him without a second thought. "No, it's not," he bit out.

"Then you better wire half my money today. If it's not in my account by five o'clock this afternoon, the deal's off. Your girlfriend and her...friends...will fly off with their new chopper tomorrow and live happily ever after on that fortress down in New Mexico, and you'll have to figure out a new way to get her back."

Carter's hands shook with fury. "Fine," he bit out.

"Fine, what?" Ricky asked.

"I'll send half your money today. But if anything goes wrong, you aren't getting the rest."

"Nothing's going to go wrong. You've got it all planned," Ricky said calmly.

"Fucking right," Carter said. "Let's go over it again."

Ricky sighed, but then said in an almost bored voice, "They're supposed to be here in the morning to close the deal, before the airport opens. They didn't even blink at the early time. I'll walk them out to the hangar where the chopper is stored. It's the only one here at the moment. I'll take care of the men first, drug the girl with a sedative, fly her out to your island, and leave with my fancy new helicopter I didn't have to pay for. I'll change the serial number, sell her again, and live somewhere warm, all fat and happy."

Carter grunted his approval, satisfied his accomplice had all the particulars memorized.

Except for the one detail Ricky didn't know—he wouldn't be leaving the country with Carter's money. Once he landed with Lara, he was as good as dead.

Carter was a wanted serial killer, and last he checked, there was a hundred-thousand-dollar reward for information leading to his arrest. And since Ricky knew where his new hideout was located, he couldn't be allowed to live to tell anyone. The man was a money whore; he'd rat him out in a heartbeat.

Once Ricky gave him what he wanted, Carter would kill him. He'd dispose of the chopper piece by piece, and then he and Lara would live happily ever after.

Well...*he* would. Lara probably wouldn't be very happy, but that didn't matter.

"All right. I'll see you tomorrow. Don't be late," he warned Ricky.

"Pleasure doing business with you," he said snarkily. "I'll be waiting for my money." Then he hung up.

Carter seethed after the phone call. He hadn't planned to give Ricky *any* money. Once he was dead, that money would most likely be gone forever. But eventually, Carter calmed. It didn't matter how much it cost, as long as he had his favorite toy back.

All Carter could focus on at the moment was the fact that, by this time tomorrow, he'd be standing over a trembling, terrified, restrained Lara Osler, and she'd be sorry she dared defy him. He couldn't wait.

* * *

Ricky scowled after hanging up on that asshole Carter. It had been difficult to keep his disdain out of his voice as they spoke. The man was arrogant, cocky, and way too confident that intimidation and fear would have everyone doing his bidding. Well, the plans Carter had painstakingly devised weren't going to go quite as the man expected.

Ricky wasn't anyone's errand boy. He had plans of his own for how tomorrow would go...and it involved even more money in his pocket.

He'd meet with Lara and the two men, of course, but he'd do things *his* way, and Carter would simply have to deal. He knew what Carter expected, but he wasn't the only one with nefarious connections.

Ricky had made his own deal behind Carter's back. A deal that included a ton of money in his account and not dirtying his hands with murder.

Tomorrow was going to be fun. Ricky couldn't wait to see the look on not only Carter's face when he learned what he'd done, but on the faces of his victims when they realized they weren't actually going to be flying off in their brand-new helicopter.

CHAPTER SEVENTEEN

That night, Lara lay on the bed in the hotel room, stuffed so full she felt a little sick, but very happy. The day had been so fun. The Space Needle was cool, but crowded, and none of them had been overly impressed with the view. How could they after seeing the city from the helicopter?

They'd wandered around Pike Place Market, been grossed out at the gum wall, and eaten at Ivar's. She'd managed to snag the bill, even though both Stone and Owl got pissed at her for waylaying the waitress when she'd gone to the restroom. They'd insisted this was a business trip and The Refuge was footing the bill, but she'd wanted to thank both men personally. And it wasn't as if she'd been spending any money recently. She had a very healthy bank account, thanks to her parents, and she felt bad that she hadn't been doing her share of paying her way.

The hotel room was dark and the TV was on. All three of them had gotten ready for bed and were watching a *Seinfeld* rerun. She loved this show; it was so stupid, and the characters so over the top, but also hilarious.

Turning onto her side, Lara studied Owl's profile.

Obviously feeling her stare, he turned to her. "What?" he asked in concern.

"Nothing. I'm just content," she said softly.

He smiled. "Me too."

She drifted off not long after, and she wasn't sure how much later it was when she felt herself being turned and Owl cuddling up behind her. She snuggled into him and immediately fell back to sleep. Not even the excitement about picking up the heli-copter the next morning could keep the exhaustion and full belly from knocking her out.

Lara didn't know what woke her a second time. The TV was off and the room was dark and quiet. The only illumination coming from a light in the parking lot peeking in from the curtains that hadn't quite been closed all the way.

Then a loud noise startled her, making her jump. It must've been what woke her in the first place. It sounded like a cross between a cry and a scream. Coming up on her elbow, Lara looked across the room toward the sound...and realized the heartbreaking noises were coming from Stone.

He lay on the other bed, tossing and turning as the distressing whimpers and groans came from deep within his throat.

"Stay here," Owl ordered as he shifted off the bed behind her.

Lara couldn't move if her life depended on it. She thought she understood nightmares, having had many of her own. But this was horrifying.

Stone's head thrashed back and forth and his hands were up in a defensive position. He jerked every now and then, as if reacting to some sort of external stimuli...like someone hitting him. No real words came out, at least none that Lara could understand. She wanted to wake him up. Shake him to make him stop experiencing whatever it was his brain was showing him, making him think he was actually suffering through some horrible experience.

But even more heartbreaking was the idea that someone had done this to him in real life. Stone was likely reliving events from when he was a POW. Whatever he was dreaming about had probably actually happened. And Owl had been through it with him.

Owl was standing between the beds now, putting himself between her and Stone. Protecting her just like he had in that basement.

"Wake up, Stone!" Owl called urgently.

His words seemed to have no effect on his friend. Stone continued to thrash on the bed, defending himself from phantom enemies, those awful noises still coming from deep inside.

"You're safe. We aren't there anymore. Snap out of it, Stone," Owl said. He reached down and touched his shoulder.

Which seemed to make him fight even harder.

To her surprise, the easygoing friend she'd spent the last month getting to know morphed into someone she didn't recognize. Stone instantly sat up, his eyes open but unfocused, and swung at Owl. And he didn't pull his punch either. He was genuinely trying to hurt his friend. To protect himself.

It was scary. And so fast. Owl managed to block Stone's first punch, but wasn't so lucky with the second. The dull thud it made against Owl's cheek made Lara flinch.

"Stone! It's me! Owl. You're good. You're in Seattle. Wake up!"

The fear and concern in Owl's tone made Lara want to cry. She was sitting up at this point, feeling powerless to help in any way. She understood now why both Stone and Owl had been so adamant about her not touching Stone if he had a nightmare, and why he had offered to sleep in the car.

It took another minute or two, minutes that felt like hours to Lara, but eventually Owl seemed to be getting through to his friend.

"That's it, wake up. You're safe. I'm not them. You're here in Seattle with Lara and me."

Stone blinked as he stilled on the bed.

"Will you get the light, sweetheart?" Owl asked, keeping a hand on Stone's shoulder as he crouched down to seem less threatening.

She did as Owl asked, and winced as her eyes adjusted to the bright light.

By the time she could see clearly again, Stone was completely awake. And he looked...devastated. His hair was sticking up all over his head and without his glasses on, he seemed even more vulnerable.

"Fuck," he swore as he ran a hand through his messy hair and scooted up on the bed, collapsing against the headboard.

"It's okay," Owl soothed.

"Like hell it is! I fucking hate dreaming," Stone said in a tone Lara had never heard him use before. It was desolate. Defeated.

"Don't hate the dreams, hate the men who put them there," Lara said before she thought better of it.

Stone turned to her. He glared for a moment, then sighed, and all the emotion on his face disappeared as if it had never been there in the first place.

Lara took a deep breath and continued. He might not appreciate her thoughts, but she couldn't *not* say them.

"Hating the dreams is like hating yourself, which makes no sense. You went from having complete control to having none. After watching you and Owl today, seeing how you easily handled that helicopter with confidence, I understand a little better now how going from having such control, to being shot out of the sky and imprisoned, is a hard thing to come to terms with.

"I hated not having control over my own situation…though what happened to me in no compares to what you and Owl went through. Personally, I'm impressed you're as well-adjusted as you are."

Stone chuckled. It was a rusty sound and not quite a humorous one, but at least he wasn't intent on killing Owl anymore. "She doesn't pull any punches, does she?"

"No, I don't," Lara answered, even though Stone wasn't talking to her. "Not anymore. Look, I'm probably not the best person to give advice, I'm still pretty screwed up myself, but I think having nightmares is normal after what you've gone through. Not normal as in nice or pleasant, but you're a pretty even-keeled man, Stone. You're charming, pleasant, you don't seem introverted, or even all that fazed by what happened to you…on the outside. You clearly don't let out your thoughts or feelings, at all. So your dreams are a way of doing that.

"I'm thinking you need to find a way to let out the poison that's festering inside you. Right now, that's only through nightmares. Maybe it's time to take up a hobby. Wood chopping, kung fu, WWF wrestling...anything that can release some of the aggression you still feel deep down over what happened."

Silence filled the room, and Lara was afraid she'd over-stepped. She just hated seeing her new friend so...helpless. Because Stone was anything *but* helpless. Not even close.

"I'm sorry. I obviously don't know what I'm talking about and—"

"No, don't apologize. You're right. I know you are. I just...it's hard."

"I know. Believe me, I do. But I'm here right now, away from The Refuge, and trust me, it wasn't easy to step outside my comfort zone and join you guys. I'm not cured, the anxiety is still there. I'm still afraid of Carter finding me, but hiding out means he won. And the last thing I want is for him to win in *any* way."

Stone looked contemplative and nodded before looking up at Owl. "You okay? Did I hurt you?"

"With your pansy-ass left hook?" Owl joked. "Not a chance."

Lara could see the bruise on her man's cheek from where she sat on the bed. Stone hadn't held back, and his punch was anything but pansy-ass. But she loved Owl even more for down-playing what his friend had done.

Stone inhaled deeply before looking back over at Lara. "Are you all right?"

"I'm fine," she reassured him immediately.

"Good. And...thanks."

"You're welcome," Lara said, thankful that Stone seemed calmer. But now that she'd seen how much anger, hurt and, yes, terror, he'd been hiding deep inside, she admired him even more.

How he could *ever* stay calm in the face of danger was even more impressive with the amount of turmoil rolling around inside him. She didn't know if he'd ever been to therapy—she assumed he had—but it was obvious he was still working through everything that happened to him.

Owl stood and went to the bathroom, returning with a wet washcloth. He handed it to Stone as he said, "For your hand. Gotta keep the swelling down because I'm not flying your ass all the way back to New Mexico. You're gonna need to do your part too."

Stone chuckled, and this time the sound was more like his old self. "As if I'd let you have all the fun," he grumbled, even as he put the cool compress on his knuckles.

Owl clasped his friend on the shoulder as he stared into his eyes. Then he nodded once and clicked off the light on the table between the beds.

As before, it took Lara's eyes a moment to adjust, and as they did, she felt the mattress depress right before Owl's arms wrapped around her and he pulled her against him once again.

A few minutes went by in silence before Lara sighed and said into the quiet room, "Does this mean *neither* of you is gonna sleep the rest of the night? Because I thought I'd cured Owl of that."

Both men laughed.

"You gonna come over here and snuggle with me to help me sleep?" Stone teased.

"No way in hell," Owl responded for her.

Lara giggled. "No, but I also don't want you to lie there staring at the ceiling for the rest of the night, like Owl used to do. If you need to get up, shower, eat, watch TV, go for a run...

do it. What do you usually do when you have a nightmare and wake up?"

"Lie in bed and stare at the ceiling," Stone said dryly.

Lara sighed and sat up. "Fine. Since we're all up, and it's likely no one is sleeping, why don't we order room service?"

"You can't possibly be hungry again," Owl said incredulously.

"I could eat," Lara said with a shrug. "Besides, I didn't say I wanted a meal. I saw they had cookies on the all-night menu. And cheesecake. I could go for some sugar. Do they still have pay-per-view movies in hotels?"

"We could just log into my Netflix and find a movie," Stone said.

"All right, but it needs to be something testosterone-y. Like, full of men blowing stuff up and explosions and fights and stuff. You need that," Lara said.

She wasn't sure how she had come to that conclusion, but when both Owl and Stone nodded, she was relieved she assumed correctly.

"I'm gonna turn the light on again. Close your eyes," she warned.

The light came back on and she sat up to glance at Owl. He was looking at her with love and adoration. Arousal shot through her... because he usually looked at her like that after he'd come deep inside her. But nothing was going to happen with Stone there, and she was more concerned about their friend than having sex.

Owl squeezed her thigh under the covers, then got up once more. He walked over to the room service menu and handed it to Lara. "You pick," he said.

"Okay," she agreed happily. Glancing over at Stone, she saw he was studying her. "What?" she asked with a tilt of her head.

"I get why Owl can sleep through the night now."

Lara frowned. "You do?"

"Uh-huh." Stone shared a look with Owl above her head.

Lara turned to glance at him, but he simply shrugged. She decided it didn't matter why Stone thought Owl's insomnia seemed to be gone, she was just glad it was...and tonight didn't count. Extenuating circumstances and all that.

"Right," she said, turning her attention back to the menu. "Chips and salsa, two orders of chocolate chip cookies, hot chocolate, and a slice of strawberry cheesecake we can all share. That good for you guys?"

"We're gonna be all hyped up on sugar by the time we leave for the airport," Stone said as he swung his legs off the mattress. Unlike her and Owl, he slept in nothing but boxers. Other than admiring his obviously toned physique, Lara felt no physical attraction for the man.

"If your hands aren't steady, I'll fly," Owl called out, teasing his friend once more.

Stone lifted a hand with his middle finger up but didn't turn around as he walked into the bathroom.

As soon as the door shut, Owl sat on the bed next to Lara. She raised a hand and gently touched the dark mark on his cheek. "Does it hurt?" she asked quietly.

"No. Thank you."

"For what?" she asked, her brows furrowing.

"For not freaking out. For saying all the right things. For going with the flow."

"Why wouldn't I?" she asked, genuinely confused.

"Most people wouldn't be as understanding. He could've really hurt you," Owl said.

"Well, that's their problem, not Stone's. And he wouldn't have hurt me. Not with you here."

"Damn straight. I love you, Lara. So much."

"I love you too. And I love your friends...but not in the same way, of course. Anyway, being at The Refuge has taught me that bad things happen to good people all the time. It's how we react to those things that define us. And I don't want to be scared for the rest of my life."

"If we were alone—" Owl started, but Stone chose that moment to return to the room.

"But you aren't," he said with a laugh. "So stop noodling with your woman and let her order our food, if she hasn't already."

"Noodling? What the hell is that?" Owl grumbled as he sat back and gave Lara some room.

"Actually, it's where you stick your bare hand into a catfish hole and hope it clamps its mouth around it. Then the fisherman, or woman, grabs their gills and pulls it up. But in this case, it seemed to fit for the two of you...kind of a cross between cuddling and nuzzling."

"You're so weird," Owl said with a shake of his head.

But Lara couldn't stop smiling. It seemed as if Stone had shaken off the effects of the nightmare he'd had, and she couldn't be happier to see him and Owl joking with each other once more.

"Hush, you two, and let me call room service. The last thing we want is someone overhearing your weirdo conversations and calling the police," Lara joked as she reached for the phone.

Owl kept his hand on her shin as she made the call and, within twenty minutes, the three of them were sitting on Stone's bed with a spread of junk food in front of them while *Die Hard 2* played on TV.

It wasn't exactly the end of the day she'd envisioned, but feeling as if maybe, just maybe, she'd been able to help Stone rather than be on the receiving end of everyone's concern felt amazing. It gave her confidence that hopefully in the not-too-distant future, she'd be back on her feet and the horrible anxiety that always seemed to be lurking beneath the surface would slowly dissipate.

CHAPTER EIGHTEEN

Owl was tired, but not exceedingly so. He'd gone more than one night with only a few hours' sleep before, and while he'd gotten used to sleeping throughout the night lately, his body could still operate on little rest.

He'd been extremely worried about Stone last night, but somehow Lara had managed to not only pull him out of the depression his nightmare always caused, but she had him smiling and joking not even half an hour later.

He'd always known she was amazing, and last night just proved it all over again. She had a huge heart, and he'd do whatever it took to protect it, no matter what the cost.

Lara had fallen asleep during the movie, and seeing her lying so trustingly next to his best friend had Owl feeling more content than he'd felt in a long time. Lara had turned in her sleep, snuggling against Stone as if she'd known he still needed comfort. There was no jealousy in Owl's heart as Stone placed a gentle hand on the back of her head and continued to watch the movie.

They'd talked quietly so as not to wake her, about the helicopter they were buying, about how well the trip was going, about when the hangar back at The Refuge would be completed, and other mundane things.

It wasn't until Owl had carried Lara back over to their bed and turned off the light once more that Stone said, "You're a lucky man," in a soft voice.

"Trust me, I know. There's someone out there for you too," Owl had felt compelled to say.

But Stone snorted and said, "I doubt it. Who would want to put their life in their hands, just by sleeping next to me night after night?"

Owl wasn't sure what to say to that, but Stone had shut down the conversation by adding, "Maybe we can get an hour or two catnap before we have to get up and get going."

So Owl had curled up behind Lara and held her in his arms as she slept. He didn't fall asleep again, and he didn't think Stone did either, but they were both more than ready to head toward home.

They'd returned the rental car the evening before and were taking a taxi to the regional airport that morning. They got up at the crack of dawn and packed their bags and showered before heading down to the lobby to check out. The taxi pulled up just as they exited the hotel, and they all climbed in.

When the car pulled up to the airport, Owl noticed that there wasn't anyone around. It was early, but it seemed odd that there was no movement inside the main building. Just when he was contemplating asking the taxi driver to hang around for a moment, Ricky Norman appeared from around the side of the building. He waved at them as he approached.

"Good morning! It's going to be a great day to fly," he said jovially.

"Figures he's a morning person," Lara mumbled under her breath.

"If you'll follow me to the hangar, you can help me get the bird out and ready to go," Ricky told Stone and Owl.

Nodding, Owl fell in step beside Lara as they headed through a gate in the fence surrounding the runway and toward a hangar a short distance from the main building.

"We'll get the paperwork done first and by the time that's finished, and you guys have done the preflight checks, the tower control employees should be here," Ricky told them.

"Is it normal that they aren't here yet?" Stone asked.

"For this airport? Yeah," Ricky said with a nod. "There's a larger airport not too far away that most people use, but I've always liked this one. It's not as hard to get on the flight schedule and it's a lot quieter."

Owl would normally agree, but something about how deserted the place was at the moment didn't sit well with him. Lara must've felt the same way, because he felt her move a little closer to him. He grabbed her hand and squeezed it in reassurance. She shot him a grateful smile. Owl would feel much better once they were in the air.

Ricky led them into the small hangar. It was very dim inside the building without the big hangar door open, but Owl saw the chopper waiting. Pride welled up inside him. Soon this beauty would be theirs.

They all walked over to a tiny administrative area alongside one wall, and Owl tried to be patient as Ricky shuffled through a pile of papers.

Owl wasn't sure what made him turn and look behind him. Maybe some kind of subtle sound...clothing rubbing together as someone moved, a light footstep.

But by the time what he was seeing sank in, it was too late.

A muscular man wearing what looked to be a black three-piece suit was swinging a large rubber mallet at Stone's head.

He opened his mouth to yell a warning to his friend, but his shout came out more as a grunt when he felt Lara's hand ripped from his own.

Spinning, he saw Lara against Ricky's chest. He had one arm around her neck and the other held a syringe. Owl froze as Stone fell to the floor with a loud thud. The man with the mallet had obviously managed to take him off guard.

Owl's blood ran cold. This was literally his nightmare come true.

His mind raced through his options, which were pretty damn bleak right about now. He should've paid heed to his uneasy feeling earlier.

He wouldn't let his mistake be Lara's downfall.

"I wouldn't," Ricky warned as he gripped Lara tighter when Owl took a step, ready to leap at the man who held the woman he loved. Lara's face had leeched of all color and she was trying desperately to struggle out of Ricky's grip.

"Stop moving unless you want to get stuck with this," he growled.

Owl swiveled slightly, keeping everyone in sight. His attention wavered between Lara and Ricky, Stone—now lying motionless on the floor—and the man with the mallet.

"I suppose you're wondering what the hell's going on," Ricky said almost conversationally.

"Let her go," Owl seethed between clenched teeth.

"Sorry, can't do that. I'm getting a lot of money for her. She'll be taken reeeeeal good care of though."

Lara whimpered, and the sound nearly broke Owl's heart. They'd all been so careful! And now it was clear the very person they'd trusted with the sale of the chopper had been working with a serial killer.

Owl had no doubt that's what was happening here. Carter Grant had found someone to do his dirty work for him. And if he didn't figure something out in the next few seconds, it was highly likely she'd be thrust right back into her worst nightmare. And he knew she wouldn't rebound so well a second time.

"They're all yours," Ricky said to the man who'd knocked out Stone.

"Boss only wants one."

"*What*? That's not the plan!" Ricky bitched, the irritation clear in his voice.

"Plans change," Muscle Man said, not sounding like he cared about Ricky's anger.

Owl had to take out Ricky. It was dangerous, especially with that needle so close to Lara's skin, and he didn't know what was in it. If it was something like fentanyl, it could kill her in minutes. If it was a sedative, her being knocked out would make escaping from this clusterfuck a challenge.

Who was he kidding? Escaping was already highly unlikely. Because there was no way Owl was leaving Stone in these assholes' clutches. If he was conscious, Stone would order Owl to get the hell out of there with Lara. But he couldn't leave him. Not after the hell they'd been through together in the past.

If he could at least get Lara away from Ricky, she could run. Get help. He'd hold out as best he could against the two men... and hopefully that would be long enough for someone to come and help.

Even as his muscles coiled to leap at Ricky, he heard another subtle sound—and just as suddenly, the man in the suit had a gun pointed at his chest.

Before Owl could blink, the man pulled the trigger.

He expected to feel the pain of a bullet tearing into his body, but instead, when he looked down, Owl saw a dart sticking out of his chest.

Howling in anger, he yanked it out, but already he could feel whatever sedative the dart contained moving through his veins. He tried to force himself to remain standing. It was no use. He fell to his knees, but didn't feel any pain as he hit the concrete.

Looking up, he saw horror in Lara's expression and it reverberated in his soul.

He'd failed her. And Stone. Then he knew nothing more as he fell face first onto the concrete floor.

Lara screamed as the man in the fancy suit shot Owl. She expected to see blood, but the dart lying on the floor at Owl's feet told her all she needed to know. He'd been drugged. When he crumpled to the concrete, she fought even harder against Ricky's hold.

"No!" she yelled as Owl lay motionless at the other man's feet.

"Sorry, but yes," Ricky said gleefully in her ear.

"I'll give you a million dollars if you let us go!" Lara said desperately.

"Sorry, honey, but I'm already getting that much to deliver you. Besides, I don't need Carter Grant on my bad side."

Lara shivered at hearing confirmation that Carter was behind this. She'd been terrified this might happen, and she'd been right.

The man in the suit tucked the gun back into a holster at the small of his back, then bent over Stone. He grabbed him under his armpits and began hauling him toward the dark end of the hangar.

"It was good working with you," he said, as he dragged Stone away.

"Wait, you're coming back for him, right?" Ricky yelled as he nodded toward Owl's body.

"No."

Ricky continued yelling threats, but the man in the suit didn't seem to care. He simply continued dragging Stone. Now that Lara's eyes had adjusted a bit to the dim light, she could see what looked like a black sedan on the other side of the helicopter.

"Shit, fuck, damn!" Ricky swore.

Lara squirmed harder against him. She had to get free. Had to help Owl and Stone. Could *not* let herself be taken to wherever Carter was waiting for her. She wouldn't survive being his prisoner again. No way. Remembering what he'd done to her before was too much to contemplate right now.

"Calm down!" Ricky shouted.

Lara *wasn't* going to calm down. No way in hell. She knew what was at stake.

Just when she thought she might manage to get away, she felt the prick of a needle in her upper arm.

Ricky shoved her suddenly, and she fell to the unforgiving floor on her hands and knees—hard. But she didn't hesitate to scramble away from Ricky, toward Owl. She shook him frantically. "Owl, wake up!"

He didn't even twitch.

Ricky laughed behind her, and Lara felt sick to her stomach. She slowly turned and stood, putting herself between Owl and the evil man who had no problem delivering her to the hands of a serial killer. As far as she was concerned, he was as bad as Carter.

"Hate to tell you, sweetheart, but he's not going to wake up anytime soon," Ricky said with a sneer.

Lara hated hearing Owl's endearment for her on this man's lips. "You won't get away with any of this."

He simply laughed harder. "I already have. Look around, you see anyone coming to your rescue? No. Because they aren't here. They won't be for at least another hour. And by then, we'll be long gone."

The bay door on the other side of the hangar lifted, and the black car slowly drove out.

Panic welled inside Lara and she felt her heart beating frantically in her chest. Stone! He was being kidnapped, and there wasn't a damn thing she could do about it! "If you think I'm going with you quietly, you're dead wrong," Lara seethed.

He stood just feet away with his arms crossed over his chest and that damn smirk on his face. "You're the one who's wrong. That sedative I gave you should be taking effect any moment now."

Lara's insides froze. She'd felt the slight pain in her arm but had dismissed it, too relieved to be out of Ricky's grasp and closer to Owl. But even as she had that thought, she realized her body felt...weird. As if she was looking down on the scene from above. She swayed on her feet.

"Why don't you sit before you fall down?" Ricky said helpfully.

Lara glared at him. Information. She needed information! Somehow, she'd find a way to share it with someone from The Refuge. Brick. Pipe. Maybe even that tech guy everyone was friends with. *Someone.*

Her thoughts were sluggish now, but she remembered her phone. She needed to get it out of her pocket, try to call someone without Ricky noticing. Cora! No, not her best friend...maybe Tiny?

She thought she was being sneaky, but Ricky laughed again as he came toward her even as she reached into her pocket. Lara tried to back away, but she tripped over Owl. She fell on her ass and moaned in pain, and Ricky easily manhandled her onto her side, groping her ass as he pulled her cell out of her back pocket.

"Too bad I can't keep a nice piece of ass like you for myself," Ricky mumbled as he dropped her phone to the floor and stomped on it.

Lara stared at the pieces as if she was in a trance. The room was spinning, and she knew it was only a matter of time before she passed out. But thinking about where she'd wake up, and with who, had her fighting the effects of whatever Ricky had given her.

"Where are you taking us?"

"Well, it was only supposed to be you, but there's no way I can leave your boyfriend here to be found. That'll ruin every-thing. So I guess he gets to come too."

Hope clawed its way upward from Lara's belly. Her odds were better with Owl by her side. She refused to think about what might happen to him at the hands of Carter Grant, but she was selfish enough to be relieved that she wouldn't be alone. At least for a little longer.

"Someone is going to know we're gone," Lara said as confidently as possible, although she had a feeling her words were slurring and she wasn't quite getting her threat across as well as she wanted to.

"Of course they are. But not anytime soon. The chopper your friends bought will be gone, and everyone will assume you three left as planned. It'll be hours before anyone realizes something's amiss, when you don't arrive at your stopping point for the evening. And yes, I have no doubt your plans were discussed and passed on to the others at the stupid retreat you were holed up in for so long."

"Refuge," Lara corrected. "Not retreat."

"What the hell ever. It doesn't matter. *You* don't matter. You're a means to an end, and that end will be a lot sweeter for *me* than it will be for you and your boyfriend."

"Please," she begged. She wasn't above begging if it would help. Would keep her away from Carter Grant. "Please leave us here."

"Nope. Not happening. I've got a sweet payday waiting for me." Ricky crouched down two feet in front of Lara, studying her with a smirk. "I can see why Carter's so obsessed with you. Blonde hair, blue eyes, tall, slender...you're a wet dream, sweetheart. Which I heard is his kink." Ricky laughed at his own joke. "Let go, Lara. It'll make what happens next all the more easier if you're unconscious."

"Carter's not gonna give you any money. He doesn't leave

266

loose ends. He killed the last guy who delivered me to him... what makes you any different?" It was getting harder and harder to keep her eyes open, and she had a feeling her words were slurred, but she couldn't give up. Both her and Owl's lives were on the line.

"You should be more worried about yourself than me, sweetheart," Ricky said.

Lara blinked, and it took more than a few seconds to force her eyes open again. The drugs in her bloodstream were doing what they were made to do. "You won't get away with this," she repeated feebly.

"I already have. The only wrench in my plans is boy-o here. Carter isn't going to be happy when he joins the party, but as I said before, I can't leave him here to be discovered. Doesn't matter. I'm sure he'll be fish food not too long after we land."

"Where're we going?" Lara managed to ask.

Ricky leaned in and palmed the back of Lara's head and lowered her almost gently to the floor. She felt boneless, completely unable to fight back. The unscrupulous man hovered —then leaned down and *licked* her, from the corner of her lips, up her cheek, stopping beside her eye. Lara desperately wanted to wipe his touch away, get rid of the slimy feel of his saliva on her skin. But she couldn't move. Her limbs felt as if they weighed a thousand pounds.

"To Carter's brand-new island. He lives there all by himself. No servants, no neighbors. He wanted to make sure you couldn't run away this time."

Lara whimpered. At least she thought she did. She didn't hear any sound escape her mouth.

"It won't be hard to throw your boyfriend's body into the ocean. The sharks will take care of him," Ricky said. Then he stood suddenly, and he looked like the devil himself as he stood over her and Owl.

"And your friend? He's as good as gone too."

"Where?" Lara whispered with the last of her strength.

"Sold. That wasn't part of Carter's plan, but what he doesn't know won't hurt him. Got a pretty penny for him. I met a guy... real asshole. Loves money almost as much as I do. And he needed a man. Didn't say why, and I didn't ask, but I'm guessing he doesn't want him as a guest at a tea party. And my bank account got a lot fatter thanks to *that* transaction." Then Ricky glared at Owl. "*Fuck.* Can't believe that asshole left him here for me to deal with!"

That was the last thing Lara heard before the drugs overwhelmed her.

* * *

Ricky ran an arm across his brow and swore under his breath. The boyfriend was heavier than he looked and it wasn't easy getting him into the helicopter. He didn't bother strapping him in, simply got him up and on the floor of the back seat. He didn't care about the broad either, but he knew Carter did. And if he delivered her with any bruises, or if it looked as if he hadn't taken great care with her, he'd pay the price.

He'd strapped her into the front seat and even went so far as to put a set of headphones over her ears. Time was running out, and he needed to get going before people started showing up at the small airport. Though, he took a moment to run a greedy hand over Lara's tits, squeezing and groping.

She really *was* pretty. It was a shame he wasn't able to take her for a spin before he delivered her. Ricky wouldn't have cared that she was unconscious, pussy was pussy, and he preferred that his women didn't fight when he took them. But Grant was expecting his property to be delivered without a mark on her... and Ricky liked to make his marks.

Slamming the passenger door, Ricky ran around to the front of the chopper and picked up the handle of the platform dolly the helicopter sat on. He took one more look around the hangar, making sure nothing seemed amiss. He'd put the three suitcases into the chopper, picked up the pieces of the cell phone he'd taken from Lara—that she'd been dumb enough to think he'd let her use—and had packed the papers from the sale of the chopper.

The money The Refuge had sent to purchase the helicopter was already in his account, and along with the money Grant was paying him—and what he'd gotten from Jason Feldman, the man who'd bought Jack "Stone" Wickett—he was more than set.

He'd fly his packages to the island, get the rest of his money, then take off, flying south across the border. He'd sell the chopper once he got to Mexico, maybe to a cartel; those assholes had plenty of money and would probably love having a helicopter in their arsenal. Then he'd spend the rest of his life drinking, fucking, and enjoying the shit-ton of money he'd accumulated, most of it thanks to this single job.

In a few hours, it would be done. He wouldn't think about the woman sitting next to him and what she was about to go through. Or the unconscious man in the back. They weren't his problem. Ricky Norman only cared about money. And he was about to have more than he could ever spend. Retirement was only one delivery away.

Satisfied with himself, Ricky pushed the helicopter out of the hangar, removed the dolly from underneath, and rolled it back into the building. Then he closed the bay door, climbed into the chopper, put a pair of headphones over his ears, and smiled as he started the process to get into the air. The sooner he delivered the broad to Grant, the sooner he could get the hell out of the country.

CHAPTER NINETEEN

Ryan paced back and forth next to her Ford Explorer. She bit her thumbnail as she argued with herself about what she should do. Doing what was *right* would mean exposing herself. Revealing who she really was. And that was the last thing she wanted. She loved her job here at The Refuge, and she had no doubt that speaking up would mean losing it.

Not only that, but she'd lose the best friends she'd ever had. The people who lived and worked here had embraced her. Had treated her like she was family...and not a freak. Someone to be wary of. Ryan had done her best to protect her new friends from afar, but this was...

She needed help.

Taking a deep breath, and ignoring the nausea in her belly, Ryan jogged toward the main lodge. Brick and the others were having a staff meeting. Jess, Carly, and Ryan were supposed to be there a little later to give them an update on the housekeeping. That was one thing Ryan loved about working here, the men who owned the place welcomed everyone's input. They were genuinely interested in how every part of the operation was running, and that meant hearing straight from the people who worked there.

But she needed to talk to Brick, Tonka, Spike, Pipe, and Tiny —*now*. It couldn't wait.

Ryan gave Alaska, who was sitting behind the registration desk inside the lodge, a distracted wave as she headed for the conference room. She vaguely heard her friend ask why she was so early for the meeting, but she didn't stop to explain. It was likely this was the last time Alaska would ever talk to her in a friendly manner. The information she was about to reveal would change everything. And not for the better, as far as Ryan was concerned.

She pushed open the door, then made sure to close it behind her as she stared at the five men sitting at the long rectangular table. Ryan had gotten to know them all fairly well over the last year or so, and she'd shared both highs and lows with the staff.

For a second, she wavered. She could keep quiet and not lose the best thing that had ever happened to her.

But her conscience got the better of her. She needed to speak up. It was the right thing to do. She'd deal with the fallout like she always did—alone.

She'd find somewhere else to hide.

"What's wrong?" Brick asked when Ryan didn't immediately speak.

She figured she must look freaked out for the unflappable Brick to sound so concerned.

"Owl, Stone, and Lara are in trouble," she blurted—then winced. That wasn't exactly how she'd wanted to start this conversation.

To her surprise, the men didn't immediately shout or demand answers. It was Tiny, of all people, who pushed his chair back and approached. He took her arm and gently led her to a chair at the table.

Ryan wanted to cry. He was being so nice...but she knew it wouldn't last.

Out of all the men at this table, Tiny was the one Ryan had been drawn to the most. He reminded her of the hero in one of her favorite movies, *Sixteen Candles*. Everyone joked with him about that, and it was obvious he hated the comparison.

And while the movie had gotten some slack in recent years for being racist and sexist, and Ryan couldn't deny there were parts of it that were definitely insensitive at the very least, she'd still always been drawn to the hero. Her very favorite part was the end. When the hero showed up for the heroine, and that kiss over her birthday cake...it was enough to make Ryan swoon every time.

Seeing Tiny day in and day out gave her those same tingly feelings. But Spencer Denny, otherwise known as Tiny, was nothing like the kid in the movie. He was twice as alpha and twice as broody, though always considerate of everyone at The Refuge. There were times she caught him looking at her in a way that seemed more than friendly, but otherwise, he never did or said anything else to give Ryan the impression he might want to be more than her employer.

She'd heard through The Refuge grapevine that he had some serious trust issues, and because she had enough issues of her own to deal with, she hadn't ever tried to see where any mutual interest might go. Especially when they both went to great lengths to ignore said interest.

And now, Ryan knew as soon as she told these men why she

was there and what she knew, *any* kind of trust Tiny may have eventually given her would be gone in a puff of smoke. And the kicker was, she couldn't even blame him.

"Talk to us, Ryan," Tiny ordered. "Why do you think our friends are in trouble? Did Lara call or text?"

Taking a deep breath, Ryan did her best to turn off her feelings. Keep to the facts. That would make this go faster. Then she could pack her things and disappear again.

"My name isn't Ryan. It's not Samantha, Julie, Riley, Rebecca, or Maryann either. Those are all names I've used in the last few years. I came here on false pretenses. I researched The Refuge and decided it would be the perfect place to lay low. Alexis...the housekeeper who left? The one who got that sudden inheritance? It wasn't from a long-lost relative. It was *me*. I did that. I arranged for her to get that money so she'd quit, and I could take the job."

"What the hell?" Spike said under his breath.

Ryan didn't stop. She'd come this far, she had to keep going.

"I'm good at computer stuff." That was the understatement of the century, but explaining just *how* good she was right now would be a waste of time.

Instead, she met Tonka's gaze. "When Jasna was kidnapped, I tracked Christian. I was in the car when Henley found out about her daughter missing, and who she suspected. The cops getting a search warrant would've taken too long, and it was a simple thing for me to track his phone. I went to the house where his phone pinged and saw Christian leaving. I peeked in the window and spotted Jas. I tracked Christian to a fast-food place, then I went and got Jas out. I called the police and gave them the tip about where to find Christian, and about the cabin. Then I left Jasna where I knew you'd find her."

"*You're* Anonymous? The mystery person who texted me?" Tonka asked incredulously.

Ryan nodded. Then she turned to Spike. "And it was me who tracked Reese's tile."

"Holy shit!" he swore.

"And you texted Stone in Arizona," Pipe said. It wasn't a question. "And unblocked those jammers Grant had at the house, allowing me to talk to him."

Ryan nodded.

"How'd you know about the bunkers?" Brick asked.

Ryan shook her head. "It's not important right now."

"The hell it's not," Tiny said in a low, hard voice.

She'd been avoiding looking at the man next to her, but now, Ryan turned and saw he'd leaned back in his chair, as far away from her as he could get, his arms crossed over his chest. He was as closed off from her as possible while still being in the room.

It shouldn't have hurt, she knew exactly what his reaction to her deception would be, and yet it was still a blow.

"I was worried about Lara. About her leaving The Refuge. I put an alert on her phone to let me know her whereabouts. And I knew this morning was when they were going to pick up the chopper. I wasn't going to pry, I swear...I know it's wrong, but...I was curious about how things were going. I hacked into the microphone on her cell and listened in."

"Is that even a thing?" Pipe asked.

Ryan glanced at her hands. "It is if you know how. All phones have microphones. And computers. And tablets. And those gadgets you can buy that will run your house and answer your questions when you ask? Those really *are* listening to everything you say and do. Companies use the info to market useless crap to people. And don't get me started on how easy it

275

is to be a spy these days. Everyone has electronics around them, at all times."

"Get on with it," Tiny growled.

Ryan swallowed hard, even as she shriveled a little more inside. She *hated* when people were mad at her. When they yelled. She'd spent most of her life being treated like shit, being screamed at, being told she was nothing but a worthless piece of shit...so much so that she had her own PTSD when it came to others being angry.

"Right. So I was listening to their banter on the way to the airport. All three were happy and excited to be heading home today. I heard the seller greet them. But when they entered what I assume was the hangar where the helicopter was located...shit hit the fan."

Everyone, except Tiny, was leaning forward now.

"What happened?" Brick asked urgently.

Ryan quickly told them everything she'd overheard. "Then the Ricky guy must've smashed Lara's phone—I heard it hit something, most likely the floor in the hangar. And by the time I was able to hack into Owl's, I'd missed a lot of stuff. But he was bragging about what he was going to do—and it definitely involved flying Lara to an island where Carter Grant would be waiting for her. He told her that Carter would kill Owl and dump his body in the ocean."

"And Stone? Where is he?" Tiny asked.

"I don't know. Ricky said he sold him to some guy. But he didn't say where he was going or what the buyer wanted him for."

"Bloody hell!" Pipe swore.

The others muttered much worse swear words under their breaths.

"I can't track Stone. The guy who took him must've taken his phone and either smashed it or turned it off. And Lara's is surely broken."

She felt Tiny stir next to her. "And Owl's?"

"It's still on," Ryan said.

"Are you still listening?" Tonka asked.

She nodded.

Brick opened the laptop in front of him and shoved it almost violently across the table toward Ryan. "Use that to let us listen too."

Ryan stared at the computer in dismay. She should've thought this through a little better. "I can't," she said softly. "I mean, I need to use mine."

"You're telling me a hacker can't use any old computer to ply her trade?" Tiny asked roughly. "I'm not buying it. If you're as good as you say you are, and if you're telling the truth, you'll pull that shit up. Right. Now."

Ryan folded in on herself at the hostility in Tiny's voice. It wasn't that she couldn't use Brick's computer...it was that if she did, if she used any unsecure device, she could be found. It would only be a matter of time before she was tracked.

But that was *also* her fault. She should've brought her own computer with her. She'd been so freaked out, so worried about Owl, Stone, and Lara, that she'd left her apartment quickly, her only goal to get to The Refuge as fast as she could and let the others know their friends were in danger.

Her timetable for leaving just got moved up, but so be it. If sacrificing her personal safety meant she might be able to save the others, she'd do it.

Besides...she'd betrayed these people. She owed them this much.

She pulled Brick's computer closer and her fingers raced over the keys as she went to the dark web and pulled up the program she'd designed and hidden amongst thousands of other home-made spying programs, all available for a price to thieves and others who used them for nefarious purposes. She'd purposely made hers inoperable...unless you were as good as she was, or knew exactly what commands to type in.

It took less than two minutes to access the microphone in Owl's cell phone, but the tension in the room was as thick as a mountain snowstorm. The hostility coming from Tiny felt like tiny knives digging into her skin.

Finally, she pushed play on the program and winced as the only sound that came through the speakers was an extremely loud hum.

"What the fuck is that? I thought you were good at this shit?" Tiny grumbled.

"Chopper," Brick said almost calmly.

"Can you trace it?" Pipe asked.

Ryan kept the mic open and opened a new tab and once again began typing furiously. She pressed her lips together and sighed as she turned the laptop around to show the others a map. "I don't have an exact location, only where the phone last pinged." There was a red dot on the map in the middle of a swath of blue off the West Coast.

"Ricky said there was an island," she said.

"Shit, there are what, hundreds of islands out that way?" Tonka asked.

"Probably thousands," Spike said grimly.

"I'm calling Tex. Maybe he has some ideas," Brick said.

Ryan involuntarily winced.

"You know him?" Pipe asked, seeing her expression.

"Personally? No. But I may have hacked into his databases in order to find info he couldn't...to feed to you guys," Ryan admitted.

Surprisingly, Brick smiled. "Oh, he's gonna want to hear all about you. What was it he said when he was trying to help us find Jas?"

"That whoever Anonymous was, he was better than him," Tonka replied.

Ryan's belly churned. She wasn't sure she wanted to talk to Tex face-to-face...or phone-to-phone. He wasn't the kind of man who would take kindly to someone else hacking into his stuff. She'd feel exactly the same.

"If we're looking for an island, we need to get the Coast Guard involved," Tonka said. "I still have some connections. I'll make some calls, see what I can get rolling."

"I'll call the FBI. Let them know about Carter, and that Stone's been kidnapped," Spike said.

"And I'll get in touch with Homeland Security. They should have the capability to track that chopper," Pipe said.

Ryan swallowed hard as all the men around her picked up their phones and began to do what they could to find their friends. She peeked over at Tiny, only to find him glaring at her.

"What's your name?"

"What?" she asked, surprised at the question. With everything else she'd just told them, *that* was what he wanted to know?

"Your name. The one you were born with. I want to know what it is. *Now*."

"Why?" she whispered.

Tiny leaned forward, and it felt as if they were the only two people in the room. She was frozen by his icy turquoise eyes as he stared as if he could read her mind.

"Because."

That wasn't an answer, and they both knew it. Ryan could make up a name, she'd been doing it for years now. But for some reason, she blurted a name she hadn't dared even think since the day she'd fled...much less said out loud. "Ryleigh. Ryleigh Lodge."

Tiny leaned back and nodded. "Smart to keep your current name as close as possible to your real one...*Ryleigh*."

That was pretty much the main reason she'd chosen Ryan. It wasn't a typical female name, but it was as close to Ryleigh as she could get. She'd had too many close calls when she hadn't answered to the other names she'd made up in the past.

Feeling uncomfortable, and needing some space, Ryan pushed her chair back and started to stand.

Tiny's hand shot forward and grasped her arm. Not hard enough to hurt, but enough that if she wanted to pull away from him, it would take a bit of force. "Where are you going?"

"To pack," she said, the words coming out a lot weaker than the firm declaration she'd intended.

"Oh, you aren't going anywhere," Tiny growled. "We need you to find Owl and Lara...and that asshole Grant. And then we're obviously going to need you to track down Stone to get his ass back here. And you have *a lot* more questions to answer before you're allowed to leave."

She didn't like the glint in Tiny's eye as he said that last part, but she wasn't going to walk away if these men wanted her help. She should've tried harder to find Carter Grant before now. That was on her. She'd have to shoulder that guilt...along with all the guilt she already carried.

She nodded slowly, and Tiny let go of her arm. But even after he'd sat back in his seat, her arm tingled where he'd touched her.

It wasn't a good sign. How could she still be so attracted to this man, when it was obvious he hated her?

Pushing her worries aside, Ryan took a deep breath. She needed to use everything she'd ever learned when it came to computers to help Lara and Owl. Nothing else mattered right now.

CHAPTER TWENTY

Lara's mouth was dry. So damn dry. She licked her lips, but it didn't do much good. She turned her head, wondering why she felt so horrible, and blinked her eyes tiredly before closing them again.

At first, she had no idea where she was and no memory of how'd she gotten there. But with each tick of the clock, scenes flashed through her brain.

Of the hotel room and late-night snacks. Of the chopper in the hangar. Of Stone being dragged away. Owl lying motionless on the floor. Ricky standing over her, telling her he was bringing her to Carter Grant.

That last thought made her gasp and her eyes flew open.

The first thing she saw was Owl. He was on the floor, staring right at her, while she seemed to be on a couch of some sort.

He quickly held his finger to his lips, then mouthed, *Are you okay?*

Lara swallowed and thought about his question for a beat before nodding.

Then, the reason he wanted her to be silent made itself clear.

"I *told* you I only wanted her!"

She'd recognize that voice anywhere.

It was *him*. Carter Grant.

Lara shivered and every muscle in her body tensed. She'd known this was where she'd end up eventually, but now she had so much more to lose.

"And I told *you*, if I'd left him in that hangar, someone would've found him by now and probably already be tracking this chopper. As it is, I have a small window to get out of the country before everyone and their brother is looking for it!"

Turning her head slowly, Lara looked behind her where the voices were coming from, but she couldn't see Ricky or Carter. The back of the couch where she was lying prevented her from seeing them...and them from seeing her.

She jerked in fright when something touched her arm, whipping her head around, relieved to see it was just Owl, who'd crept closer. She didn't remember the flight here—wherever *here* was—but she was more relieved than she could put into words that he was with her. She supposed that made her a shitty person, to be glad the man she loved was also in the hands of a sadistic serial killer, but Owl was the only person who made her feel safe.

"We need to get to the window," Owl said tonelessly. His voice was so soft, Lara could barely hear him. But she nodded eagerly.

She had no idea what the plan was, if they even *had* a plan. She suddenly remembered what Ricky told her before she'd been rendered unconscious, that they were going to an island. It wasn't as if they could run to a neighbor's house and ask to use their phone. Ricky had also told her that Carter lived on the island alone.

But if going out a window put her farther from Carter Grant, she was all for it. She'd swim back to Seattle in frigid, shark-infested water if that's what it took to be free of him.

"You're taking him with you when you go!" Carter yelled at Ricky.

"Fine, but it'll cost you."

"What? No fucking way!"

The two men continued to argue, and Owl helped her roll off the sofa without landing on her face and without making a sound. When she was on the floor, Owl hugged her. Hard. Then he pulled back and looked into her eyes. He held her face in his hands, and Lara felt as if she could see his soul in his gaze when he said, "I'm not going to let him hurt you."

She nodded...even if she didn't believe him one hundred percent. Oh, she believed that he would try, that he'd do anything within his power to keep her safe, but the reality was that Carter Grant had evil on his side—and he wouldn't hesitate to kill Owl.

That thought had her wanting to move, *now*, while the two men were occupied with their bickering. It looked like she and Owl were in some sort of library or office. There were book-shelves covering one entire wall and dozens of boxes stacked everywhere she looked. The place was also dusty, as if it had been abandoned for years. She had no idea if Carter had bought the place or was squatting here, but it didn't matter. All that mattered was getting away.

Using the various boxes as cover, Lara and Owl moved toward a large window that was already cracked open—maybe to try to air out the musty room. She glanced back and finally saw Carter and Ricky, both standing about six feet behind the couch, arguing. They were so engrossed in each other, they hadn't noticed their captives were on the move.

Thankful for the clutter, the large size of the room, and the escalating anger of the two men, Lara held her breath as she and Owl made their way across the large room toward freedom.

"You can literally just shoot him in the head and dump him in the ocean, but instead you want me to load him back on the chopper and take him with me. And do what? There's no autopilot on the helicopter, genius, so I can't shove him out while in the air, and if he wakes up while we're flying, I'm fucked! You want me to take all the risks with the guy, fine—but I want another mil before one of those skids leaves this island," Ricky argued, sounding oddly unsure and confident at the same time.

"A million?! Are you fucking high?"

"Too much? No skin off my back. I'll just be leaving alone then...once you pay me the second half of my fee."

"I'm not paying you another goddamn dime."

"Fine. I'll take the bitch and you can deal with *him*."

"You're not touching her!" Carter screamed, sounding unhinged. "She's mine! *Mine!*" He whipped out a pistol and aimed it at Ricky, his hand shaking with anger.

"Easy, man," Ricky said, holding up his hands as if in surrender.

Owl had reached the window, and still neither man had noticed. But it was only a matter of time. Lara hated hearing the possession in Carter's voice as he claimed she was his, but since he was completely absorbed in his argument with Ricky, she was grateful for that small mercy.

As Owl tried to open the window wide enough so they could

slip through, Lara couldn't take her gaze from Carter Grant. He looked more menacing than she remembered. Probably because of the eye patch. For a second, satisfaction swam through her. Cora had done that, trying to protect Pipe from being overpowered. She couldn't imagine hurting someone up close and personal like that...

But then she looked back at Owl. He was frowning and his brows were furrowed as he strained to hoist the damn window higher—and she realized she'd do whatever was necessary to make sure he didn't sacrifice himself for her.

It was looking more and more likely that they were both completely screwed here. The window wasn't budging, and if it didn't, she had no idea how in the world they were going to get away.

"I'm not giving you another dime. In fact—"

At that moment, Owl managed to finally shove the window up a few inches.

Unfortunately, the high-pitched squeak the frame made as it rose was loud enough to get *both* men to stop arguing—and turn in their direction.

Lara froze, and for a moment, no one moved.

Carter looked so furious, Lara thought he was going to have a heart attack right then and there. But of course, she and Owl weren't so lucky.

He shifted so the pistol was now pointed at *her*. "Get over here," he ordered.

But Lara wasn't going anywhere. Especially not anywhere *he* wanted her.

Owl stood and pulled Lara to her feet. The window wasn't open far enough for either of them to get out, and if they made a run for the door, they'd have to pass both Ricky and Carter.

"I said, *come here*. Now!" Carter yelled at Lara in a vicious tone.

Again, she didn't move. She huddled behind Owl, scared out of her mind.

Ricky chuckled.

"Shut up!" Carter screamed at the man.

"This is classic. It seems you're at an impasse."

Carter was clearly tired of the other man's taunting. He pointed the pistol back at Ricky as he growled, "You think this is funny?"

Between one blink and the next, Ricky had pulled a weapon of his own from the small of his back, pointing it at Carter. "Hilarious," he said.

The two men stood just a few feet apart, pointing pistols at each other's heads...and they each slowly inched back even as they circled each other, gazes locked. They were completely focused on their standoff.

As they moved, they had to step around boxes in their way, which moved them farther apart...and away from the path to the door.

Lara's heartrate increased. Her adrenaline spiked. Maybe, just maybe, they'd be able to reach the door after all.

Owl awkwardly wrapped an arm around her from his position in front of her and began to shuffle them away from the window, along the wall, closer to the door. "When I tell you, run. Get out. Hide," he whispered.

"I'm not leaving you," Lara blurted.

"The hell you aren't," Owl muttered.

"I'm *not!*"

This probably wasn't the time to assert herself, but Lara couldn't continue to live if Owl was killed trying to protect her.

Once upon a time, Owl standing between her and the man who'd made her life a living hell was the only thing that keep her breathing from one day to the next, but now? She was a different person. Not necessarily strong enough to take on a serial killer on her own, but she'd be damned if she sacrificed Owl.

Every muscle in his body was taut as he slowly inched them toward the door, Ricky and Carter's attention still on each other and the guns in their hands.

Ricky's gaze flicked to them, then immediately back to Carter. "What now, Grant? Your plaything's getting ready to flee the coop. But if you take your weapon off me, you know I'll fucking kill you the second you do."

Carter's face was so red now, Lara began to think that maybe he *would* drop dead of a heart attack. It would be the miracle she and Owl needed.

"Fuck you," Carter seethed.

And he pulled the trigger.

Ricky obviously anticipated his move, because he was throwing himself behind the couch before the bullet left the barrel.

Carter fired at Ricky again—then shocked Lara by turning his weapon toward her and Owl. Before she had time to squeak in fright or for her ears to stop ringing from the first shot, another rang out.

Instead of feeling pain blossom anywhere on her body, Lara grunted when Owl shoved her hard toward the door.

Carter had ducked behind a stack of boxes, and Ricky was still behind the couch, leaving the path to the door wide open. Lara barely avoided slamming into the door frame as she ran. She instinctively fumbled for the knob. She had to get out of this room!

Immediately, another shot rang out, this time from Ricky's general direction. Expecting to be killed at any second, Lara almost sobbed in relief when she finally got the knob turned and the door opened into a hallway.

"Go!" Owl said, pushing her through with a hand on her back.

"Which way?" she yelled, sure she was speaking way too loud, but with her ears still ringing from the gunfire, she couldn't regulate her tone.

"Right!" Owl yelled back.

Ricky and Carter were still shooting in the room, but Lara had no idea if they were shooting at her and Owl, or each other. She supposed it didn't matter. All that mattered was getting the hell out of the house.

"They're getting away!" Ricky taunted, his tone gleeful.

"It's a fucking island. There's nowhere to go!" Carter yelled back. "I'll get what's mine when you're *dead*!"

She supposed it was a good thing the two assholes were trying to take each other out, but Lara couldn't help but panic. Carter was right. If they were on an island, and she had no reason to doubt that they were, there *wasn't* anywhere for them to go. She supposed there had to be a boat somewhere. Carter had gotten here somehow, after all.

"There! This way, Lara. Hurry!" Owl said as he urged her toward a large room at the end of the hallway. She could still hear Ricky and Carter yelling at each other and the occasional gunshot, so she prayed they had a bit of time to find a place to hide.

Lara glanced back at Owl. He looked fierce and determined —and she'd never loved him more.

Then she noticed he was limping.

She almost tripped when she saw the blood trail he was leaving in his wake.

"You're bleeding!" she exclaimed.

"Yeah," Owl said grimly. "We need to get the hell out of here."

Lara was still trying to wrap her mind around what she was seeing. Owl had one hand on her back and the other was clasped against his thigh, obviously trying to staunch the blood coming from a gunshot wound. But it wasn't working. His pants were soaked and he was pretty much dragging his leg as he hobbled behind her. Even if they did find a place to hide, he could die from blood loss—and the trail Owl was leaving would lead Carter straight to them.

Panic made Lara's breathing speed up. She felt dizzy and hopeless. Owl had been *shot*. He'd stood in front of her like a human shield and taken a *bullet* for her. Even now, he was doing everything in his power to get her away, to make sure she was safe, when he should be worrying about bleeding to death!

"Owl," she said on a pant, but he shook his head.

"No, keep going, sweetheart."

"But your leg!" she protested.

"I know. But you're okay, that's all that matters."

It wasn't. Owl was here because of her. Because Carter wanted *her*. He shouldn't be hurt. Helplessness threatened to overwhelm her.

"Bingo! There! Left, Lara. The door. We need to get out before one of them kills the other and comes after us."

He was right. Lara did her best to pull herself together. If Owl could be this calm after being freaking shot in the leg and with blood pouring out of his body, she could keep her wits.

She got to the door Owl indicated, tore it open—and blinked

in surprise when she saw what was on the other side.

A large circle of land, cleared of trees and bushes.

And the Bell 505 that she, Stone, and Owl had test-flown yesterday.

God. Was it just yesterday? Suddenly it seemed like weeks ago. So much had happened in such a short time.

"Go, Lara! Go!"

Instinctively, she ran toward the chopper. Owl reached past her once they got to the bird and wrenched the door open. He practically threw her up into the front seat and slammed the door. Lara watched with her heart in her throat as he limped around to the other side. He opened the door and tried to climb inside.

His face was ghost white, and every time he tried to lift his good leg to get up into the seat, he stumbled backward.

"Fuck," he breathed, as he lifted his gaze to hers.

Lara moved quickly, leaning over the seat and reaching down for his arm. She was terrified by how little strength Owl had. Between the two of them, they barely got him into the chopper.

He immediately began to flick switches and push buttons... and in seconds, the rotors slowly began to spin.

"*Fuck!*" Owl swore again, closing his eyes as he slumped in his seat.

"Owl?" Lara cried frantically.

"I can't," he murmured. "I'll kill us both."

"Can't what?" Lara asked. "Owl? Can't what?!"

"Fly," he said, his expression one of devastation. "I'm sorry! So sorry, Lara...I failed you."

"What? No you didn't! You can fly! You were *born* to fly."

"Gonna...pass out," he told her. "If I do while we're in the air...we'll crash."

Lara stared at him. They couldn't have gotten this close to escaping only to fail now. "We need to stop the bleeding," she said, determination making her voice shake. "Lean forward."

She reached for Owl's belt and worked it out of the loops.

"Now's not the time to...get me naked," Owl panted.

Lara couldn't even smile right now. She lifted Owl's right leg and winced as her hand came back covered with blood. She wrapped his belt above the wound and pulled it tight.

"Tighter," Owl said between clenched teeth.

Lara pulled with all her strength and managed to clasp the belt closed. Thankfully it wasn't one with holes. It had some sort of latch that kind of clamped down on the leather. When she'd first seen it, she'd made fun of Owl, saying that it was neat that he owned a belt that could grow with his waistline. But now she was more thankful than she could say for the ingenious design.

"Now what?" she asked. "Owl? What do I do now?"

He lifted his head—and for a moment his gaze was as clear as it always was. "Hold on...I'll get us out of here."

Lara's heart clenched. She loved Owl, thought he was incredible, but the more his complexion paled, the more she honestly feared he was right—he couldn't fly them anywhere.

"I'll get us in the air...then you'll have to fly. You've done it enough...times...in the sim. You know what to do. The anti-torque foot...pedals...control the tail rotor. The stick between your legs controls forward and...backward...right and left. And the lever next to the sea...is up and down. You can do this, sweetheart. I believe in you. You're...the strongest woman I've ever known."

She couldn't! There was no way she could *fly* this helicopter. "I can't, Owl. I can't!" she cried, tears springing to her eyes.

Owl met her gaze again, then nodded. "It's okay, sweetheart.

It's okay."

It wasn't *okay*. Not even close.

A sound to her right made Lara turn and look at the door they'd exited, and she saw Carter burst into the yard. But instead of coming toward the chopper, he turned back toward the house and aimed, shooting his pistol.

She looked back at Owl, who hadn't taken his eyes from her, then back at Carter—and made her decision. The only decision she could.

"Right. Let's do this."

Lara was sweating profusely and felt as if she was going to throw up all over the controls. But Owl looked as calm as he had yesterday, when he was in the air. He looked down at the controls and nodded to himself. He'd told her what every ding sound, and what every word on the screens had meant the day before, but right now, all Lara could hear was her heart beating in her chest.

Looking back at the house, she saw Ricky now had one arm extended around the door frame, using the house as cover as he shot back at Carter. Both men were desperately trying to kill the other. What had started out as a vicious argument had turned into a life-or-death shootout. And Lara knew whoever won, they'd soon turn their sights on them. She kind of wanted Ricky to win. But he'd definitely kill them so he could take the helicopter.

And if Carter won...

Lara shivered. She couldn't think about that right now.

The rotors spun faster and faster, and Lara still couldn't believe she was even considering trying to fly this thing. She had hopes that maybe Owl wasn't as bad off as he thought; that once they were in the air, he'd be able to get them back to Seattle.

But when she glanced at him again, those hopes faded.

He looked bad. His eyes were at half mast, his jaw clenched, as if it was taking all his strength to stay conscious. He was as white as a sheet and sweating profusely.

If they made it off the ground without being shot, she really was going to have to fly them out of there. It was likely she'd end up killing both her and Owl...but if she didn't at least try, they were *definitely* dead.

"You can...do this," Owl said. "I believe in you. Put...the headphones on...tell whoever, you can get to answer...what's happening...that you're a novice...they'll...help..."

Lara nodded and reached for the headphones. She placed them over her ears and immediately the sound of everything but Owl's harsh breaths faded.

She looked back at the house.

To her horror, one of Carter's bullets finally found its mark, and Ricky fell in the doorway.

Carter turned to the helicopter and pointed his gun.

"Here...we...go!"

Lara put her hands on the controls and felt them move as Owl began to take off. He lifted the collective lever next to his seat, which she also felt with her own hand. He applied slight pressure to one of the pedals to counter the torque of the engine, just as he'd taught her to do with the simulator back in his cabin at The Refuge.

Even with Owl's expertise, it wasn't a smooth takeoff. He was fighting unconsciousness and the loss of blood had definitely had an effect on his hand-eye coordination. The chopper lurched, and for a second, Lara thought they were going to crash before they'd gotten two feet off the ground.

It wasn't pretty, and if any pilot witnessed the helicopter's assent, they'd probably be wondering if the person at the controls was drunk or high—but Owl had done it. They were airborne.

Lara had no idea what made her look down once more. She would never forget the absolute fury on Carter's face as she escaped him once again.

But it was Ricky, slowly rising to an elbow on the ground, that had her blinking in surprise.

She couldn't hear the shots, but she saw Carter jerk and stumble before he fell face first onto the grass.

Ricky collapsed back to the ground, and then they were both still.

She didn't have time to process what she'd just seen—Ricky and Carter killing each other, a fitting end to such evil men—before she heard a low groan through the headset and turned back to Owl.

He was slumped to the side. He'd gotten them off the ground, but now he was completely unconscious.

Lara's hands shook as she realized *she* was now flying. By herself! Without Owl there to give her tips on how not to crash.

"Oh crap, Owl! I can't do this," she whispered.

But he didn't respond.

For a moment, panic nearly overwhelmed her, and she forgot everything Owl had ever taught her while they'd been sitting safely on his couch, as she laughed and crashed the simulated helicopter time and time again. He'd been so patient, explaining why she'd gone down and urging her to try again.

Carter Grant was dead. She had to believe that. He wouldn't be hunting her anymore. She could be free. She and Owl could live happily ever after, just like the characters in all her favorite movies and books.

But only if she got her head out of her ass and got them safely off the island.

Determination welled up. She needed to get Owl to a hospital. He'd protected her, kept her safe for months. It was her turn to do the same for him.

Taking a deep breath, she spoke. "Hello? Is anyone out there? Mayday, Mayday! I'm in a helicopter and we just took off from an island, I don't know where it is, and the pilot is unconscious and needs an ambulance. My name is Lara Osler, and I don't know what I'm doing and I need help!"

Her fingers were curled around the controls so tightly, she was relieved she didn't need to let go in order to communicate via the headsets. There was a switch that made conversation private to the occupants of the chopper, but Owl had flicked it to public before he'd passed out.

"Hello? Mayday! I'm having an emergency. Can anyone hear me?"

"I hear you."

Lara almost sobbed at those three words.

"I see you're in a Bell. What's the emergency?"

"I'm not a pilot! I've never flown a real helicopter before. My boyfriend and I were kidnapped by Carter Grant. He's a serial killer and wanted by the FBI. We were taken to an island and he and another bad guy killed each other. At least I think they did! But Owl was shot and he's bleeding really badly and I'm flying, but I'm not good at it and I'm afraid I'm going to crash and kill us both and I don't know where we are or how to read the screens to know where to go!"

She was overexplaining, speaking way too fast, but Lara couldn't seem to stop. "I've only flown a helicopter in a simulator, and I'm so scared!"

"Take a deep breath. You're doing fine. You're keeping her level, which is good. On the screen in front of you, there's a green radar-looking thing. There's a line in the middle of it that's probably moving back and forth. See it?"

The man's voice in her ears was low and soothing, which went a long way toward calming Lara. "Y-Yeah, I think so."

"Good. Your job is to keep that line as flat as possible. Understand?"

She nodded, her mouth suddenly too dry to speak.

"Right. Let up a little on the stick between your legs. That's it. Good. You were going a little too fast. Can you lift up on the lever to your left just a bit?"

"I don't want to go any higher!" Lara exclaimed, feeling panicky again. The higher she went, the more it would hurt if she crashed.

"Just a tiny bit. I want to make sure you're way above the level of the waves. Good. Okay, Lara, here's what we're going to do. I need you to turn to the right. Right now, you're coming straight for the city, and I'm thinking you don't want to fly over any buildings."

"No!" she practically yelled.

"Right, so I'm going to lead you to a small airport south of the city."

Nausea churned in Lara's belly once more.

"I'm not very good at landing," she admitted.

"Piece of cake. I'll help you."

"What's your name?" she asked, suddenly desperate to know.

"Lucas."

"I'm naming my first son after you," Lara blurted.

Lucas chuckled. "Awesome. Now, here's what I need you to do."

The next twenty minutes were some of the scariest of Lara's life. She kept glancing between Owl, who was still unmoving next to her, and the screens in front of her, passing on the information Lucas requested.

Everything that had happened to her in the past was put into perspective during that flight. Being at Carter's mercy? Piece of cake compared to this.

When she caught a glimpse of the mainland, she almost panicked again, thinking about what would happen to any people on the ground if she crashed. But Lucas talked her off the ledge and managed to calm her enough to turn the chopper more to the right and follow the coastline south.

When she neared the airport where Lucas wanted her to land, Lara's hands were starting to cramp from clenching the controls. But the man's voice never wavered. He'd cleared the air space, thankfully, so she didn't have to dodge planes taking off or landing. Lara could see an ambulance and several police cars and firetrucks parked by the main building. They both freaked her out and were a huge relief at the same time.

"Okay, this is it. You're hovering, right?"

"Yeah."

"Good. Slowly—*very* slowly—lower the lever next to you and apply slight pressure backward to the stick between your legs at the same time." The nose of the helicopter tilted ever-so-slightly up, and the tail dipped as she approached the landing zone. "That's it. Easy...slower, you're doing great, Lara."

She wasn't. The chopper was lurching slightly back and forth and she wasn't bringing it down slow enough, but suddenly all Lara wanted was to be *down*. She understood now why people got off airplanes and kissed the ground.

As the chopper neared the tarmac, the rotor wash changed the way the controls felt. This was the part in the simulator when she usually messed up and crashed as she tried to land. Sweat dripped from her temple, but she didn't dare take a hand off the controls to wipe it away. The truth was, she was utterly terrified. Not for herself, but for Owl. She didn't want to kill him after all he'd done for her.

The rotor wash made the helicopter buck back and forth a bit, and as the skids touched the ground, Lucas said, "You're almost there! Back off on the power and push the lever next to your seat to the floor."

The chopper settled hard—and it took a moment for Lara to realize she'd done it. She'd actually landed! Lucas congratulated her through the headset.

"You did it, Lara! You're down! There should be lots of people approaching you now. But you aren't quite done yet. Back all the way off on the power. Did you do it?"

"Yeah," Lara croaked.

"Good. There's a red switch on the control panel, I need you to flick it; it will shut off the fuel to the engine. It'll make it safer for the first responders to get to you."

Lara did as Lucas instructed, vaguely remembering Stone doing the same when they'd landed after their test flight. The rotors of the helicopter began to slow, and Lara had a brief moment of disbelief that she'd actually flown a freaking *helicopter* and landed without crashing.

Turning, Lara saw that the cavalry of cars and trucks had almost reached her, their lights flashing and, she assumed, sirens blaring, but she couldn't hear them while wearing the headphones.

"Thank you," she whispered.

"I didn't do anything," Lucas said, which made Lara want to cry and laugh at the same time.

As if he knew how she was feeling, he continued, "Seriously. This was all you. That sim program your boyfriend has must be amazing. I don't know anyone else who could've done what you just did."

"He's a Nightslayer," she whispered.

"A what?" Lucas asked.

"A Nightslayer. One of those fancy helicopter pilots in the military."

"You mean Night Stalker?"

"Oh, yeah. That. Sorry."

"Wow. They're amazing. You obviously had a great teacher," Lucas said. "Now take off the headset and talk to the first responders, Lara."

"I want to meet you," she blurted. "You saved my life. *Our* lives."

"You did that all on your own," Lucas said, refusing to accept her praise. "But I'll do what I can to make a meeting happen. Now, go."

Almost robotically, Lara unclenched her hands from around the controls and took off the headset. She turned to Owl just as their rescuers reached them.

After that, things moved very fast. She was whisked from the helicopter as Owl was removed and placed on a stretcher. She was escorted to an ambulance, where Owl was placed in the back. She had to sit up front, but she turned and watched through the small window as the paramedics worked on Owl.

There had been so much blood. His seat in the chopper was soaked, and the sheets on the gurney quickly turned red as it continued to flow.

There was no way anyone could live with that much blood loss...could they?

Once they arrived at the hospital, Owl was wheeled down a hall, while Lara was gently but firmly led to a small room. She spent at least two hours going over everything that happened with the police. Then when the FBI arrived, she had to start all over. She had no idea where the island was located, but she told the authorities the name of the airport where they'd been kidnapped, and said Lucas could probably tell them at least the area where he'd picked up her signal. She also begged them to find Stone. Gave them the little information she had, which wasn't much, and tried not to take their unencouraging looks personally.

When the door opened for what seemed like the hundredth time, Lara didn't even look up. She was exhausted, scared, and having one hell of an adrenaline dump. She didn't want to talk to anyone else. She only wanted to see Owl. She was told he'd been brought into surgery to try to repair the hole in his artery, but that was all she knew.

When she heard her name being spoken in a gentle yet familiar voice, Lara looked up in surprise. Standing in the doorway was Alaska.

And everyone else from The Refuge.

Well...almost all of them. As her gaze flicked from face to face, she didn't see Tiny, but the remaining men and their women were there.

Lara burst into tears, unable to hold them back anymore. Seeing her friends, knowing they'd have her back, she let her guard fall. She was finally safe...

But without Owl, she wasn't sure she could ever be whole again.

CHAPTER TWENTY-ONE

The first sound Owl heard when he regained consciousness was an annoying, relentless beeping. The second was quiet laughter. And he'd recognize that laugh anywhere.

Lara.

He felt floaty from whatever painkillers were coursing through his veins, but he remembered everything...up until he'd passed out. But Lara had obviously flown them to safety, just as he knew she could. He was so damn proud of her, he could burst.

He managed to crack his eyes open and saw Lara sitting next to his bed. Now that he was waking up, he realized his hand was held gently in hers. She was looking at their friends, smiling tiredly at Cora, who was sitting next to her. Owl saw Pipe standing behind Cora, his hand on her shoulder.

Involuntarily, his fingers tightened on Lara's. Her head immediately whipped toward him.

"Hey," Owl croaked. He hated how dry his mouth and lips felt, didn't like the smell of hospitals—he'd had enough of them after he'd been a POW to last a lifetime. But waking up to Lara, and his friends, made the experience not so awful.

"Owl!" she practically yelled. She leapt from her seat and leaned over him. "Owl?" she said a little softer.

"Are you okay?" he asked.

His Lara chuckled and shook her head. "Yeah, it's *you* we're all worried about. You had to go and catch a bullet with your leg and because you're an overachiever, it nicked an artery and you almost freaking bled to death!"

"Sorry," Owl said. But he was smiling as he said it. He was so damn happy to be alive that he couldn't get upset about a bullet wound. But then his smile dimmed as he thought about everything else that happened.

"Grant?" he asked.

"Dead," Pipe said from behind Lara.

She slowly eased back down in the chair next to the bed but didn't let go of his hand, which Owl appreciated.

"We all flew up to Seattle the second we found out you guys were in trouble. But before we could even put any plans in motion, Tex called and told us you were on your way to the hospital. While you were lazing around, sleeping in the OR, we rescued Lara from an interrogation by the FBI, got her fed, and even though we insisted she lay down and get some sleep, she refused to leave your side. She got us caught up with everything that happened. Brick and Spike are working with Tex to try to find Stone. Tonka's on watch with the other ladies, back at the hotel."

It was a lot to absorb right then. Owl frowned. "You haven't found Stone?"

"Not yet. But we will," Pipe said firmly.

"And Grant's dead?" he asked, needing to circle back to that.

"Very. He and that asshole he hired to double-cross you and Stone killed each other. You're lucky you only got hit by *one* bullet, if what the detectives say is true."

"What do they say?" Owl asked.

"That the house is so full of holes it looks like Swiss cheese."

"Thank you. But if you do that again, I'm gonna be really mad," Lara told Owl.

"Do what?"

"Take a bullet for me," she told him.

"Don't you know? I'd do whatever it takes to make sure you're safe. And I'm so, so proud of you. You flew," he said softly.

"And landed," Lara said. "Not very gracefully though."

"Anytime you get on the ground and can walk away, it's a perfect landing."

"You didn't exactly walk away," she said dryly.

"But that wasn't because of anything you did," Owl countered.

He didn't take his gaze from hers. He was in awe of his woman. He remembered taking off, but nothing beyond that. He was kind of pissed he didn't get to see her fly. He bet it was glorious. Forcing himself to break eye contact, Owl looked at his friend. "He's *really* gone?" He needed to be sure. Absolutely sure.

"Yes. I went to the morgue to ID his body myself, since I'm one of the few people who've had the displeasure of meeting him in person. It was him. He's really dead."

Relief surged through Owl, but on the heels of that was trepidation. If Carter Grant was dead, that meant Lara was free. She could go back to DC. Pick up the pieces of her old life if she wanted. And that scared the crap out of him.

As if reading his mind, she said, "I can't wait to get back to

The Refuge. I think I've had enough people-ing for a while. I wanted to stay until we found Stone, but Brick promised me that he's gonna find him, and it would be better if I was back home so no one had to worry about me too. Oh! Wait until you hear what Cora told me about Ryan! You aren't going to believe it. And the FBI has confiscated the chopper until their investigation is over, but they swore they'll release it back to us as soon as possible. And they said they'd get back the money you paid for it, so we'll get a *free* helicopter! Oh, and I invited Lucas to come to The Refuge so I could meet him, and you can too. He's the guy who answered my mayday plea and helped talk me through flying and landing. I told him I'd name our son after him—I hope that's okay. I'll let you pick a middle name. Our suitcases were still in the chopper, so when you're discharged, you'll have something to wear. The staff said they'd bring a bed in here for me so we can be together..."

There was a lot to unravel, and a lot Owl wanted to talk to Lara about, but all he could focus on at the moment was the fact she wanted to go back to The Refuge...and that she'd called it home. The rest could wait. Especially since she sounded off. Almost hyper.

"You have a hotel room?" he asked Pipe.

"Of course."

"Take Lara there and sit on her until she sleeps. Better yet, let *Cora* sit on her."

"What? No!" Lara protested.

"Sounds good to me," Cora mumbled with a grin.

"At least eight hours," Owl insisted.

"Owl! I want to stay here with you," Lara complained.

"You need to sleep. I'm okay. Grant is dead. You're safe. Pipe will make sure you're good. I need you healthy, sweetheart. If you get sick because you're worrying over me, that won't be good."

Lara closed her eyes and slumped in the chair.

"When you've gotten some sleep, and more food, and a shower, we'll talk. I want to hear all about what happened when I took my little nap in the chopper. I want to know about Stone, Ryan, and this Lucas person. But not until you're a little more coherent. Okay?"

She opened her eyes and frowned.

"Please?" Owl begged.

Lara reluctantly nodded.

Relief swept through him. "Good." He wanted to talk to Pipe, but his eyelids felt heavy and he had a feeling he would be asleep as soon as Lara left his side. "Come here," he ordered.

Lara stood again and leaned over him.

"Closer," Owl said.

She brought her face closer to his.

"I love you," he said softly. "I knew you could do it. I had no doubts whatsoever that you could fly that chopper."

"You're crazy," she said with a small shake of her head.

"I watched you on the sim. You have good instincts and steady hands. If I didn't think you could have done it, I wouldn't have put us in the helicopter in the first place. I would've found a place to hide. Gotten in a boat. Tackled Grant and stolen his gun. Something. But that chopper was our fastest and best way out of there. Away from those lunatics. And even though I was losing blood fast and knew I would lose consciousness, I still chose to take off. Because you, Lara Osler, can do any damn thing you put your mind to."

A tear dripped off Lara's face and landed on his cheek, but she didn't pull back. "Owl," she protested weakly.

"Are you pregnant?" he asked.

Her lips parted on a small gasp. "Why would you ask that?"

Her non-answer told him all he needed to know.

"We're getting married. Lucas isn't going to be born without his parents being legally hitched."

"We made a doctor look her over, and when he asked if she could be pregnant, she hesitated," Cora said from behind them. "So he made her pee in a cup."

"I *knew* I knocked you up that one time," Owl said smugly.

Lara rolled her eyes. "You're supposed to ask," she told him.

"Will you marry me?" he asked without hesitation.

"Of course."

"That's why I didn't ask. I already knew your answer," he said. Then it hit him. *Truly* hit him. "We made a baby," he whispered.

"Yeah, we did," Lara agreed.

"Lucas Jackson Kaufman," he said firmly, for the stranger who saved them...and his best friend, who was still missing. "Luke for short."

"It's perfect," Lara breathed.

"No, you are. Now kiss me, then go sleep. And make sure you eat. I need you and my son to stay healthy."

"You're going to be obnoxious with my pregnancy, aren't you?" Lara asked.

"If you mean overprotective and paranoid, yup," Owl agreed without hesitation.

But Lara didn't seem irritated. She simply shook her head and leaned down, kissing him softly. It wasn't a deep kiss, wasn't passionate, but it was one of the best kisses he'd shared with her yet.

"Go. Let Pipe and Cora take care of you. I'll be here when you get back."

"Love you. I'm so glad you're okay."

"Love you, and me too."

She stood and backed toward the door, with Cora at her side, grinning at them both like a fool.

Pipe followed, and right before stepping through the door, he turned. "I'll tell the nurse you're up," he said.

Owl nodded. "Pipe?" he asked before his friend left.

"Yeah?"

"I need two things."

"Name 'em."

"I need you to find Stone. And talk to Tex. I know he can get the paperwork done fast...when you bring Lara back, I want to marry her."

Pipe nodded. "I'm doing my best on the first, and I'll make sure the second is done."

"Thanks."

Pipe studied him for a moment, then walked back into the room and over to his bed, putting a hand on Owl's shoulder. "I'm almost sorry that bastard is dead. I'd kill him slowly this time for what he put you and Stone through. Not to mention Lara."

Owl nodded. He wanted to kill Grant himself. But he had to be satisfied with the fact that he was dead.

"Henley's been anxious to talk to you. To make sure you're all right. This had to bring back some not-so-good memories," Pipe said.

"Honestly? I was more worried about Lara. I was unconscious for the flight to the island and only woke up right before Grant and Ricky started their shootout. Then I was focused on getting Lara out of there, and after I was shot, the pain kept me fixated on what needed to be done. I'm good, Pipe. Promise. Now I'm just worried about Stone."

"Yeah."

"Is there any word? Anything at all?" Owl asked.

"No. It's as if he disappeared into thin air," Pipe admitted.

Owl's lips pressed together in dismay. "Shit."

"But we're doing everything we can to find him. And we will. I promise."

Owl wanted to do his part. But from this hospital bed, he couldn't do a damn thing. "What's this about Ryan...?" he asked.

Pipe shook his head. "It's a story for another time, brother. You're about to crash. But it's a doozy. Tiny's with her, back at The Refuge."

"She's okay though?"

"Yeah."

"Good. Thanks for looking after Lara and my son."

"Can't believe we're going to have *another* baby at The Refuge in nine months," Pipe said with a shake of his head and a small smile.

"You could add to that number," Owl suggested.

"Oh, I will...but first, everyone needs to calm the hell down and stop having crises for us to deal with."

Owl chuckled. "Amen to that."

Pipe squeezed his shoulder. "Glad you're all right. It was a hell of a chance you took with Lara flying that chopper. You've told me more than once that it's difficult as hell."

"It is, but I wasn't lying to her. I knew she could do it. I watched her on the sim, Pipe. She was good. Besides...we didn't have a choice. There *was* nowhere to hide on that island. I didn't think we'd have time to find a boat, and I didn't have a weapon.

It was a stroke of pure luck that Grant and Ricky were both hotheaded assholes who turned on each other."

"And we got a free helicopter out of the deal," Pipe joked.

Owl nodded. "We just need to find Stone so we can enjoy it."

"We will. I'll get with Tex and he'll get the paperwork for your wedding. I'll be back with everyone and an officiant tomorrow."

"Thanks."

"No need to thank me. You being here is thanks enough. Later."

"Later."

Pipe left, and Owl barely remembered the nurse coming in to check on him and make sure his vitals were all in the correct ranges. He fell into a healing sleep, and instead of dreaming about serial killers and helicopter crashes, he dreamt of holding his infant son in one arm and his wife in the other.

EPILOGUE

Lara sat in the lodge and smiled as she looked around at everyone. There had been times when she wasn't sure she'd ever see it again. And now she was not only back, she was married and pregnant. It was hard to believe.

Things had been crazy since they'd returned to The Refuge, and she finally had time to reflect on everything that had happened. The ten days or so since she'd been re-kidnapped had been full of ups and downs. She'd learned she was pregnant, Owl was recovering quickly, but had still been in the hospital for almost five days. She'd split her time between staying at the hotel—when Owl insisted—and the small cot next to his hospital bed.

She wasn't really surprised when she'd gone back to see him after he'd first woken up, and Owl informed her that the arrangements had been made for them to get married right then and there. She'd agreed, they'd FaceTimed with her parents, and right there in the hospital room, surrounded by many of their friends, they'd pledged their lives and love to each other.

It honestly was just a formality. Lara had already mentally vowed to love him for the rest of her life. But she didn't care if she got married in a hospital room, in a huge chapel, or an office in some government building. After all the huge weddings she'd attended with her family growing up, and seeing all the pomp and circumstance and stress that went into them, she was more than happy to have a low-key ceremony with those she'd come to love the most in attendance. And the fact that Cora was there was icing on the cake.

Yes, she was a romantic, and loved seeing the big ceremonies on TV and reading about them in books...but the reality was, all she wanted was to love someone, and to be loved in return. And Owl fulfilled that and more.

All their friends who'd descended on Seattle had gone back to New Mexico once they were reassured both she and Owl would be all right. Brick had stayed, coordinating with the authorities about finding Stone, and making sure Lara took care of herself and didn't neglect her own health while she spent as much time as possible by Owl's side. He'd also made the arrangements when Owl was finally discharged and able to fly back to New Mexico.

Once back at The Refuge, she and Owl had gone straight to the cabin and crashed, not coming out for two whole days. It felt amazing to sleep in their own bed and be back in their home.

Now they were up at the lodge at an impromptu welcome-home party. It felt a little weird to be celebrating when Stone was still missing, but as Alaska had pointed out, Stone wouldn't begrudge her or Owl a celebration for coming home alive, married, and with a baby on the way.

Robert and Luna had made an enormous amount of food to welcome them back, and everyone was mingling and just happy to be together. Even some of the guests were there, enjoying the festive atmosphere, even if they weren't completely sure what it was they were celebrating.

Robert approached, and Lara stood, hugging him hard. "Thank you for the box of Christmas Tree Cakes I found in our cabin," she said with a smile. "I appreciate you sharing your stash with me."

"Just glad you're back, missy," he said gruffly.

A little bit later, Lara thanked Carly and Jess for making sure their cabin was spotless when they arrived.

"It was the least we could do," Carly said.

"But I know you're probably even busier, now that...well... that it's just the two of you cleaning," Lara said a little hesitatingly.

"It's fine. Ry still helps out when she can," Jess reassured her.

Lara was a little sad that Ryan—aka, Ryleigh—wasn't at the small party, but she guessed the woman probably felt uncomfortable around everyone now, after lying to them for a year. It was still unclear why the woman had lied in the first place, and what or who she was hiding from, but Lara completely understood why she'd chosen The Refuge. It really was a refuge from life, from anything that was troubling you.

She held no ill will toward Ryan, or whatever she should be called now. She simply hoped the woman eventually found the peace and happiness that Lara herself had.

Henley and Reese approached, and before she knew it, Lara was engulfed in a three-way hug.

"I can't believe you're pregnant!" Reese exclaimed. "I'm so

happy for you and Owl...and myself too! Our kids'll have someone else to play with."

"*I* can believe it," Henley said a little smugly. "I told you how Owl looked at you when he was in our sessions."

"How'd he look at her?" Reese asked.

The two women stepped back a bit, inviting Jess and Carly into their circle as they talked.

"He couldn't take his eyes off her. And you know the look... protective, pissed that someone would dare hurt *his* woman, and so damn in love he could barely sit still."

"Oh, *that* look," Reese said with a chuckle. "Yup, I know it well."

Lara felt herself blushing, even as she searched the room for the object of their conversation. She saw Owl sitting in a chair on the other side of the room. He was talking with Tonka and Pipe. As if he felt her gaze on him, he looked up and mouthed, *You okay?*

Lara nodded and turned her attention back to the women in front of her when she heard them all laugh. "What? What'd I miss?"

"Nothing. You guys are adorable," Carly told her. "I hope I can find a partner who loves me as much your man loves you."

"You will," Jess told her. "Just don't rush into things. Patience is key. You're still young, you have lots of time."

Lara nodded her agreement as she heard the door to the lodge open. She turned her head reflexively to see who'd come in, but she didn't recognize the man. She hadn't seen him around The Refuge since she'd been back, but it was likely he was a guest.

Brick approached him, and though she couldn't hear what

they were actually saying, she froze when she recognized the tone of the man's voice.

Even though she'd never seen him before, she knew exactly who he was.

Not caring that she was probably being rude by turning her back on her friends without a word, Lara quickly headed toward the stranger and Brick.

The man saw her approach, and he smiled. He was a big man, around six-four. Was probably in his early sixties or so, his navy-blue shirt pulled taut over a big belly, and his hair black liberally streaked with white. In any other circumstance, Lara would probably be intimidated by him. But without hesitation, she walked straight up to him and wrapped her arms around the man as tightly as she could.

"Thank you," she murmured between her tears. "Thank you so much."

"You did all the work, darlin'," the man drawled.

It took a hand on her back, a hand she knew as well as she knew her own name, to give her the strength to step away from the stranger. Lara wiped her face, trying to compose herself, then held out a hand. "Hi, I'm Lara."

"I'm Lucas, it's so nice to meet you," the newcomer said with a huge smile.

"And I'm Callen Kaufman...Owl. You have my undying gratitude. Anything you ever need, you've got it."

Lucas chuckled. "Don't need much. Got a loving wife, two kids, and five grandkids...I'm good."

Lara struggled to keep more tears from falling. This man had literally saved her life. Hers and Owl's. He'd been the miracle she needed when she'd called that mayday over the headset in the chopper. He'd been so calm, so soothing. He'd helped her when she'd needed someone the most, and she'd never forget him.

"We're pregnant," she blurted. "And it's a boy. Well...it's too early to know that for sure, but Owl insists. And his name is going to be Lucas Jackson."

The big man stared at her for a moment with his mouth open, before his cheeks turned pink and he swallowed hard. "I... well...alright then. Thank you. Congratulations!"

Lara beamed at him. "Can I show you around?"

"I'd like that."

"I'll put your bag in the cabin," Brick said.

Lara had almost forgotten he was standing with them. Obviously, he'd had a huge part in getting Lucas here, and she thought again how lucky she was to have found such amazing friends here at The Refuge.

"Thanks. Don't know how you managed to find space for me, but I sure appreciate it," Lucas told him as he shook Brick's hand.

"Anytime you want to bring your family here, let me know. We're usually sold out months in advance, but we've recently acquired a free helicopter," he said with a grin. "So I think some of that unused cash will go toward building a couple of special cabins reserved for friends and family. After what you did for Lara and Owl, you're among those who qualify."

These men. Some people might be wary of a bunch of former military men who lived in the forest and ran a hotel of sorts...but not her. The men and women of The Refuge had the biggest hearts of anyone she'd ever met. She made a mental note to get with Savannah, The Refuge's accountant, and make a sizeable donation to get those friends and family cabins built sooner rather than later. The Refuge might not need her money, but she had plenty of it to share, and she wanted to give back to those who had given her everything.

"Are you hungry?" Alaska asked Lucas, joining them. "Trust me, Robert and Luna have outdone themselves tonight. Let him eat, then you can introduce him to everyone," she told Lara.

She nodded and watched as her friend led Lucas toward the buffet.

"I hope you aren't mad that I tracked him down and invited him," Brick said.

"Mad? Are you kidding? No way. I'm thrilled!" Lara said.

"Good." He hugged her, shook Owl's hand, then wandered over to where Alaska was talking a mile a minute to Lucas as he filled a plate at the buffet.

"Did you know he was coming?" Lara asked Owl when they were alone.

"Yeah."

She narrowed her eyes at him. "You're good at keeping secrets."

"And you suck at it, I'm guessing."

"You'd guess right."

"That's all right. I'm looking forward to surprising you for the next, oh, hundred years."

Lara rolled her eyes. "I refuse to live to be a hundred and thirty-five years old."

"Not me. I'll take every year, every month, every minute I can, if they're all by your side."

Lara grinned. "Flatterer."

In response, Owl leaned in and kissed her lightly. "Welcome home, sweetheart."

Home. The Refuge was definitely that and more.

"How's your leg?" she asked gently.

"Sore. But I'm okay."

Lara's brows furrowed.

"Honestly, I'm fine. I want to talk to Lucas. Need to thank him again for talking you through that flight. I won't overdo it. I'll let you know when I'm ready to head back to the cabin."

"All right. Owl?"

"Yeah?"

"Love you."

He smiled. "Love you too."

Using the temporary cane he'd been given, Owl headed over to the table where Alaska, Cora, and Lucas were sitting. Smiling, Lara headed back to where she'd abruptly left her friends. She felt like the luckiest woman in the world. She'd been to hell and back, but had come out the other side with not only a man she loved more than anything, but she'd been reunited with her best friend, and had a brand-new group of men and women who would have her back no matter what. It felt amazing.

* * *

Later that night, Lara snuggled against Owl on the couch in their cabin. She was still amazed the man who'd answered her mayday call had made the trip down here to meet her and Owl.

She put her hand on her still-flat belly and sighed when Owl placed his own large hand on top of hers. She smiled at him.

"What's that smile for?" he asked.

"I'm just so happy. I feel as if a huge weight has been lifted off my shoulders, now that I know for sure I'm finally safe from Carter...as is everyone here at The Refuge. Is it wrong that I feel that way because a human being is dead?"

"No," Owl said without a drop of hesitation. "I envy you.

Not that I think my captors are going to come here to the States and track me down, but knowing some of them are still out there, that they're spreading their hate, maybe hurting someone else...it sucks. I'm *glad* Grant is dead. I only wish I could've been the one to make that happen for you."

"Don't," Lara said with a shake of her head.

Owl kissed her temple reverently. "I do," he insisted. "He hurt you. Scared you. I saw the pictures the FBI had of the room where he'd planned on keeping you, on that island." He shuddered. "Ricky Norman was an asshole, but he did us a favor."

Lara nodded absently. How everything had gone down was messed up, but the truth was, if it hadn't happened exactly the way it had...things might be completely different right now.

"Have I told you how thrilled I am that you're Mrs. Kaufman? And that little Lucas is growing in your belly?" Owl asked as his hand moved down her belly and slipped under the waistband of her leggings.

"Yes," Lara said, her breath hitching as his finger brushed against her clit.

"I don't think I have," he said. Lara could hear the smile in his voice.

Reaching down, she grabbed his wrist. He paused, but didn't remove his hand from under her clothes.

"We can't. The doctor hasn't cleared you for...this," Lara said.

"*I* can't. But you can," he retorted. "Now lay back and relax. I need this. Please, let me."

How could she resist when he put it that way? She let go of his wrist and reclined with her head on his lap, careful not to put pressure on his injured leg. She looked up at him. "Touch me, Owl."

"With pleasure."

It didn't take long. Lara hadn't realized how wound up she'd been. Even though she and Owl were safe, it had still been an extremely stressful week. His fingers expertly brought her to the edge, then threw her over. But he didn't stop after giving her one orgasm. He teased and touched and stroked her until she was shaking and trembling once more, his fingers buried deep within her.

When she began to come down from her orgasmic high, she saw him lick clean the fingers that had been inside her. He then helped her sit back up and curl against him. Lara noticed his dick was hard in his sweatpants, and grimaced.

"It's fine," Owl told her, not missing her reaction. "You can make it up to me when I'm better."

"I will," she vowed. "You'll come so hard you won't be able to walk."

He chuckled, tightening his arm around her.

"Owl?"

"Yeah, sweetheart?"

"I want to keep playing that simulator game. Eventually, I want to get my pilot's license. I never again want to feel as helpless as I did when you passed out. I'm not saying I want to fly tourists or anything, but I want to learn enough to be able to take off and land without thinking I'm going to crash."

"Done."

"And I want to continue to work with kids here at The Refuge. Guests' kids, and eventually our friends' children...if they want me to."

"They will."

"You..." Her voice trailed off as she tried to figure out how to ask what she wanted to without upsetting him.

"I...what?" Owl asked. "You can talk to me about anything.

Nothing's off limits. Nothing. You want to know more about my time as a POW? Ask. You want to ask if I'll build you a huge house out here in the woods, I'll do it without pause. Whatever you want, it's yours."

"I don't want a huge house," she told him. "I mean, if we have those five kids you planned, we'll need to add on a room or two, but I love this cabin. I can't imagine ever living anywhere else."

"Not even Washington, DC? You had a good job, your family's there. Friends."

Lara turned a little in his arms so she could meet his gaze. "My parents love me, but they don't understand me at all. And I didn't really have friends, just Cora. And she's here. And yes, I loved my job, and my kids there, but there are children everywhere. Besides...you're here. Why would I want to be anywhere else?"

"I love you," Owl said. "So much, you don't know."

"I do know, because I love you just as much."

They smiled at each other.

"What were you going to say or ask?"

"Just that...you didn't sleep well at the hospital. You woke up in the middle of the night a few times and couldn't get back to sleep. I know you've slept okay since coming home, but that's probably because you've been on painkillers. Do you think your insomnia is back?" Lara had been worrying about that. He'd been doing so well, and she hated to think about him reverting back to his previous problem and suffering from lack of sleep.

To her surprise, Owl grinned.

"What? This isn't funny," she said.

"Lara, I was in a *hospital*. Someone came in every hour or so to check my vitals, or to ask me how I was feeling, or to change my IV fluids. Of course I didn't sleep that well."

"Oh. I never heard them."

"I know," Owl said with a grin. "You sleep like a rock."

"I don't like it when you aren't sleeping."

"I know that too. And I'm sure my insomnia will return at times. My brain has a hard time shutting off. When I think about how close I got to losing you..." His voice trailed off.

"You didn't," she said softly.

"I didn't. And I'm very grateful for that. But..."

"But Stone is still out there somewhere," Lara finished for him.

"Yeah," Owl whispered. "We promised that we'd always be there for each other. And I let him down."

"No, you didn't," Lara told him, sitting up and frowning. "You were unconscious, Owl. And so was he."

"I know. But I can't stop thinking about what he might be going through. We don't know who took him or why. Where he is, or if he's even still alive."

"He is," Lara said with conviction.

"I love your optimism, but you don't know that," Owl said sadly.

"I do. I heard what that guy said when he was dragging him away. He said his boss only wanted one of you. He has to want him for *something*...and not to just kill him, because that would be stupid. He could've had him killed right there in that hangar. He's alive. And we'll find him. Ry will."

"I can't believe Ryan was the one who found Jasna and tracked Reese," Owl said with a shake of his head.

It was obvious he was changing the subject, and Lara didn't push him to talk more about his friend. She had no doubt whatsoever that they'd find Stone...she just worried about what kind of shape he'd be in when they did. But he had the support of all his friends, and there was no better place to heal than here at The Refuge.

"Right? Apparently, she's a super-level hacker, whatever that is. I heard Brick talking to Pipe about her, and he said even the infamous Tex was impressed with her abilities."

"Which says a lot," Owl agreed.

"Tiny's not happy though," Lara mused.

"No, he's not."

"If he hates her so much, why did he insist that she move into his cabin?" Lara asked.

"I think because he doesn't trust her not to simply up and disappear. He wants to make sure she sticks around to find Stone."

"I don't think she'd do that. Leave, I mean. She wants to find him just as much as the rest of us. I think she feels guilty for not being able to get to us before everything happened. Which is silly, because there was no way she could've known that Ricky was working with Carter."

"You know that, and I know that, but she doesn't. And I doubt Tiny hates her...in fact, I think that's part of his issue right now."

"Oh! I didn't even think about that."

"Right. You ready for bed?"

Lara blinked at yet another abrupt change of topic. "You tired?" she asked.

"Exhausted."

At that, Lara was up and moving like a flash. "Why didn't you say something before? Come on, I'll help you up. Does your leg hurt? Do you need another pill? I'll get you some water."

"Easy, sweetheart. I'm fine. Just tired."

"Right. Sorry."

"Don't be sorry for caring about me. The time will come when the roles are reversed and you're big with my baby, irritable, and I'll love every second of rubbing your feet, bringing you whatever it is that you're craving, and spoiling you rotten."

"I don't like my feet being touched. That's gross."

Owl chuckled. "Right. Noted." He stood and pulled Lara closer. "I love you, wife."

"Wife...I love the sound of that. And I love you too, husband."

"Take me to bed," Owl said with a grin.

"With pleasure."

An hour later, Owl lay in bed with his wife snoring against him. But he couldn't sleep. He was mostly content. He was married and had a baby on the way. Lara was finally safe, and she was everything he'd ever wanted in his life that he never thought he'd have.

But...even through all the good things that were happening, even after spending the evening with his friends, he felt guilty. He was happier than ever, but Stone was still missing. Being held against his will, possibly dead. It hurt. Badly. The only reason Owl had gotten through being a prisoner of war was because Stone had been by his side.

And now he was out there somewhere. Probably hurting. Maybe scared. And alone. It sucked. He couldn't imagine being here at The Refuge, flying that damn helicopter, without him.

His teeth clenched and determination rose within him. He'd

do whatever it took to find Stone. They'd get him back. There was no other option.

Hang on, brother. We won't stop looking until we find you.

Somehow, just thinking those words made Owl feel better. Stone would know his friends were doing everything possible to find him. He'd stay strong until they did just that. The alternative was unthinkable. Owl needed his friend. He felt as if there was a hole in his heart with Stone missing.

Lara shifted against him, and Owl tightened his arms around her as he felt his eyes finally get heavy. Not sleeping through the night had tired him out more than he'd ever admit. He'd gotten very used to a full night's rest since he'd started sleeping with Lara in his bed.

His wife.

It was almost unbelievable that he, a broken former POW, had found what he'd always wanted without even really trying. It gave him hope that everything would turn out all right in the end. Stone would return, and everyone would live out their lives happy.

Owl fell asleep with a small smile on his lips, thinking that his wife had infected him with her romantic heart. But he wasn't ashamed; she was the best thing that had ever happened to him.

* * *

Ryan sat at Tiny's table and tried to ignore the daggers she could feel digging into her back from his gaze. He'd insisted she move into his cabin because he didn't trust her...didn't trust she wouldn't up and leave in the middle of the night.

But she wasn't leaving. Not until she'd done everything she could to find Stone. She felt responsible. No, she hadn't kidnapped him. She didn't have anything to do with what happened in Seattle. But she couldn't help but feel that if she'd acted on that niggling feeling she'd had that something wasn't right, she could've figured out earlier that Carter Grant had hacked into Brick's email and found out all about the purchase of the helicopter and their plans.

But she hadn't...until it was almost too late.

And her spilling the beans about who she was, and everything she'd been doing for her new friends at The Refuge, was all for nothing. By the time everyone had arrived in Washington, Lara had rescued Owl by herself and Stone was gone.

Gritting her teeth, Ry concentrated on the screen in front of her. Her days here in New Mexico were numbered. It was only a matter of time before her father located her. She'd used Brick's unsecured laptop to hack into the microphone on Owl's phone, knowing it would open herself up to being found.

Her father had taught her everything she knew, and while she was very good at what she did, her dad was even better. And he had thirty million reasons to track her down.

So she had to find Stone, then get the hell away from The Refuge before her dad did what he did best—ruined everything he touched.

"So...Ryleigh...I've been dying to ask you something..." Tiny started.

Ry tensed. After learning her name wasn't Ryan—a name Tiny admitted he'd never liked—he'd decided to call her Ryleigh. Not Ry...the name she'd asked everyone to use. It was like he was purposely baiting her. Trying to annoy her. And it was working.

She felt like crying. She liked Tiny. He was untrusting, paranoid, and a little rough around the edges, but he was loyal. *Extremely* loyal. And she understood that his anger toward her was coming from that feeling of being betrayed and his worry for his friend.

It wasn't her fault Stone had been taken, but she was a convenient target for Tiny's frustration and concern, and she felt enough guilt to suffer his attitude.

Besides...she was used to others taking out their anger and emotions on her for no good reason.

The last two weeks had been extremely tense around The Refuge. The relaxed atmosphere she'd learned to love had been shattered. Because of everything Owl and Lara had endured, because Stone was still missing...and because of her betrayal.

Ry knew she could slip away when Tiny wasn't home, could help find Stone from anywhere, but she couldn't bring herself to leave until it was absolutely necessary. The men and women here...they were family. At least, that's how she felt. And even though she was no longer spending time with them, she wouldn't leave until Stone was found.

The guilt that she hadn't been able to find him *already* was eating her alive. She'd spent the last two weeks frantically searching the dark web and using all the contacts she had to find any thread she could pull that might lead her to the man who'd taken Stone out of that hangar in Washington.

"Are you listening to me?" Tiny asked.

Sighing, Ry pushed her laptop away and closed it. She turned toward the man who confused her, scared her, and made her want to curl up in his arms and beg him to hold her as tightly as he could.

"Nothing?" Tiny asked in a quieter tone, glancing at the computer.

"Not yet. But I'll find him," Ry said firmly. "Whoever took Stone will mess up sooner or later. I just have to follow the threads back from Ricky Norman. He had to communicate with whoever took him. I'll find how he did it, and that will lead us to the person who has him." She paused, closing her eyes briefly as she rubbed at her tense shoulder. "You wanted to ask me something?" she said, opening her eyes wearily, wanting to get this latest interrogation over with so she could attempt to get some sleep.

"I'm wondering what has you so scared that you'd give a stranger a buttload of money, just so you could take her job here at The Refuge. What, or who, are you hiding from?"

Ry's shoulders tensed even further. His question was amazingly insightful. She never said she was hiding; she told him and the other men that she thought The Refuge was a good place to *lay low*. Most people would assume she'd done something bad. Or was maybe targeting The Refuge to steal from or scam them in some way. But not Tiny. He'd somehow guessed that she was on the run.

"I'm not scared," she said belatedly.

The disappointment at her lie flashed across Tiny's face.

Ry *hated* lying to him. But she couldn't tell him the truth. He'd want to help. Even if he hated her, he wouldn't let her come to any harm. She knew that instinctively. But he couldn't help her. No one could.

As soon as she found Stone, she'd be gone. She had to lie for his own good. For *everyone's* own good.

"Right," he said, sounding angry. "You didn't eat tonight."

Ry shook her head, despite being glad for the subject change. "Not hungry."

"You can't find Stone if you don't eat," Tiny told her before getting up and going into the kitchen. Ry watched as he made a ham and cheese sandwich, slathered with ranch dressing, before bringing it over to the table where she was still sitting. For a moment, she thought she saw concern in his eyes. But when he practically threw the plate on the table and growled, "Eat, Ryleigh," she knew she had to have been mistaken.

She wasn't a prisoner, but there were times, like now, when she felt like it.

Tiny went back to his chair, where he resumed glaring at her. Ry tried to ignore the hurt she felt. She'd find Stone, then get out of everyone's hair.

The farther she was from The Refuge, the safer everyone would be.

* * *

Ten Days Ago

Stone groaned as he rolled against something hard. His head was pounding and he didn't know why. He was lying on his side in the fetal position, surrounded by pitch black. Blinking to try to see something, anything, Stone suddenly remembered what had happened.

Well, not everything. They'd been in a hangar ready to sign the papers to take ownership of the new helicopter for The Refuge when everything had gone dark.

Reaching up to his head, Stone felt something sticky in his hair. Blood.

Turning on his back in the small space, he realized that he was in a box.

No...what he thought was the sound of a fan running was actually coming from under him. A road. The wind.

He was in the trunk of a fucking car.

His heartbeat sped up and he suddenly couldn't breathe. It was almost too hard to believe, but he'd been taken captive—again. Wasn't once enough?

Why was this happening to him? Where was Owl? Was Lara all right? Was this Carter Grant's doing?

Stone's mind spun as his panic increased. He couldn't stop it. Within seconds, he was hyperventilating.

He frantically tried to claw his way out of the trunk, with no luck. He couldn't use his feet to effectively pound on the lid of the trunk because the space was so cramped. He was stuck.

Even as he gasped for air, Stone came to the realization that he was fucked. He couldn't handle being a prisoner again. He couldn't do it! Couldn't go through the kind of torture that he'd endured before. He had no idea who had taken him or why, but it didn't really matter.

His limbs shook, his head throbbed, and the panic attack consumed him.

His thoughts shut down completely, his brain too busy trying to manage what was happening to his body. To funnel oxygen to his blood cells to keep his lungs working.

In that moment, in order to deal with the trauma of being taken captive once again, his brain blocked everything but the most basic necessities for life.

Blessedly, he passed out.

When he woke, the memories of the former-soldier everyone knew as *Stone* would be pushed into the far recesses of his mind...replaced only by the recollections of the civilian known as Jack Wickett.

* * *

Poor Stone...kidnapped with no idea he has a whole group of friends who are worried about him and frantically searching for him. And make no mistake, everyone at The Refuge wants to find him. Luckily, he's got someone on his side, even if she doesn't know Stone's background, she'll do everything in her power to keep him safe from the man who wants to hurt him... the same man who hurts *her* every chance he can. Pick up Deserving Maisy to see how it all plays out.

Scan the QR code below for signed books, swag, T-shirts and more!

Searching for Lilly
Searching for Elsie
Searching for Bristol
Searching for Caryn
Searching for Finley
Searching for Heather
Searching for Khloe (May 2024)

Game of Chance Series
The Protector
The Royal
The Hero (Mar 2024)
The Lumberjack (Aug 2024)

SEAL of Protection: Legacy Series
Securing Caite
Securing Brenae (novella)
Securing Sidney
Securing Piper
Securing Zoey
Securing Avery
Securing Kalee
Securing Jane

Delta Force Heroes Series
Rescuing Rayne
Rescuing Aimee (novella)
Rescuing Emily
Rescuing Harley
Marrying Emily (novella)
Rescuing Kassie

Rescuing Bryn
Rescuing Casey
Rescuing Sadie (novella)
Rescuing Wendy
Rescuing Mary
Rescuing Macie (novella)
Rescuing Annie

SEAL of Protection Series
Protecting Caroline
Protecting Alabama
Protecting Fiona
Marrying Caroline (novella)
Protecting Summer
Protecting Cheyenne
Protecting Jessyka
Protecting Julie (novella)
Protecting Melody
Protecting the Future
Protecting Kiera (novella)
Protecting Alabama's Kids (novella)
Protecting Dakota

Delta Team Two Series
Shielding Gillian
Shielding Kinley
Shielding Aspen
Shielding Jayme (novella)
Shielding Riley
Shielding Devyn
Shielding Ember

Shielding Sierra

Badge of Honor: Texas Heroes Series

Justice for Mackenzie

Justice for Mickie

Justice for Corrie

Justice for Laine (novella)

Shelter for Elizabeth

Justice for Boone

Shelter for Adeline

Shelter for Sophie

Justice for Erin

Justice for Milena

Shelter for Blythe

Justice for Hope

Shelter for Quinn

Shelter for Koren

Shelter for Penelope

Ace Security Series

Claiming Grace

Claiming Alexis

Claiming Bailey

Claiming Felicity

Claiming Sarah

Mountain Mercenaries Series

Defending Allye

Defending Chloe

Defending Morgan

Defending Harlow

Defending Everly
Defending Zara
Defending Raven

Silverstone Series
Trusting Skylar
Trusting Taylor
Trusting Molly
Trusting Cassidy

Stand Alone
Falling for the Delta
The Guardian Mist
Nature's Rift
A Princess for Cale
A Moment in Time- A Collection of Short Stories
Another Moment in Time- A Collection of Short Stories
A Third Moment in Time- A Collection of Short Stories
Lambert's Lady

Special Operations Fan Fiction
http://www.AcesPress.com

Beyond Reality Series
Outback Hearts
Flaming Hearts
Frozen Hearts

Writing as Annie George:
Stepbrother Virgin (erotic novella)

ABOUT THE AUTHOR

New York Times, USA Today, #1 Amazon Bestseller, and #1 *Wall Street Journal* Bestselling Author, Susan Stoker has spent the last twenty-three years living in Missouri, California, Colorado, Indiana, Texas, and Tennessee and is currently living in the wilds of Maine. She's married to a retired Army man (and current firefighter/EMT) who now gets to follow *her* around the country.

She debuted her first series in 2014 and quickly followed that up with the SEAL of Protection Series, which solidified her love of writing and creating stories readers can get lost in.

If you enjoyed this book, or any book, please consider leaving a review. It's appreciated by authors more than you'll know.

www.stokeraces.com
www.AcesPress.com
susan@stokeraces.com

facebook.com/authorsusanstoker
twitter.com/Susan_Stoker
instagram.com/authorsusanstoker
goodreads.com/SusanStoker
bookbub.com/authors/susan-stoker
amazon.com/author/susanstoker

Milton Keynes UK
Ingram Content Group UK Ltd.
UKHW050835310124
436936UK00024B/352